THE Hofburg Treasures

THE Hofburg Treasures

A NOVEL OF HIGH TECH ESPIONAGE

STEPHEN P. ADAMS

MOODY PRESS
CHICAGO

ISBN: 0-8024-3677-3

1 3 5 7 9 10 8 6 4 2

Printed in the United States of America

To David Samuel Stephen Adams
December 3 to December 17, 1993
and his mother, my wife, Mary Jane

ACKNOWLEDGMENTS

To Ken and Liz Weber and Gregg and Jennifer Carrick for their advice and assistance and for their support, love, prayers, and encouragement through a difficult time.

Also to our friends at Grace Church and Moody Press, especially Dennis Shere, who kept us in their prayers. And to our children, Daniel, Katie, Laura, and Stephanie, who made sacrifices of their own.

PROLOGUE

London, A.D. *2047*

The night was cold, and Peter McBride was riding the midnight Maglev train, hurtling through Metro tunnels just outside London in excess of 600 kilometers per hour.

Over the top of his *Mutual Fund Monthly,* Peter stole occasional peeks at the golden-haired woman with the gimlet eyes and high cheekbones several seats up on the other side. She lugged an oversized briefcase, the expandable kind lawyers use for hauling around chunky transcripts and other voluminous documents. One hand was jammed deep into a pocket of her thick, black cashmere coat.

Peter visualized a handgun secreted there. At this hour, she would be foolish not to be armed, if there was anything at all valuable in that case.

The supposition was that there was, indeed, something of considerable value in her possession. This woman, Ilse Engaard—aka Alice Endicott—was suspected of being an industrial spy for an Asian member of the Pacific Consortium. Her only documented affiliation to this point had been with the European Union, but according to government sources she was a well-known mercenary with few loyalties.

In this case, she was believed to be the conduit for the stolen Human Genome master tapes from the Sontag Research Institute, tapes that contained the entire genetic code for every citizen in the Mid-Central region of the United States and Provinces of America.

Just what its purloiners intended to do with this information was a troubling question. Perhaps it would turn out to be as simple as extortion—if the heist succeeded.

Could those tapes, Peter wondered, be reposing even now in that fat satchel? His heart rate ratcheted up. There was no mistaking that this was, indeed, Ilse Engaard.

McBride & McBride had been brought into the picture at the behest of Sontag's insurer, Griswold International, a first-time client. Glad as he was for the job, Neal McBride, Peter's adoptive father, had muttered several times about the sad commentary that was on USP law enforcement. It was a virtual vote of no confidence in the FBI, primarily over information security. The Griswold executive who had retained them confided that there was far greater assurance of confidentiality with McBride & McBride than there was with the federal government.

And probably a far greater chance of cracking the case too, his father had added ruefully.

Sometimes it seemed as if Neal McBride knew everyone in town. This time one of those connections paid off with a tip regarding a Scandinavian woman who had checked into a motel near the airport shortly after the heist.

Conventional wisdom would have assumed that the tapes were already en route to San Francisco or LA for a flight to Tokyo or Hong Kong. But Neal McBride's wisdom was anything but conventional. The theft clearly had been an inside job, and McBride's intelligence indicated that the booty was still in Columbus.

Peter and another rookie were assigned to the Metro tunnels while McBride continued working his informants.

And now, Peter sat a few short meters from the prime suspect. He had never been that close to something this hot, and his hands and feet were oozing perspiration.

Finally, the Maglev came to rest in its berth beneath the Heathrow terminal, and the doors popped open. His heart racing, Peter closed the distance rapidly toward this gimlet-eyed woman lugging her load with surprising speed toward the airport concourse. He couldn't let her get enmeshed in that throng. He *must* act now.

He came up hard behind her. "Ilse!"

In a blur, the woman spun around and fired that imagined pistol from somewhere within the folds of her cashmere coat.

Peter was caught flatfooted. It was unthinkable that this woman would just turn and fire without even knowing who had called her name. He could have been anybody.

It was just as unthinkable now that he should die this way, with his hand frozen on the butt of a pistol still snug in its holster. Whereas Engaard's first shot might have been solely to unnerve, her second would surely find its mark.

Peter's next thought was an odd worry that his father would understand that he had done his best.

Then came the concussion. Peter blinked reflexively.

When his heart resumed beating, he realized he was still unscathed. Nor had the blast, it seemed, even come from Engaard's gun. In fact, Gimlet-Eyes's weapon was now clattering on the pavement several meters away, where it had been sent spinning.

"Freeze!" commanded a familiar voice.

Out of the shadows stepped Neal McBride, his automatic pistol trained on Engaard's chin.

"I don't mean you," McBride snapped at Peter. "Her! Take her."

Peter, coming to life, silently rejoiced as he produced his own weapon and relieved Engaard of her jumbo tote. He popped the latch and peered inside with a penlight. Inside were a dozen or so mainframe-size tape cartridges, the old magnetic kind. He drew a bead on their red labels.

"Sontag Institute," he read aloud.

"Bingo," breathed McBride, still poker-faced.

The older man handed their captive a handkerchief and told her brusquely to do something about that bleeding. Then he turned his eyes expectantly to Peter as a signal.

Peter did not need to have a picture painted for him. "March!" he ordered, taking charge of Gimlet-Eyes at gunpoint.

"Schwein!" the woman snarled in a deep, unpleasant voice. But march she did, holding the reddening rag tightly about her hand.

Following beside Peter, Neal McBride at last allowed himself to crack a wee smile when he apparently thought his young partner wasn't looking.

Peter realized then that he should have known Neal would never leave him twisting. But it was the closest he had come to death since that time nearly ten years ago when he had been held captive in a mind-control experiment in a castle dungeon.

1

Columbus, Ohio

Dyana Waldo's deep, dark eyes fastened on Peter McBride the moment he stepped into the outer office. They were penetrating eyes that often left him feeling exposed, reminding him of things he preferred to forget, of someone very much like this young woman.

"Hi, Champ," Dyana hailed him. "Have we made the streets of America safe once more for young children and beautiful secretaries?"

Peter smiled despite himself. Just like her older sister, Dyana could read him like a text download. She seemed to know just when to jolly him into a better outlook.

"Beautiful secretaries? You mean like dazzlingly gorgeous and multitalented femme fatales who work for world-famous private investigation agencies?" he suggested. "Maybe on the fifth floor of Columbus office buildings at High and Long?"

The truth was that she was especially lovely today in a white-and-chocolate print dress that emphasized her dark complexion and brown, brown eyes.

"Yeah, like that," she said with wide-eyed innocence.

"Not a chance." Peter removed his hat and flopped wearily onto the divan, since there were no visitors at the moment. "It's criminals one, McBride and McBride zero at the moment."

Dyana's mouth turned down in an exaggerated pout. "Poor baby."

Peter had spent the first three days of this week playing the role of new management trainee at a machine tool robotics plant in Worthington in hopes of nailing an embezzler. Things had gone quite well at first. It had been an Academy-Award-caliber performance, if he said so himself.

But this morning, when the thief turned out to be the boss's son-in-law, Papa CEO pulled the plug and sent Peter packing with the assertion that he had to be mistaken. It just wasn't possible. So much for state-of-the-art criminal detection. Peter wondered when McBride and McBride would ever see payment on that invoice.

He returned the secretary's unblinking brown-eyed gaze beneath her brunette bangs. And all at once Peter found himself looking no longer into the eyes of the lovely Dyana Waldo, the well-groomed and fashionable McBride and McBride icon, but those of her older sister, Carlotta, the painfully beautiful and sensitive artist. And the unobtainable love of Peter's life.

Sometimes Peter wished it were anybody but Dyana at the front desk. Other times he was grateful for even the memory. He shuddered. This was the kind of thing that happened entirely too often.

He rubbed his eyes as if to break the spell. "Any messages?"

"No—well . . ." Dyana paused, glancing at the clock. "You're not going out again, are you?"

"No. As a matter of fact, I could probably fit a few things into my schedule this afternoon—like a Mack truck and an army transport plane. Why?"

Dyana's expression faded to a vague evasiveness. "Oh, Neal is expecting an important visitor any minute. He'd like you to join the meeting."

"Visitor? What kind of visitor?"

Dyana shrugged. "Maybe that's for you to find out, Sherlock."

Peter was getting irritated. "Come on. Last I heard, I was vice president of this outfit."

Dyana glanced to the right, then to the left. Then she hunched forward over the desk with a conspiratorial twinkle in her eye.

"Scotland Yard," she whispered.

Peter was dumbfounded. "Not *the* Scotland Yard?"

Dyana nodded solemnly. "*The* Scotland Yard."

It took him a moment to get it. She wasn't kidding.

★ ★ ★

Neal McBride remained trim and athletic in middle age, still somewhat tall and handsome, but no longer so dark. In the past few years the splashes of gray at his temples had taken over the entire neighborhood. At forty-six he looked more the picture of the mature county Common Pleas judge that he had played in real life ten years ago.

Now he was president of his own firm, McBride and McBride, Inc., Private Investigators. But this was not the simple craft of divorce cases, stolen jewels, and missing persons. As with most such firms in the intensive niche-marketing, global-economic business climate of 2047, McBride and McBride were specialists, experts in things such as corporate counterintelligence, industrial security, trade secrets, stolen patent rights, and alternative dispute resolution.

On alternate Mondays, McBride held court upstairs on the eighth floor of the Atlas Building as one of a growing cadre of private-contractor "rent-a-judges" superintending civil cases in this litigious society with its hopelessly clogged court dockets.

In countless ways, McBride and McBride had grown and prospered beyond its founders' expectations. McBride was learning how to delegate more and more important business to his adopted son so that he could spend his own time in more leisurely pursuits—such as honing his fly-fishing skills—and ponder the possibility of an early retirement afforded by his more recent prosperity. Yet, as much as he coveted the rare environs of trout streams and horse trails, nobody seriously believed Wilson Neal McBride was quite ready to hang up his trench coat or his social conscience.

Peter McBride, just two years out of law school, looked younger than his twenty-seven years. Gone were the riotous brown curls and the motley garb of the erstwhile rock musician, replaced with military-length haircuts and conservative business suits. He was over six feet tall and had the lanky frame of the modern triathlete—cycling, swimming, and powerblading on motorized in-line skates.

But there was no hiding his innate disregard for convention and ceremony, and the quick, uninhibited wit cruising just beneath the surface. His were eyes that alternately challenged and teased, that still had not abandoned the search for truth and love in a world that no longer held much regard for either.

Peter watched his father's eyes scan the face of their visitor on the other side of the conference table. The man was a close-cropped, graying gentleman with calculating eyes and a reserved air, a kind of guarded shrewdness. This was not your stereotypical London bull, Peter thought. He looked more like a stockbroker or art dealer.

Peter realized that observation was not far from the mark when Neal slid the man's business card his way.

He saw the name—Eustace Witherspoon, Detective-Sergeant —beneath the Union Jack and the All-Seeing Eye of the European Union. But it was the italic inscription in the lower right-hand corner that caught his attention—*"Interpol/International Art Registry Unit."*

This should be interesting, Peter reflected with mounting curiosity.

"We're not used to receiving visitors from overseas, let alone Scotland Yard," McBride said. "I've only been to London once myself—and that was just for a quick turnaround on business with Peter a few months ago. Not exactly time for sight-seeing."

There was a rap at the door, and Dyana entered with a tray of coffees, which she quickly distributed and then left.

"Thanks awfully," Witherspoon said.

Unable to resist, Peter gave the conversation a small shove.

"Are you certain you have the right place? Surely you didn't come all the way to the States and Provinces just to see us."

"Quite right," Witherspoon said between careful sips of his hot beverage. "Quite right. This is actually a side trip for me from Detroit, which is hosting an international conference on art and antiquities crimes. I was a panelist for one of the sessions, and I'm killing two birds with one stone."

"I see," said McBride. He glanced at Peter, as if to suggest waiting for their guest to volunteer his exact business.

Witherspoon set down his cup, extracted a pair of half-glasses from his breast pocket, and perched them toward the end of his substantial nose. He looked down at his notes on a pocket computer. Then he looked up again after a moment of scanning.

"Mind if I ask you a few questions about that trip to London?"

Peter exchanged another glance with his father.

"Not at all," McBride said. "What would you like to know? I presume you're aware that we've already given the State's Attorney a teleconference deposition."

Witherspoon cleared his throat. "Quite right. I'm looking at it even now." He held up his small booklet. "There are just a few other matters—starting with the Sontag Research Institute. How was it that you came into their employ?"

"Oh." Crow's-feet appeared by McBride's smiling eyes. "That's a classic case of not what you know but who you know. Madelaine Ostrander was a former student of my wife's at Ohio State University. Her husband, Walter Ostrander, is now chief of operations at the Sontag Research Institute and a personal acquaintance. He knew my line of work and gave me a call as soon as the genome-tape theft was discovered. His confidence level in the authorities' ability to solve this crime was quite low."

Witherspoon wore a faintly ironic expression. "How fortunate for you."

McBride betrayed no reaction. "And fortunate for Dr. Ostrander, as it turned out. While the authorities were still deciding who had jurisdiction, we were able to bring home the bacon."

"I beg your pardon?"

Peter interpreted. "We cracked the case."

Witherspoon looked at Peter as if for the first time. "As I understand it, you had a major role to play in this drama yourself. I'd like to hear how you located Ms. Engaard."

"Teamwork. We already had a fat file on Ilse Engaard from some of her earlier capers with stolen secrets from Ohio industries. After our employee interviews, Neal was convinced that she was the prime suspect."

"Yes," Witherspoon interrupted, "that's all in your deposition. But there's another question that was never addressed. All of Engaard's prior missions had been for the Asian Consortium. In fact, she had dual residency in Tokyo and Singapore. Why would she even have been a suspect in this case?"

"That's where you're mistaken," Peter said. "Engaard would work for just about anybody for the right price—and the right drugs. If your files don't show her carrying water for the friendly folks in your own EU syndicates, then shame on your files."

"But once she became a suspect in the genome case, what would make anyone think she would go to London?"

Peter and Neal traded glances.

"Good sources. Some intelligent guessing," McBride said.

"And a good deal of prayer," said Peter.

Witherspoon looked befuddled and straightened in his seat. "That's another thing. It's been said that you two gentlemen belong to some religious order. What about that?"

McBride's crow's-feet reappeared along with the tug of a smile at the corners of his mouth. "Not exactly. We're just simple followers of Christ."

"We like to say it's not religion; it's relationship," added Peter.

"Oh." Witherspoon relaxed a bit. "Sure. We still have some of those in the UK. Quaint."

"May I ask why you're asking?" McBride pursued.

"I'm sorry to be so mysterious, but there are some new developments in other areas for Interpol—which also has its own internal security issues. If things work out, all will come clear later. If not, it's better that you not know. Let's just say that this genome business may not be an isolated incident."

"Are there other cases?" Peter asked.

Witherspoon shrugged noncommittally. "Let me pursue this business about 'intelligent guessing.' Again, I don't want you to read anything into my hypothetical questions—and everything we discuss must stay right here in this room."

The detective paused, scanning the faces of both McBrides, who nodded.

"For the sake of argument," Witherspoon continued, "suppose that multiple genome registries were disappearing from different venues. If you had to guess, what would you suspect as a motive?"

"Not knowing anything about the thieves themselves?" asked McBride.

"Correct."

Neal and Peter exchanged looks again.

Peter took a deep breath. "Some mad-scientist insomniac is tired of counting sheep and wants to count chromosomes?" he suggested, ignoring their guest's unamused stare. "Or maybe there's an international fruit-fly shortage—a slump in drosophila-belly futures in genetics markets. No, wait. I know. The Antichrist is getting ready to set up his empire, and he's getting everybody's number."

"What?"

"Sir, you have just witnessed one of our secret weapons," McBride said a bit sheepishly.

"What is that?"

"Free-braining," said Peter.

Witherspoon looked alarmed. "You say."

"Free-braining—a cross between free association and brainstorming," McBride explained, smiling. "You'd be amazed how it limbers up the mind for nontraditional thinking. Sometimes it produces startling solutions to seemingly insoluble problems."

"As well as a lot of twaddle, I would guess." Witherspoon looked unconvinced. "I hope my brain never gets that limber."

"Seems to me," Peter said, "that you are somewhat nontraditional yourself."

Witherspoon blinked over his half glasses. "What do you mean?"

"According to your own ID, you're supposed to be an International Art Registry agent. And your stated reason for being here involves a conference on art crime—all of which seems to me a far cry from genetics and genomes."

"Quite right, my good fellow," the detective said after a moment. "You're quite right. But you're anticipating me. My next proposition was to ask you to suppose that some famous religious properties also had disappeared, in this case from a high-profile public institution in a European capital. If these two very different kinds of theft—genomes and religious treasures—could be shown to be related in any way, what do you suppose might be the motive?"

"What kind of religion?" asked McBride.

"Old Christian. Ancient, one might even say."

Peter straightened in his chair. "Let me guess. These ancient treasures—could they be relics with legendary powers? Something maybe supposedly supernatural?"

"You might say that." Witherspoon raised an eyebrow. "Hypothetically, of course."

"Of course," McBride said.

Peter's eyes were alight with curiosity. "I couldn't even begin to answer your question, but I'd certainly love a shot at working a live case like that—with some real facts."

"Go ahead and venture a wild guess," Witherspoon persisted. "Perhaps with your 'nontraditional thinking.'"

"That's easy," said Peter. "I'd be looking for a religious crackpot—maybe with a scientific bent, but certainly a religious nut of some sort. I'm not sure that narrows it down much. They're a dime a dozen these days, you know."

"That's about the same thing the *Hilfsgeistlicher* said."

"Who?" asked Peter.

Witherspoon ignored the question. "Why wouldn't you first consider a plain thief or some other kind of mercenary?"

McBride instead had a question of his own. "Has there been a ransom demand?"

Witherspoon paused. "In this hypothetical scenario—no."

"Then it's something more than a mercenary's filthy lucre."

"And why do you say that?" asked Witherspoon, holding up his pen like a lecture pointer.

Peter jumped back in. "Because if this is all such famous loot, then its resale value is practically nil. Normally, that would only leave artnapping—'give me a million dollars or *Mona Lisa* takes a long walk off a short pier.' But if there's been no ransom demand, then we have what you might call a real mystery—or else a real slow artnapper."

Witherspoon betrayed the ghost of a smile. Turning to McBride, he asked, "What do you know about international crime families?"

McBride shook his head. "Such as?"

"The Mafia, the Yakuza, P3, the offshoots of the Medellin cartel, the Greens, the Islamic terror groups, the IRA, the Red Brigade, and such."

"That's a little out of our league," McBride said. "Our industrial espionage cases frequently involve foreigners but usually white-collar types from otherwise reputable multinational corporate giants—and occasionally a foreign government operative."

"But we're quick studies." Peter did not wish to let the opportunity slip away too easily.

"Well . . . ." Witherspoon folded up his glasses and tucked them back into his breast pocket. "One last hypothetical question. If the need arose, would the two of you be available to fly abroad on short notice to participate in a significant long-term investigation? Assuming adequate compensation, of course."

"Perhaps—" McBride began.

"Anytime," said Peter. "Just say the word."

Hands were shaken once again, cordialities exchanged, and their visitor escorted out the front door.

Back in the echoing stillness of the empty conference room, Peter paced, wondering.

If this was some kind of test, did they pass?

* * *

First thing the next morning, Dyana announced a call from Vienna.

It was *Doktor* Werner Liebenfels, who identified himself as chief curator of the *Weltliche Schatzkammer of the Hofburg* in Vienna.

"Mundane Treasury." That's what the name suggested to Peter's rusty college-German ears. The Hofburg institution sounded familiar, but not nearly familiar enough. He figured they would have to confess their lack of upbringing.

On the big conference-room wallscreen appeared a white-haired, grandfatherly sort, who spoke with lightly accented English. He had the kind of delicate gold-framed glasses that Peter pictured on the noses of old Tyrolean elves. Was this the *Hilfsgeistlicher* to whom Witherspoon had referred? The old man's voice was dry like the leaves of an ancient tome, and his words tumbled one after another like polished stones.

"I am told that the two of you may be available for an assignment involving some considerable time away from home, *nicht wahr?*"

"Natürlich," said McBride. "If you really think we can be of some service. I would not want to mislead you."

"Did you get our names through the gentleman from the UK who visited us yesterday?" Peter asked.

Liebenfels blinked and nodded faintly. "But we must refrain from discussing these things except in person."

"Assuming we're the right persons," McBride said.

"We would not have purchased two Lufthansa tickets in your names if we did not believe we had found the right people to assist with our situation."

Audacious, Peter noted silently. Probably just his kind of guy.

"Uh . . . just when is this Lufthansa flight?" his father asked.

"Around noon your time," said Liebenfels. "From Kennedy."

"I mean what day?"

"Oh, tomorrow. Is that a problem? Our friends indicated you could leave on short notice."

"Well . . ." McBride's wheels seemed to be turning rapidly. "I guess I neglected to ask how short. If I call a staff meeting right away, cancel some appointments, and delegate some other things . . . sure, I guess we can do that."

Attaboy, Neal, Peter rejoiced. *Go for it.*

And while McBride and Liebenfels tied up all the loose ends the way only two natural-born administrators can, Peter concentrated on maintaining the slackness of his facial muscles and keeping the fire out of his eyes.

He reflected once again upon the truth of "McBride's Axiom": Never ever betray the fact that you enjoy your work, or someone will figure out how to put a stop to it.

2

Vienna

It didn't seem long since they'd taken off from New York, but the Lufthansa suborbital already was hurtling toward the crest of its arc over the Atlantic, where it would begin its descent toward the European continent.

Peter studiously ignored the movie—a weak Hollywood attempt at dramatic comedy with heavy doses of wise guys, loose women, and coarse language—and concentrated on the small stack of travel literature in his lap. He wanted to arrive in Vienna with some basic grasp of the Austrian capital and its major features, including Liebenfels's institution, before their meeting tomorrow morning.

In the next seat, McBride glanced through each piece as Peter finished one and handed it to him, as if he were already familiar with the material. He had spent most of his time pecking at a laptop keyboard, perhaps catching up on some business details.

"May I get you gentlemen something to drink?" asked a slender, mop-topped flight attendant whom Peter initially mistook for a woman.

McBride looked up from his keyboard. "Why, yes. How about a cream soda?"

"Make that two," said Peter.

The attendant gave them a funny look. "Right. And then I'll come back with your blanky and tuck you in for a bedtime story, OK?"

By the time Peter had forgotten about the exchange and resumed reading his travel guides, the attendant surprised him by returning with two clear plastic containers of redpop.

"Thanks," said McBride offhandedly, as if he'd never doubted.

And it wasn't just any old redpop, Peter noticed. It was Yankee Doodle Dandy Creme Soda, Neal's preferred brand, the kind with Old Glory emblazoned on the front.

Or, as some now called it, "Nouveau Glory"—sixty stars on the blue, and a large red maple leaf superimposed on the stripes. Peter had been a college freshman at the time of the historic merger of the two North American nations into the USP—United States and Provinces. He wondered how the flag designers would handle it if the rumored Big One ever came to pass—the union of North, Central, and South America. That could be the end of a flag and the beginning of a tapestry.

Such a North-South merger supposedly had been in the works even before the Canada-US consolidation, and pundits continued to talk it up as if it were continually just around the corner. The pressures for it were obvious. Out of competitive necessity to keep up with the trilateral economic juggernauts of the European Union and the Pacific Consortium, the Americas long ago had become a unified free-trade zone.

It was also obvious where all this was heading. While the world powers had coalesced into three major economic blocs, popular sentiment for a one-world order had intensified. In some ways, globalism had worked for the betterment of humankind in terms of eliminating some of the worst pockets of poverty, disease, and malnutrition. But at the same time had come rising overpopulation, plagues of sexually transmitted diseases, intractable pollution problems, widespread crime virtually to the point of anarchy, and the proliferation of nuclear weapons among some of the more unpredictable members of the family of nations.

Peter returned his attention to the subject at hand. The page before him told of the Hofburg's *Weltliche Schatzkammer*—"worldly treasury," apparently in the sense of big, important objects of value as opposed to smaller, parochial stuff. He got the idea that the term also had an imperial sense. The Hofburg served as the repository of regalia dating to the Holy Roman Empire, the Austro-Hungarian regimes, and the Habsburg dynasty.

"Hey, Neal," he said.

McBride grunted distractedly.

"Who—" Peter interrupted himself to take a closer look at the screen of the laptop. "What are you doing?"

"Brushing up on my German, *Jüngling*."

"Oh. Maybe I could see that for a few minutes when you're done. I need to do that too."

"You think a little brushing up will do it? I'd say more like a shave and a haircut."

"Thanks for the encouragement."

"No problem. Actually, I intended to do a little drill with you tonight in the hotel after dinner."

"Great. But first, help me brush up on my European history. Who were the Habsburgs?"

McBride scratched the end of his nose thoughtfully. "Uh . . . one of those important European families. Very important."

Peter sighed. "Good grief. Sorry I asked."

"That's all right. Like I always told you—you never learn anything if you don't ask questions."

* * *

In the flesh the next morning, Werner Liebenfels looked smaller and more fragile than he had on the videophone two days ago. Rising from behind his desk, the *Hilfsgeistlicher* appeared barely more than five feet tall. Peter's impression of a Tyrolean elf was only reinforced, though without the joviality. He wondered if Liebenfels never smiled or whether he was just preoccupied with the trauma of whatever crime may have been committed.

"Have a seat and make yourselves comfortable, *bitte*." He waved Peter and Neal to several sturdy, plush chairs arranged about a small conference table at the opposite end of his spacious office. "I shall send for refreshments."

While Liebenfels pushed a button on his desk and murmured something in German, Peter followed McBride slowly toward the darkly reflective table. He let his eyes roam the paneled office, taking inventory of the tome-lined bookcases, the glassed-in displays of various pictures and artifacts, and an elaborate suit of armor polished to a brilliant sheen occupying an entire corner, posed as if it still contained a medieval knight at the ready.

Liebenfels pushed another button, and a video monitor sprang to life at the end of the table.

Peter was confronted with the image of a golden crown inset with jewels and bedecked with an ornate gold cross. There was no mistaking the royalty here. This was a majestic diadem, one befitting more than a king, perhaps a king of kings.

He couldn't begin to guess what regal head actually had borne this crown—what potentate, emperor, kaiser, czar, or pope. It had surely been one of those important Dead White Males who once filled history books until such forms of education were deemed oppressive and American schools stopped teaching and promoting Eurocentrist culture.

Liebenfels took his seat at the opposite end of the table and scanned the faces of his guests. If he had intended to speak, he was interrupted by the arrival of the refreshments—a tray of flavored coffees, cookies, chocolates, and small pastries delivered silently by a young Asian man with heavy-lidded eyes. Just as silently and quickly, the youth was gone.

Peter munched on a petit four, grateful to be doing something less risky with his mouth than venturing observations about art and history.

At last, Liebenfels broke the munching-sipping silence with a single word. "Charlemagne."

Spoken loudly but with somber reverence, the name hung in the air like the echoing note of a herald's trumpet in an ancient hall.

Peter recognized the name. "*The* Charlemagne?"

"That's Charlemagne's crown?" McBride gestured to the wallscreen. "It's been stolen?"

"Before we get into the crime itself, are we all familiar with *Herr* Charlemagne?"

Liebenfels smiled sadly when McBride answered falteringly, "A French—no, German—well, a European king a long time ago. I think."

The old man actually cringed when Peter suggested, "One of the Habsburgs?"

"I thought as much," he said, half to himself. "The Philistines of the New Age have effectively destroyed public education and institutional memory in the West. It was Charlemagne's grandfather who saved Europe from the Saracens thirteen hundred years ago, when the masses were forced to choose between Christ and Muhammad. And half of Europe bows to Mecca today! Including our friend from Scotland Yard."

"Witherspoon?" said McBride. "He's a Muslim?"

Liebenfels shrugged and nodded. "Mullahs now outnumber priests twenty or thirty to one in Britain," he said with a sigh. "Austria too."

"That might explain some things about Witherspoon's attitude," McBride said meditatively.

Then in a louder voice Liebenfels called, *"Spiel Programm. Englische."*

With that, the image of the Crown of Charlemagne began glinting, rotating as if on a carousel, and a British-accented voice began to intone in velvet whispers, as if to a large but hushed audience, over subdued symphonic background music.

"Carolus Augustus. Charles the Great. The name that has come down through history best known to us as Charlemagne. King of the Franks. Founder of the Holy Roman Empire. A Christian Caesar—the ninth-century emperor of Western Europe, born of the German race, whose seal bore the motto *Renovatio Romani Imperii*—'Renewal of the Roman Empire.'

"This German prince who ascended the throne at the age of twenty-nine towered over his subjects—like Saul, the first king of the Israelites—at an alleged height of seven feet. With Charlemagne came the end of pagan barbarian rule that had toppled Christianized Rome. And with him began the political foundation of the Middle Ages and the establishment of the First Reich. Atop that lofty brow sat the crown you see now before you.

"While the origins of the forging of the Crown of Charlemagne remain obscure—"

"Halt!" called Liebenfels.

The Crown ceased revolving, and the velvet voice fell silent.

Peter's flesh was erupting in goose bumps. McBride was staring at the wallscreen as if mesmerized.

"We can discuss its jewel carats and other physical properties later," said Liebenfels. Then once again he addressed his interactive video. *"Die Heilige Lanze. Englische."*

Replacing the Crown was a more puzzling image. This was obviously a sort of lance, possibly of crude iron, but suggestive of some kind of power that Peter was hard put to identify. His persistent gooseflesh seemed to be intimating something almost diabolical.

"Some say whoever holds this spear holds the power to rule the world," Mr. Velvet was purring once more. "Superstition? Perhaps. And yet this Holy Lance, which some call the Spear of Longinus or the Spear of Destiny, is one of history's most remarkable and intriguing artifacts. Certainly it is one of the most legendary.

"Throughout history, the Spear has been a prized possession of forty-five European emperors in the thousand-plus years following the reign of Charlemagne. Some considered it to have magical properties.

"According to legend, long before Charlemagne the Spear was acquired by Constantine, the Roman emperor who converted the empire to Christianity. After Charlemagne it was held by Otto the Great, the first actual emperor of the Holy Roman Empire, and then by a succession of others.

"Legend also speaks of dire consequences for the one who lost possession of the Holy Lance. Charlemagne dropped it in a fall from a horse shortly before his death. Centuries later, Napoleon aspired to rule the world, but he failed to obtain the Spear, which was moved to Vienna to keep it out of his grasp—before the fateful battle of Waterloo. The Hohenzollerns, the kaisers of the Second Reich, also failed to obtain the Lance, which the Habsburgs refused even to lend for display."

"See," said Peter. "I knew the Habsburgs would be mixed up in this some way."

Liebenfels gave him a peculiar look. "*Ja.* It was the assassination of a Habsburg, Archduke Francis Ferdinand, that started World War One. And today this family is as much 'mixed up' in the European Union as it was in the Holy Roman Empire centuries ago."

The smart-video recognized the conversational pause as its cue to proceed. "And then in the last century, Adolf Hitler invaded Austria, 'liberated' the Spear from this present site in the Hofburg, and returned it to Nuremberg. A year later he invaded Poland and touched off World War Two.

"Ironically, it is said that when Hitler committed suicide in his Berlin bunker, it was the very hour that invading American troops captured the *Reichskleinodien*—imperial treasures including the Spear. Within months, the Americans, victorious in Europe and possessing this talisman, ended the war in the Pacific by unleashing the unthinkable power of the atomic bomb. By January 1946, they had returned the *Reichskleinodien* to Vienna."

"So," Peter interjected, "why are these called the Holy Lance and the Spear of Longinus?"

"That takes us back to the first century A.D.," the video responded, "and to its legendary original owner, a Roman soldier named Gaius Cassius Longinus, who witnessed the crucifixion of a Galilean carpenter called the King of the Jews. And with this Lance, it is said, the soldier pierced the side of this condemned man, attesting to his death.

"Last year marked the one-hundredth anniversary of the return of the *Reichskleinodien* to the *Weltliche Shatzkammer*—"

"Halt!"

Peter sat transfixed. Surely this was one of the more bizarre stories he had ever heard.

Neal was staring at the frozen image on the wallscreen, his mouth half open.

And then Peter was struck by a troubling thought. *What kind of man would steal objects such as these? And for what sinister purpose?*

He was even more confused when Liebenfels rose to his feet and declared, "Come. Let us now examine the physical objects themselves."

So had the Crown and Spear not been stolen after all? What crime, then, had been committed? It made no sense.

Following Liebenfels and Neal out the office door, Peter hoped he was about to get some answers. He also began to wonder if Liebenfels were something other than a rational—or scrupulous—individual.

They walked without speaking down a long stone-walled corridor. Their heels tapped out an offbeat rhythm of hollow echoes as if they had entered a large cave. It was an early weekday morning, but not so early that there shouldn't have been other people, regular museum visitors, trafficking these corridors. Perhaps that explained the velvet rope Peter had seen at the opposite end of the hall.

When they rounded a corner and abruptly found themselves at their destination, he saw another purple velvet rope barring the gallery entrance. Next to it was posted a sign in German. He could make out enough of it to get the general drift. "Exhibit temporarily off display."

Liebenfels unhooked one end of the cordon rope and gestured for them to enter. Inside, there was no question as to where to direct their attention. Two large display cases in the center of the room stood without their plexiglass tops. Peter noticed that two such enclosures were stacked one atop the other against the far wall.

"Behold, the *Reichskleinodien,*" said Liebenfels grandly. From the tone, Peter couldn't help but feel that the pronouncement was made with a degree of irony.

Despite his eagerness, Peter was taken aback when Liebenfels blithely reached into the display and snatched the crown off its red velvet base. He was even more surprised when the curator suddenly reached up and placed the crown directly atop Peter's head.

In another moment Liebenfels had removed a truncated spear from its leather case and had thrust it into his hands. Peter instantly recognized it from its pictures as the Spear of Longinus. It was upright in his hand, cold and heavy. Peter felt shocked, sacrilegious, and foolish all at the same time.

"Heil, Peter," said the old man, his bitter irony now unmistakable. "Upon this precast gypsum aggregate I shall build my church."

"He's still speaking English, I think," Peter said to McBride, "but I don't understand him."

Liebenfels appeared agitated.

McBride cleared his throat. *"Doktor* Liebenfels, if your problem isn't a theft, what exactly is it that you want us to investigate?"

By the time Liebenfels had snatched the Spear back from his grasp, Peter sensed what was coming and why.

"Fahlschung!" he snarled and cast the lance to the tiled floor, where it clattered and rolled. But now it was in two pieces, the spearhead having separated itself from the iron shaft.

McBride's darting eyes suggested he might be losing his judicial composure.

"It's a fake." Peter removed the crown from his head. "I would expect that this crown is a phony too."

"But why?" McBride furrowed his brow.

"That," said Liebenfels, his face a shade pinker, "is what you're to help determine."

* * *

Back in Liebenfels's office, Peter studied the ersatz crown and spear from every angle, absorbing every detail, while McBride and the curator talked fees and travel expenses. Peter was dimly aware that he was hearing some rather large numbers.

But he was more intent on the puzzle before him than on business arrangements. Even having been told that this substitute imperial crown was nothing more than cheap brass with stained-glass gems glued on, Peter was captivated. And even having seen the real thing in Liebenfels's video, he found this replica mightily convincing. His own untrained eye doubtless would have been fooled a thousand times.

The Hofburg staff, according to Liebenfels, had been fooled no more than a week. That, the curator said, was the elapsed time since the last routine inspection and maintenance had been performed, which Liebenfels assured them unquestionably would have exposed the forgeries. In fact, the very attendant most directly responsible for the upkeep of the articles had noticed only three days ago that something looked amiss and had sounded the alarm. Closer inspection proved she was right.

The Spear was an equal fraud. "Pot metal," Liebenfels had called it. Considering how it had fractured on impact, he was probably right.

Peter turned the two halves over and over in his hands. If the forgeries had been planted simply to thwart or delay detection of the theft of the genuine articles, it was unlikely that anything would be gained from further inspection.

He noticed another unfaithfulness to detail. The replica was not cracked in one place where it should have been. According to Liebenfels and the video, the legitimate spearhead was actually in two pieces connected by a silver sheath. In this reproduction, there was a sheath—probably of aluminum—but inside there was no break in the spearhead.

Something else was missing too. Where he should have found metal threads wrapped around the spear blade to secure a hammer-headed nail to the blade's interior, there were only threads. The forgers had not bothered with the detail of the legendary nail from the cross of Calvary. This would be a dead giveaway to a trained eye. Maybe this was the very feature that had tipped off the attendant.

Peter found that the end of his little finger would just fit into the shank sleeve, stopping when he reached the first knuckle. At that point, a small line or ridge could be felt on the inner surface. Was it his imagination, or did this hidden feature actually move ever so slightly under the pressure of his touch?

Peter withdrew his finger and reached for his pocketknife. With his Swiss army tweezers inserted as far as they would go into the tube, he attempted to gain a grip on this little mystery. After a half dozen false starts, one of the tweezer tongs finally slipped between the object and the interior surface. That proved, as he had suspected, that the object was something separate. It reminded him of a poster rolled up inside a packing cylinder.

In the background, he was vaguely aware that the conversation of the other two men had changed subjects.

"*Ja*, there's no question," Liebenfels was saying. "Like every other item in the *Schatzkammer*, the original articles are registered by three-dimensional computer profile in the International Art Registry in London. Witherspoon has confirmed that these are not the same articles that have been here since the last century."

Maddeningly, the tweezers had slipped off the end of the object, and Peter regrouped to gain a better purchase.

"But why us?" McBride asked. "What do you expect from us that Interpol can't provide?"

Peter, concentrating with bated breath, did not dare look up to capture an expression. But he heard the faintness of a sigh, and then Liebenfels's voice again.

"There are some—how shall I say?—internal security issues involved with Interpol that render it somewhat . . . *unzuverlässig*. Untrustworthy. I think you know what I mean, or you would not be in business. I wanted to hire a private agency, and Scotland Yard recommended you. For this assignment it is important to have someone with an appreciation of religious properties, *nicht wahr?*"

Bingo! Suddenly Peter had the hidden object out the end of the tube by a couple of centimeters, enough to get a peek. Now he could see that he was extracting a small white slip of paper that telescoped to a spiraling point while the far end remained fast inside the sleeve. He stuffed the paper halfway back, twisted it into a tighter coil to relieve the pressure on its tail end, and pulled again. *Voila!* Liberated.

"Excuse me," said McBride. "What have you got there, Peter?"

"I don't know. Some kind of 'message in a bottle' maybe."

The three huddled with the slip of paper in the center. Peter unrolled it three times before he was able to keep it from snapping back into its original coil. On the slip, which was about the size of a phone notepad sheet, were a half dozen lines of characters resembling mathematical symbols.

"Greek," muttered Liebenfels, taking the paper from Peter to peer at it more closely. "Does either of you read Greek?"

Both Peter and Neal denied it. Peter said he knew someone who did.

"I'd like to take that with me," he told Liebenfels.

"*Ja*. I'll just make a copy for myself first," said the older man, then scurried out the side door into the next room.

"What do you think it means?" asked Neal.

Peter shrugged. "Let's give Rick Stillman a call."

McBride nodded. "Rick Stillman. Yeah."

When Liebenfels returned with the paper and gave it to Peter, he was almost smiling. Peter wasn't sure how to take that.

"Just a couple more questions, *Doktor* Liebenfels," McBride said. "Then we'll be going. We want to walk the premises and then begin interviewing employees."

"Certainly."

"Is there anything you're neglecting to mention?"

The old man thought a moment and then shrugged. "Such as what?"

"Do you have any suspects in your own mind?"

Liebenfels's eyes narrowed, and his grim expression returned. "None at all."

The reply came a little too quickly to Peter's way of thinking.

McBride apparently agreed. "Speculate. Considering that they're too famous to be sold and there have been no ransom demands, who would want to steal such objects?"

"That, sir," said Liebenfels, "is something I am trying very hard not to think about."

Peter's flesh formed goose bumps again as his imagination began to conjure up a bogeyman in the Hitler tradition for the New World Order. He could appreciate why Liebenfels might prefer not to pursue that line of thought.

"Perhaps our Greek message will shed some light," he offered.

Liebenfels's frown deepened. "I do not want to be—how do you say?—a wet blanket, but in our present case it is possible that these spurious articles may be the only thing we will ever have to remind us of the originals."

"All right," said McBride. "Last question. There also seems to be a concern about stolen genome data. That's how our firm came to the attention of Scotland Yard in the first place. But what do stolen crowns and spears have to do with genomes?"

Liebenfels looked impatiently at his watch. "I do not know that they have anything to do with each other. That is something you will have to take up with Witherspoon."

Peter wondered why he felt they were not being told the whole story.

3

Paris

The private accommodations were all taken on the first Maglev shuttle to Paris, but the next train, only an hour later, had what they needed—a private business cabin with a small desk and phone.

"Are you sure he'll be there?" McBride asked.

"He should be by now," said Peter. "At least that's what Peggy said."

Addressing the communicator, Peter read off the eight-digit number for the Rhema Institute in Brussels. There was silence on the line while the connection was processed. Small lights hop-scotched on the phone panel like fireflies on a July evening. Out-side, a blur of Austrian countryside hurtled past the cabin window as the train shot silently along its supermagnetic corridor.

In another moment they were hearing Peggy Finnerty's fa-miliar voice. *"Rhema Institut Curatelle."*

"Peggy, this is Peter. Is Rick in yet?"

"Hi, Peter. Yeah, he just got here. Hold the line."

Peter unfolded the paper and scanned the Greek characters. For the first time he noticed that the symbols actually appeared to be handwritten in a neatly flowing calligraphy rather than mechan-ically word-processed. He hoped he had managed to flatten the sheet sufficiently to pass through a scanner.

Peter had not seen Richard Hanley Stillman since the Rhema Institute opened its European facility several years ago and Still-man moved to Brussels with Moira and their two red-haired little tykes.

Stillman, a developer of the revolutionary computerized lin-guistics system called Cybersynchronics, had perfected a method for universal Bible translation. Now, as Peter understood it, Rhema's work consisted largely of documenting the remaining unknown tongues and then physically getting the actual translations into the hands of the people. Peter hoped he and Neal could fit Brussels into their itinerary somewhere.

"Bon jour!" said a familiar Southern-accented American voice. The smiling face of Rick Stillman with his lively brown eyes and sandy hair appeared onscreen above the now unblinking lights.

"Guten Tag!" said Peter.

"Hi, Rick," said McBride. "It's good to see you."

"Where are you?"

"En route to Paris from Vienna," said McBride.

"Great. What brings you to civilization? Business or pleasure?"

"Business, unfortunately."

"Which means you can't talk about it, right? Are you coming to Brussels by any chance?"

"Only if we have to, sorry to say. We need to get to London, actually."

Peter held up the paper from the spear for Stillman to see. "But we also need a dose of Cybersynchronics."

Stillman nodded. "Sure. Just scan it to me, and we'll take care of it right now."

"That's what we hoped you'd say."

Peter carefully fed the document into the slot under the red lights and watched as Stillman manipulated something at his end.

"ALEX," Stillman said to his computer, "identify context."

Peter watched a puzzled expression cloud Stillman's face as he read something on another monitor.

The linguist appeared to key a couple of buttons before addressing ALEX again. "Retransmit." Then Stillman turned back. "OK. Who's into Greek Stoic philosophers?"

"Not I," McBride assured him.

"Do they have anything to do with the Habsburgs?" asked Peter.

"Epictetus," said Stillman. "It should be coming over now."

A new paper clocked out the other end of the scanner. Then the original slip began tractoring out the front. Peter snatched up the papers, barely conscious of the closing pleasantries being exchanged between McBride and Stillman. McBride was lamenting that Stillman had been so helpful with his long-distance translation that they didn't have a good excuse to go to Brussels this time.

"We're a full-service operation here," Stillman was saying. "Just send your tax-deductible charitable contributions to the Rhema Institute."

"We already do," said McBride. "How's Moira?"

"Great. Still teaching part-time at the *Ecole Polytechnic* so she can be home most of the time with the little rascals. And how's Judith?"

"Fine. Enjoying retirement. In fact, she was so encouraged by the response to her first book that she's now writing another."

"Oh? What about?"

"Something linguistic and very ancient. You'd know what it meant, but I certainly don't."

"Well, you'd just better make sure you get to Brussels at some point this trip."

"We'll certainly try."

As soon as Stillman was gone, Peter moved to summon the image of the mysterious text for the two of them to read together. "Display transmission," he called out.

Across the screen appeared the words attributed to Epictetus:

> *Behold the rod of Hermes. Whatever you touch with it will be turned to gold. Whatever you bring I will turn to good. Bring illness, death, poverty, and shame. Bring trials and tribulations—all these things shall be turned to profit by the rod of Hermes.*

"The rod of Hermes?" said McBride. "What's that?"

"Not only do I not know the answer to that question," said Peter, "but I don't even know who Hermes is."

"Was," corrected McBride. "He's dead. I think."

* * *

Dr. Gwydian Brandt inserted another slide into the microviewer and watched as the forty-six familiar small squiggles appeared on screen.

"Twenty-seven A," she directed the processor.

Instantly a coiling maze of double-helix segments materialized, rotating in slow motion about an imaginary axis.

"Initiate defect scan."

Brandt sat back and lit a cigarette, blowing the smoke away from the equipment and toward the ceiling.

"One positive," vocalized the processor a moment later, reiterating the message in the screen crawl. "CF—recessive."

Brandt muttered an expletive and took another drag on her cigarette, feeling the smoke fill her lungs. Her dark brows knitted together in thought beneath severe, gray-streaked bangs, intensifying the fierce creases in her leathery face. She was a powerful woman, who still worked out in the gym regularly even in her fifties, although she could no longer quite bench-press her body weight.

This was a vexing puzzle. Scientists were supposed to like challenging problems, but Brandt, a geneticist for the EU's Population and Health Ministry, didn't like this one a bit. Even when dominant, the cystic fibrosis gene was not a particular concern anymore because of the availability of modern medical treatment—and certainly not as a recessive. Four other lethal recessives had been turned up in this patient's scanning, but nothing unusual. And the only dominant one—a predisposition to atherosclerosis—was also highly treatable.

In fact, in terms of congenital problems, sexually transmitted diseases, and immunity dysfunction, this specimen seemed exceptionally clean. So why was this young man listed as a USP procreation restrictee?

Brandt tapped her cigarette ash off into the white porcelain cup, the one that droopy-eyed fellow named Kim had brought her from the Hofburg. Now that it had fulfilled its purpose—that is, providing an oral epithelial cell micro-sample from the young man for analysis—she intended to throw it away. For now, it was an ashtray.

The woman's gaze swept her cluttered study and fastened on the other Hofburg items, the ones that she would hold onto for dear life until claimed by their rightful owner. Only when the Ruler to Come had appeared would she unlock the antique glass case and hand over the ancient regalia.

Could this young man be the one? It certainly seemed far-fetched, but Zell had been intrigued by the report of this dashing young fellow from the USPA. She wondered what Zell knew that she didn't. Whatever it was, he certainly wasn't about to share it with her. The salamander!

But that was all right. She would have the last laugh. Let him figure out what had become of the *Reichskleinodien*. She'd be the last one to tell him.

Brandt stubbed out her cigarette and dictated a phone number to her communicator. After the second ring, a woman answered.

"PH Internal Affairs Division," said the woman. "Gwendolyn speaking."

"This is *Doktor* Brandt. Let me speak to Ivar, please."

"Certainly."

After a few long moments, a familiar man's voice spoke. "It's about time. What did you find out?"

"Garbage," she said. "In effect, totally negative."

There was a pregnant pause. "You kept me waiting hours for garbage? Is that the best you can do?"

"No," Brandt snapped. "But I just love to hear you whine when you don't get something. What do you think? Look, there's nothing there. Unless you want to spend a few hours and see for yourself. Be my guest."

"I wasn't questioning your technical expertise, believe me. But what do we do now? Any suggestions?"

"Maybe. We do know that this fellow is a procreation restrictee. If I can't figure it out from his genome, maybe you can find out from your Population and Health cronies in the USP."

"Well . . ."

"Or are you afraid you don't have the requisite clout and they might laugh in your face?"

"It's not that." Now he sounded quite defensive.

"Then what?"

"Just—what possible rationale would I use to argue a security exemption?"

"Be creative. Use your imagination for something productive for a change."

"Gwydian, some day—"

She snorted. "I'm going to go too far, right? In the meantime, what are you going to do?"

Silence. Then finally, "All right. I'll make the call. What was that name again?"

"McBride," she said. "Peter Carpenter McBride."

* * *

London

The ride through the English Chunnel had been noticeably slower, but the breakneck speed resumed on the other side, and before Peter knew it, they were in London. He and Neal had no trouble finding an autocab at Victoria Station. The only moment of apprehension came when they asked for Scotland Yard and the computer asked, "Great or New?" On further questioning they realized they did not want the original edifice near Trafalgar Square but the one called "New"—even though it was a century old—on Broadway between Victoria Street and Saint James Park.

In the United Kingdom, Scotland Yard served as the National Central Bureau for Interpol. Witherspoon, they had learned, divided his time between home base in London and Interpol headquarters in France.

Now Peter and his father sipped coffee and awaited their host in a cramped conference room with walls overrun by maps of various police districts distinguished by multicolored circles and arrows. Peter wondered why this conference couldn't have been handled telephonically and then concluded that he should be thankful—maybe they were about to receive some worthwhile and sensitive intelligence.

McBride voiced the hope that their hosts might offer the use of some temporary office space.

At last Witherspoon appeared, accompanied by the faint aroma of some pungent seasoning, perhaps garlic and curry. Peter noticed as they exchanged greetings, shook hands, and seated themselves that the man seemed somewhat more relaxed than he'd appeared in Columbus. So now it was Peter's turn to be reserved. Certainly, at the moment, he didn't much feel like free-braining.

"So, gentlemen," Witherspoon said. It was a subject that had no predicate, a simple serve over the net.

"Thank you for taking time to meet with us," returned McBride.

Witherspoon managed a perfunctory smile. "I trust you had an uneventful trip, unmolested by criminal, terrorist, or public transit."

McBride smiled back. "Yes, thank you. It was our first trip through the Chunnel. That was interesting—"

"For essentially a long hole in the ground," Witherspoon concluded.

"Essentially."

With an air of finality, the detective produced his half glasses, attached them to his nose and ears, and opened a file folder on the table before him.

He looked up over the spectacles. "I trust your discussions with *Doktor* Liebenfels were productive."

McBride nodded. "Although 'bizarre' might be more the word for it."

"Questions?"

McBride nodded again. "Do you have any suspects?"

"And what does any of this have to do with genomes?" added Peter.

Witherspoon smiled patiently, if not somewhat patronizingly. "If we had the answers to those questions, there would have been no need to bring in freelancers. Yes, there is no lack of suspects. But there is a singular lack of any prime suspect. As for genomes, it may be nothing more than a coincidence or a false assumption, but it certainly does seem to be open season."

"Has there been a rash of these thefts?" Peter asked.

Witherspoon frowned thoughtfully, meshing his fingertips and then nodding faintly. "You might say that. It's almost as if someone were trying to put together a complete record for all of humanity. Except . . ."

Peter pursued. "Except?"

Witherspoon gave a dismissive wave and then sifted through his folder until he found the right paper.

"It would be like trying to count the grains of sand on the seashore or the stars in the sky. We asked a government scientist from the Population and Health Ministry about the feasibility of creating a complete genetic record for all ten billion people in the world, and she assured us it was highly unlikely, if not impossible.

"For what it's worth—which isn't too much to me—it goes something like this: The genetic code for each individual consists of about six gigabytes—six billion bytes—of information. Therefore anyone thinking of running an analysis of the entire set would require a computer with the capacity of—let's see—6×10^{19} bytes just to store the data."

"Which exceeds anything we have today?" Peter asked.

"That's what she indicated," Witherspoon agreed.

Peter noticed Neal jotting down something on his notepad. He guessed it was some numbers to double-check with *Monsieur* Stillman.

McBride looked up. "You have no indication of a connection between the genome thefts and the Hofburg case?"

"Correct. That's our case too by virtue of its being an art-and-antiquities crime, but at this point—except for a security concern—it would be almost more of an insurance issue. We simply don't have the manpower to scour the world for missing relics and treasures. We have put out notices to all the National Central Bureaus, but—"

"You mentioned legions of possible genome suspects. Who would that include?"

"Half the politicians in the world, if you consider population control."

"What do you mean?"

Witherspoon put down his notes, removed his half glasses, and issued a slightly derisive snort. "Americans always seem to need history lessons. All right. Go back to the turn of the century. Do you remember what happened after Communism fell in Eastern Europe? What replaced it?"

McBride shrugged. "Capitalism?"

"That's a very broad term, my friend. It might also be said to include things like the black market, urban gangs, and organized crime cartels."

"Yes, but those things existed under Communism as well."

"Quite so. But after generations of state ownership, who else would have the wherewithal—the venture capital, you might say—to acquire the means of production? Certainly not the impoverished masses."

There was a rap at the door, which opened to admit a young, light-haired woman wearing a gray business suit with the aplomb of a fashion model. Peter initially judged her to be support personnel, until she inserted herself at the table and fixed the three men with a killer smile.

"Excuse my tardiness," the woman said in a melodious voice with the inflections of some place around Liverpool. "I had to finish my Whitehall report."

"Indeed," Witherspoon said. "Gentlemen, Sergeant Wendy Carlisle from one of our special units. I asked her to sit in with us today because she'll be assisting in this case. I think you'll find her perspective interesting."

Peter was finding her more than that. There was a magnetism in her gently sculpted features, her pale blue eyes, and her graceful movements that he found nearly irresistible. Another of those irrational male reactions, he reminded himself. So then, why did he enjoy it so much?

Witherspoon was speaking again. "I was explaining how terrorists, drug lords, and arms merchants actually bought up major portions of the economies of Eastern Europe as golden opportunities to launder their income. But similar things also occurred in the West as the EU—then called the European Community—set up shop."

"The Mafia," Peter suggested.

"Among others. In fact, even before the EU became a real United States of Europe, the Mafia had become indistinguishable from the government in southern Italy. It was only a matter of time before the same thing happened at the national level. Then, with the lowering of all trade barriers across Europe, international crime cartels received their biggest boost through wide-open access to the world's largest consumer bloc. Would you say that's accurate, Sergeant?"

Wendy Carlisle nodded and flashed one of her heart-melting smiles. "Essentially, all the old crime and terror groups—Irish Republican Army, Red Brigade, Medellin Cartel, Palestine Liberation Organization—have more or less blended with the establishment."

"Or," Witherspoon qualified, "have become the establishment."

"OK," McBride said. "I get the picture that you suspect some of these master criminals and criminal-politicians in the genome thefts. But I still don't understand the motive. Does this have something to do with the security concern you mentioned?"

"Or population control?" asked Peter. "What did you mean by that?"

"Well," Witherspoon began tentatively, "we're starting to get into classified areas here that I'm not really at liberty to discuss. Suffice it to say that there are many players, and some would like to get the upper hand. It could get dangerous before it's all over."

"A few things about population control have leaked into the popular press," Wendy Carlisle said, "with some degree of reliability."

"Such as?" said Peter, establishing a somewhat disconcerting eye contact.

The young woman glanced at Witherspoon before speaking. "It's an open secret that governments have felt compelled by crime, terrorism, and social unrest to respond through the mass media and public education. So we find a new emphasis on things like 'maximum adaptability to rapid social change' and 'remediating antisocial individualism.' Ironically, it's the kind of herd mentality that used to be promoted in the old Communist systems."

McBride was nodding as if this rang a bell with him.

The woman nodded too. "Obviously the first step in population control is to identify trouble spots. I would suggest, then, that genome analysis might be one powerful tool in any such effort—identifying predispositions to antisocial behavior as early as possible."

"The irony being," Witherspoon added, "that some of the individuals behind these things may themselves be hardly the picture of responsible social behavior. But there again we verge on speculation."

"Fine," said McBride, smiling. "Peter and I have had some very positive experiences with speculation."

Peter suppressed a smile.

Witherspoon and Carlisle exchanged glances.

Witherspoon acquired a distant look in his eyes and a more serious set to his face. "Personally?" he said. "I believe a lot of things could be explained by exploring *die Jüdische Frage*."

"The Jewish question?" said McBride. "What's that mean?"

"It means," said Ms. Carlisle, "that if you're looking for conspiracies, there's one that tops them all. There's one group that has its agents in the highest echelons of government, commerce, finance, the media, entertainment, social services, and academia all around the world. They pretend allegiance to whatever country they happen to inhabit, but all the while they are really working to promote their own subversive cause. When you stop to think about it, there's really only one group that meets the qualifications of a truly international conspiracy across the trilateral blocs."

"The *Jew*," said Witherspoon, his lips twisting.

"*Zionism*," said Ms. Carlisle in tones normally reserved for dread diseases.

The words hung in the air like an obscenity. Peter felt his hackles rising. It was as if a veneer were being stripped from an ugliness, a corruption that he had not asked to see.

"Personally," said McBride, breaking the tension, "I always thought it was the Rotarians."

Witherspoon's eyes flashed, and a smirk visited his mouth briefly. Then he said, "But enough of this idle speculation. It's all so much rubbish, isn't it?"

"Yes," agreed McBride, closing his notebook. "We certainly appreciate your patience and your time. It's time we should be going."

Witherspoon and Carlisle escorted them down the hall.

As they were leaving, Peter's curiosity wouldn't stop nagging him about this captivating woman at his side. Despite the perplexing display of anti-Semitism a few moments ago, he found himself half hoping that he and Ms. Carlisle would indeed be working together. At the front door, he took her warm, soft hand and shook it gently.

"To what unit did you say you were attached?" he asked.

"She didn't say," Witherspoon pointed out gratuitously.

"Can't you guess?" said the woman.

Peter shook his head. "No."

"Paranormal," she said with another megawatt smile. "I'm a police psychic."

4

Cleveland Heights, Ohio

Brilliant streams from the studio skylight etched large, white rectangles on the bare oak floor. In one of them curled a Siamese cat and in another a black Persian, slumbering to the strains of Brubeck and Mingus and Monk.

At one end of the studio, Vida Beasley, a tall, angular African-American with cornrows, was practicing clarinet with a canned score of old composers.

At the other end, Carlotta Waldo, a dark-haired woman with a Mediterranean cast and intense brown eyes, was applying electric blue acrylic to a canvas with a No. 3 brush.

Vida, an instructor at the Cleveland Institute of Music, merely nodded the beat for several measures, marking time while the recorded instruments played on. Then she blew and worked a final crescendo of notes from her clarinet, ending with a melancholy fade. She upended the instrument with one hand and flipped through her music with the other, looking for a particular Copeland piece.

Then she stopped.

Carlotta, sitting frozen before her canvas, had that look again.

"Stat," Vida called, halting the music program.

She set down the instrument and walked casually over behind Carlotta, who was perched on her high stool, brush hanging limply toward the floor, eyes staring unfocused at the unfinished painting. They'd been housemates for only a few weeks, but Vida had become accustomed to Carlotta's mysterious mood swings.

Vida peered at the image on the canvas and felt a chill, literally. It could have been Michelangelo's *David,* if Michelangelo had been an ice sculptor. A sinewy figure with bluish-white skin appeared suspended in some gauzy medium, like a fly in amber. Pale eyes and expressionless face were framed by stylized albino curls.

"Um-*hm,*" said Vida. "Now that's what I call one white man."

Carlotta, also an instructor at the Cleveland Institute of Art, said nothing but looked at her brush as if wondering how it had ended up in her hand.

Looking more closely, Vida noticed something arresting about the subject's face. Aside from the deep-freeze aspects and other differences in detail, it clearly resembled other countenances she had seen on prior canvases.

"It's *him* again, isn't it?"

Carlotta visibly stiffened. "No," she said quietly but firmly.

"Come off it, girl. Any fool can see what it is."

"I don't know why you say that," Carlotta said, a little indignantly. "It's supposed to be symbolic—the hidden person of the heart."

Vida snorted. "The hidden person in *your* heart, maybe. A psychologist would have a field day with this. Here's this idealized man—unapproachable, unobtainable—who's become a human ice cube, just like somebody else I know."

Carlotta turned a puzzled face to Vida. *Me?* her eyes said.

"Yeah, you, Rembrandt. What's that called? Projection?"

"Are you saying I'm the ice cube?"

Vida gave a little snort. "It makes a lot more sense to me than that hidden person of the heart stuff."

"That doesn't make me an ice cube."

"No, you've done that by staying home and making like an old maid."

It was Carlotta's turn to snort. "I don't notice you exactly painting the town."

"If I had the kind of invitations from young men that you do, the town would have a new coat every night."

Carlotta lowered her eyes, looking chastened. "I'm sorry. I didn't mean that."

"No problem."

Silence rushed back into the studio. The Siamese stretched in the sunlight, then balled itself up again. Nearby, one black Persian ear twitched and waved involuntarily like a radar dish searching for a signal.

Carlotta stood up, set down her brush, and returned her attention to the canvas, wiping her hands on a rag.

Vida sensed an opportunity to find out something she'd wondered about.

"How come you and Peter never got serious?"

Carlotta frowned at the canvas, a stiffness entering her voice. "I told you this is not Peter."

"OK, OK. It's the hidden person of the heart or whatever. You're evading my question."

Carlotta sat down again. "We were serious. That was years ago. Now we're just friends."

"Why don't I believe that?"

"Believe what you want."

Vida decided to pursue. "So what happened years ago?"

Carlotta was silent for a long moment before speaking. "We were going to be married, but Peter was denied a procreation permit."

Now they were getting somewhere. "Why was that?"

Carlotta shrugged. "Something genetic. They were afraid our children would have expensive medical problems that weren't in the state budget, I guess."

"So?"

Carlotta blinked in incomprehension.

"That explains why you wouldn't have children," Vida continued, "not why you didn't set up housekeeping."

"You mean live together?"

Vida nodded. "That's what most folks would do."

Carlotta's shoulders seemed to cave further under her oversized denim smock. She turned her baleful brown eyes back to the canvas. "We had moral reasons. Besides, if I'd become pregnant without a permit, you know what that would mean."

"Mandatory abortion."

Carlotta nodded. "And sterilization."

"You had a problem with that?"

"Yeah, especially Peter."

Vida was reluctant to keep pressing, but it was a little late for that. "What was the problem?"

A new spark appeared in Carlotta's eyes. "Why do you want to know?"

"I'm concerned about you. Tell me to mind my own business, and I'll go back to my twentieth-century composers."

Vida was gambling that Carlotta would not pull the plug. She was sure they were very close to something now.

Carlotta appeared torn between speech and silence for a long moment. "There were . . . religious reasons."

"Oh." Vida began to get the picture. "Peter is one of those?"

"Both of us were."

"Were?"

"Well, Peter still is, I guess. I'm not so sure about those things anymore."

Ordinarily Vida would have been relieved to know that her roommate was not a religious kook, but somehow she sensed that there was more to it.

Now Carlotta's tongue appeared to have loosened. "Peter says once a believer, always a believer. He calls me a 'backslider,' but he says salvation is irrevocable."

"Does that make sense to you?"

"No. I don't know." Carlotta's voice was pinching. "There's not a lot that makes sense to me anymore."

"So if you can't have Peter McBride, you won't have anyone at all?"

"Maybe I'm just not interested."

Vida sensed that Carlotta's tears were welling.

"So when did you last talk to him?"

"A couple weeks ago. He's in Europe now for a while."

"How do you know that?"

"Dyana told me."

"You talk to Dyana a lot, don't you?"

"She *is* my sister."

Vida tried a different tack. "You ever been to Europe?"

"No."

"The quarter ends in a week. Why don't you let that graduate assistant take your classes for a while? Maybe Dyana could hook you up with Peter. She has to know his itinerary, doesn't she?"

"Are you saying I ought to go track him down?"

Vida shrugged. "Why not? You might as well be with him. Seems to me you're carrying him around on your shoulders all the time anyway."

"You remember saying I could tell you to mind your own business?"

"OK, babe. Have it your way." Vida sighed and picked up her clarinet. "Run program," she called.

As the initial strains of Aaron Copeland filled the room, building up to the first clarinet's part, Vida shot a glance at Carlotta. Her housemate was biting her lip. There was a telltale glossiness under each eye. She wondered what Carlotta would do.

The Siamese, no longer in the shifting patch of sunlight, got up, stretched, and yawned. Stiff-legged, it walked around to the other side of the Persian and curled up once again, just as the Persian itself had done a little while ago in their slow-motion game of leapfrog.

★ ★ ★

Brussels

The view from Richard Hanley Stillman's office window was enchanting. Stately white swans like porcelain figurines glided almost imperceptibly upon an emerald lagoon rimmed by immaculate topiary, a cobblestone walk, and an occasional wrought-iron bench with young lovers staring either into the miniature lake or the depths of each other's eyes. Across the water, flanked by miniature fruit trees, stood the magnificent sun-washed Greek revival edifice of the Academie d'Beaux-Arts, mirrored in the green stillness.

Peter tore himself away from the window as a door opened behind him.

"Bienvenue!" cried Stillman, pushing into the room and opening his arms wide.

"How continental, Rick," said McBride, joining the hearty embrace. "No kissing, though, please."

"Peter!" Rick cried again, giving him a big hug.

"Good to see you, Dr. Stillman," said Peter, anticipating a rebuke.

"That's Rick to you, my boy," said Rick sternly. "Don't make me feel any older than I already feel, seeing you look like such an old man. Let me look at you."

Rick eyed him up and down, then turned to McBride.

"Definitely looks more like a lawyer than a rock musician now. I kind of miss the old look in a way."

Rick himself didn't look much older, though it had been five years since Peter had last seen him in the USP. And five years before that the three of them had had their big adventure, facing death together at the hands of cultists in a castle stronghold. That had been excitement enough for a lifetime.

The quiet, professional life appeared to agree with Rick. At just over forty, he projected greater confidence and self-assurance. There was very little gray in his sandy hair, few creases in his thin face, and hardly an extra pound upon his slender frame. Peter guessed that he still worked out regularly. And then he remembered Rick's mentioning Brussels's great cycling routes in one of their recent phone conversations.

Things with the Rhema Institute, however, had changed considerably. While the organization was still headquartered in Chicago, its action was occurring here. Rick's boss, Darnell Jones, was in the Third World coordinating the introduction of the Scriptures into people groups where most of the members could neither read nor write. Now, as translation chief, Rick had become, in effect, Jones's boss.

"Quite some layout you have here," McBride observed. "I suppose the restrooms have marble floors and gold fixtures?"

It was a question that had occurred to Peter too. How did Rhema justify the elegant antiques, the mahogany and teak, the black and green marble, the fireplaces and chandeliers and spiral staircase on a missionary budget? In fact, Rick's own office, with its oriental carpeting and elegant paintings and statuettes, looked more like a parlor where aristocrats in formal attire should be sipping port and smoking Cuban cigars.

Rick was unperturbed. "Not quite. Fortunately, our benefactors are accommodating. Actually, we're just tenants in this facility from year to year at quite favorable rates."

McBride looked surprised. "How did you swing that?"

"Have you ever heard of Sir James Crisp?"

"The conservative British member of the European Parliament?"

"The same." Rick lowered his voice at this point. "You don't need to repeat this, but he's arranged for us to occupy it for at least the next several years. It used to be the old British embassy in the days before Unification. So it's still technically the property of the UK. A small British office and a ton of records are still maintained here, thankfully."

"What do you mean?"

"If they ever close out operations totally, the whole facility will probably go on the block, and we'll be looking for a new situation."

There was still one thing that Peter didn't grasp. "Why the sensitivity?"

"Sir James is a believer and a powerful ally. We don't want to cause him embarrassment of any sort by getting his name mixed up in any religious controversy."

"Don't worry," McBride said. "We still know how to keep a secret."

"Terrific." Rick directed his guests toward the waiting seats. "So do I. Maybe you can clue me in as to what you're up to."

"If you're in no hurry."

"Certainly. Drinks?"

Peter nodded, and Neal smiled.

Rick moved behind his desk, opened a small cooler, and retrieved a liter container of red fluid, possibly cream soda.

As Rick filled three glasses with crushed ice, McBride began summarizing the human genome and Hofburg cases with the economy of detail of a judge instructing his jury.

Then Rick's eyes were riveted to McBride's face as if he were studying a book. Stillman would let no detail pass unnoticed.

Peter detected the faint passage of a smile across his face as McBride recounted the Scotland Yard version of genome data analysis.

Rick began scratching a few notes on a yellow legal pad while McBride finished. "So that's why you're concerned about big numbers and databases," Rick said at last, tactfully not pressing for additional details. "I'm glad you gave me a day's warning about the question you posed. It gave me time to do a little checking."

He got up and retrieved a file folder from his desktop. Then he extracted a pair of reading glasses from a breast pocket. That was new.

"Lesson Number One," he said, looking up over the glasses. "Never trust government figures. You were told that the entire genetic code for every human on earth would take 6×10^{19} bytes of computer memory. Says who? Where did Scotland Yard gets its data?"

"Ostensibly from the EU Population and Health Ministry," McBride said. "Is that not a correct number?"

"As far as it goes. I'll give them the benefit of the doubt and assume that something got lost in the translation."

"What do you mean?"

"Well, there's no question that we're dealing with extraordinarily large numbers here. In fact, the PH number on the surface would appear to be an understatement, considering that it's only taking into account storage capacity. Any computer to handle a database that large would require enormous capacity for processing and analyzing the data. We're talking big here—like something approaching the number of stars in the entire universe. Do you have any idea of the magnitude of that?"

"Not at all."

"OK. Each galaxy is supposed to contain an average of one

hundred billion stars. And how many galaxies do you suppose there are in the universe?"

"I don't know. A thousand? Several thousand?"

Rick's eyes were showing crow's-feet now. "Peter?"

Figuring Neal had guessed low, Peter aimed high. "A million?"

"Not even close. At least two trillion. Some say as many as ten trillion. Using the smaller number, the product is 2×10^{21}. That's two with twenty-one zeros after it. Even your nineteen zeros —on the surface—would be a stretch. I was doing some figuring, and I come up with approximately two years, running night and day, for one of our supercomputers to process that much data."

Something nagged at Peter. "Why do you keep saying 'on the surface'?"

"Because I did a little research and discovered something that the Population and Health bureaucrats, of all people, ought to have known—that in practical terms the real number has to be much, much smaller."

"Why smaller?"

"It's a very simple but fundamental fact. Ninety-nine-point-five percent of the human genome program is dedicated to defining the human being; the remaining half percent accounts for the distinctive differences among individuals. That's approximately *thirty million* bytes of information, as opposed to six billion."

An idea was dawning on Peter. "Thirty megabytes? That's not so much, is it?"

"Not really—about the equivalent of three volumes of the *Encyclopedia Britannica.*"

"OK," Peter said. "So you can factor out the other ninety-nine-point-five. How feasible would it be to computerize that for ten billion people?"

"We can do it here," Rick said flatly. "Cut it by a factor of two hundred for the half percent, which works out to enough data to keep a supercomputer running for about three-and-a-half days. And there are a couple of other favorable factors not taken into account."

"Like what?" asked McBride.

"Like incomplete data and parallel processing. I know that much of the Third World data has yet to be assembled. So we're talking maybe two-thirds, at best, of the total base, counting the EU and the Americas. Now we're down to two days of work. Then let me crunch the data with multiple computers networked together, and I believe I could work this out in an afternoon and still have time for at least a half-round of golf."

"I see," said Peter. "It does make one wonder why their experts wouldn't know that."

"If an outsider like myself can figure it out, anyone can."

McBride was frowning. "We already suspected we weren't getting the whole story—such as why the genome thefts and the Hofburg case should be related at all. This only reinforces those suspicions. Do you have any hunches about the genome thieves themselves?"

Rick's eyes focused out the window toward something near the distant lagoon. "Somebody's obviously looking for a very small needle in a very large haystack. Whatever it is, it takes on a sinister cast when associated with the stolen imperial regalia. Obviously there's already a lot of paranoia about another Hitler rising up—or an Antichrist figure."

"If this gets out," Peter said, "there's going to be a whole lot more paranoia before it's all over. Considering the One World movement and all the power intrigues going on, any government would be crazy not to be concerned about this sort of thing."

Rick's eyes lit up. "There's a theory for you. Do you remember all of the twentieth-century American political assassinations?"

They nodded.

"I recall that at least one of the assassins was influenced by Madame Blavatsky and the Theosophists. She'd suggested that such terrorism, even though isolated, could create the illusion of a grand conspiracy. Then that 'grand conspiracy' could undermine people's confidence in legitimate authority. And when that occurs, the conditions are right for a demagogue to seize power."

Despite himself, Peter shivered. This was not a pretty scenario, but it had the ring of truth.

"It's been done before," he agreed.

"In our present case, however," Rick Stillman went on, "there's one major element missing."

"What's that?"

"Public knowledge. So far, it's all a big secret. Should that change, watch out."

* * *

Paris

Yussef Halima was nothing if not suspicious—not to mention superstitious. There was no way he would make any attempt on the old *imbécile* so long as she remained holed up in her den. Yussef did not want to take chances. Too much was at stake. He would take her on his terms, away from all of that, when she was without defense.

So Yussef waited in the parking lot behind a graystone apartment building in the center of the Montmartre, looking up at the early morning sky and pretending to change a tire on his rental car. At any moment she should be rounding the corner, heading for her own car and for work. And then he would be upon her, as swift as a shadow, as sure as a viper.

Across the small lot was the woman's late-model, steel gray Chakra. In its gleaming finish Yussef could make out the distorted poached-egg reflection of the sun at dawn. He kept his distance. Touch it, and the Chakra would howl like a banshee, waking the entire neighborhood. Only its owner could disarm the security alarm. There were five other cars, whose owners might eventually awake and arrive.

Praise Allah, this woman was an early riser, and there was no other activity among the dumpsters and fire escapes at the back end and lee sides of the slumbering old structure. Still, he would have to make it look natural, just as though they were comrades in car pooling, in case there were other eyes at this hour peering from a kitchen window.

And then she was rounding the corner just as he'd pictured her, hefting a bulky briefcase and making a beeline for the Chakra.

Yussef hoped she'd see him. See him absorbed in tire repair and discount him. That way there'd be less startle response at the crucial moment.

There. She saw him and moved on.

Instantly he was on his feet and across the lot. He intercepted her by the Chakra. "Act natural or you die." Yussef impressed her ribs with the pistol in his jacket pocket. "Now walk around to the other side, open the door, and get in."

He talked softly and showed her his teeth in a manufactured smile.

Hatred glared back from beneath her gray-streaked bangs, through her severe, chrome-framed glasses. But she obeyed without a fuss, moving deliberately to the other side of the Chakra and pressing the disarm button. The door swung open.

"Get in," he said. "Quickly."

Yussef followed her in and shut the passenger door as she slid behind the wheel. Now she was swearing like an iron worker. The profanity was in German, and he couldn't follow most of it. But he got the general idea.

"You can have the car," she said, switching to French. "Take it and drive it to perdition, but let me go. Here—I give you what's in my purse too."

Yussef showed her his weapon, and she froze. It was a gasser, and an expensive one. These compressed-air, tumbling-dart jobs were not the kind of weapon employed by garden variety carjackers. He could tell by her expression that she now understood the gravity of her situation.

"Start driving!" he commanded. "Circle the block. No funny moves."

After the second left turn, Yussef ordered her to pull over. He figured he could find his way back to the apartment building from here on foot, cutting through the alley into the back lot.

"What do you want?" she said in a voice that had lost its huskiness. There was a pleading look in her eyes, replacing their former haughtiness.

"Don't worry, *imbécile,*" he said, suppressing a smirk. "I only want the keys to your flat. Hand them over now, and you can go."

She had to know what he was after. She also had to know that he had no intention of letting her go call the police while he was breaking in. Knowing she was a dead woman, her only move could be to hurl the purse into his face and grab his gun. He expected that.

She did not disappoint him.

With one hand he blocked the traveling purse. With the other he fired his gasser. Far more quietly than a conventional pistol with a silencer, the weapon delivered its deadly sting.

The woman's head slumped against the driver's window, a small pool of blood collecting in her right ear, where the dart had entered.

★ ★ ★

Inside the flat of the late Dr. Gwydian Brandt, Yussef unfurled his gunnysack and reverently approached the glass case. In the dim light the articles were unimpressive—a crown with a cross and the business end of a spear. Yet what power they represented. What a fool this Brandt woman had been to let them out of her sight. He would not make the same mistake.

At the first resistance of the cabinet door, he reduced the compression on his gasser and fired directly into the lock. Without further ado, he opened the cabinet, snatched up the articles, and held them aloft long enough to praise Allah and congratulate himself on a job well done before slipping them into the sack. On his way out, he snatched one more item, a pack of cigarettes off the old woman's dining room table.

He resisted the temptation to hurl himself to the bottom of the back stairs in one leap. Getting into his car, he was flooded with fantasies of invincibility—of driving through a brick wall, watching bullets bounce off his chest, liberating Jerusalem from the infidels. He suppressed them all, reminding himself of his mission as a humble operative.

Yussef backed around in the lot, then lit one of the old woman's cigarettes. Gripping it in the corner of his mouth, he grasped the wheel with both hands and pulled out onto the half-asleep street.

Maybe he was invincible, but he still wasn't going to take any chances. If he had to sleep with the articles in his bedroll, he would maintain unswerving vigilance until they were safely delivered into the hands of the Imam.

5

Vienna

Werner Liebenfels looked like a man whose shoes pinched. His jaw appeared clenched, his eyes harried, his normally crisp business suit rumpled, and his white hair slightly disheveled. The Hofburg curator was holding a dossier and looking up from behind his desk when Peter and Neal entered the office.

"Perhaps I expected too much," he said wearily, sighing. "It may be too late."

"What do you mean?" Peter asked.

Liebenfels handed over the dossier. "Giselle DuChesne. I think you interviewed her."

Peter took the file. "Sure. Sharp lady. Almost too sharp."

"We not only interviewed her," said McBride. "We were tracing her references. There were things in her personnel file that seemed questionable—like being overqualified for an assistant archivist position. What about her?"

"*Gegangen*. Gone without a trace. She must have sensed your suspicion and decided to make her move."

Peter had a sinking feeling. "Assuming she's guilty."

Liebenfels looked bemused. "Have you a better candidate?"

"This could be a break—or a ploy," McBride said. "Did you notify Interpol?"

"*Ja,* but she had the entire weekend to flee before anyone here missed her."

Peter shook his head. "She could be in Sierra Leone by now. Or Pago Pago."

"We also have to assume that Giselle DuChesne may be an alias, which means a forged passport," said McBride. "So Interpol may not even be looking for the right person. We'll re-interview everybody on the off chance that someone might have gleaned something useful about her while she was here. She's got to be our insider."

Peter agreed. "There was never any question about an inside job. It's just a question of who she might have been working with on the outside."

Liebenfels looked as if he were considering saying more. "That's what worries me."

McBride gave his admonishing-judge look. "If we're going to be of any help, we have to know what you know."

Slowly Liebenfels got up from behind his desk and turned to stare out the window.

"I *know* next to nothing," he muttered after a moment. "Suspicions abound, but where would one begin?"

"Give some examples," Peter prodded.

Liebenfels turned back from the window and laughed humorlessly. "You want me to talk like a madman? Very well. There is no lack of candidates for imperial power. How about our esteemed EU chancellor, Waldemar Neumann, who would lead humanity into the glorious One World Order? Or the Imam of Babylon, who is rallying all the forces of Islam into a great jihad against the West? Or Emmanuel Ponzi, pontiff of the New Order of Rome, who would unite all faiths into one? Or Salvatore DiFalcone, the mafioso who seems to pull all global economic strings from prison? And, of course, there are always the Jews.

"But do I *know* anything to accuse any of them? No. I prefer to think that when this whole thing is solved, it will turn out to be nothing more than a clever addict's fund-raising scheme for his next drug shipment."

"But you don't really think that," Peter suggested.

"If you repeat anything of those things I just stated, I shall deny it."

McBride pushed the issue. "What's got you so philosophical?"

Liebenfels sighed. "Apparently you have not heard. Perhaps you have not been watching the news."

"Uh-oh," said McBride. "Have we had a leak?"

Instead of answering directly, Liebenfels gave his communications console a voice command in German, summoning to life the video at the end of the conference table. In deference to his guests, Liebenfels called up an English news channel, and in another moment they were seeing a tight-panning exterior view of the Hofburg as a British-accented woman began painting a scene of world-historic grandeur that was obviously a set-up for something ominous.

"Though museum and police officials are keeping mum," she said, "it is believed that the stolen items include the ancient and priceless Crown of Charlemagne and the Holy Lance, the spear that legend says pierced the side of Christ and has been the possession of many European emperors and kings. The articles currently on display in their place are said to be merely cunning replicas. No price has been set on the loss, but one antiquities expert said it has to be in the millions."

The scene changed to obvious stock images of the regalia.

"Sources say don't look for any official government comment on this one. High officials may be quaking in their boots, worrying as to whether, after half a century of unification, a new totalitarian or hooligan politician is about to upset the delicate European power balance and attempt to assert imperial powers."

Then came the part that took Peter completely by surprise.

"But the most unusual aspect to the entire mystifying case was a clue apparently left behind by the thief—or thieves—consisting of a quote from the ancient Greek philosopher Epictetus."

The words themselves crawled across the bottom of the screen as the woman spoke.

"'Behold, the rod of Hermes. Whatever you touch with it will be turned to gold. Whatever you bring I will turn to good. Bring illness, death, poverty, and shame. Bring trials and tribulations—all these things shall be turned to profit by the rod of Hermes.'

"Nobody seems to know what this means. But the larger question is why would a thief go to the trouble of leaving behind such a clue in the first place? For One World News, this is Crystal McKenzie."

Why, indeed? And how in the one world did Crystal McKenzie come into possession of that fact?

Instantly Peter was back in Brussels, watching swans gliding effortlessly across a green lagoon. Rick Stillman was uttering his prophecy—"So far, it's all a big secret. Should that change, watch out."

Suddenly this was getting deep. He also recalled Witherspoon's observation that things could get dangerous before it was all over. If a hidebound institution such as Scotland Yard was now using police psychics, anything was possible. Peter found himself wondering what Sgt. Wendy Carlisle would make of these bizarre developments.

McBride broke the heavy silence. "I assume no one in your organization has been speaking to the media."

Liebenfels sighed again. "Certainly not. Standing orders, by oral directive. Of course, I also assumed that no one in my organization would have been involved in so shocking a crime in the first place."

"This could be wider than you think," Peter said.

Liebenfels's frown deepened.

"Unless Giselle DuChesne herself orchestrated the media leak, the other possibilities are even more disturbing."

"That's right," McBride agreed. "Think about it. Anybody who knew about this Rod of Hermes business is a potential suspect. That includes the three of us, our friends in Scotland Yard and Interpol—"

"And Rick," Peter interjected.

Liebenfels raised his eyebrows. "Rick?"

"Dr. Stillman of the Rhema Institute in Brussels," McBride said. "He's a technical consultant, the one who translated the Epictetus quote. I would trust him with my children's lives—in fact, I have—but no suspect gets an automatic free pass, no matter how improbable."

One idea kept nagging at Peter. "Let's not be too quick to rule out the thieves as leaksters."

Liebenfels looked bewildered. "What sense does that make? Would they not want to avoid publicity?"

"Look," Peter said, "they left a clue in the phony lance. Anything's possible. We know too little about who took these things—and why—to start ruling anything out. There's been no ransom demand. So maybe they want to make some kind of political statement. Who knows?"

"This One World report by Crystal McKenzie—how widely was it circulated?" McBride asked. "Did other news organizations report the story too?"

Liebenfels rolled his eyes. "That was one of the longer reports, but it is being picked up all over Europe and probably elsewhere. Short articles also have appeared in many major newspapers."

Peter shook his head. "Wait till the tabloids get hold of it. This is bound to get pretty squirrelly."

Liebenfels stared blankly.

"Sonderbar," said McBride. "That reminds me—we need to have a media strategy."

"No comment," asserted the *Hilfsgeistlicher.* "I answer no media questions, make no statements."

"Fine," Peter said. "What do you do when the paparazzi and the scandal sheets descend on you like a locust plague, harassing employees, disrupting business, and manufacturing pictures and stories?"

Liebenfels looked pained. "I could get a restraining order, no?"

McBride shook his head. "You want to cool the story off, not heat it up further."

This time the old man nodded resignedly. "*You* want to take the heat? Be my guest. What would you say?"

"The truth," said McBride, "but as little of it as possible. A lot depends not so much on what you say but how you say it."

Peter laughed. "Yeah, boringly. Neal's a former judge and a master at boring. He can make a New England farmer sound like a blabbermouth."

"Klatschmaul," McBride translated. "Excuse him. The lad gives me too much credit. But, yes, I would like to handle the media."

"Certainly." Liebenfels looked somewhat relieved. "Are you prepared to spend some significant time on these premises?"

"By all means. In fact, if you could free up some office space, I would like to set up a base of operations right here."

"Agreed. The assistant archivist's office has suddenly become available."

"Then I'll start re-interviewing the employees and handling any media inquiries—once we've agreed on an official statement. Peter, it may be time for us to split up. What kind of a game plan would you propose?"

Peter had, in fact, given some thought to strategy.

"I'd like to go underground, find out what's being said on the streets. We won't really know whether this is basically an antiquities heist or something different until we've worked some informants. Probably our Interpol friends can get me started. And I want Rick to help us get to the bottom of this Rod of Hermes business. That's key."

McBride pursed his lips and nodded. "That sounds like a plan. But while we're at it with Giselle DuChesne, there are a couple of other young ladies who may bear some checking out."

"Who?"

"Wendy Carlisle and Crystal McKenzie. Why don't you see if you can get Sgt. Carlisle to help you trace the leak to Crystal McKenzie, and in the process try to get a reading on Sgt. Carlisle herself."

Peter was nonplussed. "You're not suggesting we actually work with a psychic?"

McBride shook his head. "Just find out what we're dealing with. It's better if we have her involved in a limited, controlled way until we figure it out. That anti-Semitism business was more than a little unsettling."

"Yeah. It also might be interesting to know just what kind of paranormal discipline Sgt. Carlisle practices."

McBride nodded, then looked at his watch. "If it seems like I'm giving you the lion's share of work, that's probably true. Other duties call on the home front. I'll have to divide my time soon between here and the USP. But I think you can handle it."

Peter certainly hoped so. Nevertheless, he was suddenly beginning to feel a bit small and vulnerable.

* * *

Frankfurt

With no one ahead of him on the people-mover, Amos Sloat was able to glide forward in that slow-motion gait that felt like a disorienting sprint when he looked at stationary objects on either side.

Sloat, a dark-haired man with penetrating eyes and hawkish nose, reminded himself for the umpteenth time that this part of the job was necessary. If there was anything he loathed more than Arab terrorists, it was Neo-Nazis. And this man Dieter Pflaum was one of those. The worst part was when they said "Heil, Hitler!" and he was compelled to respond in kind.

Dieter Pflaum was a flight plan programmer at the Frankfurt airport, computer-coordinating runway schedules for probably two dozen airlines, Sloat guessed.

He exited the people-mover, clutching his clipboard, and took an escalator to the next concourse. He paused at the top to casually scan the crowd beneath him. If anyone was tailing him, he couldn't spot it. After some years of instantaneous memorizing faces and focusing on the most nondescript ones for possible patterns, Sloat had confidence in his ability to pick out a tail. It was the ones that maybe he didn't spot who worried him.

Heading down the final corridor to the Flight Planning Department, he slowed his pace, reminding himself to get into character. He had to be Dennis Scovill, an American fascist who idolized the German Nazi underground and who just might be an operative or informer for some Western intelligence agency. He was sure that was what Dieter Pflaum suspected. If he but knew.

Since Sloat had lived half his life in Israel and half in the USP, he had no trouble with the American accent. He just kept in mind some of his favorite protagonists from twentieth-century films, actors such as Jimmy Stewart, Humphrey Bogart, and John Wayne. As long as he could hear their voices in the back of his mind, his own English stayed snappy, slangy, and devoid of European or Middle Eastern inflections.

As Sloat leaned his weight into the door, he remembered to tuck the pencil behind his ear, just like the real messenger service guys. In navy blue corduroys, royal blue windbreaker, and Italian soccer cap, he looked the part. Inside, he caught the eye of the secretary whose desk was nearest the counter.

"Package for *Herr* Pflaum," Sloat announced, laying his thick manila envelope on the counter.

He turned the clipboard around and extended his pen to her. As soon as she had initialed it, he was out the door and breezing back down the corridor. The envelope contained an old newspaper, a photograph, and a two-sentence, handwritten note.

The newspaper was filler. The photograph was of one Mustafa Ghöttas, a Turkish guest worker in Germany. The personal note was from Dennis Scovill—Sloat—summoning Pflaum to meet him at Schuster's Cafe.

Pflaum. The name stuck in his throat like something he wanted to spit into the gutter. He hoped the idiot got caught and sentenced to hard labor—but not before he had loosed the hounds of hell upon Mustafa Ghöttas.

He retraced his course back down the escalator and through the length of the terminal on the people-mover. This time he stood still and let the machine do the walking. He had time to kill until Pflaum caught up with him.

It was time to be alone with his thoughts again and his eternal wonderment over that perennial preoccupation of the human race—hatred.

He had first seen it in the schoolyard, that smirking, conspiratorial camaraderie of bullies as they marked out a fellow pupil who was too slow or too awkward, who had ears that were too big or legs that were too short, or whose shabby clothes marked him as lower class, or whose speech had some unfortunate quirk or impediment.

And then would begin the mental murder, the mocking, the taunts, the jeers, the ostracism, the cruelty, as effective as any wolf pack once it has surrounded the deer and drawn first blood. Slowly you could see the victim shrivel inside, sinking into a pool of depression and self-hatred until he believed the mockers and gave up his soul permanently to despair and desolation.

Somehow young Sloat had never been able to fathom this primal mob-think, let alone participate in it. He had been a big kid with a big heart, and he'd always tried to befriend these victims. Once he'd even bloodied a bully's nose, earning himself the grudging respect of the playground crowd but winning few friends in the process.

Then he grew up and learned how much worse it was in the adult world. Catholics hated Protestants. Arabs hated Jews. Blacks hated whites. Feminists hated male chauvinists. And vice versa. No matter the group, there seemed to be a corresponding adversary. Just by being born into the world, you came with a heritage of enemies. You learned either to avoid them or, if that were impossible, to make sure that any assault by your enemy cost him something in return.

And, of course, there was no better example than tiny Israel, the whipping boy of the nations, the skinny kid with glasses who had to learn some tricky moves just to survive.

In all the time that Sloat had worked for Shin Beth national counterintelligence, he had never killed. Sometimes, as now, he did things that might well result in serious physical mishap to an enemy of the state, but he had never served as the actual triggerman. Not that he necessarily wouldn't or couldn't; it was just that he preferred the role of agent provocateur.

At Schuster's Cafe, Sloat picked up a newspaper and slid into a seat in the back. At this time of the morning, midway between breakfast and lunch, the place was half empty. He ordered a cup of coffee and a piece of strudel and began browsing through the sports and business sections. When he finally turned to national/international news, one story practically jumped off the page at him. He read it twice. Incredibly, someone had broken into the Hofburg in Vienna and removed the Crown of Charlemagne and the Holy Lance.

The possibilities overwhelmed his imagination. He was well enough read to know that something truly sinister had to be afoot. No one could hope to sell articles like these on the black market. Wouldn't anyone shrewd enough to pull off such a crime also be sharp enough to figure that out?

Sloat glanced up from the paper, looked both ways, and then began, as inconspicuously as possible, tearing the article from the page. Something told him that this was worth checking into.

"Clipping coupons, eh, *Herr* Scovill?"

Sloat barely managed to contain his surprise. Dieter Pflaum stood beside his table, looking down upon him with a haughty smirk upon his thin, Teutonic lips. He was a tall man, well over six feet, and built like a natural athlete—one of those men who didn't need to subject his body to regular punishment, like Sloat, to stay in shape. His other features were less remarkable—very short, mousey brown hair and gray-blue eyes that seemed empty of any emotion except a predatory cunning.

Sloat covertly pocketed the clipping and forced a grim smile. "I see you got my message."

Pflaum nodded and sat down.

A waitress came and was dispatched for another coffee and strudel.

Sloat watched as the man extracted the mug shot of the Turk from his shirt pocket and laid it before him like a specimen on a slide.

After a moment Pflaum spoke again. "This Mustafa Ghöttas—why should he be of interest to me? What has he done?"

Sloat smiled again. He had little doubt now that this was going to work nicely.

"Do the names Deirdre Kurtz and Wilhelm Deardorff mean anything to you?"

Pflaum's face instantly darkened. "I knew them personally. We were friends. Their deaths will be avenged. Are you saying this Turk—God help him—was responsible?"

Sloat shrugged. He didn't have to say another word. Pflaum believed it now because he wanted nothing better than to do so.

Nevertheless, Pflaum asked, "What proof do you have? How do you know he did it?"

"I have no proof I can show you, nor can I tell you how I know. That's just the way it has to be. I think you can appreciate that. You can certainly choose to ignore it if it's proof you need. It makes no difference to me or my friends what use is made of this information. That's entirely your business."

Pflaum licked his lips, but Sloat was sure it wasn't because of the coffee and strudel that had just arrived. The man chewed and sipped in silence for a minute before speaking again.

"Where do I find this Mustafa Ghöttas?"

Sloat suppressed a smile this time and extracted his date book from the breast pocket of his jacket. He wrote down an address on the notepad in the back, tore it off, and handed it to

Pflaum. It was a public housing complex on the wrong side of the tracks, a notorious venue for scores of guest workers, with whom the German citizens maintained an uneasy truce that occasionally erupted into vandalism, hooliganism, and worse.

"Well, *Herr* Pflaum," Sloat said, slipping his date book back into his jacket, "if you choose not to pursue this and some further misfortune befalls your comrades, don't say I didn't try to help you."

Pflaum uttered a vicious oath. "This Turk, I swear, is a dead man."

"In that case—" Sloat allowed himself a modest smile "—we never had this conversation."

"Natürlich," said the flight programmer, hoisting his coffee mug in salute to Sloat, who was picking up his check and rising to his feet. "Heil, Hitler!"

"Heil, Hitler," said Sloat through his teeth as his stomach churned. It was probably too much to expect that he might have been spared that final indignity.

* * *

Across town an hour later, Sloat sat on a park bench, tossing popcorn to some pudgy pigeons and waited for the Israeli Embassy attaché Morris Farber. His thoughts kept returning to Mustafa Ghöttas, aka Muhammad Ben Nabil. Sloat had misled Dieter Pflaum on only a few details, such as Nabil's victims. They weren't two; they were three. They weren't Germans; they were Israelis—two soldiers and a twelve-year-old girl.

The two soldiers had lingered for days in a Tel Aviv hospital after their arms and legs and much of their faces had been blown off by a bomb under the hood of their Jeep. The girl had died more quickly, her throat slit when her value as a hostage had been expended and Nabil had made his way into Lebanon.

In Beirut he had acquired his new identity and a Turkish passport and emigrated to Germany as a guest worker. But Amos Sloat had put his ear to the ground and his nose to the trail and found him.

And now Dieter Pflaum and the Neo-Nazis were about to

find him too. Sloat wondered what means of retribution they would choose. He hoped it would not be too quick and painless.

He did not immediately react when a man's weight suddenly depressed the bench beside him. He continued methodically tossing out popcorn to his feathered friends. He heard the rustle of paper. Peripherally he could see the man opening up a newspaper.

Only then did the man speak. "How is work?"

It was Farber's voice.

Still looking straight ahead, Sloat responded, "My part is accomplished."

"You have met your quota?"

"I have filled the order. Now we await delivery."

"How soon?" Farber sounded pleased.

"Tomorrow. Maybe the next day. Very soon."

"Who's delivering?"

"Superman. Keep watching the newspapers."

Farber fell silent, apparently satisfied.

But Sloat had the feeling that he was not done and that another assignment was in the offing.

"There is a man in Paris who needs your services," Farber said at last.

"How soon?"

"Immediately."

At that, Farber refolded his newspaper and got up from the bench. A half-dozen pigeons moved back and regrouped.

Sloat, resisting the impulse to look over, could tell that the older man was pausing in his tracks, as if looking around. And then he was gone.

Only then did Sloat look across the bench. There beside him lay the newspaper. In one motion, he grasped it, stood up, and emptied the remaining kernels from his popcorn bag before the scattering birds. He glanced about and quickly walked off in the opposite direction from Farber.

Back in his car, Sloat opened the newspaper and began leafing through it. On page two a story circled with red marker riveted his attention. It was an account of the Hofburg incident by another news service but containing essentially the same facts about the Crown and Spear and the Epictetus quotation. A most curious coincidence. But why did that concern *him*—or the longbeards of Israel?

Before he even turned the page, the other piece of the puzzle dropped into his lap, literally. Out from between the back pages slid a sheet obviously copied from an intelligence report with certain names and other sensitive data blacked out, in case it fell into the wrong hands. Sloat was accustomed to working in the dark and understood the need for caution, but at times he couldn't help feeling a little resentful.

The report contained a good deal of police background, but, unlike the case of Muhammad Ben Nabil, there was no indication of what this new terrorist had been doing to warrant the attention of Shin Beth. All he could glean was that it was another A/E—apprehend or eliminate—and that it somehow concerned the security of Israel or one of her friends.

That and the fact that the man's name was Yussef Halima.

6

London

The floor of the timeworn sanctuary trembled, and the walls reverberated to the majestic strains thundering from the ancient pipe organ. Several dozen parishioners rose to their feet, clutching battered red hymnals and joining their voices roughly in tune.

> "Jerusalem the golden,
> With milk and honey blest!
> Beneath thy contemplation
> Sink heart and voice oppressed.

I know not, oh, I know not
  What joys await us there;
What radiancy of glory,
  What bliss beyond compare."

Peter McBride didn't feel particularly at home inside the hallowed walls of St. Mark's Anglican Church. Something was too formal and ritualistic—mechanical, almost—about this Wednesday vespers service. But it was as close as he could manage to his familiar back-home, midweek evening meeting here in this quarter of London.

At least the hymn was familiar. Barely glancing at the words, Peter let his eyes roam the auditorium from the ornate stained glass and massive wrought-iron chandeliers to the dark, hand-carved woodwork of pulpit and altar. He found the elaborate accoutrements distracting, and he redoubled his efforts to secure his own spiritual value out of this service regardless of its deficiencies or his own prejudices.

"O sweet and blessed country,
  The home of God's elect!
O sweet and blessed country
  That eager hearts expect!
Jesus, in mercy bring us
  To that dear land of rest;
Who art, with God the Parent,
  And Spirit, ever blest."

As the reverberations ceased and the hymnals closed, Peter sat down, feeling vaguely as if something had changed in the old familiar hymn. Wasn't that supposed to be "God the Father" in the last verse, or was his memory playing tricks on him? Or was the British version different from the American?

In the hiatus, the pastor, robed in white and gold, stepped up to the podium and cleared her throat.

This clergyperson was the Rev. Lucille Trevor-Bledsoe, a middle-aged woman with close-cropped, dark brown hair, probably dyed, and a hard, unhappy face. As she began speaking, Peter reminded himself to give this spiritual leader the benefit of his personal doubt. It wouldn't hurt to put up with a little social gospel talk for once. There was no harm in that, as far as it went. It was just what it left out—the need for spiritual regeneration. In any case, he did not feel his own faith necessarily threatened by this sort of thing.

For a while all appeared harmless enough. Pastor Trevor-Bledsoe talked around the edges of Christianity. She addressed the cries of the oppressed for social justice and the needs of the hungry to be fed, the naked to be clothed, and the homeless to be sheltered. She spoke of the deep longings of humankind to be liberated from injustice, insensitivity, materialism, and corporate greed. And she reminded her flock to look within to find that universal, divine spark.

That's when it started to go rapidly downhill.

"As the Ba'hai faithful say, religion is the divinity within us reaching up to the divine above. But the grim reality of everyday experience is that 'the whole creation groans and suffers the pains of childbirth.' We still await a deliverer, as we sang in the opening hymn. We groan like those in Bible times, 'Where is the hope of his appearing?'

"At the Christ's birth, the chosen people of Israel were awaiting a Messiah to save them from Roman oppression. They despised and rejected a Savior who failed to save them and merely died on a cross, unable even to save Himself. Like those Jews, we too need an authentic messiah to bring peace and justice to a divided world and hope to our own broken hearts. Where is the hope of his appearing?"

There was more—mainly about pulling oneself up by one's own spiritual bootstraps and cultivating some nebulous "Christ consciousness." But Peter heard little of it. His ears still stung from the slur against Christ, the denial of His resurrection and of the hope of His return. He couldn't help but feel that this Rev. Trevor-Bledsoe was setting up her flock to hear a different voice and follow a different shepherd.

He looked discreetly about him at the attentive parishioners. Did they understand that they were receiving a different gospel? It wouldn't appear so. In some cases there appeared to be very little consciousness at all, let alone Christ consciousness.

Peter was mildly surprised to find that the worship time was concluded with an opportunity for "testimonies" and prayer requests. He couldn't help wondering what was the hope of their praying?

Abruptly Peter, the inveterate Scripture memorizer, found verses coming to him. He began formulating a statement and decided to seize the opportunity. He knew he would be considered impertinent, but he chose to obey the prompting.

"Excuse me," he said, rising. "But I have a word from the Lord."

There was a hush while heads turned his way.

"'Know this first of all, that in the last days mockers will come with mocking, following after their own lusts, and saying, "Where is the promise of His coming? For ever since the fathers fell asleep, all continues just as it was from the beginning of creation."'"

Trevor-Bledsoe's lightly amplified voice attempted to override his. "My good man—"

But Peter pressed on. "'The Lord is not slow about His promise, as some count slowness, but is patient toward you, not wishing for any to perish but for all to come to repentance. But the day of the Lord will come like a thief, in which the heavens will pass away with a roar and the elements will be destroyed with intense heat, and the earth and its works will be burned up.'"

Trevor-Bledsoe looked harder and unhappier. "I would just point out that this is a time for testimonies and prayer requests, not orations."

A very round-headed old man with a bumblebee-striped bow tie raised his hand partway and then looked toward Peter. "I would like to ask the young man—are you saying, sir, that Christ, in fact, is coming again?"

"No," said Peter, "the Word of God says it."

Trevor-Bledsoe's voice was acquiring an edge. "I would remind our American friend that wild-eyed fanatics for centuries have been declaring that the end is at hand, and still the world goes on."

"But that doesn't mean the end might not really be at hand."

His calmness belied the wild-eyed-fanatic stigma. "There is only one last thing that stands in the way."

"I say," said the old man again. "What is that one thing?"

Peter could almost feel invisible forces drawing sides as he consulted his pocket New Testament for the next verse. "Let no one in any way deceive you, for the day of the Lord will not come unless the apostasy comes first, and the man of lawlessness is revealed, the son of destruction, who opposes and exalts himself above every so-called god or object of worship, so that he takes his seat in the temple of God, displaying himself as being God."

Peter had a feeling that the old man was probably one of the only true believers in the place.

"And just who is this 'man of lawlessness?'" the man pursued.

An unhappy murmuring was arising among the parishioners, who seemed confused by the proceedings.

Trevor-Bledsoe held up an admonishing hand. "This concludes our time of testimonies."

Peter ignored her. "He's the one we've heard about here tonight—the so-called authentic messiah, the alternative Christ who will promise a kingdom with peace and justice and warm fuzzies."

"I've heard of that," said the old man sharply, oblivous to the disapproving stares. "That's the Antichrist."

"That's right," Peter agreed. "And he may well be alive in the world today."

"No!" said Trevor-Bledsoe, reddening. "That's not right, and we are not about to countenance this kind of clamor."

As if a self-fulfilling prophecy, the pronouncement was greeted by an upsurge in murmuring, like the gust when a smoldering house fire suddenly bursts forth to involve the entire structure.

"Poppycock!" rose one voice above the din.

"Freak!" cried another.

Peter heard the old man say, "Now, wait just a minute—" and then his voice was lost in the tumult.

There was a smacking sound as though someone's face was being slapped, although Peter couldn't see who or where.

Another smack. There was a flurry of activity several rows

behind him as parishioners seemed to be separating two figures who were still thrashing about.

He wondered what Trevor-Bledsoe would do now that things really had gotten out of hand. He didn't have long to wait.

The red-faced pastor pointed at two older chaps in the front row, who dutifully rose and began working their way back down the aisle. Peter recognized them as the regular ushers. He was just wondering how effective these elderly fellows could possibly be as sergeants at arms, when they stopped at his pew.

"Come with us, please," said the younger, a small, wiry fellow with reddish, oily hair carefully combed over a bald spot.

"I was just leaving anyway," Peter said pleasantly.

"No, this way," said the older man, a stronger figure despite his years. He gripped Peter's elbow and aimed him toward a side door.

Peter decided to cooperate rather than get accused of elder abuse.

They entered a dimly lit corridor.

"Where are we going?" he asked.

The younger man opened an office door, switched on a light, and turned back to Peter.

"We're calling the bobbies, of course," he said matter-of-factly.

"Now wait," Peter said in disbelief. "Why the police?"

The older gentleman looked at him as if scrutinizing an errant schoolboy and then shook his head. "Creating a public uproar. The bobbies may not be very sharp at serious crime, but they do know how to nail traffic offenders and disturbers of the peace."

A knock at the door stopped the phone call temporarily. Both ushers conferred in hushed tones with someone outside.

"Um," said the older man on his return, "you can go now."

"I can go?" Peter repeated, then began moving toward the door. "So you're not calling the police?"

"Don't have to," said the younger man. "They're already here."

Nothing made much sense, but Peter kept walking. It just didn't seem credible that the police actually would make an arrest.

Out in the darkened corridor, he was joined by a woman whose face he could not make out while his eyes adjusted to the dimness. She escorted him around a corner, out a side door, and onto the street, where her upturned face came into sudden focus in the soft glare of a streetlight. It was an unusually fair face, and one he recognized immediately.

"Good evening, Peter."

"Sgt. Carlisle!"

"Wendy," she corrected. "And you're . . . uh . . . under arrest."

"What!"

"Sort of," she said with a little laugh. "If this is the best way you know to amuse yourself in London, it's a real crime. Come along, now."

* * *

A few blocks away on Seaton Row was a reasonable seafood restaurant, the "Squid Pro Quo." They were shown to a table in the back of the dimly lit establishment. The place felt comfortable and intimate. It was a place where one could speak freely.

Sgt. Carlisle—Wendy—smiled wryly at Peter when he ordered a ginger ale with his mussels platter. She ordered white wine with her calamari.

Wendy Carlisle looked like neither police officer nor psychic. If anything, she looked a prim, young schoolteacher whom beaus two centuries ago would have been inviting to ice cream socials. Her medium-length, light brown hair neatly framed a gentle face of fine complexion, delicate lips, and large, sensitive eyes. She wore a simple, beige print dress that accentuated her slender figure. The entire effect was quite pleasing, wholesome—just the kind of woman that appealed to Peter. He had to remind himself that she was not really on the same team, spiritually at least.

"So," he said as the waiter receded with their order, "you wanted to know what I was doing at Saint Mark's this evening?"

"Besides disturbing the peace and creating a spectacle, yes," she said lightly. "Eustace said you and your father were very religious."

"Eustace?"

"Stacy. I'm sorry—Sgt. Witherspoon."

"Oh. Yeah. Well, 'religious' is not exactly the word I'd use."

"What, then?"

Peter paused thoughtfully as the ginger ale and white wine arrived.

"'Blessed,' maybe. 'Redeemed,' certainly."

He watched Sgt. Carlisle's expression change to puzzlement, but she said nothing.

"So," said Peter, changing the subject a bit, "I might ask you the same question. What were *you* doing at Saint Mark's?"

"Why, that's my church. I've been going there for years."

Peter struggled with the concept. "But you're not a . . ." He paused.

"'Christian'? Why not?"

"I don't mean church membership."

"What *do* you mean, Peter?"

"I mean being a believer in Christ and one of His followers."

Wendy Carlisle lifted the wine glass to her lips while keeping her eyes fixed on him. She drank deeply, then closed her eyes for a moment in apparent satisfaction. When she opened them again, there was something transfixing, almost hypnotic in the depth of her gaze and the assurance of her smile.

Peter felt the undercurrent of a deep and mysterious attraction.

"I am all of those things," she purred. "And more."

"So now I have to ask what do *you* mean?"

Her smile broadened, and she fed it more wine. "I am a follower of truth, wherever it may be found."

Peter found himself wanting not to offend this lovely creature, yet needing to draw a line, tactfully. "So what does that exclude? Anything?"

The wine was at her lips again. She leaned on her forearms with the glass thoughtfully near her face.

"'In abundance of counselors there is victory.' That's what the Bible says."

"It also says that the Lord Himself is the 'Wonderful Counselor,'" Peter noted. "Do you mean you're a follower of other counselors?"

Her pale blue eyes turned vague and distant. She shrugged. "To varying degrees. Buddha. Muhammad. Lao Tzu. Confucius. Crowley. Krishnamurti. As the mystics say, 'One light, though the lamps be many.'"

Wendy quaffed again, and Peter noticed that her glass was nearly drained.

"But Christ said, '*I* am the way, the truth, and the life,'" he said carefully. "Was He lying?"

Her eyes narrowed.

Either way he had her. If Jesus Christ was not the truth, then he was lying—and certainly not perfect. But if she acknowledged that He was telling the truth, then why didn't she also acknowledge His sovereignty?

Suddenly she laughed a little tinkling laugh that partly disarmed him. "They told me you were a lawyer, in addition to being a private investigator. Don't you ever give it a rest?"

They were both saved from the awkwardness of the moment by the arrival of their salads. Wendy's empty wine glass was replaced by a full one.

"What about you?" Peter said after a couple of bites. "What makes you tick? Tell me how you get to be a police psychic."

"What do you mean?"

"If you're really psychic, wouldn't you just know what I meant?" Peter asked with a straight face.

"Psychic, yes. Omniscient, not quite." She laughed again. "I guess you *don't* give it a rest."

"I mean is this from a correspondence course or something? A laying on of hands? Where do the police find psychics? Can anybody hang out a shingle?"

"I suppose you might call it a gift. Just speaking for myself, I have simply managed to produce leads in cases that nobody else could find using conventional techniques. Otherwise my training was no different from that of any other officer. There is no Clairvoyance 101 at the police academy, I assure you."

"I see."

The rest of their food arrived. If she was the one drinking wine, why was he feeling giddy? He didn't feel right about this situation, yet he found himself wanting to believe her. Maybe he shouldn't have accepted her dinner invitation, but refusing would have been a bit ungracious after she had essentially saved his hide back at St. Mark's.

They tackled mussels and calamari for a minute or two in silence, except for Peter's teasing remark likening calamari to fish bait.

After another minute, Wendy broke the silence. "What's your plan for the Hofburg case at this point?"

Peter frowned thoughtfully at his plate. "Did you see the news leak?"

Wendy nodded silently.

"In the short run, that's a real problem. But in the long run, it could provide an opportunity to break this case open, if we could figure out how somebody like Crystal McKenzie got clued in. We know that the heist was partly an inside job, and we might be close to establishing a motive. Frankly, Wendy, I was hoping that you could help me investigate the news leak."

Wendy finished chewing a bite of calamari, washed it down with another draft of wine, and then looked deeply into his eyes. "Frankly, Peter, there's nothing I would enjoy more." Her smile was devastating.

Peter felt his heart melt. With an effort he vowed under no circumstances to allow himself to accompany this young lady home tonight.

* * *

The next morning Peter presented himself sharply at eight o'clock at the front desk of the Art Registry Unit at Scotland Yard, fully expecting to go directly into a work session with Sgt. Wendy Carlisle. In fact, he looked forward to it with greater anticipation than he cared to admit.

Once the auto-secretary verified the identity of his voice-print, Peter was admitted through the outer security door into a vestibule. There a uniformed officer with a bureaucrat's glower directed him toward the same conference room where he and Neal had met the first time with Stacy Witherspoon. He had expected instead to be meeting Wendy in her own office.

Inside, he understood. She was there with Witherspoon.

Wearing a green plaid jumper, white blouse, and knee socks, and with her hair tied back in a ponytail, she looked more like a parochial schoolgirl than a police officer. Come to think of it, she never looked like a police person.

"Good morning, Mr. McBride." Witherspoon barely looked up from the documents spread before him on the table.

"Morning."

Wendy, much warmer, gave him a smile and a wink.

His heart beat a little faster.

"Have a seat, please," said Witherspoon. "Coffee?"

"No, thanks." Peter wanted to get right to things. "You have something new regarding the Hofburg?"

Wendy took a seat beside him.

"We might," Witherspoon said. "It's all in what we're able to make of it."

Peter looked at Wendy and, not being a psychic, failed to read her mind. He shrugged in bewilderment.

"I'll explain," she said, touching his forearm reassuringly with her fingertips while Witherspoon continued to sort through various documents and photographs. "There's been a murder in the past forty-eight hours in the Montmartre section of Paris. The victim was a woman, age fifty-three, by the name of Gwydian Brandt. A German. Show him a picture."

Witherspoon keyed up a file on the wall monitor. On the large screen appeared two mug shots, frontal and profile, of a powerful, leather-faced older female with dark brows, gray-streaked bangs, steel-framed glasses, and a scowl. Somehow it wasn't difficult to imagine someone's wanting to shoot her.

"This woman was a geneticist for the EU Population and Health Ministry," Wendy continued. "She was found shot to death in her own car about a block and a half from her building, and her flat appeared to be burgled. We've just received a report here from the *Sureté*—the French National Central Bureau."

"But what's this got to do with the Hofburg?"

"Quite a lot, actually," Witherspoon interjected, pushing a stack of photos across the table toward him. "These came from the woman's flat."

Peter instantly saw what they were—photos of the Crown and Spear, taken from various angles. Most appeared to have been taken in the Hofburg display gallery. He recognized the cases and trappings.

"Mr. McBride," said Witherspoon, "I've got a call in to your father in Vienna. He apparently has rapport with half the staff of the Hofburg. We want him to see if anybody there can recognize Brandt from her photo. Who knows—maybe she was a regular visitor. Maybe she even took the pictures."

Peter nodded, hearing the words distantly. "So what's this one? Where was it taken?"

He held up a photo of the Crown and Spear that was quite different from the others. Instead of reposing elegantly in their separate Hofburg displays, the articles appeared one atop the other on different shelves of the same modest piece of furniture, much like a personal curio cabinet in a private home.

Wendy took the photo from him and shut her eyes as if deep in contemplation, a corner of the picture touching her pursed lips.

"We need to go to Paris, Peter," she said abruptly, her eyes popping open.

"Why?"

"Those treasures had to be in Brandt's flat. I'm sure of it."

He was taken aback. "How do you know that?"

She was adamant. "I just know. They had to be. That picture—it had to be from her flat."

An idea was taking shape in the back of Peter's mind. "Genomes. Considering her position, could Gwydian Brandt also be our connection to the genome thefts?"

"A connection, maybe," Witherspoon allowed. "It's a start, at least."

But Wendy wore a curious expression, a cross between irony and concern. "Show him the rest."

Witherspoon pushed another pile of documents across the table.

Most of it was incomprehensible scientific notation, tables, data, equations with Greek functions, and other esoterica.

"There are a number of individuals here," explained Witherspoon, "whom Brandt apparently was studying. But one in particular jumps out."

Witherspoon pulled a document from the pile and tapped its header field with the back end of his pen. He was right. The name did jump out.

PETER CARPENTER McBRIDE.

Peter was floored. Maybe it was someone else with the same name? Scanning farther, he could see that the other vital statistics matched. All the way.

Before he could ask the obvious question, Witherspoon beat him to it. "Any idea why someone like Brandt would be interested in *your* genetic information?"

Peter shook his head. Words would not come easily.

"Anything unusual," Witherspoon persisted, "about your genetic make-up?"

Peter stopped shaking his head and looked up. "Nothing I know of. Except—"

"Yes?"

"Except that a young woman and I were denied a procreation permit a few years ago by the USP Population and Health Authority."

"On your account or hers?"

"They wouldn't tell us—and I have never applied for another permit with anyone else . . ."

Abruptly the words stopped coming. Peter sat immobile, watching Witherspoon continue to sort through his documents, imbibing Wendy's subtle fragrance, and thinking.

It did indeed look as if he would be going to Paris. And the sooner the better.

7

Paris

Yussef Halima lit another cigarette and angrily crumpled the empty pack. When he had squeezed it down into a tight little wad, he slammed it into the wastebasket hard enough to produce a dull clang. Then he resumed his pacing, a beady-eyed man in his early twenties with a small mustache and a perpetual sneer.

Two days he had wasted in this lousy flat, stymied on all fronts. Not only could he not get a call through to any of his contacts in Iraq, but he had encountered unanticipated travel complications too. He had been mostly through the line at Charles De-Gaulle Airport for Flight 448 to Beirut before he realized that there was no way his footlocker would ever pass security inspection. With no small embarrassment he had managed to extricate himself by feigning illness and asking for a prorated refund for a future flight.

What was wrong with him? Had his brain left town without a forwarding address? It was the kind of misstep that happened when he became overconfident or distracted by other concerns, such as trying to think too far ahead and forgetting what lay immediately before him. It was also the kind of lapse that could bring his mission to an ignominious end in a jail cell.

So much for invincibility. He might survive physical combat, but he doubted that the royal treasures afforded any protection from the legal ramifications of stupidity.

Yussef walked the floor of the dreary pensione's cramped living room, smoking and thinking. Surely, he reasoned, there would be some simple way to camouflage the articles and ship them out so they would not be subjected to intense security inspection. Yes, but he had vowed not to commit the same mistake as the old woman and let the articles out of his sight. The most he had been willing to risk was to drive with them in the trunk of his car.

Yet the more he paced and the longer he smoked, the more inescapable became the conclusion. He would have to get over his superstitious fixation about the regalia, and he would have to start by deprogramming his thinking. Otherwise he could end up convincing himself that he was doomed to fail, and that just might become a self-fulfilling prophecy.

So how would he disguise the articles? Yussef blew out smoke and stared through the window to the gray shades and rickety fire escapes of the next building.

He knew that drugs sometimes were packed with corpses, in the hope that the sensitivities of the customs people would preclude a thorough inspection. But then he realized that the reason he knew about that scheme was because of its well-publicized failures.

Besides, he didn't **really** want to kill somebody just to provide a cover for smuggling. There was nobody else he knew at the moment here in Paris who needed killing. He also could imagine that the logistics of that scheme would be as difficult as the smuggling itself.

What else? It wasn't as if he could dismantle the articles and ship them in pieces. He obviously was going to have to encase them in something.

An idea began to grow upon him. What was that colorized movie he had seen a long time ago? *The Maltese Falcon*. In that story a priceless bird had been embedded in some kind of black, disposable material. What was it? But it didn't really matter. There were unquestionably better substances available today for such a purpose.

Now the idea began to form into a plan. He would go to an art supply house and ask for a quantity of Miracle Cement, the synthetic sculpting material that adheres only to itself. Yussef recalled reports that objects secreted in Miracle Cement could be removed no worse for wear once the cement was broken off.

If he could just get the disguised articles on a cargo ship bound for North Africa, he would be almost home free. Any number of contacts in Tunis or Tripoli could help him get his booty on to Baghdad and Babylon.

In fact, he realized, there was no reason he should not be able to take a bullet train yet this day to Marseille and have the goods loaded for shipment first thing in the morning. Then he could return to Paris, arrange a flight for himself, call again for his Iraqi contacts, and check out of this lousy pensione. In just two or three days he should be able to reclaim his package in safer environs.

Buoyed by the distant prospect of success, Yussef stubbed out his cigarette, hauled the faded brown footlocker out of the closet, and went out the door. He deposited his precious luggage in the trunk of his rented red Zodiaque coupe and headed for a shopping center on the other side of town where he knew there was an art supplies outlet. Probably there were closer places, but this one he knew he could find, and it was a pretty big place, likely to have what he needed.

Yussef was tooling along the Boulevard de Rochechouart toward its confluence with the Boulevard de la Chapelle when he spotted a familiar car in his rearview mirror. There was so much about this entire operation that made no sense that he told himself to forget it. If someone were really tailing him, would he choose to do it in a car as conspicuous as an electric blue Karma convertible? Yet he had been in the terrorism business long enough to know that reverse psychology was not out of the question. In fact, wasn't he himself inclined to write this off for that very reason?

He had a bad gut feeling that just wouldn't go away. He knew this was at least the third time he had seen that car.

Fortunately, by the time he got to the Levecque shopping center, the Karma was nowhere in sight.

Yussef parked immediately in front of the entrance to Gaspar's Art Supplies. He knew he would be perspiring the entire time he was separated from the regalia.

He told himself to start getting used to it. If he couldn't get used to it now, what would he do once his case had set sail for Tunisia or Libya?

★ ★ ★

Peter negotiated the unfamiliar, winding boulevard with fingers tightening on the steering wheel.

"Now wait a minute." He tried not to let his irritation interfere with his driving. "I didn't tell you that Neal was handling all media relations. How did you know that? Clairvoyance?"

"I never reveal a source," Wendy Carlisle said half-teasingly.

Maddeningly, this entire conversation was going nowhere. And then it occurred to Peter—they were having their first argument.

He had wanted to try the direct approach with Crystal McKenzie and to confront her with questions about her Hofburg report for One World News. Sure, reporters have the right to conceal sources, he argued, but he and Sgt. Carlisle could certainly try a little haggling. There might be some things about the case that they could disclose without compromising the investigation. Nor would it hurt to plant a big hint that reporters like Crystal McKenzie could be flirting with a national security problem if they weren't careful. The important thing was to get a parley going.

But Wendy had vigorously opposed the idea, arguing that they would be inviting a worse media problem by keeping the story alive. Peter grudgingly admitted that she might be right. Still, it bothered him that she seemed to ignore the need to pin down the news leak, something crucial to the entire case.

So he had been especially irked when Wendy pointed out that Neal McBride needed to be the sole media contact on this case. She was correct, of course, but how did *she* know that? He wasn't prepared to accept the possibility of ESP, nor did he really want to think about that. It was too much of a reminder that this woman should be strictly off limits for him.

By the time they arrived at Rue de Chantilly in Montmartre, they had fallen into a fragile silence. They parked in a small lot behind the apartment building, and went in search of the *propriétaire*.

Peter had barely ceased knocking at the first-floor flat when the door flew open, revealing a stone-faced little man with beady eyes and two days' growth on his chin. They asked to see Number 405. Wendy handled the French.

The manager looked about to slam the door in their faces when Wendy flashed her badge. His face sank, and he retreated behind the door for a moment to reappear with a key. With a wave, he handed it over and bade them adieu. If they didn't need him, they could help themselves. Just return the key when they were done.

Upstairs they opened the door onto a living room that had known very little in the way of living. Books and papers and manila file folders littered the place, overflowing from the desk and shelves onto the couch and other furniture. Book titles in *Deutsch* were confined to subjects such as biochemistry, hereditary diseases, and epidemiology—consistent with the reading habits of a government geneticist.

While Wendy rummaged among those items, Peter stuck his head through the other doors—bedroom, bathroom, kitchen—just to make sure there wasn't a dog, a body, or an insane relative hanging around. There wasn't. The *Sureté* had already scoured the premises, but it never hurt to be careful.

When he returned to the living room, Wendy was staring at a large antique curio cabinet in one corner. Just as she was extracting a photograph from her purse, Peter made the connection. The cabinet.

"*Voila.*" Wendy held the picture aloft.

Peter moved closer to see. They were indeed identical—the same rounded top, beveled glass, and carved curlicues on the end posts. This was clearly the cabinet that had held the Crown and Spear in the photo. He also noticed that the lock, adjacent to the cracked pane, was extruded as if something had violently forced the mechanism.

He was looking over Wendy's shoulder at the picture and standing close enough to feel her body heat and hear her breathing. All of a sudden it was too close. Peter stepped back, deliberately clearing his head.

"That's enough for me," he declared. "It's now a murder case."

"Yes," said Wendy with a condescending edge. "Unfortunately we're no closer to locating the objects, and the whole affair is getting more complicated instead of simpler."

Peter said nothing, but watched the young policewoman resume her wandering about the room as if following unseen clues. She gravitated to a computer console on the long desktop next to the microviewer, then turned at last to Peter.

"Do you know anything about computers?"

Peter shrugged. "A little."

"I believe," Wendy said, "that you may find something helpful in its files."

"What makes you—" Peter began, then stopped himself. "Oh, never mind."

He decided to fire up the machine and see what he could see. Not knowing its voice-actuation protocols, he assumed control of the keyboard the old-fashioned, manual way. Wendy continued roaming the room as though still sniffing a trail, but Peter had the impression that mostly she was watching him.

The information files were as he had expected—Greek equations, tables of data, endless columns of numbers, headings in German, a few things in languages he could not identify. Unfortunately there was little indication of the use for which this information had been intended—or for whose eyes. Other files contained genetic maps and other technical graphics. He found the file on Peter Carpenter McBride, which gave him the willies all over again.

At that point, he became aware that Wendy had pulled up a chair and moved in beside him, quite close.

"I believe all of the files have been downloaded by the *Sureté* and copied for us," she said.

"Then why are we poking around in it too?"

"I don't trust the pencil pushers of Interpol to find anything that doesn't jump up and bite them on the tail," she said quietly but earnestly. "I do have, however, a good deal of confidence in our collective abilities—your investigative skills and my . . . intuitive ones."

"So what is your intuition telling you now?"

She took his question seriously. "That what we're looking for may be a lot more obvious than you'd think. And that it probably isn't contained in those copied files at all."

"OK. I give up. What *are* we looking for?"

"A clue. Any clue. Right?"

He shrugged again. "True enough."

Oddly, when he returned his attention to the database, it was as if the trees had fallen into place and he could see the forest for the first time. He exited the data files and began looking at the other utilities and applications. Sure. Why hadn't he thought of that before? If he did a header search, he might be able to reconstruct some identities, assuming sly old Gwydian Brandt had been electronically exchanging data with anyone. And if any of her reports had been used as blind memos, he might be able to glean still more with an index search, canceling suppressions.

"Watch this," said Peter, cracking his knuckles in parody of the concert pianist before the magnum opus.

Wendy leaned in closer. Their shoulders were now touching.

Peter meticulously constructed a series of commands that initiated a string sequence of searches. Once in motion, it didn't take long. The screen became a blur of fields and directories lighting up in spots for fractional seconds and then moving on. Sure enough, there were enemy planes, and they were showing up on radar. As the printer sprang to life, Peter leaned back, feeling Wendy's softness against his arm.

In less than a minute, they had a full list on two eleven-inch pages. There were more than a few electronic data transmission numbers—most probably innocuous—but also fourteen names of individuals. Most of those related to EDT numbers with the same prefix. If he had to guess, Peter imagined they would belong to other EU Population and Health functionaries. Most names appeared only once.

A notable exception was an Ivar Koznik, who appeared several dozen times.

Probably the most intriguing individual had no electronic address at all—a person by the name of Zell. Peter assumed it was a last name, but there was no guarantee even of that. It might be nothing more than a code. The only thing he could tell was that "Zell" had a high priority in Brandt's indexing. And she was no longer around to explain why. If nothing else, at least there were some potential witnesses they could begin interviewing, probably starting with this Koznik fellow.

"See?" said Wendy, her admiring eyes devouring his. "I knew you could do it."

Her face was very close. And then she smiled, a smile that could thaw the polar ice caps.

It was certainly having its effect on Peter McBride.

* * *

Vienna

The König von Ungarn hotel on Schulerstrasse was not hard to find. Carlotta had only to point herself in the direction of the Stephandom—St. Stephen's Cathedral—the focal point of the Vienna skyline with its majestic Gothic spires and ostentatious nineteenth-century tiled roof.

There in St. Stephen's shadow stood the historic hotel, like a drugstore postcard, and Carlotta homed to it. Looking neither to right nor left, she entered and whisked through the parquet-floored vestibule. She wasted no time crossing the brass-and-marble lobby and presenting herself at the front desk. As she completed the check-in process, she could contain herself no longer.

"Are Neal and Peter McBride still registered?" she asked almost casually.

"I will check for you." The pleasant young blonde clerk had an easy smile and schoolbook English.

She consulted a monitor behind the counter and smiled again. "Mr. Neal McBride is still registered here, but Mr. Peter McBride checked out two days ago. Would you like for me to leave a message for Mr. Neal?"

Carlotta's heart sank, and it was hard for her to speak. "No—no, thank you. Uh . . . wait. Could you just ring Neal McBride's room and see if he's there?"

The young woman did so and looked up after a moment. "I am sorry. There is no answer. I believe he may call in for messages, however."

Resignedly Carlotta asked to have him ring her when he called in. She probably would go out sightseeing, but if he left his number she would return the call.

She followed the bellhop to her room on the third floor, feeling jet-lagged, empty, and ridiculous.

As soon as he had deposited her bags and shut the door behind him, she threw herself on the firm, fresh-smelling bed and buried her head in the pillow. Would it feel better if she cried? Maybe a little. But in another moment it was no longer an option; it was an inevitability, beyond questioning.

Why had she bothered to come here? Maybe this was just a temporary frustration, but it felt like desolation and just more gross stupidity on her part. The tears were flowing freely now, wetting the pillowcase. Why had she listened to Vida? Was she really so impressionable and naive that she could be talked into crossing an ocean on a whim? Now she felt more alone and hopeless than ever.

The bucket was reaching the bottom of the well and bringing up the deep things. Maybe she was unlovable. Maybe Peter was better off without her. If they couldn't marry, what was the point of chasing after him? He should just find someone else—and so should she. Why torture herself further?

Now the ache had found a voice, a wail muffled by the pillow that became a choking rasp as she stopped only to draw the next breath. And then came the little staccato bursts of sobs that wound slowly down as her grief approached exhaustion. It wasn't long before that point too was reached, and Carlotta let it all go. There just wasn't any more, and she was done.

She was drifting toward a land's end of consciousness that verged on slumber. And then she was over the edge.

* * *

Not too many minutes later, it seemed, Carlotta became aware of the tingling of her left arm where it had fallen asleep. She changed position to restore circulation and considered her next move. It appeared that she wasn't going to fall back to sleep.

She found herself doing something she hadn't done for a long time—praying. Not because she much believed that anything would happen but out of sheer desperation. It hurts, Dad. Make it better. Maybe she still was a Christian, at least in the foxholes of life.

After a minute or two of that, she found the strength to get up. The anguish wasn't really better, but it was manageable. She needed to consult her friend in the mirror.

Her friend looked back at her like a wraith. Her dark brown Cleopatra bangs were matted and stringy, her eyes red and puffy, her complexion washed out and cadaverous. How could anyone love anything like that? Maybe God could, if He cared. Did He?

She needed a shower, she decided. She began stripping off her clothes, glad to be out of their travel-stickiness, and draped them over the back of a chair.

The shower was a good idea. It seemed to melt away the toxins of the past few hours. It felt wonderful to rinse the clean-smelling shampoo from her hair, to feel the watery needles bombard her face and to open up her pores.

When she next consulted her friend in the mirror, it was a new woman. Color was restored to her cheeks, a renewed clarity to her large brown eyes, a rich sheen to her blow-dried hair. She pulled a new dress over her head, letting it drop like a curtain to the top of her knee.

She studied the total effect. She was blessed with the type of physique that probably would remain slender all her life. At a graceful five feet six inches, she had looked good enough in stylish dresses to prompt a few people to suggest a modeling career. But she far preferred capturing the beauty of other things on canvas.

The dress was a cheery lavender print summer-weight with extra feminine touches of chiffon and lace. It was also the dress she had expected to wear for greeting Peter, though ordinarily it might be a little frivolous for straitlaced Vienna. But now she wanted to wear it anyway, feeling it would provide a welcome boost to her spirits.

She consulted her travel literature and stashed one museum brochure into her purse. She knew exactly where to go to kill a few hours. For years she had yearned to visit the Albertina, home of the world's largest collection of drawings, sketches, engravings, and etchings. It was a surefire way to lose herself for a while, and she was certain that someone at the desk could tell her how to get there.

★ ★ ★

Neal McBride, standing beside his borrowed car, spotted her coming down the front steps of the Albertina. Carlotta Waldo, the lovely and mercurial daughter of gypsies and now respected artist, teacher, and writer, twenty-nine years old and more beautiful than ever.

He stood outside the car mostly so she'd see him, and she did, giving a little wave and changing course in his direction. But he also stood there so he could take her by the shoulders and just look at her, if she didn't mind.

She didn't. In fact, she kissed him on the cheek, wrapped her arms around his midsection, rested her head against his shoulder, and squeezed. He squeezed back.

"Carlotta," he murmured. "How many years has it been?"

"Too many," came her muffled voice. "Too many."

He'd had a daughter once, and he caught himself wanting to call her by the dead girl's name—Angie. He had fully expected to have Carlotta for a daughter-in-law, and when that failed to occur it was almost like losing another girl. That may have had something to do with his hiring Carlotta's sister, Dyana.

So what was bringing this one back into his life?

They broke the embrace and climbed into the car, a dark green Prana sedan. Neal noticed that the lapel of his sport coat was curiously damp.

He drove silently through the noon-hour rush while Carlotta expounded lightly about the masterpieces she'd been privileged to view at the Albertina. Her voice had sounded more urgent on voice mail when he'd called in for messages and found that a woman named Carlotta Waldo was asking for his number and wanted to call him from the museum.

So it was a lunch date. They went to a place called Die Magische Flöte, which specialized in casseroles, cold cuts, salads, and rich cakes. The other attraction was its outdoor patio dotted with brightly colored umbrella tables. It didn't take long to get one.

She asked him to order for her, almost as if she were too distracted to hassle with the identities of foreign foodstuffs. So he ordered two luncheon specials, a dish consisting of spaetzle and bratwurst.

They talked about art a bit longer, certainly long enough to exhaust McBride's knowledge of the subject. Then they did some general catching up on the last couple of years of life's benchmarks until McBride sensed that Carlotta was ready to be pressed.

"Well," he ventured, "I don't suppose you exactly came to Vienna to see *me*."

She smiled. "Not totally. I'd really like to see Peter."

"Good luck. He's in Paris right now, and then who knows where, working a case. It's hard to predict where he might be next."

Carlotta shrugged. "Then I'll just go to Paris and take my chances. Do you know where he's staying?"

"I'd really hate to have you go there and find he's gone on to Brussels or returned to Vienna."

"But you're in contact with him, aren't you? Couldn't you have him call me? We could make some kind of arrangements."

Neal McBride chose his words carefully. "Carlotta, what's going on with you? I thought you and Peter had agreed that things were impossible."

She looked down at the table and said nothing.

Maybe he had gone too far. "Besides," he said, "I'm not in direct contact with Peter. He's working with someone from Scotland Yard, and we're communicating through her office."

Carlotta's eyes grew round. "A woman? Who is she? What is she like?"

McBride laughed. "The policewoman? You mean what does she look like? Not bad—if you like female Sumo wrestlers. Just kidding. But she's not nearly so good looking as you—nor so much fun."

Carlotta wasn't laughing.

McBride was beginning to get the picture. "After all this time, you still love him."

She was looking down at the table again. When she looked up, there was torment in her eyes.

"I don't care about Population and Health bureaucrats and permits," she choked. "I just want Peter back."

He really didn't know what to say. He could only watch as the tears rolled down her cheeks toward her bratwurst.

8

Paris

Inspector Henri Reynard looked like a man who might not trust his best friend, let alone a foreigner. Peter didn't want to read too much into first appearances, but Reynard's countenance was clearly something less than warm and encouraging.

The man was almost forbidding. On the wallscreen his craggy forehead, crowned with close-cropped gray hair, and jutting brow gave his patrician blue eyes a brooding, accusing look. Peter imagined that this effect might be used to some advantage in the interrogation of criminal suspects.

He wondered what Reynard might have to report on the Gwydian Brandt murder investigation. Had the local police made anything of the new leads Peter and Wendy had produced? He understood the need to share their intelligence from Brandt's computer files with the *Sureté* and Paris police. But he needed reassurance that this sharing would truly be a two-way street.

One redeeming aspect was that they had been provided temporary basement office space at Interpol's General Secretariat in the woodsy Paris suburb of St. Cloud, modest as it was. Many of the upstairs offices had cheery views out into forested countryside, but this cramped room was more like work quarters on a submarine. At least it had all the necessary equipment, including a telecommunications wallscreen.

"I am afraid that there is really little to report," began Reynard, whom Peter judged to be on the riper side of fifty. "There are still no suspects and no known motive, other than smalltime robbery or attempted carjacking. I suspect it may join the long list of unsolved street crime in the big city."

Wendy verbalized Peter's objection. "Are you forgetting the Hofburg case?"

Reynard's expression became patronizing. "Not forgetting, Mademoiselle. There is just nothing substantive there."

"However, Inspector," Peter interjected, "several Hofburg employees have positively identified Gwydian Brandt as a visitor on more than one occasion, who also took pictures in the *Reichskleinodien* gallery."

"That may be," said Reynard with a derisive wave. "So. A tourist with a camera. Think of that!"

"Pictures," said Wendy, "which were, in fact, found in her flat—one of them showing that the regalia actually had been on the premises."

"Yes, yes. I have seen that picture. Do you know what it proves? Merely that items resembling those articles reposed at some point in a cabinet similar to the one in Dr. Brandt's apartment."

Peter's impatience was growing. "We could do a computer analysis—"

Reynard's expression hardened. "You play whatever computer games you like. Perhaps Interpol has time for frivolities like that. Meanwhile I have a homicide to investigate."

Peter could hardly believe his ears. "So are you telling me that you're ruling out—"

"I rule nothing out, nothing in. But criminal investigators must look for the simplest answers. And in this case, that has to be simple street crime. You are aware, are you not, that Dr. Brandt's purse had been emptied?"

Wendy too was growing impatient. "An obvious cover."

"Without compelling reason to the contrary, the obvious should be taken at face value."

"So," said Peter, "does that mean your department has done nothing with the leads we provided from her computer files?"

"Not at all. Not at all. We investigate all aspects, no matter how farfetched. Unfortunately, there is nothing here. These individuals whose names and numbers you supplied were all colleagues of Dr. Brandt, with whom she had been communicating strictly in the furtherance of her duties at the Population and Health Ministry, according to our interviews. There was nothing out of the ordinary that anyone could recall."

"Perhaps," Wendy suggested, "their memories would improve before a grand jury."

Reynard chose not to comment.

Peter found the whole direction of this conversation disturbing. "What about this Ivar Koznik or this other character named Zell?"

Reynard looked as if he was tiring of the quizzing. "This Zell—nobody has heard of him, if there is such a person. Monsieur Koznik—he is on a leave of absence, but I would not be concerned."

"Oh?" said Wendy dubiously. "Why do you say that, Inspector?"

"There are medical reasons. Nothing sinister."

"Then," Peter said, "perhaps we can talk with him. Where is he?"

Reynard's glower deepened. "Out of town—who knows where?—convalescing. Lourdes, perhaps."

Peter pressed him. "Nobody knows or nobody cares? Don't you think that's a bit much of a coincidence for such a close associate of the victim to disappear?"

"Not at all," Reynard said stiffly, his irritation visible beneath the surface. "If he and Mademoiselle Brandt were close, do you not think there would be good reason for upset?"

"To some investigators," Wendy observed darkly, "it might also be a good reason for such a person to be regarded as a potential suspect."

The wrath broke the surface. "Rot! If you wish to take an ordinary street crime and turn it into something sensational, that is your business. But I will not be party to it. I think you need me no longer."

Wendy responded smoothly. "Thank you, Inspector. Please keep us informed if things change."

Reynard nodded curtly. "Then I bid you adieu."

"Adieu," Peter said to the fading image.

"Adieu, adieu," Wendy muttered. "Probably a Jew."

"Look," said Peter, wheeling about. "What is it with you and Witherspoon and this anti-Semitism?"

Wendy smiled benignly. "Nothing, really, Peter. Just an expression."

Peter didn't think so. But he decided to save it for another time.

Wendy was asking someone over the interoffice to get them a party in Vienna. Peter could guess who.

"Your father left a message early this morning," she explained. "I have no idea what he wanted. But he was supposed to be at the Hofburg all day."

He tried to imagine what was on Neal's mind. He knew his father needed to get back home for a few days to take care of some USP business. He wondered if he had come up with anything further at the Hofburg.

A moment later McBride's familiar features assembled on the wallscreen.

"Hola," he said. "I was calling for my basic Paris update. Any developments?"

"Hardly," said Peter. "Mostly pulling teeth right now, especially with the Paris police. Are you getting ready to head home?"

McBride shrugged. "Maybe. I'd just like to know if you've managed to get anywhere investigating the Crystal McKenzie news leak."

Peter felt a little sheepish. "Not far, Neal. We've been pursuing this Brandt murder. As I said before, I suspect her murderer may be the proud new owner of the Crown and Spear. We find him, and Crystal McKenzie can go fly a big kite."

"Besides," added Wendy, "we felt it best if we left all media contacts to you."

McBride's eyebrows rose visibly. "Oh?"

Peter winced at the half-truth, but he suspected that Neal was going a different direction anyway. "Why do you ask?"

McBride had a slightly pained expression. "Crystal McKenzie is on my case. She has been pestering me for two days now, trying to find out everything we know. And believe me, she's used every trick in the book."

Something in the way he said it struck Peter. "What do you mean?"

"Well, let's just say that Crystal McKenzie made it clear that she'll do anything for a story. But I have managed to elicit some information from her, so now I'm in her debt. We're going to have to feed her something pretty quickly."

"What kind of information? What have you found out?"

"Well, she claims her sources are law enforcement officers involved in the Hofburg investigation."

"You think that's true?"

"Let me play back part of our conversation, and see what you think."

Wendy snorted. "Whatever she says, it's got to be a lie."

Peter filed that in the suspicious-remark department.

Onscreen a moment later appeared the face of a young woman with luxuriant blonde tresses, the kind of perfect features frequently associated with cosmetic surgery, and the flicker of a calculating intelligence when she spoke. Her cultured British tones suggested sophistication, education, and self-importance. In short, she exhibited the kind of journalistic arrogance that can infuriate and incapacitate an opponent unaware of the purposeful tactic.

"Well, Mr. McBride, there's simply no use pretending you know less than you do," she was saying. "I happen to know better than that. So we can stop—how do Americans say?—pussyfooting around."

"Ms. McKenzie" —McBride was responding with his best judicial restraint— "I don't know who's been telling you such things, but the simple fact is that there is—how do the British say?—precious little that *anybody* knows or even suspects about this case. So I would suggest that you might need to find better sources."

Not bad. Peter could sense Crystal McKenzie's struggle not to let her offended dignity get the better of her. The effort was not totally successful.

"I'm disappointed with you, Mr. McBride." She sniffed. "My sources are unimpeachable. They include law enforcement officials involved in the investigation of the Hofburg affair itself. You'll have to think of a better excuse."

McBride assumed a credibly surprised expression. "Really?

If that's the case, then you don't need me. You've already been hearing from—as we Americans say—the horse's mouth."

McKenzie donned a little smile that could well have masked an entirely different emotion. "No, I do need you. And I think you could use me too. What do you think of that?"

Peter appreciated the deliberate ambiguity and Neal's adroit sidestep.

"Why are you so interested in a common museum theft?"

McKenzie's eyebrows went up. "Come now. I'd hardly call the theft of the Crown of Charlemagne and the Holy Lance common."

"What would you call it?"

"Maybe not the crime of the century, but possibly the crime of the decade."

"Why would you say that?"

McKenzie's coral-colored lips pursed ironically. "By virtue of the possible list of suspects."

"And who might those be?"

"Look here, you're the one who's supposed to be answering the questions."

"I must have forgotten." McBride put on his thoughtful face. "Tell you what. I'll make you a deal, a small deal. And it's the only deal I'm going to make. OK?"

McKenzie thought about that a second and apparently concluded it might be worth it. She nodded stiffly, as if a bit suspicious. "What kind of deal?"

"Let's just say there could be lots of potential suspects. You name the ones who interest you, and I'll see what I can do by way of a response."

"That's fair," she agreed. "But I don't see what's in it for you."

"Good will mainly. You have your problems; I have mine. I can't comment on a matter currently under investigation; you can't reveal a source. Anything I give you, therefore, will not be for attribution. I'm hoping you'll be able to find a similar solution to your problem, because we have a security issue at our end. If we have law enforcement officers giving out vital details—like the

Greek inscription—the entire investigation could be jeopardized. Your cooperation would be helpful."

McKenzie, eyes lowered, thought about that for a time. Then she looked up. "It sounds to me, Mr. McBride, as if I might be better off sticking to my sources and getting my information from them."

"My guess is that you wouldn't be coming to me if that were true. Sources come; sources go. Their usefulness can be limited."

McKenzie smiled slyly. "Touché. I'll see what I can do. In the meantime, may I leave you with my favorite suspects?"

"Certainly."

McKenzie dropped her voice in a conspiratorial tone. "My sources tell me that there are two main theories."

"Yes?"

"The first goes all the way to the highest levels of the administration of the European Union—perhaps even Waldemar Neumann himself or the chancellor's closest aides."

"For what purpose?"

McKenzie looked a bit askance at McBride's naiveté. "Imperialism. Pan-European hegemony. Or as you Americans say—all the marbles."

"You think One World News has the chutzpah to air something like that?"

"You let me worry about that."

"OK. What's the second working theory?"

Her eyes narrowed again. "The Jewish conspiracy."

McBride maintained his naive expression. "Which one?"

McKenzie appeared to be wearing down. "Let's not play games. It's all the same marbles. In this case the game is keeping them out of the hands of certain Gentiles."

"Interesting theory. One gang of thieves preempting another gang?"

She shrugged. "As it were."

"So you think the Jews run everything?"

"Come now, Mr. McBride. Anything the Jews *don't* own isn't worth having. Everybody knows that."

The screen froze as McBride stopped the recording and his real-time image reappeared.

"That's the first true thing she's said," said Wendy.

"So," said McBride, "you see what we're dealing with. She may be dissembling, but I think we have to take her seriously in regard to this internal security breach. Sgt. Carlisle, considering the fact that the Austrian police have not been involved in this case, the finger would seem to point to Interpol and Scotland Yard."

"That's rubbish," she snapped.

"That may be, but we can't afford to disregard the possibility, no matter how remote. What's your assessment of Witherspoon in terms of trustworthiness?"

Wendy was adamant. "Ironclad. You're on the wrong trail, my friend."

"I'm open to suggestion."

"How about the Paris police?"

Peter spoke up. "Based just on Inspector Reynard's attitude, I'd be inclined to agree with that, except for two things. First, the Paris police did not become involved in any of this until the Brandt murder, and that was long after the One World News report. Second, Crystal McKenzie still appears to know nothing about any Paris connection."

"And let's keep it that way. What I want to know is what I'm going to tell her about Chancellor Waldemar Neumann and/or the Jewish conspiracy."

"Well—" Wendy started to say.

"And I'm not going to lie," McBride said.

Peter snapped his fingers, his eyes lighting up. "Tell the truth. Tell her—not for attribution, of course—that the investigation is centering on the Waldemar Neumann administration. You don't have to say the Population and Health Ministry, but that's what we'll be doing."

McBride nodded thoughtfully. "If One World News runs that story, it'll certainly stir things up."

"Which might not be a bad idea," Peter said. "I hear that the PH Minister—Bardo—is a tough cookie. Maybe the threat of media pressure will soften him up."

McBride looked satisfied. "Might work. In fact, I'll deliver that message to Ms. McKenzie and then buy us even more time by going back to the USP for a while. Thus far, I don't think she even knows of your existence, Peter. So continue keeping your head down."

"Just call me Ostrich—the Österreich Ostrich."

"Oh, Peter. I almost forgot to tell you. There's someone coming to see you from Vienna. She wants to see you very badly."

Peter was baffled. "Who?"

"Carlotta. Be kind to her. I think you and she should have some meaningful communication."

Peter was too stunned to speak. When Neal bade farewell, he could only nod.

"Carlotta?" said Wendy in the lingering silence. There was distrust in her voice.

"Yeah," said Peter distractedly, then began to realize the import of his situation. All of a sudden life was becoming more complicated. A good deal more complicated.

★ ★ ★

Once his feet touched the ledge, Amos Sloat knew he had it made. Still holding onto his rappelling rope, he let out the drag, stepped off, and spidered across to the landing step of the fire escape. It was a piece of cake from there. He unhooked the carabiner and fished out his lock tools. In less than a minute, he had the sliding tumbler mechanism picked and the fire exit door swinging open.

Only then did he reel in the black nylon rope, hooking it to his belt. Everything was black—clothes, shoes, even his face, which was covered with Special Forces water-soluble black grease. There was no moon, and he was the next thing to invisible.

Sloat quickly slipped inside the fifth-floor flat, confident that he would encounter no electronic security devices or alarms in so downscale a pensione. But if he did, he had a plan for that too.

He closed the door and found himself standing in a modest kitchenette. In the pale city light coming through the window, he could make out dirty cookware piled in the sink and used paper plates overflowing the breakfast table and wastebasket. There was a disquieting, stale odor in the room.

Sloat calmly switched on his pocket light and began moving through the kitchen. He had staked out this place long enough to believe its tenant was away and he was alone here. If that proved incorrect, there was yet another plan. He extracted his small flé-chette pistol—the silent kind that fired tiny but deadly metal darts—and entered the next room with the gun in his right hand and the flashlight in his left.

It turned out to be a small, nondescript bedroom devoid of many personal items. He shone the flashlight into an equally desolate little bathroom and then swept on quickly into the last room.

He was correct. Yussef Halima was not home. His next task was to ascertain whether Halima would be returning. If not, where should he look next?

He took a quick tour of the living room and found nothing but bargain-hunter furnishings—decrepit couch, chair, coffee table, credenza, a threadbare area rug, nothing on the walls but flaked paint and plaster. The credenza drawers were empty. The coffee table had no drawers. Maybe Halima *had* blown.

The bedroom, however, was a different story. A pair of dirty socks on the bureau opposite the bed and a few other articles of men's clothing inside—with empty pockets—suggested that their owner might return. But the clincher was the nightstand drawer. Inside was some cash—EU bills of small denomination and some change—plus a battered, dog-eared Koran; a small vial of some toxic-looking amber liquid; an unopened package of fuses; a half-empty disposable lighter; five wrinkled sheets of paper bearing various scribblings in Arabic; one newspaper clipping, in English, regarding the Hofburg theft; and a photograph of the Spear and Crown reposing in a kind of curio cabinet.

This swallow, Sloat believed, would be returning to Capistrano.

He flipped through the Koran just in case it held other papers. There were none. Then he scooped up the five handwritten sheets, spread them out on the bed, and began photographing them with his tiny document camera and flash. Finally he put everything back the way he had found it and stood thinking. His gut told him he wasn't done. But what else was there?

The telephone. Sloat took the instrument from the top of the nightstand and pushed redial.

Ten tones later—indicating long distance but not out-of-country—it began ringing. On the fourth ring, a recording kicked in with a breathy French woman saying, "You have reached the Marseilles office of Cluny Overseas Cargo. Our normal business hours are seven thirty A.M. to seven thirty P.M. weekdays and nine A.M. to three P.M. on weekends. If you would like to leave a message, please press one at this time. If you would like information about rates, please press two. If you would like information about specific times and destinations, please—"

So Yussef Halima was in the export business these days.

Sloat shuddered to think that his exports might include the Hofburg Crown and Spear. In that case, it was imperative that the Arab be found as soon as possible.

Should he continue to try to nail Halima, or should he make tracks for Marseilles and try to determine where this package had gone? If he got particularly lucky, he might be able to do both. But Halima would have to make an appearance very soon—which was not at all farfetched. He could return from Marseilles in a matter of hours while his cargo took days to reach its destination.

With these chess moves playing out in his head, Sloat peered through the front-door peephole onto an empty hallway.

On impulse, he slipped out the door quietly and made a beeline for the stairs opposite the elevator. He quickly wiped off the black grease with a rag, in case anyone was still stirring at this hour. Fortunately, there was not even a security guard in the narrow entrance hall of this shabby building—just a desk, a phone, and rows of mailboxes.

Sloat trotted down the front steps. The glare of the streetlight was in his eyes.

Suddenly shards of cement on either side of him kicked up as two gunshots rang out. He hit the sidewalk and rolled off into the grass behind some shrubs. Another shot sounded.

In an instant he was aiming the fléchette pistol through a break in the bushes. His aim was disturbed by another shot, forcing him to duck, but not before he squeezed off a shot of his own. He had no idea how accurate he had been, but he'd certainly had an effect. He heard a man's voice, the slamming of a car door, and the muffled whine of engine acceleration.

He popped up and squeezed off another shot at the vehicle, to no apparent avail. This kind of job really called for heavier firepower.

All he could do was try to get a description. The car was too far off now to get a license number, but he had no trouble with the make. It was a sporty, electric blue Karma—a convertible.

The question, of course, was why?

Paris

There was a definite satisfaction in pulling on the handgrips, pumping the cranks, and propelling himself and the ultralight cycle along the wide, leafy avenue. Peter, crouched over the frame, felt the coolness flowing around him like an airfoil as the elegant clutter of Paris faded into the woodsy expanse of the Bois de Boulogne.

Within the park proper were children with balloons, young men with sweethearts, old men with dogs, teenagers with guitars, seedy men with bottles in brown paper bags. And now there was a young man with a bicycle and a need to get out of the city.

Peter kept pushing the road under and behind him in search of a suitable place to have a one-man picnic and a good ponder. The broad avenue fed into smaller parkways that split out around small woods and lakes. Navigating by instinct, he turned randomly down enticing paths that drew him along almost magnetically. Shortly, he came upon a small *lagune* that seemed to say, "You're here."

It was a lake just large enough to have several families of ducks and swans riding the ripples and dipping occasionally for submarine treats. And there was a tree waiting by the shore for Peter to lean his bike against and then himself on the other side, facing the water.

His stomach told him to get his lunch sack out of his bike pannier. Inside was a fruit-drink box and a couple of croissants with lunchmeat from the corner delicatessen near the hotel. It appeared to be something like pimiento loaf, he was thankful to note. Considering his difficulties in communicating with the deli clerk, it could have been almost anything—escargot loaf, maybe.

Peter unhitched his helmet, laid it beside him on the grass, and dug in. He had worked through lunch with Wendy, and now he was famished.

The two of them had labored for mind-numbing hours, consulting data banks, reading reports, and talking to Witherspoon and several other Interpol offices in search of criminal records for anyone connected even remotely with the regime of Chancellor Waldemar Neumann, especially Jean Pierre Bardo's Population and Health people.

There was much from which to choose. He had been surprised at the number of ex-cons in EU government employ. When he finally called it quits at three o'clock, Wendy was still calling up personnel files and studying mug shots onscreen. Apparently she expected her sixth sense to tell her something about the individuals just from their pictures. Peter had left her to her own bizarre devices.

He needed to plan some next moves, and he still wanted to hit the streets and develop some sources of his own. He had heard that the south of France was a mecca for *tombaroli,* professional art thieves, and the semilegitimate dealers who served as their fences.

Let Wendy chase the PH characters; maybe it would produce something. Certainly Gwydian Brandt had implicated their organization. But since Brandt's murder, it was with cutthroats and thieves that the booty surely would be found. Peter wanted to test that theory.

And now what of this imminent arrival of Carlotta the unobtainable? He dared not let his stuffed-down feelings from the past get loose in the present. But what did she want with him?

The last thing he needed just now was more female trouble. He suspected that Wendy Carlisle's interest in him was more than just professional. Peter knew better than to let a casual physical attraction get the better of him, but when he was with her his responses seemed to have a life of their own.

But what would he do with Carlotta? And why did he seem doomed to relationships with unobtainable women? Carlotta, because of some undisclosed genetic incompatibility. Wendy, because of her spiritual incompatibility. It was tempting to think he might be able to win Wendy over, but something told him he was dreaming. And yet, didn't he have an obligation to be a witness for his faith?

It was maddening.

Still, on the whole Peter had to admit he was having the time of his life. These were great days to be a private investigator. They were such terrible days in the losing battle against crime that law enforcement agencies, caught in the throes of major budget traumas, were generally appreciative of any help they could get. Society's misfortune resulted in tremendous business opportunities for sharp operations such as McBride & McBride.

Peter could recall from the crop of twentieth-century detective novels he had consumed that PIs once were regarded as themselves just one step ahead of the law, fair game for abuse by thugs and heavy-handed cops alike. The common thread today was the crooked cop—a dangerous species that still could spell major trouble for the unwary private eye.

The phone in his pannier rang twice before he realized what it was. He scrambled to his feet and dug out the small device.

"Peter?" said a female voice. It was one he knew quite well.

It took him a moment to find his voice as his pulse quickened. "Yes. Carlotta?"

"Yes, Peter. It's so good to hear your voice. Where are you?"

"I'm—well, I'm somewhere in the Bois de Boulogne on a bike. Where are you?"

"At your hotel, Peter—the Toussaint. As Neal probably told you, I'm vacationing, and I decided to look you up. I've never been to Paris before, and I could use some expert counsel."

"I don't know, Carlotta. Neal probably told you I'm here on business, and I'm certainly no expert on Paris. It's my first trip here too."

"You couldn't even fit in dinner with me? My treat?" Her voice began to sound a bit stressed while trying to remain casual.

Peter felt a little ashamed. "Of course I'll meet you for dinner—on me. I just don't want you thinking I was here for fun and games and escorting gorgeous young women around Paris."

"Flatterer," she said reproachfully, but the stress was gone.

"Are you staying at the Toussaint too?"

"That's right."

"OK. Look, it will take me half an hour to make it back down the avenue, so why don't you check out the pool? I hear it's very nice. That will give me time to get cleaned up and—" He stopped.

"What's the matter, Peter?"

Now he felt like a major dope. "I forgot. I already have a dinner engagement with a . . . police officer."

"Well, I certainly don't want to—"

"No, no," he blurted. "It's all right. I can probably get out of that. I'll just have to make a call. I'm sure it will be all right."

"Listen, Peter. I have no objection to a threesome, if your police officer doesn't. In fact, I think I'd like to meet her."

Peter was almost too nonplused to respond. "OK. We'll see."

He stood there a moment after they had hung up, dumbfounded.

Her? Had Carlotta been talking to Neal about his personal life? What was she up to? Who was supposed to be the detective here anyway?

* * *

Peter, freshly showered and cologned and every hair brushed into place, paced the pretentious, red-velour draped lobby of the Toussaint, jumping every time the elevator doors clanged.

He did not have a good feeling about this. Why couldn't one of these women have gracefully declined the dinner engagement? Why hadn't he had the foresight and the fortitude to prevent this? Would there be a scene?

He stopped pacing for a moment and smiled. The mental image of a food fight erupting in a grand place like the Ritz helped break the tension.

But when at last the elevator doors opened and Carlotta did emerge, all of those feelings dissolved into wonder. The moment their eyes connected, her face lit up like the sun after a summer shower. Peter felt almost detached from the earth. The feeling only intensified as he resisted it. Rationally it was not an emotion that he especially welcomed.

So why did he feel like a four-year-old on Christmas morning? If Wendy had made him feel alive, Carlotta made him feel risen from the dead. Was this what the poets meant about falling in love in Paris?

It appeared Carlotta was feeling the same way, except that she seemed not to be resisting. She had always been lovely, but somehow today she looked fully capable of launching a thousand ships. She glided toward him like something out of a dream, wrapped in a smile and a cheery lavender print dress with chiffon and lace.

"Hello, Peter."

"My, you're looking . . . swell, Carlotta."

"Thank you, but 'swell'? Have you been watching old Jimmy Stewart movies?"

"Shucks, ma'am. I don't know what you're talking about."

"Never mind. Where are you taking me?"

"Taking you?"

She rolled her eyes. "For dinner. You know—like to eat?"

"Ah. That kind of dinner. Well, it's kind of a . . . a foreign restaurant."

"Oh. That sounds different."

Peter offered his arm, and she slipped her hand through, resting it upon his forearm as if it belonged there. It was amazing. It felt just like starting over.

* * *

Mansour's was Franco–Middle Eastern with emphasis on Moroccan and Algerian cuisine. It took a moment for Peter's eyes to adjust to the subdued lighting and then for a hostess to ask their names. The young woman with a cascade of permed auburn hair picked up a couple of menus and began escorting them to their table in the back.

They passed other tables occupied by a spectrum of nationalities with exotic-smelling dishes before them and serious-looking beverages in various stages of consumption. The low murmur of feeding was punctuated by an occasional guffaw or titter. Upon the walls hung small Persian rugs with hypnotic patterns and various gleaming swords, sabers, and scimitars with strangely curved blades.

Wendy Carlisle appeared oblivious to their approach. Her head was bowed over a book on the table before her. When she looked up, it was with a deliberate smile that faltered momentarily, as if she had seen something she didn't like. There was a flash in her eyes, the glimpse of some emotion she would not reveal further. And then the smile returned, but with a more controlled expression to the eyes.

"So, this is your little friend from the USP?"

Peter winced.

Carlotta extended her hand and said graciously, "Carlotta Waldo. Glad to meet you."

Wendy clasped the hand momentarily and nodded perfunctorily, her eyes scanning both their faces as Peter and Carlotta took their seats.

He endeavored to get the evening onto a better footing. "What's that you're reading, Wendy?"

She smiled, closed the volume, and held it up so they could see the title. *The Holy Scriptures*.

"It's an English version that I found at an exceptional price at a secondhand bookstore down the street from my hotel. It's my gift to you."

At this, she handed the book over to Carlotta, who accepted it with no small surprise.

"Why, thank you. I've kind of gotten away from Bible reading, but I'm determined to get back into the habit."

Wendy wore an expression that eluded Peter. Of smug tolerance?

The menus included English subtitles, but the dishes themselves were so foreign that didn't help much. He asked Wendy to order for them, since she had chosen this place.

Wendy started to describe some of the various entrees, then agreed it would be easier to order a family dinner for three with an assortment of dishes to sample.

"So," she said during the wait for the food, "Peter told me you're an artist, but he didn't say how you avoided starvation. What do you do?"

"I paint and do graphic design. But to eat, I write and teach."

Peter listened with half an ear. He was thumbing through the tome that Wendy had given her.

It took him a minute to realize that something was awry. *The Holy Scriptures* was not exactly Genesis through Revelation. In fact, there was only a smattering of any books of the Bible here—mostly excerpts from Ecclesiastes and Song of Solomon. The rest was a conglomeration from various sources—the Apocrypha, the Koran, the Hindu Upanishads and Bhagavad Gita, the ancient Egyptian Book of the Dead, Zen koans, Taoist parables. Besides the familiar Judeo-Christian way of faith, there was a lot of talk about the clear light of the void, karma, reincarnation, enlightenment.

It did not appear as though these disparate pieces were being presented as opposing views, however. Rather, Peter got the impression that these were devotional readings and one was expected to give the various traditions equal weight and reverence.

It took him only another moment to realize that he had entirely lost the thread of the conversation between the two women.

"Do you believe the legends about the Holy Grail having been secreted in the cathedral crypt?" Wendy was asking.

Carlotta shrugged. "It makes for interesting folklore, but who can even say for sure what the Grail really was?"

Wendy began to reply, but before the words were out of her mouth, their food was there. She repeated the server's identifications of the various dishes as they scooped them onto their plates.

Then just as quickly, the two women resumed their arcane discussion. Peter was beginning to feel like the outsider. Wendy, it turned out, had an interest in all things Gothic, in which Carlotta just happened to be thoroughly informed and happy to share. Now the conversation had turned to mathematical relationships in the architectural design of this particular cathedral.

He had been worried about mediating conflict, and instead he was unable to get a word in sideways.

Wendy stopped eating for a moment. "How long will you be in Paris, Carlotta?"

Carlotta shrugged carelessly. "There's much to see, but I'm under no particular time constraints. Depends mostly on how the money holds out. I'd hoped to spend some time in a few other cities—Rome, Athens, Zurich, Stockholm. Why?"

"I just wondered if you'd like to go to Chartres."

"Absolutely."

Wendy smiled. "If I do it at all, it has to be squeezed in tomorrow. I'm not really supposed to be here for sightseeing."

"That's right," Peter said, wondering how she intended to justify such an excursion at all.

As if reading his mind, Wendy spoke to him in a low voice. "Don't worry. I have reason to believe we can combine some business with pleasure on this."

Before he could question what she meant, he was interrupted by an insistent electronic chirping under the table.

Wendy dug something out of her purse. "Hello," she said softly into the small device.

Carlotta gave him a quizzical look.

Wendy spoke only a few more words into the phone, too low to be audible. When she had finished, she had just one word to report. "Witherspoon."

"Witherspoon?" Peter repeated.

But Wendy was already on her feet and wiping her mouth. "We have a new development, Peter. You and I must repair to Montmartre."

He realized that her words had been chosen as much for Carlotta's benefit as for his. Carlotta looked very much as if she were about to argue for accompanying them, but he stared her down, shaking his head faintly.

"I'll . . . uh . . . I'll get a cab back to the Toussaint then," she said, getting the hint. "Peter, please call me tonight, no matter how late it is."

He pressed some large bills into her hand. "Please settle the tab for us. And—listen, Carlotta."

"Yes?"

"I have a feeling that it may be morning before I call."

She nodded somberly.

He turned to follow Wendy's disappearing figure out the door. At least they had mostly finished their meal.

★ ★ ★

On the way to Montmartre, Peter tried to extract more information from Wendy, who was more interested in giving directions through the traffic, heavy even at this hour.

"So what did Witherspoon say?"

"An informant has reported another murder in Montmartre."

"So? Isn't that Reynard's business? Why do they think it concerns us?"

"Reynard's a fool." Wendy sounded distracted. "This is clearly something else."

"Like what?"

Peter sensed her eyes now on him before she answered. "Another hit like Gwydian Brandt. It's right up ahead. Turn here."

The place would have been hard to miss. Uniformed police had a small parking lot behind a low-rent apartment building cordoned off with yellow nylon cord. Wendy flashed her Interpol ID through the open passenger window, and they were waved through. Peter parked on the street behind an unmarked police car flashing emergency lights in the back window.

In the lot, two paramedics were loading a shrouded stretcher into the back of an ambulance. Peter walked gingerly around the red Zodiaque coupe as though it were a bomb. Its windshield had been strafed, and pellets of glass lay all over the blacktop. The doors on both sides had been left open.

Peter bent down and gave the interior the obligatory once-over. Despite bracing himself for the sight of blood, he was surprised by the quantity of it. It was pooled on the floor, smeared over the front seat, spattered on the dashboard. These triggermen had taken no chances.

He became aware that one of the *agents de police* had joined them and that Wendy was conversing.

"Comment s'appelait-il?"

"Yussef Halima," said the man.

The rest was too fast and too French to follow. Peter stood up in time to see Wendy head toward the apartment building in the company of a young officer.

"I'll be back in a minute," she called over her shoulder.

Peter walked over to one of the squad cars, where another officer sat with the door open, apparently filling out a report.

"Bonsoir," said Peter as the man looked up. *"Parlez-vous anglais?"*

"Un peu," the man said with a shrug.

"Were there any witnesses?"

"Déposants? Non. Désolé." The man went back to writing.

Peter had the feeling he was not being told the truth. It was maddening. Interpol—Scotland Yard, at least—couldn't be trusted, and Paris police didn't much care. He walked slowly across the lot toward the apartment building, considering whether he should join Wendy inside.

"He is lying," said a voice behind him.

Peter whirled.

A dark-haired man, dressed in black, was seated on the stoop of a nearby outbuilding. His white face was about all that Peter could make out in the shadows.

"Lying?" Peter repeated. When there was no immediate answer, he considered walking away but changed his mind. "What do you mean?"

The man stood up slowly, as if weary. "There most certainly was a witness, and they know it."

"Why do you say that?"

"Because I am the witness."

Peter was momentarily at a loss.

The man moved slowly closer, and Peter got a better look at the face. It was the face of a man in his mid-to-late forties, on the swarthy side, possibly Mediterranean or Semitic. Weariness showed there too, but not the kind from weakness. It was more the fatigue of great vigor depleted by great exertion. There also was a calculating look in the dark eyes that seemed to be scanning for clues, peering into the future, counting odds.

"CIA?" the man asked, looking Peter up and down.

Peter stifled a laugh. "No."

"But American?"

"Yes. I'm a private investigator—Peter McBride. And you?"

The man ignored the question. "And who is the British lass? Not a private investigator?"

"Scotland Yard."

"The Yard," the man repeated as if quietly disapproving. "What sort of investigation are you conducting?"

There was something so audacious, yet rational, in the man's manner that Peter set aside his normal cautions. "Stolen antiquities from a major institution."

The man's eyes glowed as if someone had flipped a switch. "The Hofburg? The *Reichskleinodien?* If that's the case, you're too late, my friend."

"Why?"

Peter did not get to hear an answer, if the man had intended to give one. Around the corner just then came Wendy and a police officer.

"No, Sergeant," the man was saying as they walked over to the red Zodiaque. "There was not a trace."

The officer popped the trunk and pointed inside with his flashlight, displaying its emptiness.

"Thank you, officer." Wendy looked inside and then stepped back.

Peter turned to his mysterious friend. "What do you know of all of this? And who are you?"

The man gave Peter an inquisitive look before speaking. "This Yussef Halima, now dead, did indeed have the *Reichskleinodien* in his possession. However, he was shot to death about an hour ago by two men in a blue Karma convertible. If our friends at

Interpol are worth their salt, they will find the Crown and Spear at a dock in Marseilles prepared to sail on the morrow."

"How do you know this?"

"I'm the witness, remember? Here." The man scribbled something on a card and handed it to Peter. "I'm taking a bullet to Marseilles in the morning. You're welcome to join me for the ride. Just call my room before seven."

Before Peter could reply, the man had gone, and Wendy was speaking to him.

"It was just like Gwydian Brandt's," she said, apparently referring to the victim's apartment. "There was even a picture of the regalia in his bedroom. Anyway, are you ready to take me home, Peter?"

He nodded silently, turning the card over in his hand. Oddly, it contained no address and no vocational title—just a scribbled phone number underneath the simple printed name: *Amos Sloat.*

10

Chartres

Chartres Cathedral appeared to span the universe over Carlotta's head. Its flying buttresses, vaulted ceilings, pointed arches, arching ogives, engraved voussoirs, massive pillars, and tall, vertical panels of multihued stained glass gave her a crick in the neck to take it all in. She felt dwarfed and insignificant in the midst of this awesome majesty.

Fortunately they had arrived at the cathedral just as a tour group was forming. Their guide was a plump young woman named Rochelle in decidedly masculine attire with close-cropped hair. She was the English speaker, working the other side of the aisle from a French-speaking guide.

"Many consider Chartres Cathedral to be the foremost artistic creation of the Middle Ages," Rochelle declared when the obligatory hush had fallen. "Twenty-first century visitors are still impressed by the magnificent architecture, the priceless statuary, and the colorful masterpieces of stained glass. The omnipresent Christian symbols are obvious. Yet there is something far older than Christianity here."

Carlotta glanced at Wendy Carlisle, who was equally wide-eyed, before moving along with the knot of English speakers. They had been standing in the hub of the structure. Now as they moved into the south transept, she felt all the more like a vulnerable child in the Hall of the Mountain King.

Rochelle continued, "Those who entered through the main gate may have noticed some strange symbols along the left bay voussoirs. Some of you may have recognized them as the signs of the zodiac, carved in stone, flanking the ascended Christ. . . .

"We are now approaching the restored labyrinth, where unshod pilgrims once traced out symbolically their road to Jerusalem."

Carlotta looked down at a mazelike pattern in stone that led circuitously toward the center and then back out again.

"Walking this labyrinth at certain astrologically significant times was said to open the spiritual eyes of the pilgrim. Prior to the construction of the original cathedral in the eleventh century, historians say, the Chartres cathedral mound had been the site of ancient pagan worship. Christian sites were built atop more ancient pagan ones throughout Europe as the new religion sought to accommodate the local populace steeped in the ancient ways. . . .

"You may want to go up to the triforium and observe the stained-glass windows and other overhead marvels. In another fifteen minutes, refreshments will be served in the Saint Piat Chapel. The way is marked by green arrows. Thank you for visiting Chartres Cathedral."

The group began dissolving in sundry directions. Carlotta observed an expression of peculiar concentration upon Wendy's face.

"Well," Carlotta said, "I think I'll avail myself of one of those interactive Tour Links." When there was no response, she added, "Care to join me?"

Wendy glanced up, still wearing that mysterious expression. "No. I think I'll explore the 'road to Jerusalem.'"

Carlotta realized that Wendy had been staring down at the labyrinth, almost as one mesmerized. Now she was removing her shoes.

As Carlotta moved away, she overheard Rochelle saying, "Some seekers of enlightenment reportedly walked the Jerusalem road on their knees."

Carlotta glanced over her shoulder to see Wendy dropping to her knees in the attitude of a true seeker.

* * *

Descending the staircase into the subterranean mysteries of St. Fulbert's Crypt, Carlotta felt as if she could have been at Stonehenge or the Pyramid of Cheops. Remembering the Tour Link headset, she gave voice to her question.

"How did people in the Middle Ages construct a building of such massive proportions without the benefit of modern heavy equipment?"

"Part of the answer," a synthesized male voice spoke in her ear, "lies in the simple mechanics of pulleys, scaffolds, and counterweights. The rest of the story, however, is a big question mark. History simply has not recorded just how the master builder engineered such massive stone tonnage of such complexity into place with such precision."

At the bottom of the staircase, Carlotta blinked under the stark illumination of an electrified wrought-iron chandelier of medieval design. She was standing in one of several vaulted chambers with lower arched ceilings.

Without prompting, the synthetic voice began explaining the legend of the crypt from its pre-Christian existence when Celtic and Gaulish pilgrims came to imbibe from a healing well.

Carlotta began to wonder if she were the only tourist in the crypt. She could see no one else and was beginning to feel like a child in the dark hearing heavy breathing under the bed. Did those lights just flicker, or was it her imagination?

"According to legend," the Tour Link continued blithely, "a goddess known as the Black Virgin was worshiped here."

Then from the next chamber came a spine-chilling scraping sound, as of something being dragged across the floor. Another sound—a liquid *plip-plip*—gradually rose in volume. The hairs on the back of Carlotta's neck began to stand up. In no way was she going to venture out of this room.

"Stop!" she told the Tour Link.

"Eventually," the ersatz voice continued, unheeding, "Chartres Cathedral became the repository for one of the Church's most venerated relics, the Virgin's Holy Tunic, reputedly Mary's own garment, worn at . . ."

"End program!" Carlotta cried.

"The legend of the healing waters apparently dates to Chartres village's first Christian martyrs, who were cast headfirst into the well by their persecutors. Their contact with the waters was credited for these healing properties. Go now into the next chamber and observe the site of the ancient well."

"No!"

Now Carlotta's imagination was taking on a life of its own. There was something, she felt, in that well—a presence, a loathsomeness—that made her want to flee, fast and far. Unfortunately her knees seemed to have lost their steadiness.

"Go now into the next chamber—"

Stifling a scream, Carlotta stripped the headset from her ears and hurled it through the arch into the next chamber, which responded with a burst of feedback distortion. She knew she was acting irrationally, but her gut instincts were signaling mortal danger. And now there was that scraping-dragging sound again.

Get out!

Finally her feet began to obey, and she launched herself across the chamber and up the staircase toward the reassuring daylight. Her heart was jackhammering as her pounding legs faltered on the last steps. Just a little farther! She gasped for breath at the top, certain that anything was better than falling into the clutches of that vileness in the crypt.

There was something down there. She knew it.

And yet, things were not quite what they should be up here either. Where was everyone? Surely they were not all consuming refreshments in St. Piat Chapel.

Carlotta surveyed the corridor, as panic rose once more. She told herself not to run, and yet she didn't dare let her shadow rest. She wouldn't feel safe until she had laid eyes on flesh and blood.

Rounding a corner into the main concourse, she found herself in the cavernous south choir beneath the spectacular medieval kaleidoscope of *Our Lady of the Beautiful Window.* And still not a soul in sight.

Recalling where she had left Wendy Carlisle, Carlotta made a beeline toward the far nave and the mysterious labyrinth. She could see already that no one was there, but perhaps Wendy would not be far away, doing whatever newly enlightened humans do when they have entered the promised land.

At the edge of the maze, she paused to catch her breath and look about her, like a girl on the verge of a secret swimming hole. Surely she could not be the only person left in the cathedral.

On impulse, she let her feet take a few tentative steps into the inward coursing of the labyrinth. After that, it was easy. No longer was she walking the maze; the maze was walking her.

She wondered what would happen when she reached the center. Would she disappear like everybody else? Was there a Narnia on the other side of the black hole? She told herself she would simply stand at Ground Zero and look and pray, and maybe then someone would come.

Gradually Carlotta became aware of a droning, keening sound, rising and falling on the periphery of her awareness like a Gregorian chant.

Now she was at the center. She let her eyes survey the cathedral, taking in the sweep of grandeur in its entirety. She felt as if she had arrived at the summit of the mount of wisdom, needing only to ask to receive. So then, where was Wendy?

And then she placed the keening sound. Her eyes lit upon Wendy Carlisle's solitary figure, high upon the triforium, precariously weaving her way in and around the huge stone pillars of the vaulting high above the floor. She appeared drunk—or mad?—and in reckless disregard of the precipice's edge. The unsettling sound was some despairing wail that threatened to end in catastrophe.

"Stop!" Carlotta cried, her heart in her throat.

It was doubtful that Wendy heard her.

Carlotta wasted no time. In a moment she was racing along the wall in search of some access to the higher level. Inside an alcove she found a staircase leading up to the gallery and attacked the steps as if the hounds of hell were at her back.

Within this stony incline, the wails reached her ears in louder, unmistakable peals of desolation. And then, gasping, she reached the landing. There was a channel, just wide enough for one person to pass, lower than the pillar bases. Up ahead she could see Wendy, one hand against a column, her eyes set on something across the cathedral, her toes at the very edge of the abyss.

"Stop!" Carlotta cried again.

This time she was heard. Wendy half turned, her expression impossible to read at this distance. "Go away!" she yelled. "It's too late."

"No! Wait!"

Carlotta closed the distance quickly and looked up into the woman's dilated eyes, which regarded her as they would a viper. Wendy sidled backward around the base of the pillar, farther away from Carlotta but oblivious to her footing, which threatened to drop off into space.

"Be careful!" Carlotta boosted herself up onto the pillars' foundation.

"Stay back!"

Carlotta hesitated, afraid her own actions might precipitate the disaster she sought to prevent. There was something about the voice, something not Wendy Carlisle. And an idea blossomed in her mind. From where did clairvoyants—even police psychics—draw their power? Was the woman possessed?

"Who are you?"

The woman's face twisted into an expression of disbelief and contempt. "What?"

"In the name of Jesus Christ, I command you to tell me your name."

There was a dirty kind of laugh, but then Carlotta got her answer. *"Belen!"*

In the moment of recognition of her worst fear, Carlotta lost the upper hand. Wendy was upon her, viselike fingers closing off her windpipe.

Carlotta thought she could hear someone shouting at a distance. But now the blood was pounding in her ears, and she was seeing spots. She felt herself sliding toward the edge of oblivion, and she began kicking and clawing. She could not scream.

Her head collided with stone, and time seemed to stop. She was losing consciousness. Her fingers tried to dig into the stone to halt her forward slide to the brink, but her fingernails gave way. Wendy's leering visage and hot breath were in her face. Over her shoulder, through blurring vision Carlotta caught the dizzying sight of the cathedral floor below.

People were down there now, pointing, shouting. She thought she heard other voices on the triforium.

Her oxygen-screaming brain was going full tilt.

Then, finally, she realized what had become of the loathsomeness in the well of the crypt. It had become a beautiful woman named Wendy, whose thumbs were locked around Carlotta's throat.

* * *

Marseilles

Two decorative, brass-framed portholes looked out from the dockside office onto a gray vista of tin roofs, rust-colored warehouses, and pontoon cranes bobbing slowly on the swells like giant tendrils. Peter gazed through one of the circular windows and imagined he could smell the tang of the sea.

Despite the chipper assurances of the morning supervisor at Cluny's Overseas Transport, he had an unsettled feeling. It couldn't be this easy. Or maybe he'd just been hanging around Wendy Carlisle and her precognitions too long.

"Oh, yes," the *administrateur* had said. The moment management was notified by Interpol, Cluny's had pulled Yussef Halima's footlocker off the ship and stashed it overnight under lock and key in the manager's office.

But even as he heard this, Peter found himself disbelieving that he was actually about to lay his eyes on the Crown and Spear.

Amos Sloat and Detective-Sergeant Witherspoon silently sipped their coffees and regarded each other warily. Peter was not sure how to take these men. Witherspoon had looked somewhat surprised to see Sloat instead of Wendy Carlisle. When Peter explained that she had taken an odd excursion to Chartres, the detective had just rolled his eyes as if to say that sounded just like the old girl—you know how unpredictable police psychics can be.

Sloat, for whatever reasons, had insisted on maintaining the fictitious identity of an American named Dennis Scovill. Peter gathered that he harbored some deep distrust of Interpol, but Peter was harboring some distrust of his own for this mysterious, tight-lipped "witness" with the alias.

"Here we are, gentlemen," said the supervisor at last, wheeling a footlocker into the room. He was a sawed-off, bandy-legged little man named DeCoursey, with a mustache, beady brown eyes, and the quick, impulsive movements of an artist.

Peter and the other two jumped to their feet at the sight of the nicked and faded brown luggage. Witherspoon wasted no time hoisting it from the dolly onto the visitors' couch and aiming his bolt cutters at the lock.

"Wait a minute," said Witherspoon sourly, setting his cutters down.

"What's wrong?" Peter asked.

Without answering, Witherspoon grabbed the padlock. It came off in his hand.

Peter could guess what was coming.

While Witherspoon frowned at the padlock, Sloat pulled the footlocker lid open.

Peter crowded in close, then stepped back quickly, trying not to retch. The footlocker was not entirely empty, as he had expected.

Sloat let the lid fall back, and the room light revealed the sole contents—a large dead fish, about the size and shape of a mackerel.

Witherspoon swore a vicious oath.

Sloat pressed his lips together in a grimace of disgust.

"Monsieur?" said the supervisor, looking from one face to the other. "I assure you that no one has had access to this *bagage* since it was taken from the hold. Maybe if you could tell me what you are looking for—"

Witherspoon silenced him with a curt gesture. "Forget it. This is obviously all a wretched mistake."

"Aren't you going to take statements?" Sloat protested. "Someone here may know something about the tampering with this luggage."

Witherspoon shot him a contemptuous look. "I'll give you a statement. Mind your own blasted business next time."

Peter could not believe his ears. "You're really *not* going to investigate further?"

"You catch on quickly, my friend. No wonder Carlisle stayed in Paris. She knew this would be a wild-goose chase. She could have told me. Just wait till I get hold of her."

Witherspoon motioned for DeCoursey to remove the trunk and its foul treasure.

"But—" Peter began. He broke off, feeling a hand on his arm.

"Let it go," the Israeli said quietly. "These slugs couldn't investigate their way out of bed if it was on fire."

"So why the fish?"

Sloat gave him an odd look, then appeared to be considering something. "Let's bail out of here. And you can check that message you've got."

Peter looked down at his belt, where he'd clipped his portable, and spotted the winking red light. "Oh."

* * *

Outside, Amos hailed an autocab and instructed it to take them to the Marseilles-Paris Bullet.

"The Mob," Sloat said when they were strapped in and began to speed off.

Peter drew a blank. "What?"

"You asked about the fish. Dead fish are a traditional Mob symbol. It originated with the Mafia, which used it to announce that their victim was now sleeping with the fishes."

"So Halima's killers—and the new owners of the Crown and Spear—are the Mob?"

Sloat shrugged. "Or someone who wants us to think it's the Mob."

"What do *you* think?"

Sloat studied him for a moment. "All I know is that there seems to be a variety of competing interests willing to step on each other for the prize. And I wouldn't be surprised if it gets a lot worse before it's over."

"So which of those interests commands your allegiance?"

Sloat ignored the question. "Better check your message. It could be important."

Peter hated to admit it, but Sloat was right. It could be. He punched the callback.

Instantly it rang, and the digital display indicated a Paris exchange. Then a voice was telling him he had reached Inspector Reynard's office, although the Inspector was not in just now.

"Is there a message?" Peter persisted.

"Let me see," the secretary said in clear English. "Oh, yes. Ms. Carlotta Waldo has been taken to St. Simone's Hospital, just outside Paris. She has asked if you would go see her."

Peter's heart began to race. "Are you sure?"

"Pardon?"

"Never mind. What has happened to her? Is she OK?"

"The only information I have is that she has suffered minor injuries from an accident and she may be released this afternoon after observation."

Peter began to breathe a little more easily. "Oh. Thank you. Can you tell me how to find St. Simone's."

Peter hit "Record" while the woman gave directions. He was surprised how much Carlotta was beginning to mean to him—all over again.

11

Paris

It was the middle of the afternoon before Peter arrived at exurban St. Simone Hospital. And after further contretemps arranging Carlotta's discharge, he was now fighting rush-hour traffic back into Paris in a rental car. Between his hassles and her injuries, their respective moods created a heavy silence that was gaining weight by the minute.

Peter had been relieved to find that Carlotta's visible injuries were blessedly minor—multiple contusions, abrasions, broken fingernails, and one glaring black eye. All diagnostic imaging of internal parts had turned up negative. He suspected, however, from her demeanor that her worst injury was nothing that would show up on a scanner. And right now, he just didn't have much extra wherewithal to render encouragement.

But neither could he stand the silence. "Would you like to talk about what happened?"

She parried with a question of her own. "It took you a long time to come back for me. Was there a problem?"

"You might say that. A hospital bureaucrat got difficult when she found out they were discharging you to your male companion's hotel."

Carlotta sounded surprised. "I didn't know such quaint morality still existed anywhere in the West."

Peter realized she'd missed the point. "It's not Victorianism. It's PH regs. Population and Health rules. They want to bill USP national health for your treatment. A records check showed a procreation ban for the two of us. If they think we're shacking up, that would invalidate our coverage and they don't get paid. Simple as that."

"How did you get out of it?"

"I didn't."

"What do you mean?"

Peter had almost forgotten how much fun it was to put her on. "I promised them our firstborn child."

"Oh, Peter!"

Then she began to laugh, a sound he had not heard for a long time. It was gratifying to hear it now, especially under the circumstances. Something intangible between them—a kind of barrier, some unspoken tension—had just been removed.

"No," he confessed. "I signed a waiver and gave them my central telecredit number to bill if there's any problem."

"How touching," Carlotta said with just the slightest teasing tone.

Peter began to believe that she wasn't feeling too bad. Maybe he could pry a little.

"Carlotta," he said at length, "when will you be ready to tell me what happened at Chartres? Was it really just a fall on a flight of steps?"

There was a pregnant silence before she answered. "I'm just afraid you won't believe me."

"Why in the world would you think that?"

"Peter . . . how do you feel about Wendy Carlisle?"

Peter wondered why women always answered a question with a question. "I like her, but I don't really trust her. I don't trust psychics—including ones who wear police badges."

"I mean, how *much* do you like her?"

Suddenly things were beginning to click. "Not that much. There's only been one love in my life, and she's unobtainable. You're not suggesting that Wendy—"

"That's *exactly* what I'm suggesting," she retorted. "It wasn't a staircase. It was a balcony. And it wasn't a fall. I was pushed, almost over the edge."

"But why would Wendy want to push you off a balcony?"

Her voice became petulant. "See?"

"What?"

"I knew you wouldn't believe me."

"It's not a question of believing you. I'm just trying to figure out why a Scotland Yard detective would want to kill you."

"It was wrong for me to come here. I should have known I would just get in the way and cause problems." There was a silence, followed by sniffles.

Peter knew he had said the wrong thing. "I'm sorry. You're not getting in the way. Let me try that again, please. OK?"

Carlotta blew her nose, then said with a quavering voice, "You missed your turn."

"What?"

"Shouldn't you have turned left at that light?"

"Oh. Yeah. You're right."

They fell into another awkward silence as Peter circled the block and approached the Toussaint from the rear.

They left the car in the parking garage, and Peter said he would escort Carlotta to her room. She didn't object.

Upstairs, she kicked off her shoes and disappeared into the bathroom to freshen up.

Peter called room service and ordered sandwiches and tea. He looked around. The room was a small sitting area off the bedroom, much like his own, with floral wallpaper, Second Empire furniture, and barely room to swing a cat.

He paced distractedly until she reappeared in thongs, sleeveless blouse, and shorts, looking somewhat reconstituted. She apparently had even applied makeup to her shiner. Peter recalled that Carlotta generally looked great in just about anything. She gave him barely a glance, shaking out her hair in the vanity mirror and attacking it with a brush.

"Look," he said, plunging into his rehearsed speech. "I want you to know that I do believe that Wendy Carlisle attacked you at the cathedral. I just—"

He was startled by a knock. He had already forgotten about the food. He opened the door for a white-haired, stoop-shouldered garcon, who whisked into the room with a platter laden with a large covered dish and a silver teapot, deposited it neatly on the coffee table, gave a little nod as he accepted a small bill from Peter, and slipped back out as quickly as he had entered.

"Now, as I was saying—"

Carlotta lifted the cover and sniffed at one of the little sandwiches. "Limburger?"

"I don't know, Carlotta. Listen—"

There was another knock. What now?

Peter opened the door to a familiar face—Amos Sloat. Whatever this strange man was selling, Peter was in no mood to buy just now.

"Look, Amos. Can you come back later? We—"

"Who is it, Peter?"

Before Peter knew it, Sloat had brushed past him and breezed into the room.

"You must be Carlotta." He took her hand. "You're even lovelier than Peter described."

She was smiling and blushing down to her thongs. "I don't know if that says more about me or about Peter. And *you* are . . ."

"Amos Sloat. And I'm sure Peter hasn't told you anything about me, because I've managed to keep him pretty well in the dark so far. Would you like a sandwich?"

Sloat scooped up the plate and offered it to her. She took a sandwich and began nibbling. He then thrust it at Peter, who reflexively took one and regarded it like a mackerel in a footlocker.

"Have a seat," Sloat said generously.

Peter could not believe the audacity of this strange man. Nevertheless he deposited himself on the loveseat, next to Carlotta. She didn't seem to mind.

Sloat seated himself in an armchair and began piling finger sandwiches on a plate for himself.

"So," said Carlotta pointedly, "are you going to keep both of us in the dark?"

Sloat looked mildly surprised, then smiled. "No, Carlotta. And my apologies, Peter, for being so evasive. It's a professional habit for General Security Service agents."

Carlotta wrinkled her nose. "What agents?"

"Also known as Shin Beth."

"I see," said Peter. "Israeli counterintelligence."

Sloat nodded. "At your service."

Now Peter was really wondering what he had gotten into. "Is that what they call 'the Jewish conspiracy'?"

Sloat just laughed.

Carlotta asked, "What do you mean, Peter? Isn't that kind of rude?"

"Maybe," he conceded. "I'm just wondering why Israel would be on the trail of the Crown and Spear."

Sloat shrugged benevolently. "To keep it out of the wrong hands."

Peter remained suspicious. "Whose? The Antichrist's?"

"You go ahead and worry about the Antichrist or whatever," Sloat said less softly. "We worry about the anti-Jew. The last dictator who wielded that Spear wiped out six million of us. Or don't they teach the Holocaust in the USP anymore?"

"OK, OK. You make a point. It sounds like we may have the same objective, whatever the reasons."

"Agreed. I think we should work together."

"I thought we already were."

Sloat studied them both. "I would like to hear what happened at Chartres Cathedral with Carlotta and Wendy Carlisle."

Peter looked at Carlotta and squeezed her hand reassuringly.

"I'm not so sure myself what really happened," she said tentatively. "I just—all I can say is that something weird was in the air there. I got pretty spooked in the basement crypt. And when I went back up, there was nobody around. They told me later that it was just coincidental that it was feeding time for the tourists in Saint Piat Chapel.

"Then I found Wendy up on the balcony, looking as if she were going to jump or fall. I tried to stop her, and she attacked me. Then—"

Here she stopped and gave Peter a self-conscious look. "This is where I'm afraid you're not going to believe me."

"Go on," urged Sloat.

"It appeared to me from her actions that she was . . . possessed. So I—"

"Possessed," repeated Sloat.

She looked embarrassed. "Demon possessed. So I commanded the demon in the name of Christ to identify itself."

If Sloat distrusted the statement, his voice didn't reveal it. "And did it?"

Carlotta, tightlipped, nodded.

"What name did it give?"

"Belen."

A heaviness fell on the room, as if someone had just brought word of a financial disaster or a military defeat.

Sloat broke the silence. "Then what happened?"

Carlotta gently rubbed her forehead. "I'm not—it's kind of jumbled. She was strangling me and pushing me over the edge. And then I passed out. When I came to, people were asking me what happened. I tried to tell them, but nobody had seen Wendy Carlisle. So they acted like I'd fallen and knocked myself senseless, which was probably the easiest thing to believe."

Peter was curious about something else. "Amos, what is your concern about this incident?"

"Ah. Well, I've had plenty of reasons in the past to distrust the Yard and Interpol, but it's quite another thing to think they actually might be implicated in this plot."

"You really think they are?"

Sloat shrugged. "It's sounding more that way by the hour, don't you think?"

"Well," said Carlotta, "I'm certainly convinced that this Wendy Carlisle is a fraud."

Peter couldn't let that pass. "I wouldn't go that far. She's put in long hours on this case. In fact, she was the one who made the ID on the geneticist who had the regalia in her curio cabinet."

"And how did she make that determination? ESP?" Carlotta said with thinly veiled sarcasm.

"No," retorted Peter. "Photo analysis."

"But doesn't she use psychic phenomena as part of her repertoire?"

"Maybe. But I wouldn't call that fraudulent. I accept the reality of supernatural phenomena."

Carlotta shook her head. "I may not be all I should be, but I do know that the word for that stuff is 'evil.' In fact, there's a Bible verse that I still remember from a long time ago. Something like, 'The Son of God appeared that He might destroy the works of the devil.' So I don't think we're supposed to work right alongside them. Do you?"

"I think that may be a little strong," said Peter, not very comfortable in the defender's role. "There are a lot of sincere people who are being misled right from the pulpit. I know. I sat in the church in London where Wendy Carlisle is a member and heard all sorts of heresy."

Carlotta raised her eyebrows. "Wendy Carlisle in a church? Did anybody try to drive a stake through her heart?"

"Oh, come on."

She shook her head. "I would bet money she's no more a member of that church than I am."

Realizing that Carlotta was nursing some hard feelings, Peter decided to let it go. He had almost forgotten that Amos Sloat was still there.

"What do you think about all of this, Amos?"

Sloat smiled wanly. "I try to make it a practice not to comment on other people's religion, no matter how crazy it sounds. But I'll tell you what I'll do. If you'll give me the street name, I may be able to settle the question about Sgt. Carlisle's church membership."

Peter searched his memory as Sloat turned on the flat-panel work station on the credenza and began punching in commands. "Yarborough Street. Saint Mark's Anglican Church on Yarborough Street." He looked up. "If I can't hack a church database inside of five minutes, I'm taking a slow boat back to Haifa."

Peter and Carlotta regarded each other warily as the agent hammered on the keys.

She spoke first. "You probably think I'm just a typical jealous female, don't you?"

"I'll make you a deal," Peter rejoined. "You don't peg me in love with Wendy Carlisle, and I won't peg you a jealous female."

Carlotta seemed partly mollified. "But are you so sure she's not in love with you?"

"That's just silly."

"Is it? I still don't know why she tried to kill me, but jealousy can be a motive."

The loaded silence was punctuated only by Sloat's staccato keyboarding.

Peter was still mulling Carlotta's remarks when she spoke again.

"Peter, did you read any of that book of Wendy's, *The Holy Scriptures?*"

"I glanced through it."

"What did you think?"

"It was quite an equal-opportunity Bible. It certainly doesn't discriminate against anybody. It was like Religion's Greatest Hits."

"Seriously, Peter, while you were out crimefighting last night, I stayed up reading that thing. It was the supposedly Christian parts that bothered me the most. There were so-called noncanonical gospels—a gospel of Thomas, a gospel of Barnabas, and others —that teach a different Jesus and a more Eastern-sounding theology. In one of them there was even a homosexual Jesus."

"That's pretty weird. Was there a central thrust to it all?"

"Not overtly. But you couldn't help but get the idea that there are many paths to the truth, all equally valid."

He remembered their dinner at the Squid Pro Quo. "Wendy had a saying—'One light, though the lamps be many.' I told her that sounded like the broad way to destruction, but she seems to be equally comfortable with any faith—Buddhist, Muslim, Christian."

"It's like what they call 'hugging you to death.' We embrace Christianity as long as you don't make it exclusive. Other places in the book make that very clear. Hold on."

She fetched the volume from the bedroom and opened it to a place with a marker. "I'd never read any of the Koran. It's interesting that some of the Koran selections include references to Jesus. In one place, it denies the crucifixion. And then here it refers to Jesus as simply an apostle who prophesied the coming of Muhammad."

Peter was baffled. "How do they get that?"

But now Sloat was crowing. "OK, boys and girls. It looks like that boat ride to Haifa will have to wait. That Wendy Carlisle is no more a member of Saint Mark's than I'm a member of the College of Cardinals."

Peter and Carlotta crowded around the display screen, where Sloat was scrolling through the roster.

"Maybe she was an attender rather than a member," suggested Peter.

"I have that covered. There are two hundred forty-three members and one hundred seventeen adherents. Wendy Carlisle shows up neither place. Nor does she show up in any other church record, including baptisms, confirmations, visitations, last rites—you name it. And this seems to be a church that keeps very careful records."

Peter realized that he had not quite expected this outcome. "So then, what was she doing there that evening when I visited?"

"I would humbly suggest," Sloat said, "that the young lady was tailing you."

"But why?"

The Israeli shrugged. "That gets back to my worst-case scenario. It may be that the Yard or Interpol—or both—are implicated in this whole intrigue."

"And maybe," said Carlotta, "that gets back to my worst-case scenario about the femme fatale."

"Just what do you suggest, Amos?" Peter said slowly.

"Me? I'd say stick close to this young lady here, and I don't think you'll have too much trouble from Sgt. Carlisle. Besides, if I'm not mistaken, I think she has feelings for you."

Carlotta was blushing again. She wasn't denying it.

Peter smiled. "What do you think, Carlotta? Are you up for some exotic travel and real adventure?"

Her eyes were dancing. "Whither thou goest—"

"In fact," said Peter, "I think with Carlotta's art background we might try passing ourselves off as shady art dealers and see what we can learn on the black market grapevine."

"It's a thought," said Sloat, who looked like he was having a number of thoughts.

"So where do we pick up the trail?"

Sloat's eyes became inscrutable, probing. "What do you think? Let me hear your thoughts."

Peter knew he was being tested. "Well, I'm not sure. But I think it's time to leave Paris. Undoubtedly the regalia have left the country, but I'm told the south of France and the Riviera are a hotbed for fencing art and antiquities. I might start there. On the other hand, if the Mob's behind this latest heist, would it make more sense to go to Italy?"

"I'd say not just yet. The Mob's in many countries. It may be that the *Reichskleinodien* are en route to Salvatore DiFalcone himself—in which case we'll be in Italy soon enough. But for now, I think your original instincts about the south of France are sound. We need to get underground."

Peter stood up. "I think that settles it then. Can we leave in the morning?"

Sloat nodded. "By all means."

"Oh," said Carlotta in a worried tone.

Both men looked around.

"What's the matter?" asked Peter.

Carlotta looked sheepish. "The south of France? I'll have to do some emergency shopping. I don't have a thing to wear."

12

Cannes

On the beach the relentless waves were dying in fitful swirls of spray and foam. Farther out, the Mediterranean was a dazzling expanse of blue, punctuated by the masts and rigging of distant pleasure boats. Peter now understood why the fabled Riviera shoreline was called the "Côte d'Azur."

Propping himself up on locked elbows, he scanned the pink and white and brown sunbathers cavorting in the tide, tossing beachballs, or just irradiating themselves on beach blankets under the scorching sun and the wheeling, wailing seagulls. He basked in spreading, sun-baked serenity, pleasantly reminded of the proverbial clam at high tide.

He gazed over at Carlotta, standing behind her canvas and wiggling a brush intently in a small corner. Her modest, black, one-piece bathing suit only accentuated the fact that she was arguably the most attractive woman on the beach. He wondered as she daubed at her palette how much of that desirability was in the eye of the beholder—his eye.

He watched her change brushes and apply a different color to another section of canvas. The paints, brushes, and other paraphernalia had cost them an outrageous markup at a little boutique that morning, but Carlotta had insisted that it would be money well spent if it helped them establish a local reputation as art savants. He certainly hoped so.

Besides, she seemed to draw a measure of comfort from her painting. Ever since their arrival in Cannes, she had been effervescing about the visual delights of these coastal environs: gleaming châteaus, high-walled villas, small promenades lined with Italianate white stucco homes with orange-tiled roofs, and the prolific flora, especially the exotic red bougainvillea and giant pink mimosa. She had rattled on about the masters who had found creative inspiration here—Picasso, Matisse, Fragonard, Léger, Renoir, Cocteau. And, of course, there was the deep, deep blue of the sea.

When they checked into the Hotel Normandy, Amos Sloat had stood outside while Peter and Carlotta registered as Mr. and Mrs. Carpenter. Then Sloat went in and registered as Dennis Scovill for a room with twin beds, which he actually would share with Peter. Even so, Carlotta had appeared somewhat uncomfortable with the arrangements. Now might be a good time to ask.

"Carlotta?"

"Hmm?"

"Do you have a problem with being Mrs. Carpenter?"

Carlotta's brush stopped wiggling, but with her dark sunglasses it was hard to tell where she was looking. "Not exactly."

"OK. Make me guess. You worry about the morality of an undercover alias?"

"I have no question about your morality."

"Then what?"

Carlotta's voice dropped to a somber tone. "Are you sure you really want to know?"

"Why not?"

"All right. It reminds me that I'm not Mrs. *McBride.*"

Before Peter could react, there was a commotion seaward. Two young women were arguing loudly with a policeman. Peter had a pretty good idea why. They were both topless.

"Does that still go on around here?" Carlotta wondered aloud.

"All the time," answered a man behind them in a non-French accent.

Peter turned to see another couple, both blond and thirtyish, watching the same drama unfold. By this time the two sun worshipers were being marched offbeach ahead of the policeman. It reminded Peter of a painting of Adam and Eve's expulsion from the Garden.

"I beg your pardon?" said Carlotta, looking behind her.

"I said it happens all the time," the man repeated. "Half the town is Muslim. But no matter how many years the natives complain, they can't seem to eradicate the old morality. There's always somebody asserting her rights."

The woman muttered something about Muslims that Peter didn't catch, but it didn't sound like a product endorsement. He decided not to offer his opinion on religion and morality at this point.

The man was a trim fellow with a short mustache and wire-rim glasses. His companion was petite and young with luxuriant, shoulder-length hair. Both wore golden tans and had the bearing of people of some substance, which was certainly in character for the Riviera. They began depositing their blankets and towels nearby.

The woman, apparently intrigued by Carlotta's seascape, returned for a closer look.

The man joined her. "Nice. Is she a professional artist?"

"Not exactly," said Peter. "She teaches art, and we're . . . in the business."

"Ah," said the man knowingly. "We do some collecting as well. Of course, the best pieces are never on display."

"Of course. We just need some contacts, being new here."

The couple exchanged glances and, coming to some unspoken understanding, introduced themselves as Piers and Greta Anders from Zurich—he an investment banker, she a holistic health consultant, apparently for New Age jet-setters.

Peter and Carlotta identified themselves as Mr. and Mrs. Carpenter from the USP.

Before long, Peter and the Anderses were seated comfortably on their blankets while Carlotta continued calmly painting.

"And just what kinds of art do you and *Frau* Carpenter collect?" asked Piers. "We have a few contacts ourselves here and there."

"All sorts," Peter said carelessly. "Although we are most interested in those things that are not on display."

"Actually," interjected Carlotta, turning from her canvas, "our real métier is antiquities."

"Ah," said Piers. "What kind of antiquities?"

Peter tried to maintain a casual tone. "Artifacts, memorabilia related to royal dynasties."

The man appeared not unduly fazed. "That certainly requires some resources but can be quite rewarding, depending on the period. What era? Which royal families?"

Carlotta turned again to them. "Those of the Holy Roman Empire."

"The Habsburgs in particular," said Peter, making a mental note to get back to his European history before this was all over.

"Ah," said Piers again. "That is certainly . . . challenging."

Peter was suddenly aware that *Frau* Anders was studying him with some intensity. In fact, she was moving over to his blanket and looking intently into his eyes.

"What's the matter, Greta?" asked her husband.

"Oh," she said sweetly. "His sclera. The coloration. Let me see. Yes, I see some opacity in the aqueous humor."

"What's that mean?" Peter wondered if he should be worried.

She was so close now that he could smell her subtle fragrance, some fine perfume. And he could not help but notice that she was extraordinarily attractive.

"I do not mean you are about to go blind," Greta said, smiling with tender concern. "But the eyes are the window to the soul, darling. It could be a nutritional deficiency easily remedied by some dietary supplements—lecithin, folic acid, ginseng. Apparently, your capillaries and follicles are not being adequately fed." Here she began running her fingers through his hair.

Peter felt like bolting.

"I always thought he had great follicles," said Carlotta with what Peter thought was secret amusement at his expense.

"On the other hand," Greta continued, "it could be psychic. Have you ever had your aura done?"

Peter shook his head. "I didn't even know I had one."

"Well," she said, "would you like me to give you an orgonomic massage here and see if I can release some of your stress points?"

Peter was puzzled. "'Orgonomic'? Is that like Japanese paper folding?"

"That's origami, darling," said Greta with a little giggle. "This is much more pleasurable."

"No, thanks." Peter grasped for an excuse. "I have a . . . well, my back . . . we really need to be . . . uh . . . going soon."

"Yeah," said Carlotta with a straight face. "Have to find some Habsburg stuff."

"Oh, this won't take long," said Greta, patting the blanket where she obviously wanted him to recline. "And it should be good for your back too."

"Actually," said Carlotta with some hardness in her voice this time, "his stress points are just fine, darling."

"But how about yours?" said Piers, gesturing to his own blanket. "I am equally adept at orgonomic massage."

"I don't think so," said Carlotta. "We really must be going."

"Yeah," Peter agreed. "The Habsburgs are waiting."

The couple exchanged glances again, and Piers sighed sadly.

"As you wish," he said, then looked at Greta. *"Die Brieftasche, bitte."*

Greta, digging into a handsome leather bag, extracted a billfold of equally handsome leather, and handed it to her husband along with a pen. From the billfold Piers withdrew a business card and jotted something on the back.

"Here." He handed the card to Peter. "This should be of some benefit. If Gus Grodin does not have a line on what you are seeking, I am confident that he will know who does."

"Thank you," said Peter, taking the card without looking at it.

Carlotta already was breaking down her easel and securing the painting in her drybox. Neither of them was about to prolong this scene a moment longer than necessary.

"Listen," said Piers as Peter and Carlotta grabbed up the last towel. "If you change your mind and want to play, we're staying in town at the Hotel Brabant."

Peter nodded.

Carlotta gave a little wave.

Peter guessed that Greta's melancholy blue eyes would follow them devoutly as they tracked their sandy footprints away from the sea.

* * *

They did not have far to go after changing at the bathhouse. It was just a long stroll down the chic beachfront promenade called La Croisette, past the trendy cafes, glitzy boutiques, and luxury hotels catering to actors and actresses, investment bankers and holistic health consultants. It was a trek they would have wanted to take for art's sake, anyway.

At one outdoor cafe they revitalized themselves with some tart cerise pâté and espresso among the other milling tourists on the crowded patio. Carlotta took the opportunity to practice her French and ask a waitress for more precise directions to 744 Rue Meynadier.

Moving on, they passed the Palais des Festivals, the venue for the famous annual Cannes Film Festival. Unconsciously Peter's left hand found Carlotta's right. It just seemed natural.

Eventually, following the waitress's simple directions, they managed to find their way from the promenade through a couple of turns inland and onto the Rue Meynadier. The old avenue exuded character from its quaint houses and storefront shops for exotic foods and other connoisseur items in structures three centuries old.

In time they found their number. Black-stenciled letters on the plate-glass front erased any doubt.

AUGUSTIN GRODIN III
ANTIQUAIRE

Inside were the usual overpriced mahogany secretaries, threadbare settees, fine crystal, hideous vases and statuary, racks of bizarre garments, silver utensils with obscure pedigrees, and cases of coins, jewelry, and baubles of every description from every generation since Homer.

Presiding over it all was a curly-haired girl of no more than fifteen, who stared lifelessly from behind the back counter and out the front window as if her young mind were as clotted with dust as some of the relics in the most inaccessible corners of the shop.

Behind her was a dark doorway suggesting an inner sanctum where a magus such as Gus Grodin might lurk until summoned by some rogue or another wanting to buy or sell the Hope Diamond, the Ark of the Covenant, or the Crown of Charlemagne.

Suddenly Peter was seized with the desire to make a purchase—something very special.

"Look," he said, squeezing Carlotta's hand and guiding her to one of the glass cases. "Do you see anything you like?"

Carlotta scanned the case of rings, blinking in incomprehension. "I know you're not proposing marriage, so what?"

"We should at least look the part, don't you think?" Peter stabbed a finger at the glass over a plain gold band that caught his eye. "How about that one?"

"I think it's too big, Peter. You have to try these things on. They come in different sizes, you know."

He looked up to see the zombie girl migrating in their direction.

"Say," he said to her, "we'd like to see some of these rings."

"Quoi?" said the girl softly. *"No anglais."*

"I'll handle this." Carlotta downshifted into some mellifluous French.

After trying on a few likely prospects, they narrowed the rings down to the two best fits and said they'd take them. Peter asked Carlotta to tell the girl not to wrap them—they'd wear them out the door.

That, at least, should have prompted a reaction, but the girl tapped mechanically, unblinkingly through the UTP—uniform tele-credit process—without comment. She finally handed Peter a receipt and a small black box with the two plain gold bands.

"Now, tell her we'd like to speak with her father, if he's in."

Carlotta told her.

All at once, it was as if life flooded back into the girl's face and eyes, which grew saucerlike. There was a flash of something like outrage and disbelief. And then her face exploded in laughter, giant, piercing peals of hysteria that rattled the bone china in the glass-fronted cabinets.

"Papa Gus!" she cried over her shoulder to the back room. *"Papa Gus!"*

Moments later, out of the shadowed doorway crept a crippled remnant of a man, hunched over a cane despite the fact that he probably was no more than thirty-five. His scalp was a defoliated wasteland, his frame a bony bag of emaciation. His breathing came in shallow gasps. He trailed an oxygen tank on wheels, tethered to his belt and connected by plastic tubing that looped over his ears and under his nostrils. His eyes, large by contrast in the shrunken face, were rheumy question marks above a hawkish nose and a bushy mustache that was perhaps his only healthy part.

Augustin Grodin was a coper, an unfortunate AIDS lifer, too sick to live, too responsive to die. There was still no cure, but with the latest twenty-first-century treatments it was possible for such patients to live for many years, albeit with a severely limited quality of life.

Peter now understood the girl's laughter but was appalled at her insensitivity. It made him wonder about the health of their relationship, whatever that was.

"Qu'est-ce que c'est?" said the man in a surprisingly authoritative tone despite diminished wind power.

Peter half-whispered to Carlotta, "Tell him we're black marketeers looking for hot antiquities or words to that effect."

Carlotta grimaced. "I can't say that."

"Then just ask him if he's heard anything about the *Reichskleinodien*."

"You bet your boots," said Grodin. There was obviously nothing wrong with his hearing or his grasp of English.

With a devilish look lighting his eyes, the pathetic figure worked his way over to the glass case between them and, placing his forearms on the counter, leaned across to speak confidentially.

Peter and seemingly Carlotta were too startled to move or speak.

"You a private dick, no?"

Peter was about to suggest that Grodin had been watching too many old American movies, when the man held up a hand.

"Makes no difference. I talk to police. I talk to thieves. I talk to private dicks. Is all the same to me. Some things I even buy from the *Milieu*, if they are not too dirty. But the *Heilige Lanze*—you and I will not see that again. Or the Crown."

Peter was struggling to keep up with the surprises from this man. "Why do you say that?"

A thin smile came to Grodin's lips. "Because they say they are now in the hands of the brothers. And I believe them. Is surely something they do."

"The brothers?"

The smile faded, replaced by something closer to impatience, maybe some fatigue. "Felici, you know."

"Felici. What are their first names? What do you know about this?"

Grodin removed his arms from the counter and stepped back, putting a finger to one ear. "I hear things. They kill a man in Paris, no? But even the *tombaroli* cannot fence such things. Too famous, you know."

Peter did not want the conversation to end here. "So what do you think they've done with the items?"

Grodin shrugged and turned back toward his darkened sanctum. "The business of fools is not my concern. Maybe is yours. I am sorry. That is all."

With that he withdrew, trailing his oxygen tank and making a wheezing sound. As they left the shop, Peter took one last look.

The girl had lit a cigarette and was watching the smoke curl toward the ceiling as one transfixed by a shooting star or a solar eclipse.

* * *

A phone message was awaiting them at the Hotel Normandy, but no Amos Sloat. Peter hoped Amos had not encountered trouble in his parallel probe into the affairs of the Mob. But he was cheered by the message from Neal in the USP.

While Carlotta freshened up in her own room preparatory to dining out, Peter decided to return his father's call. He propped himself up on the floral bedspread and instructed the flat panel to put the USP number through. In another minute Neal's familiar face materialized on the wallscreen.

"*Bonjour,* Monsieur Carpenter," McBride said with a twinkling eye.

"*Bonjour.* How's retirement suiting you, Pops?" Peter teased.

"It's been quite busy. I really don't know when I'm getting back overseas. How are things going there?"

"We're under control. Making some progress, but it's still scratching the surface. Did Amos Sloat pass muster with your sources?"

McBride nodded. "With flying colors. Quite a character. A real adventurer, it seems. You could do a lot worse for a comrade-in-arms, although I wouldn't necessarily assume he's ever got all his cards on the table."

"What do you mean?"

"Just the usual secret agent stuff. Amos Sloat is not his real name, for example."

Peter wasn't too surprised. "Oh? What is it?"

"Yaakov Zacharias."

"OK," said Peter, filing the name away for the future. "I'll keep that in mind. But this isn't why you called, I'm sure."

Neal's face formed a more serious expression. "Is Carlotta with you?"

"Not at the moment. She's in her room."

"All right. Considering how she feels about . . . things . . . I'd suggest you just keep what I'm about to tell you under your hat for now."

"What's up?"

McBride seemed to consider his words before speaking. "I'd been thinking about some things that Rick said about Population and Health control bureaucracies. And then we got this new case—a fellow who'd lost his health coverage because he violated a procreation stricture."

Instantly Peter was interested. "What kind of violation?"

"Failure to abort. He and his girlfriend were married without a procreation permit, conceived a child, and went through with the pregnancy even though the government expressly denied coverage and directed them to abort. They might have got off with only the loss of coverage for the maternity costs except they began complaining, and PH revoked their entire health coverage."

An idea was growing on Peter. "Were they Christians by any chance?"

"No, but you're on the right track. They're Hasidic Jews, and vocal about it. The original PH citation was for Tay Sachs syndrome. But when we arranged a consult, the doctor said that was a bunch of baloney. Our guy had been making lots of noise alleging discrimination. And here's the interesting part—he collected a number of other cases among the Hasidim to support his argument."

"Anecdotal evidence doesn't carry much legal or scientific weight without a control population and all of those things."

McBride nodded. "Correct, but wait. He took his case to the rabbis, who approved a survey in several synagogues. Seems that they found a number of similar situations—a disproportionate number. I've given the results to Rick, and he says it's pretty persuasive. In fact, he said the odds are—let me see here—at least 10^{17} against this pattern occurring by chance."

"He would. So what's it all mean? Another pogrom?"

"That's what we intend to find out. My suspicion is that this may be a lot bigger than just a few synagogues. Considering your own situation with Carlotta and some other stories Rick has heard, I suspect we may find the same thing with Christians and any other groups that might be considered nonconformist."

Peter's mind raced. "I see. What kind of things has Rick heard?"

"Well, it's a long story. But it seems that governments that have been losing the battle to control population *growth* may be moving into controlling population *behavior*."

"What does that mean?"

"Rick is supposed to be getting me some more intelligence on this, but he says there are strategies here and in Europe to weed out antisocial and nonconformist behavior and to condition populations to make them more—I think the phrase is 'more adaptable to rapid and fundamental social change.' For what reason is another question."

Peter could not resist his most immediate concern. "So you're suggesting that Carlotta and I—"

McBride held up a hand. "I don't want to raise expectations at this point. It's way too early. So I wouldn't tell her yet. But if what I suspect is true, we may have legal grounds to put up a pretty good fight for people like you two."

"Assuming our RH incompatibility isn't real and valid."

McBride blinked several times, then laughed. "Where have you been? I thought you already knew that. The government has already admitted that the original ineligibility was erroneous."

Peter was stunned. "You mean—"

"Peter, as far as we can tell, there's no good reason you and Carlotta shouldn't be able to get married—if you wanted to, of course. It's just that PH still won't lift the denial, and they won't say why. Now it's our job to go after them on it."

Peter's mouth tried to work, but nothing came out.

"Don't worry," McBride said. "We'll give it our best shot."

"Yeah," said Peter at last. "Keep me posted."

His father's picture dissolved into snowy background, leaving a heavy silence in the room.

Peter looked over at the little black box on the dresser, and his heartbeat quickened. He had to put this out of his mind. He didn't dare think about it. Not just yet.

13

Cannes

What's the matter, Peter?" Carlotta set down her fork. "I don't believe you've heard a word I said. Is there something on your mind?"

Startled, Peter caught himself staring at her in the candlelight as if seeing her for the first time and finding a vision of delight.

There was something different, but what? Certainly this black, off-the-shoulder Paris dress was something new and enchanting, emphasizing her darker shade of tan, which was also new. But that wasn't it. There was also something quite alluring about the large, gypsy hoop earrings and how they dangled at the median point of her twin sweeps of straight, black hair.

But that, he realized all too well, wasn't it either. He knew exactly what it was. It was the eye-of-the-beholder thing again, and he was out of his mind to let it show. This had to be handled carefully.

"Yes," he conceded. "There is something on my mind, and I guess we'd better take care of it right now."

He reached into the side pocket of his suede sports coat, and his fingers found the small black box.

"Close your eyes, Mrs. Carpenter," he said, "and hold out your hand."

She held out her right hand, the corners of her coral pink mouth twitching in the candlelight.

"The other hand, my dear," he said sternly.

The twitches broke into a small laugh as Carlotta changed hands, her eyes still squeezed tightly shut.

Peter slid the smaller ring deftly onto her fourth finger and then the larger one onto his own.

"You may open your eyes now."

Carlotta obliged, opening her eyes and mouth in wide circles of mock amazement at the gold bands.

"Now we're a little more credible, Madame Carpenter, don't you think?"

"Yeah, I guess," she said dubiously, wrinkling her nose and pointing a finger and a fierce squint in Peter's direction. "But just don't get any fresh ideas, mister. My big brother is a Marine."

Peter laughed. "You don't have a brother."

"Well, then," she fumbled, "I certainly hope you don't have any fresh ideas."

They both laughed again and resumed eating.

As they finished their surf and turf, Peter related the part of Neal's conversation that pertained to Amos Sloat, aka Yaakov Zacharias. He omitted the part about the suspected population control conspiracy and the possible reopening of their own case. They were just beginning their *mousse au chocolat* when Carlotta froze, her eyes widening in astonishment at something behind him.

"What is it?"

"Over in the corner. Just be discreet."

Peter turned nonchalantly and scanned the crowded restaurant. Sure enough, over toward the far corner he spotted what she had seen. At the table in question sat two couples, apparently engaged in scintillating conversation and fine food. One was a young Oriental couple, possibly Japanese. The other two were both blond, thirtyish, and strikingly familiar.

"Piers and Greta!" said Peter with some amusement.

"Not so loud," she admonished him.

"Are you thinking what I'm thinking?"

Carlotta started to giggle. "Uh-huh. They finally got a live one. And to think, if we'd played our cards right, we could have been the lucky ones."

"Do you suppose that's lecithin they're eating?"

She leaned forward and batted her eyelashes. "Hold my hand and look deeply into my aqueous humors, darling."

"Please to explain," Peter said in his worst Japanese accent, "what is this 'origami massage'? What do you do for paper cuts?"

Carlotta put her hand to her mouth, laughing so hard that Peter was afraid she would fall out of her chair. She finally took a sip of water and almost choked.

"Easy, darling," he said. "Maybe we should think about exiting this place before one of us meets an untimely end—aspirating on mousse."

"Lead on, Monsieur Carpenter. Darling."

* * *

The Mediterranean was a vast, black looking-glass, reflecting an inky firmament where a giant silver moon danced in myriad shimmering fragments like a Monet painting without colors. Mingled fragrances of mimosa from the promenade and hot grease from the restaurants were set to flight by the cool breezes coming off the waves with their subtler suggestions of salt sea and distant tropical isles.

Hand in hand, Peter and Carlotta negotiated the foamy cusp between land and sea, treading barefoot across the tumbling, rinsing sands where lazy, tepid waves lapped up to their ankles and slithered back down through their toes. The effect was disorienting, as Peter imagined for just a moment that the water was standing still and the beach underfoot was moving. But the stationary silhouettes of eucalyptus and palms against the starry sky told him that was not really so. He might be losing his heart but not his mind.

With her free starboard hand Carlotta held her skirt just above the reach of the watery tongues of the lisping swells. She had given Peter her shoes, and he deposited them carefully with his own by a conspicuous mossy boulder at the foot of the embankment just above the public beach.

"Thanks for dinner. It was . . . swell."

"Watching too many old twentieth-century movies, are we?"

"Peter?"

"Hmm?"

"Did you mean what you said after . . . Chartres?"

"What did I say after Chartres?"

"That you weren't sorry I had come here and that I wasn't really in the way."

"Well, you're half right."

Carlotta slowed, pulling him slightly off balance.

"What do you mean?" Her voice carried a note of doubt.

"I mean I'm not sorry you came, but you certainly are in the way."

She stopped dead in her tracks. Her face was in total shadow with stars peeking through errant wisps of windblown hair. When she spoke, her tremulous voice betrayed the hidden emotion of her shrouded face.

"Say the word, and I'll go."

"Whatever happened to 'whither thou goest'?"

Her voice was very quiet. "I don't want to be in the way. And I won't."

Peter sighed. "Don't you see? That won't help. No matter where you go, no matter how far away, you'll always be here." He drew her clasped fingers up to his heart. "That's where you're in the way."

"Oh, Peter."

They were walking again. He hadn't meant to be that transparent. He didn't know if he should regret it.

"Peter?"

"Hmm?"

"Don't you wish you could just sail away to a deserted island, far away from government and politics and—"

"And population control and national health bureaucrats? Yeah. But then we'd probably be arrested for violating international maritime law or spoiling a wetland ecosystem."

Carlotta was not so easily put off. "Or maybe take a time machine back to the twentieth century, when there were Christmas carols and Easter lilies and total freedom of expression, no matter how politically incorrect?"

"Yeah. The good old days. Unregenerate red-meat white males like Ronald Reagan in the Oval Office. All-male major league baseball teams. No government on people's backs, telling them to terminate a pregnancy or hire a homosexual pastor. But it probably didn't seem so idyllic at the time. The good old days always look best in retrospect."

"We just have to make our own good old days, Peter."

How she got into his arms, Peter was not sure, but there she was, feeling as if she belonged there, as if she had always been there, as if she should never leave. Then she kissed him chastely on the cheek and just as quickly was out of his arms.

And now he was biting his tongue, wanting desperately to tell her that dreams sometimes come true, that even procreation bans can be overturned, that even people like Peter McBride and Carlotta Waldo can live happily ever after.

But to say that would be wrong. What if it didn't happen? This way, at least, his would be the only heart broken twice.

"Peter?"

"What?"

"You're not fooling me."

His heart missed a beat. "What do you mean?"

"I know there's something you're not telling me."

"How do you figure?"

"That's my secret. I have my ways."

By unspoken agreement, they turned around and began the return trip to find their shoes.

Carlotta had only one thing further to say on the subject. "Whatever it is, I know it's either very good or very bad. If it's very bad, I don't want to know. I just want to enjoy whatever the Lord chooses to give us now for the moment. If it's very good . . ."

Her voice trailed off.

Peter touched her cheek. It was moist.

Carlotta sniffed bravely. "You're in the way there too."

* * *

Peter tossed fitfully with a plague of grotesque dreams and images. In one he was on the shore, pulling frantically on a lifeline attached to something far out to sea. Life and death were at the other end. From the resistance, it seemed as though he were working through molasses rather than brine.

For a while he appeared to be gaining ground, laying more and more coils of line at his sandy feet. Soon he would know. And then he did. It was Carlotta, calling to him across the waves not to let go, to save her. He was shouting and desperately pulling on the rope, but his strength was flagging, his arms turning leaden, unable to keep up.

Despite his best efforts, the rope was reversing course, sliding back through his hands, burning fiercely into his palms and fingers. It was too late. Carlotta's cries grew fainter, then died altogether. The line was gone. The sea was as silent as death.

Peter flung himself down onto the shore, weeping bitterly to the ebbing tide.

Later he was standing on the beach, looking out to sea, mourning for a lost Lenore and a sun that would never rise again from beyond the waves.

"Peter!"

Could it be? Inexplicably, his beloved was calling to him from behind. And then she was in his arms again, where he would never let go. In their kiss her fingers found his throat, becoming talons that would not be removed until death did they part.

In his asphyxiation, Peter's desperate eyes opened to see not Carlotta but some other woman he should know.

"Wendy!" he rasped. "Let me go!"

"No!" the woman spat.

"Wendy!"

"No!" the fiend repeated. *"Belen!"*

And then he was out.

In yet another scene, someone was stealing into his hotel room with a sinister delivery. Before Peter could reach for the gun in the nightstand drawer, the phantom/assassin became Amos Sloat carrying an armful of books. Peter asked where he had been all day and all night, and Sloat said something about bars and libraries. He also suggested that Peter go back to sleep.

His watch said it was only a few minutes after 1:00 A.M. He hoped the rest of the night would pass more quickly.

* * *

In the morning Peter snapped awake, realizing that the chainsaw that had been tormenting him was just Sloat snoring in the next bed. It was not quite 6:30, but he knew it was useless to try to sleep longer.

He threw on some shorts, shoes, and a T-shirt and headed quietly out the door for the beach, where he could think or at least get his brain started.

He found the shore and looked out to sea under an overcast morning sky. He was just wondering what today would bring, when night memories came flooding back, dream images of a sun that would not rise and lungs that could not breathe.

"Peter!"

Terror leaped into his throat. This should not be happening. His nightmare was calling out to him in the daylight. Slowly, as through molasses, Peter turned to confront it.

And then Carlotta was at his side, touching his hand and peering questioningly into his eyes.

He pulled her to himself and squeezed long and hard. A heart decision was forming. In that moment he knew exactly what he wanted, and he determined not to be dissuaded by any power or principality. He made a silent vow.

"What is it, Peter?" Carlotta whispered in his ear.

"Nothing," he assured her. "Nothing bad, at least. In fact, you might even say it's very good."

She broke away, giving him a quizzical look as if she didn't dare ask further. "Let's get some breakfast. I saw a little cafe on the promenade where they had some enchanting pastries."

The sun was breaking through, and he felt its warmth spread across his back. "What are we waiting for? Let's go."

⋆ ⋆ ⋆

Back at the Normandy, Peter was surprised to find that Sloat had been a busy man. Not only had he showered, shaved, and dressed in Peter's absence, but he was even now cracking some books at the desk and scrolling through a database on the wall-screen.

"My, my." Peter set down the bag of pastries and the paper cup of expresso he had brought for Amos.

"*Wunderbar, mein Freund!*" the Israeli exclaimed. He put aside his books and attacked the coffee and pastries with gusto.

"Tell me," Peter asked, "was I dreaming or did you really

sneak in here at one A.M., telling me you'd been out visiting saloons and libraries?"

Sloat chuckled. "Something like that. Do you want to hear the short version or the long version?"

"Hold it. You eat. I'll shower. Then you can tell me the whole thing."

By the time Peter returned, Amos was letting Carlotta in the door. She looked sharp in a peach-colored sunsuit and sandals.

"If this is just guy talk," she said coyly, "I'll be glad to go shopping."

"Not so fast," said Peter. "You're not getting off that easily, Madame Carpenter. You're in this just as deeply as we are now. Amos was just about to make a clean breast about his activities yesterday. Isn't that right?"

Instead of answering, Sloat scrolled through a database directory until he found something in particular. "Listen to this." He addressed the flat panel. "Entry for '*Belen.*' Audio."

Onscreen appeared an artist's conception of a ram-headed deity executed in gleaming bronze, rotating slowly about its vertical axis. A computer-generated voice identified Belen as the "One and Unknowable," a fertility deity of the ancient Gauls.

About the time Peter was becoming intrigued, it was over. "Is that all?"

"I've tried to do some cross-referencing." Sloat gestured vaguely at the half dozen books on the desk. "When they say he's 'unknowable,' they're not joking."

"I don't get it," said Carlotta. "What are you trying to prove?"

"I don't know exactly what he's doing," Peter answered. "I'm just pleased that he's taking your story seriously. You said yourself that this attack at Chartres was demonic, and I think this goes a long way toward confirming it."

Sloat smiled. "I don't know exactly what I'm doing either. But there are some things about all of this that have intrigued me from the beginning. Maybe they'll lead to nowhere, but then again they may hold the key we're looking for."

"For example?" Peter prodded.

Sloat looked like a man weighing whether or not to push his blue chips forward. "You are probably surprised to hear a spy-chaser talking like a cultural anthropologist."

It was Carlotta's turn to smile. "That was exactly where I'm coming from."

"I come by this crazy stuff honestly," Sloat continued diffidently. "My father was an archaeologist, and I briefly entered that field until . . . other situations developed. But that is a whole other story. Instead, let me ask you this: How close are you to a solution to the 'rod of Hermes' question?"

Peter had all but forgotten the mysterious Greek inscription. "Stalled on square one," he confessed with a twinge of guilt.

Sloat was standing now and looking like an imposing Old World schoolmaster. "The one clue of any import in this entire affair and you have not even got the plane out of the hangar, let alone taxied onto the runway?"

Peter was beginning to feel quite sheepish. "If you want to put it that way."

"No!" thundered Sloat, causing Carlotta to start. "I do not want to put it that way. What I want is to solve this case and recover these objects before some new madman decides to make a play for world ruler or führer or imperial majesty by whatever title."

He stopped and paced, but Peter knew he was not done. When the Israeli spoke again, he lowered his voice to a calmer pitch. "I am sorry if I sound overzealous. But revisionists have been trying to convince the world for a century now that the Holocaust was just a fantasy circulated by a bunch of Zionists. And now, through attrition, Christians are the same kind of minority that the Jews were a century ago—a blight and an offense in the eyes of many. I certainly hope history does not repeat itself."

Peter glanced at Carlotta, who wore a somber expression. He too felt sobered by the man's passionate jeremiad. "All right. Do *you* have some ideas about the Rod of Hermes?"

Sloat's face lost its scowl. "Did I say that? Well, in truth, my plane's not on the runway either—but I may have got it out of the hangar."

"Excuse me," Carlotta interrupted. "What is this Rod of Hermes anyway?"

Peter explained. "Legend says that the Spear—or Rod—conferred magical properties of health and good fortune to its owner."

Sloat nodded, and Peter could see that Carlotta was intrigued.

"So what do you think it means, Mr. Sloat?" she asked.

"That's Amos, my dear. Well, I have a couple of thoughts on the subject. First, there's the old maxim 'The medium is the message.' That means that using a pagan symbol (the Rod of Hermes) to rename a Christian symbol (the Spear of Longinus) is a statement itself."

"What kind of statement?" she asked.

Sloat's eyes began to glow. "Perhaps the question should be, Why a statement at all? It suggests that the perpetrator is either thumbing his nose at traditional values or that he actually wants to be caught and the articles to be recovered. In either case, I have the feeling that this may not be the last we have heard from him. He seems to be making a partial statement, and the other shoe has yet to drop."

"That's an interesting idea," Peter agreed. "What's your other thought?"

Sloat pursed his lips before answering. "What do you know about Hermes?"

Peter straightened up. "That much I did check out. He was the Greek counterpart of Mercury, the messenger of the gods. But I don't really know what to make of it. Do you?"

"Not for certain," Sloat confessed, a distant look coming into his eyes. "But Hermes was not just the messenger of the gods. He was the god of all the occult arts, even medical science. If you think about it, you will realize that you have seen the Rod of Hermes many times."

Peter started. "I have?"

"Certainly. The winged staff with the two serpents intertwined. The symbol of the medical profession. An interesting juxtaposition, don't you think? The lance that pierced the body of Christ, now presented as the rod of life-giving properties."

"Hmm," said Peter. "He was pierced through for our transgressions—"

"And by his stripes," Carlotta added, "we are healed."

Sloat smiled. "Old Testament. The prophet Isaiah, speaking of the suffering servant, Israel. Forever misquoted by Christians."

"Oh?" Peter challenged gently. "When did Israel die for our transgressions?"

"Never mind," Carlotta interceded. "I want to hear the rest of these coincidences. You two can argue theology later."

"Well," Sloat resumed, "you may find this interesting. Your Belen was not the head of the Gauls' pantheon. Their chief god was this fellow here, Mercury. They gave him the same top billing that the nearly identical figure was accorded by the Germanic peoples under a different name—Woden."

"OK," said Peter. "Maybe I'm missing something, but why is any of that significant?"

"I don't really know—yet," Sloat conceded. "But I'm certain it means something. Did you know that Gwydian Brandt's first name is a feminized form of 'Woden'? Or that Montmartre, where the killings occurred, was named after the temple to Mercury in Rome?"

"That's really strange," Carlotta said.

Peter was less impressed. "I repeat, why's that significant?"

"I think it strongly suggests that while we pursue leads to EU henchmen, mafiosi, and Muslim terrorists, we also take a good look at the occultists. I suspect we may find a variety of players here, knocking each other off and vying for possession of the Hofburg treasures."

Peter said, "I just hope none of us gets caught in the crossfire."

Carlotta gave him an intent look. "Amen, Peter. Amen."

14

Cannes

Peter looked first at Carlotta, then at Sloat. Both seemed lost in thought.

"Well, Amos," he said. "You haven't answered the most pressing question of all.

Sloat looked mildly surprised. "Maybe you haven't asked it yet."

"All of this about Belen and Mercury and Woden explains what you've been doing at the library. But what was it you were doing in the taverns?

The older man laughed. "What people usually do in taverns, I guess, only a good deal less productively.

"How's that?

Sloat shook his head a bit sadly. "One of the trade secrets of my craft is soaking up the maximum amount of intelligence from the drinking class while soaking up the minimum amount of drink. In this case I got exceedingly little of either—drink or information—although I certainly managed to hit enough promising locations. Nobody around here seems to have heard anything about our Hofburg thieves.

Carlotta began to chuckle. "I was just thinking that they should have talked to Gus Grodin."

"Who?

Peter began to explain about their visit to Grodin's antique shop and the peculiar conversation they had had with the man. When he got to the part about the Felici brothers, Sloat's eyes grew round.

"The Felici brothers?"

"Yes.

Sloat got to his feet. "Guido and Eduardo?"

"I don't know. We didn't get as far as first names. He was not that cooperative. Felici means something to you?"

"Indeed. Where is this antique shop? Come on. We can talk on the way.

* * *

When Sloat realized that 744 Rue Meynadier was not just around the corner, he insisted that they take a cab. To Peter's way of thinking it was reasonable walking distance, but the Israeli was clearly too impatient for that. Unfortunately the cabs around the Hotel Normandy were the old-fashioned kind with human drivers, and Sloat was not about to talk in their presence.

The drive took about two minutes, counting stoplights. It took considerably less than one minute to realize that something was different at the shop. The first indication was a lack of interior lights. The second was the black crepe encircling the AUGUSTIN GRODIN III window stenciling.

Undeterred, Sloat pressed his nose against the glass. "Someone's in there—a young girl."

He tried the door, but it was locked. He began rapping vigorously on the glass.

"They're closed, Amos," Peter said.

Sloat pounded harder and kept it up until the door opened. Immediately he inserted his foot and pushed the rest of himself inside.

Carlotta looked appalled at such a breach of etiquette, but Peter just shrugged and indicated they should follow.

"I don't know how well Amos speaks French," he said.

Inside, the curly-haired girl regarded them with disdain. She moved behind the counter and lit a cigarette, pretending to ignore them.

Sloat unleashed a convincing volley of French upon her. Peter could make out the name of Gus Grodin a couple of times.

The girl responded with a plume of smoke and several barely audible syllables.

Peter nudged Carlotta. "What did she say?

"She said Grodin's dead. Died last night."

Sloat pressed her again.

The girl answered, this time a bit more sharply.

Peter whispered, "Now what did they say?"

"Amos wants to know how Grodin died, and she said it's none of his stinking business."

Sloat was jabbering again, and Peter picked up "Felici."

Now the girl was barking at Sloat commandingly. A pistol appeared in her hand.

His hands went up, and he began backing slowly toward the door.

Peter and Carlotta did likewise.

Sloat slammed the door behind them and muttered something in yet another language, possibly Hebrew.

Peter noticed that Carlotta was a bit red in the face. "What was she saying there at the end?"

Carlotta gave him a funny look. "Nothing I care to repeat. Loosely translated, she was telling Amos to go sit on his hat."

"Very loosely," said Sloat.

They set off down the street in silence. This time no one lobbied for a cab ride. The walk would do them good, let them work off some adrenaline.

Finally Peter could stand it no longer. "Amos, who are the Felici brothers?"

Sloat gave him an appraising look. "When Salvatore DiFalcone wants something done right—especially if it involves bloodshed—or he wants to send a message with a calling card, the Felici brothers get involved."

"Salvatore DiFalcone." Peter was skeptical. "I thought he was a back number. Giuseppe Orsini—isn't he the Mob's big provolone now?"

"Orsini." Sloat made a spitting sound. "That's what they'd like you to think. Don't believe everything you hear on One World News. Orsini is window dressing, a public relations man who may be gone tomorrow if he crosses the capo *di tutti capi*. That's DiFalcone. And no doubt will be till he dies."

Carlotta quickened her pace and caught up to them. "So what's the next move, Amos?"

"That's easy. We must get an audience with the capo."

"Why would he want to talk to us?" Peter asked.

Sloat smiled humorlessly. "That's what we need to try to figure out on the bullet ride."

"To where?" Carlotta asked. "How soon?"

"As soon as possible. As soon as we can check out of the Normandy. Pack your bags, boys and girls. We're going to Milan."

* * *

Milan

Starting from southeastern France—down the road at Nice, to be exact—Milan was a straight shot, as the bullet flies, across northern Italy to Milan. Unfortunately, it was a 600-kilometer-per-hour blur under the circumstances. In a more civilized day, Peter was sure it would have been a charming trek to make in the shadow of the Alps in a more leisurely conveyance such as a Lamborghini.

The good news was that they would be in Milan in about a half hour. That might not be civilized, but it was certainly efficient. Now all they had to do was figure out how to gain an audience with the leader of the largest organized crime enterprise in the world.

Understandably Sloat would not permit them to speak of DiFalcone on the train, except by veiled allusion. Peter adopted the fanciful "*Signore* Provolone" for the purpose of discussion.

He sat in the middle seat, between Carlotta at the window and Amos with a newspaper on the aisle.

"So, fellow mice, who's going to bell this Provolone cat?"

To his great surprise, Carlotta spoke up. "I'm obviously the logical choice."

Peter was instantly opposed. "Why do you say that?"

Carlotta batted her eyelashes. "Because I'm so cute, natch."

"Nope. You don't know what you're saying. I can't let you do it."

"What do you mean?"

"Because I—yeah, you're pretty cute, and I want you to stay that way. It's way too dangerous, Carlotta."

"But that's exactly why I should do it. You two macho guys would stand a much greater chance of being turned into shark bait."

"You may not want to hear it, Peter," Sloat spoke up, "but she's right. She would be treated like a princess. It's the old way. They haven't changed in a thousand years."

"But—"

"No buts." Carlotta patted his arm sympathetically. "I think you've just been outvoted. Sorry, Peter."

He sighed resignedly. "I didn't realize this was a democracy. Let's go back to square one. Where in Milan does *Signore* Provolone reside?"

Sloat looked amused. "Not in Milan. A little bit outside the city."

"Oh. In one of those big, fancy villas."

Sloat chuckled. "Yes. You might say that. *Casa grande*. You might even say *Il Casa Grande*."

"Here we are," Sloat announced as the cab pulled up outside the giant gray walls of Aldo Moro Penitentiary, the kind of high walls that are tipped with barbed wire.

"Here?" Carlotta said in disbelief.

"Here." Sloat grinned broadly as they got out. "Welcome to the capo's big house."

Peter turned to Sloat. "Did anybody ever tell you you're a real scream?"

Carlotta was equally dumbfounded. "I just figured you were putting us on. How are we going to get in?"

"Just follow me."

They scrambled to catch up with him as he made a beeline for the guardhouse at the gate.

"Amos!" Peter protested. "This is a prison, for crying out loud. They don't let you just walk in."

Sloat, undaunted, struck up a conversation with a man in a snappy gray uniform behind green-tinted glass.

"How many languages does your friend know?" asked Carlotta.

"Makes you wonder. You had a couple years of Italian, didn't you?"

She nodded.

"Can you tell what they're saying?"

Sloat took something out of his wallet and slid it through a slot in the glass.

The man inside picked up a telephone and began talking.

"I'm not real sure. Amos said something about the Israeli ambassador. And then something about our being 'special friends' from the USP. And that we want to see *Signore* DiFalcone."

The officer hung up the phone, tore something off a printer, and scooted the paper back out the slot along with Sloat's card. The huge iron gate began clocking open with a wrenching sound, and they were waved through by a second uniformed guard.

Peter looked at Carlotta. "Maybe his people do run everything."

After passing single file through a metal detector, they were led down a short hallway into a surprisingly commodious waiting room with an entertainment console, telephones, coffee, magazines, and genuine upholstered furniture. They were the only visitors at the moment. From the looks of things, Peter concluded that Aldo Moro Penitentiary must be a facility for the white-collar criminal.

Yet another guard exchanged a few brief words with Sloat, and both men nodded.

Peter looked expectantly at Carlotta.

"So far, so good. But *Signore* DiFalcone still has to agree to see me."

Carlotta was directed to a red X marked on the floor with plastic tape. She waited there while the guard punched numbers on a keyboard, spoke a few words into a mike port, and eventually managed to conjure up on the wallscreen the image of a gray-haired man with designer-frame glasses.

Peter sized up the man. He was somewhat disarming, a grandfatherly sort, albeit a rather shrewd-faced one. The most intriguing thing about the man was that he wore a white shirt and tie rather than a prison uniform.

And then he realized that *Signore* DiFalcone was also sizing up Carlotta. He appeared to like what he saw. A thin smile relieved the tension of his poker face. He began speaking, slowly at first. Then, after Carlotta answered a question or two in tentative Italian, the words began coming in a fusillade.

Carlotta looked overwhelmed. "*Può ripetere?* she implored. "*Lentamente.*"

"She's asking him to slow down," Sloat explained quietly.

The old fox began speaking in a more measured cadence.

Carlotta, still looking a bit bewildered, stepped off the X and motioned for Peter to take her place. "He wants a word with you."

"Me?" Peter pointed to himself in disbelief. "But I don't speak the language."

Sloat nudged him. "I do. Go on over there."

He moved to the red X.

Peter could tell he was being asked something, but he hadn't a clue as to what.

"Uh . . ." Sloat looked almost embarrassed. "*Signore* DiFalcone would like to know how much you would accept . . ."

"How much would I accept for what?"

"Uh . . ."

Carlotta interrupted. "For me, Peter."

Peter saw red. "OK. Remember what the girl in Grodin's shop told you, Amos? Whatever she said, you can tell *Signore* DiFalcone that it's double for him."

Abruptly he lost his balance as Sloat yanked him off the X.

Amos stepped onto the spot and began smoothing things over in seamless Italian. Then Peter sensed that the Israeli was pressing the question about the *Reichskleinodien*. He heard the Felici name twice.

DiFalcone said a few more words with a toothy smile, and it was over. The screen went blank. A guard returned to escort them out.

On the way out the main gate, Sloat spoke again to the man in the guardhouse and wrote something on a card. Carlotta said it was Sloat's portable number, where he could be reached at any time in case *Signore* DiFalcone wished to talk.

After a cab ride back into the city, they ordered lunch at a crowded downtown restaurant on the theory that the food couldn't be too bad where it was in brisk demand. Sloat bought a copy of *Il Mondo* and nonchalantly scanned the international news pages while they waited to be served.

Carlotta was simmering with questions. "What next? Where do we go? What do we do?"

Sloat looked up with a cryptic expression. "Let's just bide our time for now. Sometimes the mountain comes to Muhammad."

Peter made a sardonic face. "Translation: Amos knows something he's not telling. Just like the 'big house' where *Signore* DiFalcone lives."

"So, you always expect the whole nine yards?" the Israeli said with a hint of mischief.

Peter ignored him, but Carlotta couldn't resist. "What does that expression really mean anyway?"

"The whole nine yards?" said Sloat cheerfully. "I doubt this is true at Aldo Moro, but they say twenty-seven feet used to be standard height for prison walls. So successful escapees were said to have made it—"

"The whole nine yards," Carlotta concluded for him. "You didn't make that up, did you?"

Sloat crossed his heart.

"What I still don't understand," said Peter, "was how easily you got us into Aldo Moro. You have something on the warden?"

Sloat smiled at the compliment. "I wasn't so sure it would work myself. But it confirmed what I had heard about the warden and his regime."

"What do you mean?" Carlotta asked.

Their iced teas and salads arrived.

"DiFalcone runs the place. That's the only reason we got in. He receives lots of visitors, and the administration doesn't ask questions. They probably take orders from him. If we had been there to see anybody else, we would not have made it past the main gate."

"Hold on," said Peter, as Sloat lifted the first bite of salad toward his open mouth. "Mind if I give thanks for the food?"

Sloat blinked, the fork frozen in its trajectory. But he didn't object.

Carlotta just closed her eyes.

"Heavenly Father," Peter prayed, "we thank You for this food. Thank You for Your lovingkindness and for keeping us from harm's way in this world full of dangers. And, Lord, I thank You especially for Carlotta and Amos, who have become so dear to me. Please guide our steps as we seek our next move. In Jesus' name, amen."

"Peter," said Carlotta gently, "I doubt that Amos prays in Jesus' name."

Amos said nothing and shoved in the fork.

"Well then," said Peter, "he can ask the blessing next time if it's a problem. It's a free country. At least, I think it is. Is Italy a free country, Amos?"

"Technically it's a commonwealth member of the European Union. But you can say it's a free commonwealth."

"So will you tell Carlotta that I didn't mortally offend you?"

"I am not offended. Jesus Christ to me is just a rehash of the prophets."

Under the circumstances it was tempting to let that pass as a noncontroversial agreement to disagree.

But Carlotta was not letting it pass. "That's interesting. Our Jewish friend looks away from Christ as just a rehash of the prophets—"

The same idea was striking Peter. "And the Muslims look past Christ as just a—an advance man for their prophet, Muhammad. But neither of them sees Christ for who He really is."

"Watch who you're lumping your 'Jewish friend' in with," Sloat said with a slight edge. "We don't need any more lumps."

"Yeah, Carlotta," Peter teased. "I doubt that Amos appreciates your analogy."

"Now, kids," Amos said, pushing back his empty plate. "Let's have none of that. Come to think of it, I don't have as much of a problem with Christ as I do with Christians."

Peter felt a twinge of guilt. "Speaking of Christians, I didn't do very well at Aldo Moro when DiFalcone tried to 'buy' Carlotta. I lost my temper, and I should apologize."

Sloat looked surprised. "To whom? I don't think the old fox could have heard you, and I'm sure he wouldn't have understood if he did."

"Then I apologize to those who did hear me—you and Carlotta."

"Forget it," the Israeli said. "I'm sure Carlotta preferred the No Sale."

"What I don't understand is how—or why—that old joker expected to 'buy' me."

"Amos?" said Peter warily.

Sloat smiled faintly. "Have you ever heard the term 'concubine'?"

"Well, yes. But that's not what I meant. I mean—in *prison?* Are the inmates completely in charge of the asylum?"

"You'd be very surprised, my dear. In any case, Peter, do me a favor and don't try to apologize or bring it up with him next time."

"Who says there's going to be a next time?

Sloat looked unshakable. "There will be a next time—and I have a feeling it may be sooner than you think."

"Right," said Peter, unconvinced. "In the meantime, do we go back to Cannes, or do we stay in Milan and go to restaurants and argue religion and politics until the mountain comes to Muhammad?"

Before Sloat could answer, there was a gentle chirping below table level.

"Excuse me." Amos unclipped the portable from his belt and began speaking into it softly.

Peter couldn't make out what he was saying, but he noticed that Carlotta was listening intently. Italian?

Then Sloat glanced up with a significant look and spoke a bit louder. *"Grazie, Signore DiFalcone. Arrivederci."*

Peter and Carlotta stared at each other.

Peter spoke first. "This wouldn't be a joke, would it?"

"You knew DiFalcone would call back, didn't you?" Carlotta added. "How did you know that?"

Sloat smiled and stood up. He plopped down his copy of *Il Mondo,* folded back to an inside quarter page. "You should read the paper sometimes. Many interesting things in the news these days."

Peter swiveled the paper around to where both he and Carlotta could see it.

There was a large color picture of a wildly perforated automobile that obviously had had an unfortunate encounter with an automatic weapon. It reminded Peter of the car in which Yussef Halima had died in Montmartre. There was lots of glass and blood. The bodies had been removed. But from the looks of things, there was little doubt about survivors. There would be none.

It had happened just outside Turin, near the French border. The caption identified the dead men as Guido and Eduardo Felici. The car was an electric blue Karma convertible.

15

Milan

This time the man behind the green glass at Aldo Moro waved them through after no more than a glance. Inside, two guards whisked them through the metal detector, down the short hall, on past the waiting room, around a corner, and down a longer corridor. At the end, a third guard in the same gray uniform scanned all three faces and then showed them to an elevator.

As the floor pressed against his feet, Peter flexed his knees and tried to imagine the living arrangements of this mafioso inmate with the business suit. His imagination was not equal to the task. What made DiFalcone think, for example, that he could install a personal concubine? Peter had heard of other crime kingpins getting preferential treatment behind bars, but this was ridiculous.

They got off on the fourth floor. He had expected to be taken directly to a cell block, but they were ushered into the first office on the left. With generous doses of rose-colored cement block, redwood paneling, glass walls, and fine executive furniture, this swank complex did a good job of helping one forget that he was in a penal institution.

The guard issued a torrent of Italian at a chubby bureaucrat with a clipboard, who nodded. He exchanged a few words with Sloat, then cocked his head, indicating they should follow him into the inner suite. Peter brought up the rear, admiring the tall ficus plants in shiny brass pots and the tastefully framed and matted wildlife watercolors on the paneled walls.

Within, sundry characters circulated about a massive desk obscured by the milling bodies and a cloud of cigar smoke.

Two inmates in orange prison garb traded bored expressions. There were several men who looked like muscle men, plus a possible lawyer or two. Several young secretary types kept coming and going.

The chubby fellow with the clipboard inserted himself into the traffic pattern, maneuvering to get his turn with the man behind the desk.

"So what's going on?" Peter whispered to Carlotta. "Can you make out anything?"

"It's hard to tell. I think there's some parole board business going down. But I'm also hearing some kind of argument about DiFalcone's cut of the racket proceeds. It sounds like drugs and prostitution."

"Why would the warden be discussing something like that?"

Sloat gave him a strange look. "You appear to be laboring under a case of mistaken identity." He hooked a thumb at the man with the clipboard, humbly waiting his turn on their side of the desk. "*That* fellow is the warden. You should know the man behind the desk."

Peter changed position, and at that moment people began to thin out. The inmates left with the lawyer-looking characters and thugs, leaving only the man with the clipboard and the secretaries. And then the man behind the desk stood up, extracting the cigar from his mouth.

It was Salvatore DiFalcone.

Signore Clipboard gestured toward Amos, Peter, and Carlotta. DiFalcone looked at them and, when his eyes fell upon Carlotta, broke into a smile. He came from behind his desk, took her right hand, lifted it to his lips, kissed it, and gave it back to her with a pat and a toothier smile.

DiFalcone said something to *Signore* Clipboard, who fetched three chairs for the guests to make themselves comfortable by the desk. He said something else in Italian, and *Signore* Clipboard disappeared. While DiFalcone struck up a conversation with Sloat, the warden came back, wheeling a coffee cart. A secretary with spike heels poured for them.

"Translate for me," Peter murmured in Carlotta's ear, deliberately hooking his arm up over the back of her chair.

"OK," Carlotta said quietly as Sloat and DiFalcone continued conversing. "DiFalcone has just apologized for being brusque earlier. He says he must not have been thinking straight." Here she rolled her eyes and blushed. "He was so overwhelmed by the charms of the young lady that he failed to grasp the significance of our earlier inquiry. And now he would like to remedy that."

Sloat said something that caused the older man's smile to turn to a calculating expression. Peter heard "Felici."

Carlotta translated. "Amos asked if the terrible misfortune that occurred to the Felici brothers had anything to do with his improved memory, or if he still denied any connection to the young men. And now DiFalcone is saying he doesn't know what Amos is talking about. Nor does he know exactly who we are or what we want."

Sloat apparently was enlightening the mafioso. Peter now recognized "Hofburg." Amos spoke at some length before Carlotta interpreted.

"Amos has kind of lumped himself in with us, saying we're private agents seeking recovery of certain valuable artifacts missing from the Hofburg in Vienna. There may have been some reason to believe that the Felici brothers had their hands on these things before they met their untimely death. And we were just hoping that *Signore* DiFalcone might be of some help in reestablishing the whereabouts of the articles."

DiFalcone frowned earnestly and rattled off some more Italian.

"He's saying it is a shame that such crimes are committed, but he is not so sure he can be of much help. He would like to see these items recovered, but he is afraid that it will be an expensive proposition. Now Amos is asking how expensive. He says there has been not so much as a ransom demand to this point."

DiFalcone gestured magnanimously and chattered more rapidly. Peter heard a couple more names he thought he should recognize, but they were lost in the chatter.

"He says there are some powerful suspects—Waldemar Neumann, Emmanuel Ponzi. He would like to know how much we are being compensated to recover these items and wonders if we think it is enough for the risks we face. Now Amos is saying we are quite satisfied with our arrangements. He is asking *Signore* DiFalcone what he is suggesting."

DiFalcone relit his dead cigar and began filling the air with more acrid fumes before speaking. This time he was quieter and seemed more direct. Peter had the impression of a deal's being offered.

Carlotta confirmed that. "He says to take whatever the museum is paying us and double it. That's what *he'll* pay. He wants Amos to name a price."

Apprehension crawled down Peter's shirt and wrapped itself around his chest, where it stifled his breathing. He began to feel as if he were the prisoner in this place. If Sloat said the wrong thing, he feared the consequences for their safe and timely departure from Aldo Moro. He especially feared for Carlotta. It was a no-win situation. The Israeli was being forced to choose between spurning DiFalcone outright or selling out their own cause.

Amos glanced over before answering.

Peter beckoned to him, and Sloat leaned back. "What do you plan to tell him?"

Amos looked pained. "It looks like my only option is to stall and tell him we don't know—we'll have to think about it and get back to him."

Peter was rapidly coming to a decision. "Our friend does not strike me as the kind of man who takes kindly to equivocation. I don't see that as any better than an outright no, which is our only responsible position anyway."

Sloat shrugged. "You are wise beyond your years perhaps. I just hope you are also resourceful beyond your enemies."

"Amos, just tell him we appreciate his offer, but we have a prior commitment that no amount of money can cause us to breach, et cetera."

Sloat sighed and began putting it into Italian.

DiFalcone stiffened.

Peter could feel the man's fierce eyes boring into him. He silently appealed to his heavenly Father to prepare them a table in the presence of their enemies.

And then DiFalcone responded.

"Uh . . . Peter," said Carlotta, "he's addressing you. He's saying he is disappointed with your decision, but he respects a man of his word. There are so few such men today. He wishes you well in all of your future undertakings, and he hopes you track down those dogs and they get what they deserve. In fact, he will have someone contact you in the near future with some additional information regarding Neumann and Ponzi."

"Thank him and ask him if we should call him since we're frequently on the move."

This time Carlotta did the talking herself.

"No," she said after DiFalcone had responded. "He says he will find us wherever we are."

"That's what I was afraid of," Peter muttered.

* * *

Rome

Carlotta squeezed Peter's arm when the historic outskirts came into sight.

The Eternal City. Throne of emperors. Graveyard of martyrs. Capital of capitals.

Peter, who had been lost in thought, was startled by the city of storybook grandeur approaching in the distance. Sloat eyed it calmly through the window, as he had many times before. Carlotta, seeing it for the first time, was transfixed by the expanding image.

She murmured, "Someone once said that Rome united all peoples into one nation and made all the world one city."

"Ah," said Sloat. "But who said, 'While stands the Colosseum, Rome shall stand; when falls the Colosseum, Rome shall fall; and when Rome falls—the World'?"

"Keats?" she guessed.

"Byron."

Peter was doubly impressed. "Amos Sloat—secret agent, amateur archaeologist, and Romantic too?"

"A personal hero," Sloat explained. "Byron died championing Greek independence from the Ottomans."

In the span of their remarks, the Milan bullet had closed the distance, penetrating the heart of the city of seven hills. In kaleidoscopic fast forward, Peter's vision was flooded with a fleeting blur of ancient monuments, picturesque fountains, grand piazzas, modernistic skyscrapers, famous museums, Renaissance basilicas, Baroque cathedrals, and one gargantuan stone derelict that he recognized as the Colosseum.

And then in a split second everything was swallowed in darkness. The train plunged beneath it all, dying in the bowels of the city and depositing itself at the foot of the great transportation terminal of the Metro.

Peter, Carlotta, and Amos unstrapped themselves and followed the other passengers out the whooshing cabin doors into the stark profusion of lights and signs, voices and tongues of the *Stazione Termini* underground. They found some handywheels for their baggage and were on their way.

Sloat, somewhat familiar with this subterranean ant heap, led the way through the milling, jostling commuters. He claimed this Metro line would take them to the foot of the moderately priced, conveniently located hotel where he recommended setting up shop.

Pine trees, Peter noted with surprise as they confronted the dark stone steps of the dignified little flower of a hotel. He had not been expecting pine trees. But the Fiorello, a former eighteenth-century mansion on the Via Vittorio Veneto, was virtually surrounded by them. They offered their tart fragrance to the light and variable winds. Sloat explained as they checked in that the pines were a spillover from the lush parklands and pleasure gardens of the nearby Villa Borghese.

"Oh," said Carlotta with a flash of recognition. "Did you do this on purpose, Amos?"

He let a bellcap take his bag and gave her a puzzled look.

"The Villa Borghese," said Carlotta. "Is that walking distance?"

Sloat nodded as the bellcap, a nondescript young man in a red velour suit, led off with their luggage. "Yes. Why?"

Carlotta beamed. "My art students could tell you why. The Borghese just happens to be the site of three major museums, including the National Gallery of Modern Art."

"Well," Sloat said to Peter, "you probably didn't realize the life of a secret agent could be so civilized, did you?"

Peter chuckled. "No, but if Carlotta turns up missing, we'll know the first three places to look."

They got onto the elevator with bellcap and luggage.

"Seriously," said Sloat, "the choice was not dictated by cultural attractions so much as security concerns. The chief of security here—house detective—is a friend of mine. Tony Novello."

They got off on the third floor. Sloat waited until the bellcap got ahead of them down the corridor before speaking again, more softly.

"I will inform Tony about our acquaintance with *Signore* Provolone and the message he intends to send us. Tony may want to alert *Signore* Provolone's agents preemptively."

"Is that wise?" whispered Peter.

Sloat nodded. "I think it sends the right message—that we don't want to be shadowed, and we don't need to be. We are forthright individuals. Of course they'll probably do it anyway, but at least they'll know we're watching them too."

Rooms 314 and 316 were the only two adjoining suites still vacant at the Fiorello this evening.

"Perhaps Tony will give us the key to the door in between," Sloat said before entering.

Peter turned to Carlotta as she opened her own door. "We would be pleased to have the pleasure of your company next door at *Signorina's* earliest convenience."

Carlotta smiled. *"Si, Signore.* Would that be before or after the first museum visitation?"

"Before, please. Otherwise, *Signorina* will miss all the super-duper top-secret stuff."

* * *

Carlotta and the room service coffee tray arrived together at Peter and Amos's room. She took care of the gratuity herself and sent the bow-tied old gentleman with the cart on his way.

Peter tasted the coffee, finding it strong but palatable, and then turned to Sloat, who was doing his own taste test. "When are you going to talk to the house detective, Amos?"

Sloat looked at his watch. "I could call him at home, but it can wait. First thing in the morning will do, if I don't catch him this evening."

"OK. Then I think the first order of business is to touch base with my employer, *Herr Doktor* Liebenfels, and give him an update—especially since we've changed countries."

Sloat raised an eyebrow. "You want me to leave?"

Peter shook his head firmly. "No. It's time that Werner Liebenfels got the real picture about things here, including you and Carlotta."

"What if I prefer to remain anonymous?"

"It's a little late for that—although you can certainly use your alternative ID if you like."

The Israeli nodded. "I like. How about channel security?"

"No problem. We have scrambled lines for Liebenfels both at the museum and at his home, which is where we'll have to call him at this hour."

Sloat appeared less than excited about the idea, but he said nothing while Peter initiated the call.

In another minute, the white-haired *Hilfsgeistlicher* was greeting them on the wallscreen and looking genuinely pleased to be getting the call. He wore, however, a slightly puzzled expression until Peter introduced his companions.

Peter wondered why both Carlotta and Liebenfels were giving him strange looks, until he realized he had just introduced Carlotta as his fiancée. His ears burning, he hastened to explain that they were posing as husband-and-wife art dealers with the able assistance of their good friend and independent consultant Dennis Scovill.

Sloat nodded in genteel acknowledgment.

"Our team has grown a bit, but don't worry," said Peter. "There will be no manpower cost overruns on this project. At least not for a while yet."

Liebenfels gave a little snort of unconcern. "I let the foundation and its insurance company worry about such things. I just want to know about the rumors. Crystal McKenzie has been calling every day from One World News, wanting to talk to your father."

"What rumors?"

Liebenfels looked somber. "That the Mob is feared to have possession of the *Reichskleinodien*. Your father says he does not want to talk to Crystal McKenzie further until she has driven Waldemar Neumann and the entire EU 'up the tree,' as he puts it. But I believe this may be her source for these Mob rumors in the first place."

"An interesting observation," Sloat said approvingly. "It's always a good sign when suspects start finger-pointing among themselves."

"The Mob connection was just what we were trying to determine," Peter explained. "We've just talked to Salvatore DiFalcone, who denied any involvement and pointed the finger at Neumann and Emmanuel Ponzi."

"You talked to who?" said Liebenfels.

"Salvatore DiFalcone," Sloat interjected. "DiFalcone is de facto head of the Syndicate, also known as the Mafia, Mob, or *Cosa Nostra.*"

"Incredibly, he seems to run international organized crime out of Aldo Moro Penitentiary," added Peter. "Let me tell you what we believe we know to this point."

Peter glanced at Carlotta and Sloat before resuming.

"Since leaving the Hofburg, the Crown and Spear have been changing hands as rapidly as coalition governments in Italy. All of our evidence is circumstantial but, I believe, compelling.

"First was the EU. We can't pin anything on Waldemar Neumann directly, but circumstantial evidence points to his Population and Health minister, Jean Pierre Bardo. If Interpol ever gets their hands on Giselle DuChesne, there might be a chance to make that case. She is the one who apparently transferred the regalia to Gwydian Brandt, a Population and Health geneticist."

"Though," Sloat interjected, "there could have been an intermediary that we don't know anything about."

"Certainly," Peter conceded. "As you may know, *Doktor* Brandt was found murdered in Montmartre. Photographic evidence indicates the items had been in her apartment. But the Paris police have written the whole thing off as a simple robbery-shooting, and the prosecutor has shown no interest. That in itself looks suspicious, but then law enforcement in general isn't what it used to be.

"Next is the Imam of Babylon—Ibrahim Nabuhadar—the ayatollah of Jihad Jerusalem. That, of course, is where Yussef Halima comes in. Forensic evidence establishes Halima as Brandt's probable killer. Unfortunately that evidence came as the result of Halima's own death. Paris police don't want to hear about radical Muslim politics, but we have fully briefed Interpol."

"One moment . . . " Liebenfels frowned. "If I understand correctly, you're saying that Yussef Halima was an agent for the *Imam?* What is your basis for this . . . Arab intrigue?"

Peter glanced over at Sloat.

"That's my department," Amos said. "I have classified sources that I would rather not get into at the moment, but I assure you that there is adequate substantiation."

Liebenfels appeared satisfied, and Peter continued.

"So the trail goes from the EU to the Imam—and then to the Mob. Circumstantial evidence implicates two DiFalcone henchmen in Halima's slaying—Guido and Eduardo Felici. And now—just yesterday afternoon—the Felici brothers turn up dead. We're waiting to hear what Interpol says about the ballistics, but there's little doubt that the Felicis can be tied to the Halima shooting. Suffice it to say that the regalia may have changed hands yet again."

"If the Syndicate is no longer in possession," said Liebenfels, "then who?"

"Precisely the question," Sloat agreed. "If DiFalcone still had the articles, he would have had nothing to do with us. In fact, it wasn't until he knew that the Felicis had been killed—and that the objects had slipped through his grasp—that he agreed to talk. And I think it is highly significant that he is now pointing fingers at Ponzi and Neumann."

"How so?"

"Because," Peter said, "it means DiFalcone himself doesn't know, and he's trying to figure it out like the rest of us. In fact, he flat out offered us twice what the Hofburg is paying to recover the objects for himself."

Liebenfels looked alarmed. "You turned him down?"

"Yes, *Herr Doktor.* Our motivation is not entirely monetary. And the same is true for Mr. Scovill."

Sloat nodded but quickly changed the subject. "So we have a big free-for-all that can only get worse. We could have any number of players piling on now, if for no other reason than to keep the articles out of their enemies' hands."

Peter thought he discerned some irony in Sloat's last statement, since that fairly described his own role in the affair for the Israelis.

"So what do you propose to do next?"

"I believe we have no choice but to heed DiFalcone's words and put some heat on Ponzi and Neumann," Peter said. "Ponzi first, since we're already in Rome, then Neumann, and maybe even the Imam later, if we're still scratching."

Now alarm had taken up permanent residence on Liebenfels's face. "You are in danger. There are too many people being killed. I do not know about Ponzi and Neumann, but DiFalcone will surely shoot you, and the Imam will cut off your legs."

"We'll do our best not to let them catch us."

Sloat added, "We'll be careful. My greatest concern at this point is for the young lady. DiFalcone seemed to be quite taken with her."

"Just so long as *I* don't get taken by *him,*" Carlotta said.

"That's approximately what I had in mind," Sloat said grimly.

"All right, Peter," said Liebenfels, winding down, "you be very careful indeed. And stay close to that lovely young lady."

Peter grinned. "It's a dirty job, but somebody's got to do it."

Carlotta gave him a mock jab to the chin, but nobody was really laughing.

16

Rome

Peter and Amos were loath to leave the Fiorello, but the artist in Carlotta was demanding to be out of doors for her first Roman sunset. The men had chosen to take a simple dinner indoors at the Fiorello's charming little trattoria rather than take the time—no one mentioned risk—of venturing out. At first, it was simply casual remarks, but by dessert Carlotta was agitating for an excursion.

"Don't fall for it, Amos," Peter teased. "This is the old bait-and-switch routine. First she gets you out to 'enjoy the sunset'—wink, wink—then, before you know it, you're inside one of those museums, staring back at the *Mona Lisa* and being force-fed large doses of culture and refinement."

"I'm surprised at you, Peter," Carlotta said reproachfully.

"Why?"

"The *Mona Lisa* is in the Louvre."

"So?"

"And the Louvre is in Paris, which is in France, as you may recall."

"Oh, yeah. France. Nice country."

"Which just shows how much you could benefit from a little culture and refinement."

"Ah ha!" Peter exclaimed. "Then you admit this excursion is just a ruse?"

"You're impossible," Carlotta placed her navy blue napkin on the table. "Anyone care to escort a lady for a walk in the park? If not, I'll find my own way."

Peter moved quickly around the table and made a show of pulling out her chair.

"Come on, then," said Sloat. "If we're to do it, let's do it right. Why don't you two meet me in the lobby in about five minutes, and I promise you a Roma sunset to remember. I need to get something from my room first," he added vaguely.

Peter had a pretty good idea of the needful item—the kind of protection that rides snugly and invisibly under one's jacket in a shoulder clip.

When Sloat returned, he motioned across the lobby for them to join him at the front desk.

Amos made some request of the desk clerk. The young woman opened a door behind her and produced three adjustable sets of powerblades, motorized, voice-actuated "smart" in-line blades that were about as far removed from ancient roller skates as baseball was from cricket.

"I trust you both know your way around on these," said Sloat, passing the blades around.

"You betcha," Carlotta said, looking pleased.

"But what's the hurry?" Peter asked. "How far are you taking us?"

"Far enough, and Inspiration Point closes at dark."

Sloat said nothing further until they were outside putting on their blades and their small red helmets.

Peter began doing some lazy-eights until the other two were up and rolling.

"Just follow me," Sloat said, wheeling off down the Via Veneto's blade-strip. "Onward, into the twilight zone."

Indeed the fading azure sky, the refreshing *pontina* wafting from the south, and the moderating warmth of the spring day all hinted of approaching dusk. Peter's forward motion produced a refreshing breeze.

He scanned the pedestrians for any suspicious sign but saw only ambling tourists, window shoppers, and casual natives. There were no other rollers in sight and nothing to arouse any concern.

Soon they approached a formidable, high-walled barricade with a grand portal.

"The Aurelian Wall," said Sloat over their helmet communicators. "It was built in the third century to keep out the barbarian hordes."

"Like us?" said Peter. "Guess it didn't work too well."

"Oh, it worked well enough for more than a century. It extended about ten miles and had several hundred watchtowers and eighteen gates."

"You sound like a tour guide," said Carlotta. "How do you know these things?"

"I've been here a few times, plus I have a memory for trivia. It comes in handy sometimes."

Peter was impressed by the age and the size of the wall. "Seventeen hundred years old? How was it constructed?"

"Ordinary materials. Cement covered by brick and stone—about thirteen feet thick and twenty-six feet high."

"That's what I wondered," Carlotta said. "Almost 'the whole nine yards.' Are you sure that expression didn't come from the conquering barbarians?"

"It's a thought."

They breezed through the high gate, which Sloat identified as the Porta Pinciana, and found themselves inside the Villa Borghese.

"We must still make tracks," said Sloat. "You can view the gardens more leisurely sometime in the daylight."

The gardens and flower beds were lush and verdant, overshadowed by orange trees and palms. There was a sweet aroma that Peter believed was orange blossom.

"It will be dark on the way back, Amos," he said.

"We can take a cab back if we want."

Finally, he led them off the main path onto one to the left that appeared to lead out of the Borghese.

"What's this?" Carlotta asked.

"We're almost there," Sloat said. "This path takes us right where we want to go, the hill above the Piazza Popolo. It's called the Pincio, and it's one of the best views of Rome."

The Israeli led them into a clearing, where they left the path and removed their blades. Down a short flight of stone steps they came to a picturesque terrace with tables and benches and a handful of people, mostly young romantics, all ostensibly drawn there for the same terrestrial event—to witness Apollo's fiery chariot sinking beyond the city, beyond the sea, in its final blaze of glory.

And then Peter got his first glimpse of the picture-postcard sunset. Between them and the burning horizon, the entire city lay spread like a royal feast. It was as if the entire sweeping panorama from the bullet train had been captured in one giant freeze frame, even more impressive in still life.

And the sky! It reminded him of one of Carlotta's palettes, swirled and streaked with violets and mauves, oranges and pinks.

She pulled a small camera from her bag and began taking pictures.

"I'd like to see you try to paint that," said Peter.

"I intend to," she said. "That's why I'm taking pictures. Sunsets have a way of evaporating on you."

"If you think this is something," said Sloat, "you should see Jerusalem at nightfall." He deposited himself on one of the benches and stretched out his legs.

Carlotta took out an artist's pad from her bag and began sketching.

Peter absorbed himself in the view. Still, his thoughts kept returning to other cities—Paris, Cannes, Milan. Especially Milan. This seemed like a good time for reflection.

"There's something I still don't quite understand, Amos."

"What's that?"

"Salvatore DiFalcone. I don't get it. How do inmates get to run a prison?"

"Not just any inmates. DiFalcone is an eight-hundred-pound gorilla who can bring an entire penitentiary to its knees with the flick of a finger."

"But the warden—DiFalcone seemed to have his heels locked. This was like a permanent role reversal."

"Look. You may not hear much about it, but the fact is that periodic inmate uprisings at some of these institutions have had some remarkable results. At Aldo Moro, it's been tantamount to a permanent inmate takeover."

"That's hard to believe."

"Pragmatically it makes a certain amount of sense. As long as the inmates stay on the inside, what's the point of sacrificing the lives of wardens, guards, and state police for the sake of a few rules about showers, yard privileges, and mail screening?"

"That sounds pretty cynical to me."

Sloat shrugged. "Check it out. I'm sure the same thing goes on in the USP—anywhere, in fact, where the Mob is a factor. They're almost a prison management franchise operation these days. Let's face it. They do a far better job of keeping order than the penal authorities."

"And that's another reflection of just how much organized crime and modern government have become almost indistinguishable."

"Now look who's cynical," said Sloat. "But you may have a point."

"So what do you expect of barbarians and pagans?"

The vivid hues of the Roman firmament were slowly but perceptibly fading like ink in water, all contrasts washing to gray. A pink-orange corona behind the skyline testified to the fiery exit of the celestial charioteer. Carlotta continued drawing bold charcoal streaks across her pad, alternating with shorter detail strokes.

A fine cloak of dark and quiet was spreading. The other *turistas* were thinning out, the low murmur of their voices becoming more distant.

Then Sloat broke the silence with his own reflection. "Speaking of barbarians and pagans," he said, "maybe you could explain something I don't quite understand."

"What's that?" Peter asked.

"This Antichrist that you Christians talk about—what's that all about?"

Peter raised an eyebrow. "What brings this on? You'd be better off understanding Christ than the Antichrist."

"My interest is strictly professional, believe me. I just want to know everything I can about the various crazies we might be up against. And I don't have to be a snake to learn herpetology."

"You certainly have a way with words," said Peter. "Some people would be offended by that kind of analogy."

"My apologies. I assume too often that people are as difficult to offend as I am."

Peter turned from the ebbing sunset and sat down on the bench beside him.

"No problem. There're really many little antichrists and one big Antichrist. The New Testament says that in the last days an Antichrist will come, but that many antichrists already have come."

"How so?"

"I think of it as all the false messiahs, impostors, cult fanatics, and crazies we see. That's been going on for centuries."

"Then who is the big Antichrist?"

"The Bible says this one will set up a regime of peace and prosperity at the helm of a kind of revived Roman empire. He'll eventually require his followers to worship him."

Sloat looked thoughtful. "Of course, I don't really take any of this seriously, but it is interesting that everybody seems to be expecting a deliverer. We Jews have our Messiah. The Muslims have their Mahdi. Christians are looking for the second coming of Christ."

"And the Buddhists look for Maitreya. And at first the Antichrist will seem to be the deliverer people have been waiting for. But he'll turn out to be an impostor, and ultimately he'll be destroyed."

"When's all this supposed to happen?"

"Nobody really knows, though each new year seems to bring us closer to the final New World Order—one world under one man. Probably the last major missing link is the temple in Jerusalem, where the Antichrist is supposed to set himself up to be worshiped. So far, at least, there has been no move to rebuild that temple."

Sloat gave him a long, curious look. "That so?"

"OK. Has there been some late-breaking news I should know about?"

"Nothing to speak of."

Carlotta spoke up. "I think that means Amos knows something he's not going to tell us."

Peter was surprised that she had been listening.

She was folding up her pad now and putting away her pencils in the failing light.

"Listen," said Amos, "many people in the twentieth century thought Adolf Hitler was the Antichrist. Seems to me this is all just an old refrain."

"And all the way back in the first century there were people who thought it was Nero," said Peter. "But there's one big difference. Let me ask you, what significant event for Israel occurs next year?"

"The centennial of its rebirth in 1948."

"That's the difference—Israel. Bible prophecy calls for a regathering of Israel before the end. In fact, the Antichrist is supposed to arrange a peace treaty with Israel. I'm sure the next world dictator will be much like the Führer—able to move the masses, only more successful."

"If you watch old newsreels of Hitler," said the Israeli, "you see an almost religious devotion from his followers. It's pretty clear that something supernatural was going on."

"Like what?"

For a moment, Peter was afraid Sloat would clam up, but then he spoke again.

"I've made a lifelong study of Hitler and the Nazis, and I'm convinced that the best-kept secret about them was their occultism."

"You mean that was what was behind their master-race ideas."

Sloat nodded. "Their inspiration came from the works of people like Wagner, the composer who revived the old pagan Nordic and Aryan mythologies. The whole concept is a mystical racism."

It had become deathly still on the Pincio. The view from Inspiration Point was transforming into a tapestry of urban nightlight. The only sound was a distant car horn and the soft crunch of Carlotta's footsteps as she moved to join the two men. A cloying aroma of unseen jasmine and gardenias put Peter in mind of a mortuary at midnight.

Carlotta touched his shoulder. "Why am I feeling like a ghost in a graveyard?"

Sloat was reaching inside his sport coat. "Don't make any sudden moves, Carlotta, but come over behind me. You too, Peter. Behind me—unless you have a firearm."

Alarmed, Peter did as he was told. "What's up?" he murmured to the back of Sloat's head.

"By the tree," Sloat said, barely audibly.

Peter looked where Sloat's eyes seemed to be fastened and saw a man in a dark windbreaker standing farther down the hill. From the shadowy profile, the man appeared to be looking back toward the Passeggiata del Pincio. But he could just as easily be staking them out.

Now the man, possibly aware that he'd been spotted, moved away from the tree and began walking casually toward them. Sloat made a subtle movement that suggested his firearm under the sport coat was now fixed on the stranger.

Peter decided this assignment had just entered the routine pistol-packing stage.

He could now see that the stranger too was carrying something that might be a weapon. He was vaguely aware that Carlotta had drawn very near and was clutching his arm.

"Stop right there," called Sloat, "and drop your weapon."

But the man kept coming.

Peter heard a round-chambering sound under the Israeli's coat.

"I said stop!" called Sloat with a dangerous tone.

"Would you really shoot an old *amico*, Amos?" said the man with a ripe Italian accent.

Sloat relaxed like an unstrung bow.

The man's face now became visible in the park lamplight. It was a broad, handsome face with a neatly trimmed mustache, straight black hair, and an ironic smile.

Sloat made a move as if reholstering his gun. "That's a good way to leave a widow and a couple of orphans, Tony," he said reproachfully.

It didn't sound as if he was kidding. The man named Tony aimed the object in his hand at their blades under the park bench. A little red light pulsated in time to a quavering beep. Peter had no idea what he was doing, but obviously it was something other than a gun in the man's hand.

"Dennis Scovill," said the man as if reading something on the device. "Peter McBride. Carlotta Waldo. Enjoying your stay, I trust, at the Fiorello?"

Sloat stood up and stuck out his hand. "Well, boys and girls, meet my old friend Tony Novello, the most fearless hotel detective in Rome—the best too, if you forget these occasional outbursts of idiocy. I thought you'd be home by now, Tony, and I was going to call you. Too many hotels to keep track of these days?"

Novello pumped Sloat's hand enthusiastically. "Me? I stay in touch electronically. You checked in at the Fiorello at five-twenty-five, and by five-thirty-five I had picked up 'Dennis Scovill' on my routine checks. Don't you ever think of changing your alias?"

"Maybe I wanted you to find me."

"It's who else might find you that worries me. I don't suppose you're here for an audience with the pope."

"Not exactly."

Peter was trying to play catch-up. "So the house blades have a homing device you can track?"

"Exactly," said Novello. "And here I am."

He shook hands with Peter and then gently squeezed Carlotta's hand, smiling almost as delightedly as DiFalcone had. *"Piacere, bella donna,"* he said softly, releasing her hand but not her eyes.

Novello turned back to Sloat. "If you're here for the Roman sunset, you might try a little earlier next time. There's more to see *before* the sun goes down."

"Wise guy," said Sloat. "We were just leaving."

"Well, if you're done roller skating, I'll give you all a ride home."

* * *

Back in the hotel room, Peter sensed from the sidelong glances that Sloat's friend was sizing him up. Perhaps Novello found the young teetotaling private detective from the USP with his beautiful companion a bit puzzling. Amos and Novello already had popped the cork on a bottle of Frascati Vino that came with the room service snack tray while Peter and Carlotta sipped iced tea.

But when Novello finally put it to him, it was not a question that Peter would have expected.

"Have you ever killed a man, *Signore* McBride?"

Maybe he said it for effect, to see how the younger man handled himself. Maybe he had a more serious reason for asking.

"I've never shot and killed anybody, if that's what you mean. Why?"

"In this business, you will have to face that prospect sooner or later. Are you ready for that?"

Carlotta was sitting with her feet stretched out and her shoes off. "A few years ago Peter and his father rescued me and several others from a castle in the USP and ended up leveling the place. Unfortunately, several dozen people died in that incident."

Peter winced. "That was a terrible accident. Many of those people were just in the wrong place at the wrong time."

Carlotta shook her head. "And a lot of them were criminals, demon-possessed psychopaths, and baby killers. The point is that he's been battle-tested, and I doubt that even *Signore* Novello can top that story."

Novello was chuckling. "I just love a loyal woman."

"Knock it off, Tony," said Sloat. "You're being obnoxious, which I realize is part of your native charm, but—"

"Speaking of obnoxious," said Novello, "are you going to tell me what brings you back to Rome? Are we going to see some further deterioration of our relations with the Arab world soon?"

"Not exactly." Sloat poured a little more Frascati. "This is even more unusual. You might say we're hunting the Antichrist."

Novello's expression was that of pure amazement.

Carlotta yawned and wobbled to her feet. "If you gentlemen don't mind, I'd like to start packing it in. It's been a long day, and I have a few things yet to tend to."

"I know," said Sloat. "So many museum brochures and so little time."

Carlotta wrinkled her nose at him and headed for her room. Novello had unlocked the door between the two suites so that she didn't have to go into the hall at night.

Signore Novello stood up in honor of her exit. *"Buona cera."*

Peter rose also. "Excuse me for a while too. If Amos needs help explaining what we're doing here, I'll be in the next room."

Next door, Carlotta turned on a table lamp, which left the room half in shadow except for the area by the loveseat.

Peter sat down and drew her to him by her left hand. She rested her head on his shoulder.

"Are you really going to bed so early?" he asked.

"Not really. I am tired, and I'm serious about the unpacking. But Amos's friend gets on my nerves. He *is* obnoxious."

"It didn't seem to bother you that much when he called you *bella donna*."

"I thought you didn't know Italian."

"Just the important stuff. Bella donna means a female ding-a-ling, doesn't it?"

"You want a punch in the nose, buster?"

"That wasn't exactly what I had in mind."

She kissed him on the right ear. "You wild man."

Peter lapsed into melancholy silence, reminded of all the hopes and dreams he dared not mention.

"Peter?"

"Hmm?"

"What would you say if I told you I knew what Neal is trying to do?"

He couldn't believe she could be reading his thoughts. She must be referring to something else.

"Uh . . . what do you mean?"

"You don't need to pretend, my dear boy. I'm talking about the procreation ban."

Now he was really floored. "I see. Let me guess. You've been on the phone, and a younger sister by the name of Dyana Waldo has become a security leak."

"Don't be mad at her, Peter. She'd just like to see us . . . you know . . ."

"Get married?"

"Well, yes. Wouldn't you?"

"I'm supposed to ask that question."

"It's only been ten years. No sense rushing things."

Peter was feeling exasperated. "Carlotta, I really didn't want to expose you to the possibility of another disappointment. I have no idea whether Neal will be able to pull this off."

"That's noble of you, but it's a little late to spare my feelings. I prefer to think he will succeed. I also prefer to think that God has not brought us this far just to disappoint us."

Peter felt there was a ring of truth in her words. He also felt himself on the cusp of one of those turning points in life. With stress-heightened senses, he was simultaneously aware of his own breathing, the tiny pulse in Carlotta's fingers, and the sound of the men's voices filtering in from the next room. He could make out Sloat's even tones, though not the words, then Novello's higher-pitched laughter.

"I think," Peter said slowly, "that this would be a good time to pray."

Carlotta said nothing but squeezed his hand.

"Heavenly Father," he said, "I agree with Carlotta. I don't believe You have brought us this far to let us down. While we look to You for all of our present needs—especially for protection in this dangerous enterprise—we also look to You for the future. Father, please do what needs to be done back in the USP as Neal tries to remove the obstacles to . . . our marriage."

"Yes, Father," said Carlotta. "In obedience to You we have kept ourselves pure. If this is Your will, confirm it by removing this procreation ban."

Peter was seized by the gravity of the situation. "Lord, I love this woman and want to ask for her hand. But I also realize that it isn't really hers to give—it's yours. Father, I leave it to You to do what's best. But I do ask You, Lord, for Carlotta."

In the heavy, ensuing silence, Peter felt as if he had just bet the farm on a dark horse.

17

Rome

When Amos shook him, Peter was performing the impossible feat of being in two places at once.

In one place he was on the phone with Neal, who was telling him to watch out, that the Population and Health people had sentenced him and Carlotta to die by lethal injection. In this conversation, Peter was trying to get Neal to tell him why. What had they done?

In the other place, it was still the middle of the night in the Fiorello, and something was happening in the next room.

Peter, snapping awake, decided this nightmare was a real event.

"Carlotta!" Sloat was yelling loudly enough to be heard in the next room and maybe beyond. "Don't open the door!"

By the time Peter's feet hit the floor, Sloat was at the door to Carlotta's suite. He turned around just long enough to point Peter back the other way. "Take the rear flank!" he snapped.

As Amos plunged through the inner door, Peter raced across their own room, jerking open the nightstand drawer on the way. He grasped the reassuring cold metal and plastic of his pistol with one hand and found the hall door with the other. Carefully he opened it—and found his worst fears incarnate.

A squat, balding man with a gun was holding Sloat at bay while barking something in Italian at Carlotta, cowering against the wall in her nightgown and pretending not to understand. Peter could see only the back of the man's head.

"Non capisco," Carlotta said pleadingly. *"Non capisco."*

Peter knew he had only seconds to make a potentially fatal decision. He slipped quietly out the door, his heart in his throat. Now time itself seemed to slow surreally, like the jerky frames of a slow-motion movie. He himself felt like a disembodied observer from afar.

The gunman took a step toward Carlotta, and Sloat reached for his own weapon. The man stopped and turned to the Israeli, and Peter knew instantly that Sloat was about to get it.

Peter's gun spoke first. It wasn't like in the old movies, with the cracking boom of exploding gunpowder in the muzzle. It was the barely audible report of a modern pistol with standard noise-cancellation electronics that generated an equal-but-opposite mirror-image sound wave. If they weren't already awake because of the loud voices, most guests in nearby rooms would not hear it.

The intruder's gun discharged wildly into the ceiling. Peter knew the man had been hit and was not surprised to see him stagger against the far wall. But he was surprised to see the flash of the thug's pistol, suddenly pointed his direction, and hear the muffled report of a third shot. This time the bullet impacted inches away, chewing a piece out of the door behind Peter and spraying him with tiny shards. Now he was seeing the man's beefy, pock-marked face for the first time, the eyes squinted in pain.

Before Peter could respond, a fourth shot sounded, apparently from Sloat. With that, the man pitched onto the tiled floor and moved no more.

Peter felt sick. Carlotta was crying. Amos put a hand on her shoulder and directed her back to her room. Peter trudged numbly behind them, and the words of Tony Novello echoed in his head. *Have you ever killed a man,* Signore *McBride?*

His mind's eye kept picturing the death mask of the man's face, the face that he had been unable to see until he pulled the trigger. Now it leered back at him, bug-eyed and pock-marked.

In this business, you will have to face that sooner or later. Are you ready for that?

The only thing that kept Peter from being overwhelmed by the horror of what had occurred was the realization that Carlotta was in greater need of comfort. In her room, he wrapped an arm across her shoulders and eased her onto the loveseat. She was weeping quietly, not sobbing.

"Do you want to tell me what happened?"

Sloat was calling someone on the phone.

Carlotta's voice was relatively calm. "I can't believe I fell for it. I was half awake—not thinking clearly. He said he was . . . not room service . . . Maintenance. That was it, maintenance. I should never have opened the door, but once I did, he wedged his foot in and—"

"What about the door chain?"

"He cut it with something like—uh—"

"Bolt cutters?"

She nodded. "Yes. It happened so fast. The next thing I know, he's pointing that gun at me and ordering me out into the hall. That's when Amos got there, and then you."

"I wonder how he expected to get you out of the hotel at gunpoint in a nightgown, unless—"

He left the rest unspoken. There was no point in telling her that she could have been an expendable hostage or that there might be a mole on the Fiorello night staff.

"Are you—are you going to just . . . you know . . . leave him out in the hall like that?"

Peter smiled faintly. "He's too big to throw away, and I'm sure not going to bring him in here. Besides, the police don't like it when you disturb a crime scene."

"The police," Carlotta said as if somewhat startled. "Will we be interrogated?"

"Well, this is a bit more serious than an overdue library book."

Sloat, having finished his phone call, joined them.

"The police?" asked Peter.

"No. Tony Novello. He'll talk to the *carabinieri*. Tony thinks they'll accept his statement for what happened."

Peter was a bit surprised. "Just like that?"

Amos shrugged. "He's a one-man police auxiliary. They'll send somebody to make an appearance, show the colors, pick up the body, et cetera."

"Yeah. More than one person on this floor would see what happened and call the cops."

"That's typical," Sloat agreed. "Don't get involved as a witness. Just look out your peephole and call the *carabinieri* anonymously."

"How can you stand this . . . insecurity?" Carlotta interrupted. "Shouldn't we check out of here and find another hotel?"

Sloat shook his head. "This is DiFalcone's doing. There's nowhere in Rome—or Italy for that matter—beyond his reach. There's really only one thing that can provide any protection from that kind of threat."

"And that is . . ." Carlotta prompted.

"Remove the source of his temptation."

"What?"

Peter understood. "That's you, Carlotta. DiFalcone is not

used to being denied. As much as I hate to say it, it might be best for all concerned if you went back to the USP for the duration."

She blinked in noncomprehension.

Sloat nodded. "That's right. DiFalcone's motivation is more than just libido. As much as he obviously wants to get his hands on the *Reichskleinodien*, I'm sure he thinks you would be his best bargaining chip, since money didn't work."

Carlotta's chin jutted out the way it did when she became resolute. "I have no intention of cutting and running. And I wouldn't think you would want to yield to that kind of intimidation."

Amos sighed. "It's more than a matter of intimidation. It's a matter of vulnerability. At this point, having you with us is like trying to fight with one hand tied behind our back."

Carlotta stiffened. "Oh. So I'm just a big, fat albatross, am I?"

"No," said Peter, "you're a quite svelte albatross."

Carlotta was not amused. In fact, biting her lip, she looked as if she were about to start crying again.

"Hey," he said, touching her cheek. "I would be sad if you ended up in a Mafia harem. Wouldn't you rather go back to the USP and help Neal clear the decks for us?"

The chin jutted out again. "No."

"Boys and girls," Sloat interceded, "we're all just a bit tired and stressed out. Do you realize it's only half past four? I suggest you get some sleep. I'll wait up in case the *carabinieri* want to talk to anybody."

"No," said Peter. "I'll stay up. Sleep is the last thing I could do right now."

Carlotta nodded dazedly, looking spent. She got up slowly and began shuffling toward bed.

Sloat gestured to the other room with a cant of his head.

"Good night, babe," Peter said over his shoulder, following Sloat into their room.

"Good night, sweetie," Sloat replied.

"Not you, blockhead."

Peter watched as Sloat climbed under the covers and realized for the first time that that was how his partner had appeared fully dressed in the corridor—he slept in his clothes. Peter wondered whether Amos always did that. And then he realized the absurd picture he himself must have presented in the hall with his pistol and his short-sleeved green PJs sporting those preposterous Holstein cows.

Peter realized he was getting more than a little punchy. Now he was beginning to regret volunteering to stay up for the police. It just occurred to him how tired he really was. Too late. He'd just have to get dressed and wait for the authorities in something more presentable than cow pajamas.

Woodenly, he sorted through the closet in the dark until he found a clean shirt and slacks, then fished socks and underwear out of the dresser drawer. It must have been a measure of his fatigue that his limbs felt like lead as he tried to make them go through the various arm and leg holes. That done, his body was grateful to collapse into the high-backed armchair closest to the door, where he could answer a knock quickly before it woke Amos.

It was amazing how weary he felt when the adrenaline wore off. That seemed to play tricks on the mind too. Sitting there half-dazed in the silent dark, he kept imagining that he heard sounds out in the hall, but every time he strained to hear more clearly, he realized it must be his imagination.

And then he was hearing Tony Novello all over again.

Have you ever killed a man, Signore *McBride? In this business, you will have to face that sooner or later. Are you ready for that?*

Finally he even imagined he was asleep.

* * *

Half past six. The morning sun and rush-hour noises, brilliant and insistent, were invading the room through the half-parted drapes when Peter snapped awake, his heart cranking up to overdrive. Without another thought, he leaped to his feet, threw open the door, and looked out into the hall.

Nothing. Had he dreamed it all? There was no body. No bloodstains. No sign that anything more serious than bad grammar had occurred here overnight.

He shuddered as jumbled memories of ugly night dreams flooded back in. There were pock-faced hit men in sharkskin suits, and big black-and-white spotted cows, and guns that roared and kicked.

It had been a hard couple of hours in that high-backed armchair. He had a headache like what he imagined a hangover might be. His neck was stiff. Worse, his conscience was bruised and seeking comfort and reassurance. He wondered one more time if the hit man had a family.

Back inside, Peter looked for Sloat and found his bed empty. But the bathroom door was closed with a pencil line of light showing underneath.

"Amos!" Peter called, then bit his tongue, thinking of Carlotta probably still asleep in the next room.

The bathroom door opened, and Sloat peered out, patting his face as if applying after-shave or cologne.

"Good morning, sweetie."

"So what happened?"

"Happened?"

"While I slept. Our . . . visitor. The body's gone."

"Oh, that," Sloat said dismissively. "The *carabinieri* came shortly after you fell asleep. I gave them a statement, and they took the body away. That's probably the end of it, because they got a corroborating witness across the hall. Self-defense and all that, just like Tony told them."

"How did they get another witness?"

"The guy who called didn't realize they could trace him through the hotel relays."

"Oh. That's good, I guess."

"You guess? You don't sound too sure."

"No, I'm just wondering how I missed all that and you didn't. I never noticed that you were a particularly light sleeper."

Sloat smiled. "I'm not. I just knew you'd probably nod out pretty quickly once the adrenaline wore off. I stayed awake and waited."

Peter's embarrassment was cut short by Carlotta's cry from the next room. "Breakfast!"

So Peter, having assumed the role of noble protector, had been the last of the three to get up. That was no help for his smarting conscience. It was going to be hard not to have an attitude today.

Tantalizing aromas greeted him as he followed Sloat into Carlotta's room. Red meat, if he was not mistaken. The room was cheery in the full morning light pouring through the drawn curtains.

Carlotta smiled "Good morning" and looked satisfactorily recovered from last night's ordeal. On the antique mahogany coffee table reposed various covered dishes.

"Compliments of the establishment," Amos explained. "They do that for all their crime victims. Tony probably had them knock something off yesterday's bill too."

Peter started to lift the cover on one of the dishes, but Carlotta stopped him. "Yours is the one in the middle."

He lifted that cover and discovered scrambled eggs, two pieces of bacon, and a small steak.

"New York strip, of course," said Sloat.

"That's in honor of the one who saved our lives," Carlotta explained.

Peter didn't know what to say. His stomach, awaking with a vengeance, said it for him.

Humbled, he was prompted to give thanks. "Thank You, Father, that You are the one who numbers our days and saves our lives and our souls and who prepares us a table in the presence of our enemies. Guide our steps as we consider when to go, when to stay, and what to do."

Then they all dug in. There were waffles and porridge and fresh fruit and orange juice and coffee. Peter and Carlotta sat on the loveseat with lap trays; Sloat, on the high-backed armchair. Carlotta observed that she wasn't sure whether the hero's portion of protein, fat, and cholesterol was a reward or a punishment.

And then Peter remarked about typical female observations, and Carlotta stuck out her tongue.

The repast was immensely satisfying and put an encouraging light on the new day. The coffee was excellent, adding to the warm glow in the gut and the spreading sensation of vitality.

Sloat helped himself to a second cup and looked at Peter. "What do you say our next move ought to be?"

Peter chewed thoughtfully before answering. "I think we ought to call DiFalcone and break the news to him that his torpedo is dead and ask him to call off his dogs."

"Or what? We'll kill another one? Have the capo thrown in jail?"

"Maybe tell him we're removing the source of temptation and sending her back to the USP."

Once again, Carlotta was not amused. "I'm not going home. So forget it."

Sloat raised an eyebrow. "If you're staying with us, I'm going to have to insist that you take firearm training. Have you ever fired any kind of weapon?"

"No. You don't get too much of that in art school these days."

"I'll see if Tony can get us scheduled for some time at one of the firing ranges."

Peter finished his plate and suppressed a burp. "There goes your museum tour."

She shook her head. "Not necessarily. Maybe the Galleria Borghese has a shooting gallery."

"Sure." Then Peter snapped his fingers with sudden inspiration. "Rick!"

"What?" said Sloat.

"Rick Stillman in Brussels. Get your portable out, Amos, and I'll see if Rick will upload some translation software to us."

"Do you know what time it is?"

"Oh—I guess it *is* another hour before they start work at Rhema. That'll give us time to get cleaned up."

"Peter," said Carlotta, "some of us have already done that."

"Oh. Well, look. Get your Bible, and we'll do some morning reading first. Then I'll get my shower."

"What about Amos?"

"He can get his own shower."

"You know what I mean."

"That's up to Amos."

Sloat looked up from his empty plate with apparent interest. "If it's not a problem, I would like to listen in. Are you going to do the New Testament?"

"Yeah," said Peter. "We're in Romans, in honor of the occasion here."

"How apropos. Maybe I can learn something. 'Know your enemy,' I always say."

Peter grimaced. "I can see why you didn't join the diplomatic corps."

Carlotta got her burgundy Bible from the credenza. "We're up to chapter eleven."

Peter studied Sloat's reaction as she began reading about the believing remnant of Israel who refused to bow the knee to other gods. The Israeli appeared to be following intently the progression of Paul's relentless logic. Eventually he was sitting up straight and round-eyed.

"Excuse me," he interrupted. "What was Paul—Jew or Gentile?"

"Most definitely a Jew," said Peter.

Sloat nodded. "There is something truly Talmudic in his argument. Go ahead."

Carlotta resumed. "'For I do not want you, brethren, to be uninformed of this mystery, lest you be wise in your own estimation, that a partial hardening has happened to Israel until the fulness of the Gentiles has come in, and thus all Israel will be saved."

Sloat looked surprised.

"That's the end times again," said Peter. "The last generation of Jews will make the Gentiles look like pikers when it comes to following the Messiah."

"And I suppose you say that's Jesus Christ."

"What does it say in the margin, Carlotta?"

"Uh . . . it says this is quoted from Isaiah 59:20, where it refers to the 'redeemer,' traditionally understood to mean the Messiah."

"So," said Sloat, "the argument comes down to whether you believe Jesus Christ to be the Messiah."

Peter agreed. "It always does."

* * *

"Run, flat panel!" called out a squeaky-clean Peter McBride.

The wallscreen above the credenza sprang to life, displaying a lovely sunlit color portrait of the Fiorello. Sloat patched the portable into the peripheral port of the flat panel.

"Calling *Rhema Institut Curatelle,* Brussels, main number," said Peter.

In less than a minute, the Fiorello was replaced on screen by a lovely sunlit color portrait of the Rhema Institute. A synthetic Rhema voice answered.

"Dr. Stillman's office, please," said Peter.

In another moment Peggy Finnerty's middle-aged smiling face appeared onscreen.

"Hello, Peter," she said. "Dr. Stillman's not here today. He's out in the field. Do you want to leave a message?"

"No. I was just hoping I could download some basic gab-ware."

"Not to worry. Rick left standing orders to honor any requests and help you any way we can. 'Within reason,' I think he said."

"So is gab-ware within reason?"

"Certainly. Hang on. I'll have Barry hook you up."

"Thanks."

The lovely sunlit Rhema portrait reappeared.

Sloat seized the opportunity to ask another question. "This Dr. Stillman. He has access to Cybersynchronic technology?"

"Access to it?" said Peter, amused. "He invented it."

Sloat looked astounded. "I guess you don't fool around."

A moment later, Barry, a young bespectacled technician, came on momentarily to give them some parameters.

Peter punched in the codes and then watched the data flow commence. "Now," he said, disconnecting, "we call DiFalcone. Is it too early?"

Sloat shrugged. "His problem."

"Would you do the honors? This should be interesting. Carlotta, would you mind listening from the next room, for security reasons?"

With a sigh, she vacated the premises.

Sloat fished the special Aldo Moro number out of his wallet and dictated it to the flat panel. In less than a minute, a hard-faced, raven-haired vixen with smeary lipstick on her scowl and pillow creases in her face answered.

"Mr. DiFalcone is unavailable right now," she said in perfect English. "Would you care to leave a message?"

Peter smiled. The only clue to the computer reconstruction was that her lips didn't move in sync with her words. Otherwise, it was this woman's own voice and inflections. Her own mother would think she'd just miraculously learned English overnight.

"Yes," Peter said. "This is Peter McBride and Amos Sloat. Tell Mr. DiFalcone that we got *his* message, and it's now reposing in a police morgue in Rome."

The woman looked doubtful. "Just a moment, please."

She made a half turn and then disappeared.

The screen went blank for a few seconds and then blinked to a different scene. Salvatore DiFalcone was having breakfast in bed. He was wearing little half glasses and apparently had been reading some papers spread before him.

"Mr. McBride," said the capo with a curious expression. "Mr. Sloat. And where is our lovely Miss Waldo?"

Without the intermediary of a translator, the effect was even more unsettling.

"She's safe," said Peter. "Which is more than I can say for your hit man."

DiFalcone's expression became less curious and more calculating. "Hit man? What do you mean?"

"Or kidnapper, whichever you prefer."

"What was this man's name?"

Peter started to say he hadn't had the pleasure of an introduction when Sloat interrupted.

"Lorenzo Lonardo, according to the *carabinieri*."

DiFalcone's eyes narrowed menacingly. "And he is dead?"

Peter nodded. "Very."

DiFalcone was silent for a long moment. "So which one of you killed Lorenzo?"

"Both of us," said Sloat. "Basic self-defense. We caught him breaking and entering Miss Waldo's hotel room and attempting to abduct her at gunpoint. You claim this man?"

DiFalcone shrugged. "I claim nothing. I have nothing to hide. I know nothing about kidnapping. Lorenzo was simply to pass along the information that I had mentioned. That is all."

"Just a friendly little visit, eh?" Sloat said acidly.

Peter remembered an earlier conversation. "What information?"

DiFalcone smiled craftily. "You are interested? I will give this information—plus *three* times what the Hofburg is paying for the holy relics."

Peter shook his head emphatically. "No deals. If your information would help us solve this case, I would love to have it. But no deals."

He braced for the capo's reaction. At the least, he expected the discussion to end right there.

But DiFalcone apparently had anticipated Peter's rejection and rolled with it. The cagey smile stayed on his face. "What will it take for you to trust me?" He sighed but did not appear to expect an answer. "You want my help but are willing to give nothing in return. I tell you what—as a gesture of good faith, I give you my information—no strings—for whatever it is worth. Rosetta!"

He turned away, apparently summoning the woman who had answered their call.

Peter took the opportunity to give a communicator voice command. "Record audio. Make hard-copy transcript."

The same dark-haired woman reappeared, this time wearing a pink sweatshirt and a pair of severe-looking, dark-framed glasses and looking older than Peter first had thought. Now she was studying something on a piece of paper. She began to read.

> "'I know that I hung on the windy tree
> For nine whole nights,
> Wounded with the spear, dedicated to Odin,
> Myself to myself
> On the tree that none may ever know
> What root beneath it runs.'"

There was pregnant silence until Peter spoke, half aloud and as if to himself.

"'The spear'?"

"Odin," Sloat murmured, frowning.

The woman showed a sour look, folded the paper, and disappeared.

DiFalcone reappeared.

"This is the information you had for us?" asked Peter.

DiFalcone nodded.

"Where did you get it?" Amos asked.

"There was a note found in the death car with the Felici brothers. This was all it said."

"Do you know what it means?" Peter asked him.

"Of course not. There's only one person I know who would."

"OK," said Peter, "who's that?"

"Cardinal Ponzi."

"Why Ponzi?"

At that, DiFalcone's eyebrows worked together like a gathering thunderhead, and his mouth tightened at the corners. Even on video, his eyes seemed to be giving off sparks. To those who knew and feared the capo, this was probably the signal to run for cover.

"Mother of mine!" he stormed. "You kill my emissary. You reject my offers. You take my information, freely given without obligation. And then you have the nerve to question me as if I were selling you a bill of goods. I think we have nothing further to discuss. Give my regards to Miss Waldo."

With that the screen went blank, leaving the capo's words hanging in the silence.

18

Rome

Carlotta breezed back into the room like a spring zephyr. "Well?" She settled herself back onto the loveseat.

"Sounds like DiFalcone wants to put us onto Ponzi," Amos said.

"No kidding," said Peter. "But what do we know about this Ponzi, really, and why would he want to talk to us?"

Sloat pursed his lips. "That's the easy part. DiFalcone thinks Ponzi has aced him out and grabbed the holy relics for himself. He may be right. You're unfamiliar with Ponzi?"

"I just know he was a cardinal who broke away to form his own religious movement called the New World Order or something."

"The New Order of Rome. When Pope Gregory the Eighteenth put the brakes to the radical ecumenical movement several years ago, it resulted in a schism. Gregory had been trying to unite all the major faiths under one big tent. But he soured on the movement when it balked at adopting the church as that tent. Ponzi—the Vatican's major domo in the movement—simply split and set up his own big top. He took the radicals with him."

Peter had a sudden thought. "Wait a minute. Is there another angle here? What is DiFalcone actually doing time for?"

"He was convicted on a conspiracy charge in an unsuccessful assassination plot aimed at Pope Gregory. There's been a lot of speculation that DiFalcone and Ponzi were in cahoots. If so, it would appear there's been a falling out since then."

Peter shook his head slowly. "So why would Ponzi agree to talk to us?"

Sloat smiled cryptically. "Perhaps you forget, sweetheart. We are not without resources of our own."

"Oh," said Carlotta. "Like at Aldo Moro. Open sesame."

"Yeah," Peter said, "but there's no Israeli ambassador to turn to this time. Israel doesn't have relations with the New Order of Rome."

Sloat's smile broadened. "We may have something better than that."

Carlotta mirrored the smile. "Do you think Amos knows something he's actually going to tell us this time?"

"No," said Peter. "But he might let us guess."

Sloat's eyes nearly smiled shut.

"OK," said Peter. "Free-braining time. Let's see. Infiltration. Shin Beth or Mossad has infiltrated the security forces of the New Order of Rome."

Sloat shook his head. "You're just guessing. But you're warm. Think harder. I want to see how you use your alleged powers of reasoning."

"OK. OK. Not the security forces. But probably an infiltration. Let's see. New Order of Rome. Radical ecumenical movement. Global interfaith brotherhood. Peace and love. Christians and Buddhists and Hindus breaking bread, celebrating diversity, seeking common denominators. Even Arabs and Jews smoking peace pipes. Ah! That's it. It's obvious."

"So quickly?" said Sloat. "For ten thousand dollars, the game point and the right to play on. What is your answer?"

"I believe that if one were to investigate, one might find a lieutenant to Emmanuel Ponzi by the name of Cohen or Levine or Goldfarb. And if one were to check further, one would find that this lieutenant was also an operative in some fashion for Israeli intelligence."

Sloat grinned. "Incorrect."

"What!"

"His name is Goldman."

Carlotta chuckled. "Oh, well. Better luck next time."

"Also, he is not an operative but an informant."

"What's the difference?" Carlotta asked.

"Amos is an operative," said Peter. "Mr. Goldman might actually be a true believer in this ecumenical New World Order stuff while also maintaining an allegiance to Israel. If pressed, he will help, but he's not going to be volunteering information."

Sloat nodded. "Essentially correct—with the proper persuasion."

"What's that mean?"

"Sorry. That's classified."

Carlotta looked at Peter with furrowed brow. "How'd you guess the Goldman angle?"

Peter shrugged. "Easy. It's no secret in the USP that one of the most overrepresented groups in all cults is Jewish. And frequently it's in some major domo capacity where they can exercise their administrative abilities. Besides, how else would Amos, the agnostic, have an automatic in?"

"So once again," said Carlotta, "all we need is for Amos to push the right buttons, and we may have instant access."

"I don't know about instant," said Sloat, "but again, essentially correct. Except this time I think it has to be a one-man approach."

"Because you know Goldman?" Peter asked.

"I only know Goldman well enough to get in the door. But Peter, you're the one who should actually go to Ponzi."

"Why me?"

"Because I think one of us by himself stands a better chance of gaining an audience, for one thing. Also I intend to start teaching Carlotta how to shoot, for another."

Peter frowned.

"What's the matter, Peter?" said Carlotta. "You think you could do a better job teaching me than Amos?"

"No, I was just thinking of something—a couple of things. Does this mystical interfaith brotherhood business remind you of anyone?"

Carlotta's eyes widened. "Yeah, now that you mention it. Our favorite Scotland Yard detective, Sgt. Carlisle, and her equal-opportunity approach to the gods. It sounds like she'd fit right in with this New Order of Rome. You don't suppose she could be involved in some way? But let's not get started on that. I had almost put her out of my mind. What was the other thing?"

"Just that Amos had said this business with Ponzi and the New Order of Rome was the easy part. If that's so, what's the hard part?"

Sloat got up and began moving slowly toward the credenza. He stopped, picked up a paper, and turned around.

"Our new clue. If you really want to earn your stripes, try your hand at unraveling that one."

"Let's hear it again," said Peter. "Replay last take, flat panel. Null video."

Preceded by the faintest hiss of white noise, the familiar voice of the woman in the pink sweatshirt was reading again.

> "'I know that I hung on the windy tree
> For nine whole nights,
> Wounded with the spear, dedicated to Odin,
> Myself to myself
> On the tree that none may ever know
> What root beneath it runs.'"

Peter realized that the paper Sloat had picked up was the hard-copy printout. The shadow of an idea was beginning to fall in a corner of his mind.

"You predicted we would hear from the mysterious riddler again, and it appears that we have. I'd guess this means that the articles are back in the clutches of the original thieves, whoever they are."

Sloat's face remained expressionless. "That's fairly obvious. What else?"

The shadow was growing more substantial. "I can't help but think that this wounding spear has some connection with the 'Rod of Hermes' in the first message. And I imagine Odin could have something to do with the Woden you've been talking about."

Sloat nodded faintly. "It has everything to do with it. 'Odin' is the Norse version—'Woden,' the Anglo-Saxon—of the same pagan god."

"So my Anglo-Saxon ancestors may have worshiped this god in pre-Christian England?"

"Quite probably. And now, as Christianity ebbs in Europe, this brand of paganism has made a strong comeback. It was never far from the fringes of modern civilization anyway. You've heard of Thor—Woden's eldest son. That's where we get the English 'Wednesday' and 'Thursday'—from Woden's Day and Thor's Day.'

All the days of the week as well as the planets are named after pagan gods—not just in English but in many languages. It's one of the cultural constants. Days, planets, gods. World forces to be appeased, invoked, manipulated."

Pieces clicked. Instantly Peter was convinced he'd been missing the boat. "I'm sorry, Amos. I guess I didn't want to listen to this Woden stuff the last time, but maybe I was wrong. What do you think this spear means?"

Sloat paced some more before answering. "I can make some general guesses. I'd say this appears to be an enlightenment motif. Woden attains the secret wisdom through some kind of self-sacrifice, being wounded with a spear and hanging on a tree."

"Nobody's mentioned the most obvious symbolism," Carlotta said thoughtfully.

Peter frowned. "Crucifixion? That's the first thing I thought of, but I dismissed it. Why would that appear in a pagan myth?"

"You tell me," Sloat said.

"Well, it sounds like a corruption of the idea of the Messiah who was pierced on a tree for the benefit of believers."

"And that explanation sounds like another Gentile corruption. Can you support that outside of the New Testament?"

Peter smiled. "Sure enough, chief. How about Zechariah saying that some day the inhabitants of Jerusalem would look on Him whom they had pierced? That's commonly agreed to be the Messiah."

Sloat made no reply. Peter noted, however, that he did not reject the assertion outright. He appeared to be thinking.

"And what's the point of this strange, windy tree with its mysterious root?" asked Carlotta. "This whole quotation sounds like an excerpt from something, but what?"

Sloat stopped pacing. "All I know now is that this appears to be a verse from the Edda—the Norse body of sacred literature comparable to the creation myths of various cultures."

Peter was beginning to feel a new sense of direction. "That's something I'd like to put to Cardinal Ponzi too. If he's got Norse paganism under his big top, maybe he can shed some light on this."

"There's just one problem," said Sloat.

"What's that?"

"You don't speak Italian."

"Does Goldman speak English?"

"Yes, but I don't know if Ponzi will let him interpret—or even if he'll speak freely with Goldman there."

Peter shrugged. "No big deal. I'll just have to take a portable and wear an earpiece. Good thing we have Rick's gab-ware."

Sloat walked toward the other room. "Let me start making some calls and see if I can get an appointment with Ponzi for you and a firing range appointment for Carlotta and me. I may have to twist a few arms."

Peter winked at Carlotta. "I have faith. When Amos starts twisting, it's as good as done."

"Just don't take any nonsense from Goldman," said Sloat through the doorway. "If he gives you any grief, tell him there's going to be trouble for Arnold."

"'Trouble for Arnold,'" Peter repeated. "What—never mind. It's probably classified."

* * *

White-whiskered Omar Goldman, sad-eyed and unsmiling, greeted Peter in the dimly lit lobby of Beth Chesed Synagogue on the edge of the ghetto. He offered only the touch of a cold, bony hand that did not squeeze back. The man was older than Peter had expected but probably not as old as he looked. In fact, the gaunt Goldman looked medieval in a dark, flowing garment like a monk's robe and a contrastingly tiny beige yarmulke decorated with intricate geometric patterns on his bald pate.

Wordlessly the man led the way farther down the corridor toward a set of double doors. Peter wondered if this was where Cardinal Ponzi held court.

"Thank you for agreeing to see me . . . uh . . . Rabbi," Peter ventured, "if that's what I should call you. Are you a friend of Amos Sloat?"

The old man half turned and gave Peter a cryptic look.

"You may call me 'rabbi,' if you like, but not in the orthodox sense. I am a priest in the Qabalist tradition."

Peter was considering whether to confess his ignorance about Qabalism when Goldman spoke again.

"And Amos Sloat is not a friend of mine," the old man said firmly in a voice like dry husks in a deep bin. Peter got the impression that the Israeli operative was some kind of sore point.

There were four sets of double doors. An inconspicuous young man in a navy blue blazer and holding a hand communicator appeared to open them, bowing slightly as they passed through. Low-key ecclesiastical security, no doubt.

It took Peter a moment to realize that he was standing in a sanctuary. His first impression was that this part of the temple was a good deal older than the lobby and passageway they had just traversed. He had to remind himself that this was a synagogue. To all appearances, it could have been almost any place of worship.

Three tiers of pews descended theater-style to an elevated platform surmounted by a massive, dark wooden pulpit. Behind the podium stood an ancient-looking altar that could have been made of stone and appeared to be for more than just holding candles. Peter recognized off to one side the arklike cabinet and reading table where the Torah scrolls would be stored. That fit. But why, then, did there appear to be a baptistry at the rear of the platform?

As he was wondering anew why he had been brought into an empty sanctuary, the subdued interior lighting rose several increments to a more businesslike level—probably the work of the Levite by the auditorium doors. Then he noticed a triad of stained-glass windows dominating the unpaneled stone wall to sanctuary stage right.

The largest panel, in the center, was a masterful depiction in deep reds, blues, and greens of Moses receiving the Decalogue tablets on Mount Sinai. A yellow sliver of lightning from heaven gave the picture a chilling immediacy.

To either side were panels of quite different themes. On the right was a yellow Egyptian pyramid on a brown background. Its peak segment levitated and radiated the mystical green spell of the all-seeing eye. On the left was a lotus-sitting, eight-armed Buddha wearing a grotesque grimace, whose version of nirvana had to involve poisonous serpents, sharp swords, and rivers of blood.

With a shiver, Peter turned his attention to a band of smaller panels emanating from the window frames and circumscribing the three walls on the sides and rear of the auditorium. Each was embossed with its own arcane symbol, many totally unfamiliar to him.

Some he did recognize, however—paisley-shaped yin-yangs, Egyptian ankhs, the serpentine caduceus, the devilish doodles of the zodiac, the Niels Bohr atomic model, Dutch-barn hex signs, psychedelic mandalas, esoteric mutations of the cross and star of David, stylized neo-pagan stars and pentagrams, and a miscellaneous cavalcade of solar disks, rainbows, swastikas, centaurs, and dragons.

Peter became simultaneously aware of Goldman's scrutiny and the fact that his own mouth was hanging open in mystification. Was this the reaction Goldman had intended?

"Questions are permitted," said the old man.

"OK. What are we doing here? What happens on that altar? What's the Qabala? And how do you explain a swastika in a synagogue?"

It was Peter's turn to scrutinize Goldman. Would he smile? Would he laugh? Would he steam in anger and call security?

Goldman did none of those things. Instead he very quietly put a question of his own to Peter.

"First tell me your own spiritual persuasion."

"Christian—Bible-believing, evangelical, reborn."

Goldman squeezed his eyes shut just for a second, as if experiencing a glitch in his pacemaker.

"Then I would expect you to have some difficulty with the concept of a faith that respects the traditions of others without laying an exclusive claim to the truth. That inclusiveness, in essence, is the foundation of the New Order of Rome. Ecumenism as opposed to chauvinism."

"Excuse me, but that sounds like the man who said there was just one thing he couldn't stand—intolerant people."

If Goldman intended to answer, it was lost in the confusion of the moment. The doors behind them swung open, and some two dozen men in saffron robes filed in. With them came the rhythmic crashings of a tambourine and a ragged unison of voices intoning a repetitive tribute to the virtues of Lord Krishna. The stubble-headed men with splashes of color on their foreheads and noses marched haltingly down the far aisle toward the front, where they mounted the platform and dropped consecutively into postures of supplication. The murmured chant of a mantra began to rise.

"Follow me," said Goldman, leading Peter back toward the front doors.

Outside, he followed Goldman farther down the corridor. "Where are we going?"

The old man gave him a quizzical look. "Did you want to see His Holiness?"

"Cardinal Ponzi? Sure."

Passing doors to several offices, they came to the end of the corridor and turned a corner. Ahead lay an elevator. Inside, the older man lapsed into silence, staring impassively at the closed door before him.

"Rabbi," Peter asked, "what is the Qabala?"

There were only two floors, so it was not a long elevator ride. But it seemed forever as Peter waited for Goldman to react. The elevator, in fact, had stopped before the white beard turned his way, the melancholy brown eyes met his, and the thin lips parted to speak.

"The Qabala," Goldman pronounced solemnly as if intoning a prayer. "It is neither a book nor a teaching, and yet it is the inspiration of many books and teachers. To those who need tangible definitions, we say it is the Tree of Life."

Peter took a long shot. "The 'windy tree' of Woden?"

Goldman made no reply. The door slid open. Somehow Peter had the impression that it would be a mistake to press further. Maybe the man would elaborate on his own.

Instead, his escort took him down another dimly lit corridor in silence. Without warning, he stopped abruptly at a small door, where Peter almost collided with him, led the way inside, and flipped an old-fashioned light switch. They climbed a half flight of steps into a small office with two desks and a bank of recording equipment. The far wall was mostly glass, looking down upon a larger, more brightly lit chamber. Two men could be seen below, conversing in high-backed chairs with a coffee table between them.

Peter took a seat at one desk, Goldman at the other. If it was hurry up and wait again, he might as well get in another question.

"Rabbi, I don't believe you ever answered my question about the swastika in the synagogue."

Goldman didn't flinch. "If you had observed more closely, you might have noticed a key difference in this solar symbol that you call a 'swastika.' It is pivoted in a clockwise manner, as opposed to the counter-clockwise swastika the Nazis inverted for their own perverted devices—not to mention their ultimate destruction."

"Is that like the so-called difference between white magic and black magic?"

"There could be worse analogies."

"Was this always a synagogue, Rabbi?"

"No, nor is it one now exclusively. This is really its third incarnation. Its first was as a Christian church—San Felipé—during the Counter-Reformation when the Jews in the Rome ghetto were forced to attend penitential sermons. About a century later the Christians were gone, and it was partly rebuilt for a small Jewish congregation that became Beth Chesed, 'House of Loving-kindness.' That body too waned, and it was closed for many years until the New Order of Rome bought it. The Order built on office space for headquarters use while preserving the sanctuary for ecumenical worship. Even fundamentalist Christians are welcome, if they behave themselves."

Peter was tiring of all this loving-kindness and tolerance. "So when do I get to see His Holiness?"

Goldman looked aghast. "You are seeing him." He gestured through the glass.

Suddenly Peter understood. The man below on the far side of the coffee table, arrayed in purple-and-white vestments, undoubtedly was Emmanuel Ponzi. Peter almost laughed, despite his irritation.

"When I said 'see' him, I meant in the way you and I are meeting now."

Now Goldman looked scandalized. "Surely you are not serious. That is totally out of the question."

Suddenly Peter's sense of humor was gone. "Listen to me carefully, Omar. I'm not here for autographs or a guided tour. I'm here on serious business—so serious that at least five people so far have died. I would prefer not to see that list get any longer."

Goldman stiffened. "If you think you can threaten—"

"Get this straight. If you don't go down there right now and tell His Holiness that he's got an urgent new appointment, things aren't going to go well for you."

"Just what do you mean?" said Goldman with a look that could strip paint.

"Trouble for Arnold," Peter half-whispered, leaning forward. "Big trouble."

The old man looked as if he had been slapped in the face. His gaze dropped to the floor, his rounded shoulders stooped another degree, and the fight seemed to leave him. He muttered something unintelligible under his breath. Then he looked up contritely. "As you say. Wait here."

Whatever leverage Sloat had on Goldman, it was effective. Peter made a mental note to press the question with Amos, classified or not. He had an uneasy feeling that he may have violated his own ethical standards unwittingly.

Through the picture window Peter noticed that Ponzi's visitor had left. In his place was a woman, apparently middled-aged, who was consulting a small ledger that could have been an appointment book. There was something maddeningly familiar about this woman, viewed in profile, but his memory would not yield whatever it was.

Peter unclipped the portable from his belt and set it on the windowsill with its lens pointed toward the action.

"Record," he instructed the instrument. "Include best-resolution close-up of female subject."

He saw Goldman enter the room, and Ponzi and the woman turned heads in his direction. After another moment of moving lips, the heads again swiveled toward Peter, and Goldman beckoned.

Peter picked up his portable and instructed it to record the next conversation and give him a translation from Italian to English.

Maybe a closer inspection would jog his memory about this brown-haired woman with the appointment book.

19

Rome

The young man outside Ponzi's chamber was not so deferential this time. At the sight of the portable riding on Peter's belt, he became somewhat difficult.

"You go in. Thassa OK," he said, removing the black plastic device and turning it over in his hands. "Thissa stay out."

But he was not totally unreasonable. After Peter gave a small demonstration of its translating functions, he grudgingly agreed to let it go.

"Who is the woman with Cardinal Ponzi?" Peter asked.

A cryptic expression flitted across the young man's face, as if he had asked something impertinent or naive. "Estelle Morgenthau, an American. She is personal secretary to His Holiness."

Inside, Morgenthau herself greeted him with a veiled expression and a voice startlingly suggestive of fire and rain.

"Peter . . . McBride? Please state your business and show some ID."

And instantly Peter was transported back ten years. He was in the basement of a castle, held captive by a vicious cult in a mind control experiment. It was there that his sister, Angie, had been warped and corrupted and eventually met her death. He could still hear the rumbling explosion that tore the castle apart and littered the landscape with bodies. And he could still see in his mind's eye the fleeing figure of the lone survivor from the evil cabal, vanishing into the woods, the woman who had been one of his chief tormentors.

Elizabeth Morningstar. Astrologer. Fetal farmer. Kidnaper. Jailbreaker. Infant sacrificer. Explosion survivor. Harder to kill than an asbestos vampire in a lead-lined coffin. Occasionally, on cold, rainy October Holiday nights when buildings blazed in the Halloween fires, Peter would remember and wonder what had become of her. Now his blood ran cold at the thought that he might be about to find out.

"Mr. McBride?"

"Yes, yes." Peter fumbled for the smart card in his wallet as if his fingers had turned to thumbs and finally handed it over.

Morgenthau inserted it into her own portable and began scanning through its files—employment and credit history, military and Social Security status, basic medical information such as blood type, hereditary diseases, allergies. Without government clearance, she would not be able to access more personal PH data. But Peter also knew that if Morgenthau was who he thought she was, she certainly knew who he was. If so, she was giving no indication.

Peter watched her intently. Her conservative tweed business suit, brown hair tastefully coiffed in a no-nonsense chignon, and more matronly appearance in general would not have suggested the Elizabeth Morningstar he knew and loathed. Her voice was the giveaway, plus an unmistakable something about the eyes, nose, and mouth, recognizable as when learning that the person you have just met looks so familiar because she is the sister of a good friend.

"Private investigator?" Morgenthau said coolly, handing back his card. "What is your business here?"

"I want to ask His Holiness a few questions."

"Concerning?"

"He may have some information that could help solve a crime."

She was unyielding. "His Holiness does not do interrogations."

"Are you suggesting that your boss has something to hide?"

She hesitated, her eyes darting to a point behind Peter, where door sounds and footsteps indicated someone's approach. Peter turned to see Goldman. The old man went straight to Morgenthau, whispered in her ear, and then left.

Across the room in the other direction, Peter could see the empty chair where Ponzi had been sitting a few minutes ago. The slightest hint of wood smoke in the air suggested that the fireplace behind the desk and chairs was real. Past the fireplace was a door, which Peter assumed led to Ponzi's personal inner sanctum.

He knew things had turned his way when the woman spoke again. "Do you speak Italian?"

"No," he said, holding up the portable. "But this does. Cybersynchronics."

He thought he detected a slight rising of Morgenthau's eyebrows at the mention of Stillman's brainchild. It might have been his imagination, but his imagination had been fairly accurate of late.

"Come," she said stiffly, turning on her heel.

Peter quickly followed Morgenthau across the room, attaching the portable earpiece on the way. As he took his seat, the woman spoke into an intercom on the black tycoon desk. "A Peter McBride is here to see you," the device translated in Peter's ear. "He's a private investigator from the USP. He is not a law enforcement officer. You don't have to tell him anything you don't want to."

Maybe she didn't understand that Cybersynchronics had her number.

In a moment, the door behind the desk swung open, and out stepped the purple-and-white-clad figure with a white skullcap several sizes larger than Goldman's yarmulke. He had considerably more hair than Goldman too. In fact, it was a nearly shoulder-length cascade of frizz about the color of rodent pelt.

Peter judged Ponzi to be in his early fifties. He had icy blue eyes, an aquiline nose, and a smug mouth. Peter was reminded of an arrogant investigative reporter he once knew, a muckraking journalist who never let the truth stand in the way of a good story.

"Peter McBride," Morgenthau formally announced as Ponzi stood before his chair.

"Piacere," said the man, extending his hand.

"Pleased to meet you," came the translation almost simultaneously in Peter's ear.

He was relieved to see no ring on Ponzi's hand. Had there been, he couldn't commit any breach of etiquette by failing to kiss it.

"Thank you," Peter replied. "Glad to meet you too."

"Grazie," spoke the portable on Peter's behalf for Ponzi's benefit. *"Piacere anche."*

Ponzi sat down, and Morgenthau indicated that Peter should be seated.

"Your Eminence," Peter began, "could we speak privately?"

Ponzi's eyebrows hiked up a notch, and he exchanged a glance with the woman.

Suddenly Peter believed he knew why the young guard had reacted so oddly when asked about Morgenthau. In this exchange, Peter thought he discerned something personal, even intimate, as between people who have shared much in life.

"For me this *is* privacy," said Ponzi. "I hope that is acceptable to you."

Peter gathered that if it was not acceptable, he was perfectly free to go jump in the lake of his choice at no extra charge. As much as he hated the idea of opening up in the presence of this woman, he had no viable choice but to go along.

Ponzi, apparently taking Peter's silence for consent, asked, "What may I do for you?"

Peter took a breath and began. "You have heard, I assume, about the stolen articles from the Hofburg in Vienna?"

There was another exchange of glances again before Ponzi replied.

"The Crown and Spear," he agreed, nodding.

"My firm has been retained to recover those articles. Unfortunately, it seems that a few other people have been trying to get their hands on them too. Some of them have died doing so."

Ponzi smiled unconvincingly. "I certainly hope that you are spared such a fate."

"I was simply hoping that you might have some information that would be helpful in that effort."

Ponzi's eyes narrowed. "Why would you suppose that?"

"Your name has been mentioned a few times."

"I can't imagine why. Who says such things?"

"Salvatore DiFalcone, for one."

Peter noticed Ponzi's hands grip the arms of his chair momentarily. "You would believe anything that hoodlum has to say?"

"I don't know. But he did say that you were the only person he knew who would understand the clues."

"What clues?"

"Twice the thieves have left fragments of ancient poetry alluding to Hermes and Woden and other bizarre things. After taking the tour here with Rabbi Goldman, I think I can understand why DiFalcone might say that."

"What do you mean?"

"The New Order of Rome seems to cover the religious waterfront. I'm wondering if that might even include dead religions such as the old Greek and Norse systems."

Ponzi's superior attitude peeked through. "There is no such thing as a dead religion—certainly not anymore. The New Order of Rome has seen to that. We have revived all the ancient traditions. God is now worshiped in as many ways as He or She has names, in all His or Her aspects."

"'One light though the lamps be many'?"

Ponzi ignored the remark. "What are these clues?"

Peter fished two folded sheets of paper out of his breast pocket. He started to hand them over to Ponzi and then stopped himself, realizing they were in English. Instead he read the stanzas aloud. First, there was Hermes with his magic, healing rod. And then there was Woden with his spear and his gruesome, self-inflicted rapture.

Ponzi sat implacably during the reading, betraying no reaction.

"Gungnir," the New Age pontiff murmured when it was over.

"I beg your pardon?"

"Gungnir," he said again. "Teutonic mythology. Woden's magic spear. My advice to you is to leave this alone before you get hurt. There may be some powerful forces here, but it's probably not what you think."

"Quitting is not an option. Tell me about these powerful forces."

Ponzi stood and began to pace, a scowl darkening his features. After a minute, he stopped and looked at Peter.

"Have you ever heard of the Fourth Reich?"

"No."

"Or P3?"

"No, I haven't. What are they?"

Ponzi took on a sly look. "I may tell you, but only on one condition."

"Which is . . ."

Ponzi shot another glance at Morgenthau. "That you work with me on this problem. Without me, you do not stand a chance."

Peter wasn't sure how to take this. "Do you mean you would help me return the articles to the Hofburg?"

"Not at all," Ponzi snapped. "That's what started the problem in the first place. That's the surest way to have them fall into the hands of Waldemar Neumann and his henchmen."

"And so the only solution is to turn them over to Emmanuel Ponzi, who will save us from tyrants?"

Ponzi gave him a baleful stare that clearly said he was not a man to be trifled with or mocked. Just for a moment, Peter entertained thoughts of playing along with Ponzi for the information value as long as he could. Then he thought of Estelle Morgenthau and realized how untenable this would be. Yet, should he necessarily burn this bridge?

"I will have to discuss your proposition with my . . . associates," Peter said carefully. "You are saying Chancellor Neumann may be behind this affair?"

Ponzi nodded, seeming to warm a degree or two. "One day we may awaken and find Waldemar Neumann sitting on the throne with the Crown and Spear, being hailed as the reincarnation of Caesar and the Führer and *il Duce.*"

"What ruler are you waiting for, sir?"

Ponzi appeared not to hear the question. "One more thing I would like you to consider. The New Order of Rome needs men of virtue and valor. When the great faiths of the world are united behind one strong leader, it will be an irresistible force. A great contest is coming between the kingdom of God and the kingdom of man. Choose your own allegiance wisely, Mr. McBride."

"I think the question is the kingdom of which god?"

Morgenthau stood, apparently signaling the end of the interview.

Peter rose and took the opportunity to get in one more question. "Are you asking me to join you? Are you yourself that strong leader?"

Ponzi smiled beatifically, as if to say, "If you have to ask, you don't deserve to know." But he said nothing further.

Suddenly Peter was aware that the young man in the blue blazer was wanting to steer his elbow toward the door.

"Thank you, Your Eminence," said Peter as he willingly moved that direction.

He took out the door with him a parting vision of two pairs of viper eyes.

* * *

Columbus, Ohio

The usual fight seemed to have gone out of Crystal McKenzie. A deadened look was in her eyes.

"It's just not a story I can do," she was saying on the wallscreen.

"Editor trouble?" asked Neal McBride.

McKenzie winced. "No, why?" she said defensively.

"Just wondering. It has the earmarks. Reporters hate to admit to outsiders that their own organization may be as imperfect or corrupt as the ones they report on, maybe more so."

"My story is the Hofburg case. Period."

"Let's try this one more time. Until I can get this Population and Health issue resolved, I'm staying right here in the USP to work on it. That means no Crown and Spear, no international intrigue, no juicy story. That means I couldn't help you if I wanted to. Help me, and maybe I can help you."

McKenzie gave him a sour look. "And so you want me to blow this procreation permit thing open for you with some journalistic percussion caps."

"You'd already agreed to look into it. Remember?"

"Maybe I lied."

"You don't even have to do a story. Just a few pointed questions in the right places should do the trick. I'm sure none of these people want publicity. But it might actually be a good story. We have definite evidence of Jews, Christians, and other nonconformists systematically being denied procreation permits as part of some population control scheme."

"I cover Europe. This is a USP story."

"Wrong again. I'm telling you that the Population and Health authorities of the USP and the EU are conspiring to control their populations through various means, including health care, procreation permits, public school indoctrination, and media manipulation. And furthermore, we're on the verge of proving it."

McKenzie looked as if it was past her bedtime. "Yeah. That's what they all say. Listen, Judge. Don't call me. I'll call you. OK?"

McBride worked hard to maintain a look of disappointment. "If that's the way you want it. But I think you're making a big mistake."

"I'll be the judge of that. Later."

Only when her image had blinked off the screen did McBride allow himself the luxury of a faint smile. Actually, having a One World News exposé of the Population and Health conspirators might not be a bad idea. He never really thought Crystal McKenzie would go for it, but getting her out of his hair in a way of her own choosing was the next best thing.

His office door inched open, and bright-eyed, brown-haired Dyana Waldo waltzed in, looking as if she might have a thing or two on her mind.

"Yes?" McBride said.

"You had a couple of other calls while you were speaking to your video vixen."

"OK. Who?"

"Radman Gerrick from the US Attorney's office—and a young fellow by the name of Peter McBride."

McBride brightened. "Did Peter say what he wanted?"

"No. Probably just a progress report on things at his end. But he also seemed pretty curious about any progress on your special project. Of course, I couldn't tell him a thing."

"Sounds like Peter's not the only curious one."

Dyana put a hand on a hip and stuck out her chin. "It would be sort of nice to know how much longer things are going to take. If I get my maid-of-honor dress now, will I still fit in it by the time this is all over?"

"I don't know, but at this rate you might start checking out the walkers and orthopedic dress shoes."

She gave a little snort of frustration and rolled her eyes. "You're hopeless."

McBride turned serious. "Listen. You haven't been talking to Carlotta about any of this, have you?"

Dyana got a guilty look. "Well . . . not exactly, but she's a really good guesser, you know."

McBride put on his Boss face. "Dyana, Carlotta may be your sister, but there are things that must not go out of this office. That is crucial to everything we do. Do you understand that?"

"Yes, sir," she said, looking truly chastened. "I'm sorry. I'd never do anything to compromise this firm. It's just . . . Carlotta and I have been pretty close. It's hard to keep secrets from her."

"I understand."

"Do you want me to try Peter now?"

"No. Get me Radman Gerrick first. Then maybe I'll have something to talk about with Peter."

It only took a minute before the hatchet-faced assistant D.A. with the scheming brown eyes appeared on the wallscreen—except that this time there was something more subdued and tempered in his expression.

McBride was instantly suspicious.

"Hello, Neal. How're things in the rent-a-judge business?"

"Hi, Rad. Busy. They keep trying to get me to do it more than a day a week, but there's not a chance. My private business is keeping me busier than I ought to be in my dotage."

"So I hear. They say you're becoming a multinational corporation."

"Not quite, although we do have some substantial EU business. What occasions your sudden interest in my well-being?"

Gerrick chuckled nervously. "I'm always interested in your well-being, Neal. But since I don't believe in countenancing rumors, I thought I'd go to the source."

"What kind of rumors?"

"Oh, that you're about to file some big case against the government—like a federal class-action suit."

McBride's guard went on red alert. "Rad, do you comment on government cases that you work on?"

Gerrick shook his head. "Uh-uh. Never. So I gather there *is* a case."

"Gather what you want. At this point, I'm just trying to get administrative relief for some clients. Litigation might take years. If the government forces these families into that position, we're going to be talking mega-damages."

"Ouch! Sounds serious."

"You might call it life and death."

"You're not getting cooperation from the government?"

"I'm barely getting the time of day. Lots of runaround, double-talk, stalling."

"May I ask from what agency?"

McBride hedged. "Why do you ask?"

Gerrick's conniving eyes looked away uncertainly. "Maybe I can help. If it takes muscle, we'll get muscle. They'll sure as shootin' give Justice the time of day. And . . . well . . ."

"And? What else?"

Gerrick smiled sheepishly. "Actually, the Big Guy got me onto this. I think there are people over here who are afraid of you, Neal. I'm not sure why."

McBride smiled too. "Thanks. Well, if we're laying cards on the table, the ministry in question is Population and Health. You want to be a pal, put some heat on the appeals bureaucrats in Procreation."

"Heat? We're talkin' acetylene here. Boiling oil. What do you want 'em to do? Roll over? Sit up and beg?"

"It's a discriminatory pattern of permit denials. Just give them my name. They'll know what it's all about."

Gerrick looked as if he wanted to say more and thought better of it. "All right, counselor. It's as good as done."

"Terrific. Thanks much, Rad. I guess you're not such a bad guy, after all."

"Don't worry. I'll find a way to soak you for it later. See you."

McBride sat in the silence of his own thoughts, considering how much credence he should place in this little fortuitous development. On one hand, he was suspicious. It was almost too good to be true. Radman Gerrick was anything but a buddy, just another slick lawyer in a town full of them. In fact, he had a reputation as an opportunist—nothing outright dishonest, but he certainly was not one to let anyone's grandmother stand between him and success and promotions.

On the other hand, this scenario also made a certain amount of sense. He could picture the rumors of his investigations in the Christian and Jewish communities striking fear of multimillion-dollar lawsuits in the hearts of government lawyers. It was a legitimate fear. He had nothing to lose. If Gerrick failed, McBride still had an excellent class-action case in the making with tremendous damage potential, even with today's courts. And any *federale* with half a brain had to know that.

"Dyana," he called.

"Yes, Chief."

"See if you can get Peter for me now."

They just might have some things to talk about.

20

Columbus

Just for a moment McBride was disoriented by the face on the wallscreen. It was one he used to know but now belonged to someone else. These were the game-face eyes of a young investigator who no longer gazed through the window of innocence but from the battlement of experience. They were lawyer eyes without the scheming and shifting of a government barrister such as Radman Gerrick.

It was a face of strength without guile, of kindness that wasn't afraid of the dark. This was someone McBride would be glad to have beside him in the trenches.

"Howdy, Pops," said Peter McBride.

"Greetings, Peto. You got that case about cracked?"

"Um . . . not exactly. Some interesting developments but nothing earthshaking. I was just going to ask you the same thing about the procreation business."

McBride chose his words carefully, not wanting to raise expectations too high. "We've got the survey results. We've got the affidavits. We've got the Covington group assessing damages. I think we've got a decent case. Right now, I have a . . . new opportunity to pursue administrative relief, which would certainly be more timely for us."

Peter looked interested. "What kind of opportunity?"

"Well, there's an assistant D.A. who thinks he can snap his fingers and make those recalcitrant Population and Health bureaucrats straighten up. We'll see. If he's right, we can save ourselves a lot of time. But I wouldn't hold my breath."

"Sounds encouraging though."

"Maybe. So what's happening with you?"

Peter sighed. "All we've found so far are some of the other people who are trying to get their hands on the Crown and Spear. And all trying to buy us off. Salvatore DiFalcone has offered us three times what the Hofburg is paying—"

"Three times? Sounds like we're on the wrong side."

"Yeah, and then he fingered Emmanuel Ponzi, who also denies any involvement. Ponzi, in turn, is accusing Waldemar Neumann. But Ponzi's offering me a place in his organization if I play ball and help him find the regalia. I don't even have to think about that one. But DiFalcone is dangerous. He's taken a liking to Carlotta, and he sent a goon to kidnap her, to maybe use her as a bargaining chip—or something worse. We had to . . . dispatch the goon."

McBride's heart went into a syncopation. "You what?"

Peter nodded gravely. "Gunplay ensued. Sloat and I shot him."

"Everybody all right?"

Peter nodded again. "Yeah. Except for Lorenzo Lonardo. He's dead. But I doubt that's going to stop DiFalcone. I'm sitting in my hotel room now, waiting for Carlotta to come back from the firing range with Sloat. He's teaching her to shoot."

"You going to let her stay there under those circumstances? Don't you think she should come home?"

"*You* try convincing her. I'd be tickled chartreuse and magenta."

McBride chuckled. "Just wait. It only gets worse. You sure you want me to proceed with this procreation fight?"

"Yeah, but can't you keep a little tighter security? Carlotta found out about it."

"I know—from Dyana. I've spoken to her. If you really want to start something, we could fire her."

"No, thanks. She's a good kid. I know she's totally trustworthy otherwise. Now let me lay something else on you."

"OK."

"I'm going to replay something for you, and I want you to tell me if you recognize this person. I also want you to record it."

McBride was really wondering now. "All right," he said, then addressed the flat panel. "Record incoming."

In another moment he was seeing a middle-aged woman in a tweed business suit and a conservative, upswept chignon. It was shot at a distance, but even when the camera zoomed in on her, the image remained somewhat indistinct and unfamiliar. No bells rang.

"Peter, I don't recognize this person. Maybe with some computer enhancement and redigitization, I would. I don't know."

"Think Elizabeth Morningstar."

"Elizabeth Morningstar? From Chateau Fahlgren and the Pre-Life Science fetal farm?"

"The same."

"Now that would be strange. I guess I never had the pleasure of meeting her. But what would be the significance?"

"I don't know. It's just the wrong kind of coincidence. It makes me think we must be getting close to something."

"Where was this recorded?"

"At Rome's Beth Chesed Synagogue, near the Tiber in the Jewish ghetto. It's the world headquarters of the New Order of

Rome. This outfit is trying to merge all of the world's religions into one superfaith. Shades of Wendy Carlisle. Boy, would she fit right in. That's the other thing that bothers me. It's like all the wrong pieces are trying to fit together."

McBride could relate to that. "Witherspoon was astounded when I told him Wendy Carlisle had attacked Carlotta. He insists that she's the straightest possible arrow. I'm not sure he believed me."

"Then what's she up to?"

"That's interesting too. Witherspoon says she and another officer are on the trail of Giselle DuChesne and are making some progress. There could be no better breakthrough than catching the original thief."

"So what's your analysis, Pops?"

McBride rubbed his chin thoughtfully. "Well, for starters we can almost discount DiFalcone and Ponzi if they're scrambling for the goods the same as we are."

"What do you mean, 'almost'?"

"Just that this could be a diversionary strategy."

Peter frowned. "Maybe. That's not what my gut tells me. I think they're really grasping at straws."

"Either way, it seems we're going to be forced to deal with Chancellor Neumann."

"Ponzi was clear about that. He warned me about playing with fire, but that might have been for effect—to scare me into throwing in with him. And—oh, wait, there was one other thing. He mentioned two other groups—the Fourth Reich and P3. Do those mean anything to you?"

"No. Do they have something to do with Neumann?"

"That's what it sounded like, but the price of finding out was joining up with Ponzi. Actually, that's something I bet Sloat can ferret out."

"OK. But the big question is just how you plan to get to Chancellor Neumann."

"My secret weapon again—Amos Sloat. I'm not sure how he does it, but he seems to excel at opening doors. This man's got more connections than the phone company."

"Then let's hope he can pull another rabbit out of the hat."

"And pray that we can make some progress out of all of this."
"Let's pray now."

★ ★ ★

Rome

Carlotta and Sloat walked through the hotel room door like two fishermen back from the sea with bursting nets. She was in tomboy gear—jeans, camouflage shirt with rolled-up sleeves, blue bandana, and running shoes. Under the gypsy kerchief her hair was pulled back in a ponytail, and a smile lit up her face.

Peter wondered again if anything—housecoat, curlers, cold cream?—could dim her beauty. In his eyes, maybe not.

"Bang," he greeted, hammering a thumb over his forefinger.

Carlotta laughed, came over to where he sat, and planted a kiss on top of his head.

"So I gather you had a fun time shooting paper men in the heart."

She shrugged. "I discovered a gift I didn't know I had—or a great deal of beginners' luck."

Sloat smiled. "Carlotta did quite well, and I don't think it was luck. Men don't like to admit it, but this happens all the time with women on the firing range. Some people think it's superior hand-eye coordination."

Carlotta lined up an imaginary paper man with a forefinger and blew it away.

"Which is something artists are supposed to have," she said. "Come to think of it, some of my bad old portrait sketches would make good targets."

Sloat plopped himself into a chair and placed a handgun on the coffee table. Peter went over and picked it up. "A fluffer, huh?"

"Yeah. The price was right. Carlotta wanted to buy pretty things with pearl handles and steel barrels—cowboy jobs that fire black powder and brass-and-lead bullets and cost a small fortune."

Peter turned it over in his hand. The fluff gun was a low-grade gasser—a compressed-gas weapon with small tumbling flechettes. Plastic-bodied, it had a comparatively short lifespan, though was just as deadly as pistols costing a hundred times more. No matter. It was the kind of gun generally purchased with the intention of firing only a few times, when one's life most depended on it. In this case, it seemed an apt purchase.

Sloat picked up the phone and ordered room-service sandwiches and coffee. Peter was still hefting and sighting the fluff gun when the Israeli got down to business.

"How was His Holiness?"

Peter smiled. "That was one weird synagogue. Ponzi and Goldman are both strange ducks. Which reminds me, Amos—what does 'trouble for Arnold' mean anyway?"

Sloat looked a bit evasive. "Did it work?"

"Like a stink bomb in a crowded auditorium. Rabbi Omar was an arrogant pedant one moment and a pussycat the next. Who's Arnold?"

"Arnold Goldman. His son."

"Open wide, Amos. I'm going to pull that tooth. What kind of trouble were we threatening for poor Arnold Goldman?"

Sloat's face suddenly twisted in contempt. "'Poor,' my eye. The man is a traitor to Israel. Only a few people know that—including his father. I am forbidden to say anything further, but sooner or later Arnold Goldman is going to turn up dead."

Peter suddenly didn't like himself or Sloat very much. "Next time, Amos, I'm going to ask a few more questions before I let you put words in my mouth."

Sloat had a blank look. "Something wrong?"

"I don't believe in threatening families. I guess the ethics of a counterintelligence agent for the state of Israel are a bit different from those of a private investigator from the USP."

"Or more to the point"—Carlotta spoke up—"those of a Christian."

Peter nodded, mute.

"There's an old Russian proverb," said Sloat, "to the effect that you don't blame a wolf for not acting like a lamb. I make no apologies for what I do."

"The difference is that wolves don't have a choice," Peter said. "People do."

"I disagree. People are products of their genetics and their experiences—they do what they have to do. Period."

"Almost true. If you include the experience of the new birth, the possibilities for change are boundless."

"'Born again?'"

Peter nodded. "Yeah. But notice how you said that—the same way some people say 'Jew.' With contempt."

"That's quite different."

"Is it? Maybe you forget that I'm 'born again.' Carlotta too. Maybe you thought only crazy people were born again. Or do you think we're crazy too?"

Carlotta looked disapproving. "Peter!"

"That's all right," said Sloat. "No, I don't think you're crazy. In fact, some of what you say actually makes some sense. Much as I hate to admit it."

It was Peter's turn to be surprised. "What do you mean?"

"And no, I'm not about to convert. But I'm impressed that you have a faith that seems to work for you. I wish I could see life in such black-and-white terms. I'm sure there's a good deal of security in that."

"Don't patronize me, Amos. Sometimes things are *not* too good to be true."

Sloat shrugged. "If you say so. But I really want to hear about Rabbi Omar turning into a pussycat."

"And what this Father Ponzi had to say," Carlotta said.

"*Cardinal* Ponzi," Peter corrected with a sigh. "Same deal as with DiFalcone. He didn't have anything to do with the disappearance of the *Reichskleinodien,* naturally, but he'd sure like to have something to do with their recovery. Fame and fortune could be mine if I would only join his cause. In this case, the finger points to Waldemar Neumann. I told His Eminence I'd have to think about it."

There was a knock at the door, and Carlotta let in the waiter with the coffee and sandwiches.

Peter's stomach began knocking on the door. "Let's get the cover off that platter."

He watched Carlotta's eyes grow round as, between bites, he

laid out his suspicions about Estelle Morgenthau. She remembered Elizabeth Morningstar only too well.

For Sloat's benefit Peter described Morningstar's occult group of a decade ago. These devotees of Ashtoreth and Molech had operated a fetal farm and conducted a gruesome experiment in artificial intelligence until Neal and Peter put them out of business. Peter had been seventeen at the time.

Carlotta looked genuinely pained by the old memories. "How are you going to prove anything about this Estelle Morgenthau? And what are you going to do about it if you do?"

"I don't know," Peter admitted, chewing more slowly. "Neal is going to have some photo analysis done, but photo analysis won't tell us what all this means. For that, we're going to have to put our heads together and use our best powers of analysis."

Amos assumed a half smile. "OK, Sherlock. But sometimes coincidences are no more than just that—coincidences. What I want to know is whether Ponzi furnished anything more substantive than a cheap shot at Chancellor Neumann."

Peter was a bit surprised. "You don't think there's anything to the Neumann angle?"

"I didn't say that. In fact, I have a feeling that we may find ourselves on our way to Brussels very soon. I just want to have all the facts first."

"There are no more facts to have—unless you happen to know anything about groups called P3 or the Fourth Reich."

Sloat's eyes froze. "What about them?"

"Ponzi wouldn't say. Just dropped the names and clammed up. With this fellow you have to know the secret handshake before you find out the good stuff. Why? Do you know something about these groups?"

Sloat was out of his chair and pacing the room slowly. About the time Peter wondered if the Israeli was going to answer at all, he spoke.

"The Fourth Reich should be obvious. These are fire-breathing neo-Nazis. They do the salute, goose-step, beat up Jews, pass out hate literature, yell 'Sieg, Heil' and 'Heil, Hitler.'"

"You speak as though you've had some firsthand experience."

Sloat gave Peter a penetrating look. "Nothing I can talk about. You know I don't work for the Friends of the Library. It's the big, bad wolf again."

"I would expect this to be an area where you'd do a good deal of counterintelligence."

"Except that in the case of the neo-Nazis, the word 'intelligence' would be a stretch. We call it a Jehoshaphat mission."

Carlotta's face took on a puzzled frown.

Peter guessed the connection. "The king of Judah who was spared fighting the armies of the Moabites and Ammonites because the Lord confused them and they ended up killing each another instead of the Jews."

Sloat's eyes were twinkling. "Not bad—for a Gentile."

"Thanks. But what about P3? What's that?"

"Nobody's supposed to know about that. It's a secret society organized like a Masonic lodge but without the funny hats. And there's nothing funny about it. They're in the governments of a couple dozen countries. They're the antidemocrats, the militarists, who are looking for strong-man rule."

"So why the name P3?"

Sloat hesitated. "We're speaking confidentially here? If I'm ever quoted on the subject, I will deny everything."

"Sure."

"There was a mystery lodge of Freemasonry in the nineteenth century known by the name 'Propaganda.' Then in the twentieth century an international organization of thugs, right-wing fanatics, anti-Communists, money launderers, and high-rolling entrepreneurs mimicked the organization and called it 'Propaganda Due'—or P2. In some countries it functioned almost like a state within a state, using blackmail to bring government workers and politicians under its sway.

"They were also an interlocking force with the Mafia and some of the military regimes, making the world safe for organized crime. They ran out of gas with the collapse of Communism—no longer had a common enemy to rally against. You can pretty well guess what's happened in our own century—history repeating itself yet again in the latest incarnation, P3. This time it's not anti-Communism; it's just naked power-grabbing and population control."

"Does P3 have anything to do with the Fourth Reich?" asked Peter.

Sloat shook his head. "They're fellow travelers, but the Fourth Reich types are total losers and misfits. The chief difference is that P3 can fire automatic weapons and chew gum at the same time."

"OK. That brings us back to the EU. Is Chancellor Neumann a member of P3?"

Sloat looked at the ceiling and sighed. "I'd love to be able to prove that. I have little doubt. He has P3 people in his regime, including high-ranking military officers, party apparatchiks, and key aides to the Population and Health minister."

"So you do put credence in Ponzi's allegations?"

"They fit. I can say that. What we do know is that Neumann is an intensely ambitious man from an intensely ambitious family. Even his name, 'Waldemar'—like 'Vladimir'—means 'mighty ruler.' It would not surprise me to find out that he's attempting to gain possession of the *Reichskleinodien*. I might be more surprised if he weren't."

"So we have at least three distinct organizations vying for global domination—the criminal Syndicate, the ecumenical/religious New Order of Rome, and now this militarist/political P3."

"And don't forget the Imam of Babylon and his hordes of Yussef Halimas who think he's their long-awaited Twelfth Imam, ready to lead them to world dominion under the sword and the crescent."

Peter shuddered. "And if we actually do find the Crown and Spear, we can expect to become a target of any or all of those groups—and maybe end up just like Yussef Halima. Right?"

Amos shrugged. "Would you like to throw in the towel and go back to the safe life of the gentleman barrister? That's up to you. You can have your air-conditioned offices and soft chairs and golf courses and country clubs, where the worst that can befall you is tennis elbow or cirrhosis. If you want to return to the USP and go back to chiseling widows and orphans out of their estates, I'll understand."

"No, thanks. I'm not complaining about the hazards. I just want to know what they are. And for your information, I don't play golf, I don't play tennis, I don't drink, and I don't chisel little old ladies out of their estates. Besides, we don't do probate."

"Just checking. Don't say I didn't warn you."

Carlotta blew away another imaginary paper man. "Don't worry, Peter. I'll protect you."

"You're the only thing I'm worried about," he said. "I still don't feel that great about your being here."

Carlotta frowned. "We've settled that one. I'm staying—and fighting if I have to."

Peter sighed wearily. "Yeah. OK, next subject. Hats—as in pulling rabbits out of. Amos, you have any more rabbits in that hat?"

"Hmm?"

"You got us in to see DiFalcone and Ponzi. What do you think about Neumann? Should we even try to talk to him? If so, how do we get to him?"

Sloat chewed his lip. "I've given that a good deal of thought, and I think it's unavoidable. Again, we can use my backdoor diplomatic contacts. The only problem is I can't afford to be exposed in the process. That means you'll have to be the front man again."

"No problem," Peter said without hesitation. He'd half expected that.

"You did so well with Cardinal Ponzi that I'm sure you'll be all right."

"Thanks for your vote of confidence. Where will you be in the meantime?"

"Right there behind you. Carlotta and I will be your back door—sharpshooters and lifeline-throwers. Not that I really expect any trouble."

Peter looked at Carlotta. "Is that acceptable to you?"

Carlotta was smiling brightly. "Yes, sir. Brussels, huh? That should be grand. Just one thing—"

"No, Carlotta," Peter interrupted. "Don't start worrying about your wardrobe. Now that you're a working member of this team, I think what you're wearing now is suitable attire."

Carlotta scowled at her scruffy jeans. "Grungies in Brussels? I don't think so. Haute couture is this lady's cover, my dear fellow."

Sloat got up. "I'm not getting involved in this. I'm going to check the bullet train schedules and make a couple of other phone calls. You two might start figuring on packing up and moving out."

Peter followed Carlotta part way into the next room.

She turned around and stopped. "Peter," she said, touching his cheek. "Why the worried look?"

"Lorenzo Lonardo," he murmured.

"Oh, Peter. Don't start thinking about that."

"Somebody has to. DiFalcone, Ponzi, Neumann—we're going up against some pretty tough players. If they're as stymied as we are . . ."

"We don't know that Chancellor Neumann is stymied. Maybe he's the one with the goods."

Peter shook his head. "If he is, he's not going to just hand them over to us. And if he's not . . ."

"What's the matter, Peter?"

"Just a feeling I can't shake."

"What kind of feeling?"

"That maybe we're not wrestling against flesh and blood."

For an instant, Peter thought he saw something like fear in her eyes. Then just as quickly, she reached down and picked up something from the bed. It was a blouse, one of those Euro styles with extra strips of material running diagonally, in fuchsia.

"You like this?" she asked with a smile that looked a little forced.

Peter nodded and smiled back. There was no sense undermining her confidence. Things were going to be difficult enough.

21

Rome

Kabir Ali Halima pulled his Texas Rangers baseball cap tighter on his skull so that his dark, predator eyes peered out from a deeper veil of shadow. He took a deep breath, angled his long white box with red ribbon vertically into the revolving brass door, and pushed.

One hundred eighty degrees later he was striding across the plush lobby of the Fiorello toward the front desk. He could feel his pulse rate accelerate as the adrenaline began to flow. Not even predators were totally immune to pre-game jitters.

"Yes, sir?" said the dark-haired young woman clerk with an expectant half smile.

"Flowers for Ms. Carlotta Waldo," said Kabir, fingering the box tag, "in room . . . uh . . . I can't make it out."

There was the slightest flicker of hesitation in the woman's face. "I'll take care of that," she said, reaching for the box.

Kabir handed it over gently, taking care not to let his face tilt directly into the light. This woman clearly was not going to volunteer the room number. That would have been too easy.

"Is she still checked in?"

The woman thought a moment. "I believe she left a little while ago, but I don't think she's checked out. Let me see."

She murmured something to her display screen, then looked up. "Yes, she's still here. I'll make sure she gets these."

That was good enough.

"Thank you," said Kabir, touching the bill of his cap. "Uh . . . where is the men's room?"

"Down that hall." She pointed. "The door on your left before the trattoria."

"Thanks," he said again, turning on his heel.

Kabir walked halfway down the corridor, looked over his shoulder to make certain that no one was behind him, then spun around and retraced his steps.

As he made his way back to the main lobby, he removed his reversible jacket, turned it inside out from its khaki to its plain navy side, balled up his hat, stuck it into an inner pocket, and shrugged back into the jacket.

In the lobby, he strolled past the front desk with his face averted and wandered nonchalantly over to the rack of local tourist literature. He feigned absorption in a brochure about Vatican City, all the while stealing glances at the front desk in hopes of spotting the flower box. He couldn't see it, and he hoped that it was just out of sight on a desk behind the counter.

In about the time it could have taken Kabir to memorize half the brochure, a young monkey-suited bellcap finally appeared behind the desk. Sure enough, he scooped up the flower box and scurried off.

Trying not to appear obvious, Kabir refolded the brochure and headed toward the corridor where the bellcap had disappeared. There the young man in red velour had managed to summon an elevator, whose door was just opening. Kabir glided in behind him.

"Tre," the bellcap told the elevator. If he even noticed Kabir, he made no sign of it.

On the third floor Kabir allowed the man to leave, making no move until the doors began sliding closed once again. Then he stuck his hand into the opening at the last moment, interrupting the sequence.

"Stop," he instructed, waiting a long moment before speaking again. "Open."

As the doors parted silently, Kabir produced a rubberoid mask from another inner pocket and pulled it down over his face. Instant Albert Einstein.

By the time he was out in the hall, he could see the bellcap halting outside a door and reaching into his jacket pocket. Kabir closed the distance quickly, reaching into his own jacket.

"Open the door," he breathed over the man's shoulder, giving his spine a nudge with his pistol. "This is a gun."

The bellcap stiffened but quickly unlocked the door and stepped inside.

Kabir pulled out a length of nylon cord.

"Sit down on the bed with your hands behind your back," he instructed the terrified youth. "If you make a sound, you die."

★ ★ ★

Tony Novello got off the elevator on the third floor and headed for 314 and 316.

He hoped he was mistaken, but this development had the wrong feel about it. It sounded like a new version of the old telegram routine. Get the hotel staff to lead you to the right room and then take care of the bellhop.

He stopped at 316 and put his ear to the door. He was sure he could hear muffled sounds of movement. He moved over to 314 and inserted his master keycard in the door slot. With his left hand Novello grasped the doorknob, and with his right he extracted his pistol from its shoulder clip. He pushed.

The room was empty. He knew Amos and his friends were away for the day. Maybe the flower man was looking for something of theirs. Maybe he was searching for the same thing that Amos and his friends were seeking. In that case, he would be sure to come through to Amos and Peter's room when he was done in Ms. Waldo's.

Edging silently into the room, Novello could see that the middle door had been left ajar. He moved catlike toward it.

He was glad he had given Cerelia standing orders to alert him if any items were delivered for his special guests. Fortunately, she had remembered her instructions well and had not rung for the bellcap until Novello had been alerted and had given her the go-ahead. And now he was discovering how well his fears had been founded.

Sounds of drawers and closets opening and closing came to him from the next room. There were other, unidentifiable sounds of sifting and sorting, piddling and poking. Ransacking sounds. Novello edged closer.

The sounds stopped. Cautiously, with his gun under his chin, Novello took a peek through the crack of the door.

Albert Einstein blinked back at him. And then the door slammed in his face.

Novello threw himself against the door before it could be locked. It burst open, knocking the man several steps back across the room.

"Alt!" Novello barked, then ducked, anticipating gunplay.

In the same instant, Einstein fired. The bullet passed precisely where Novello had been standing a moment ago. The detective returned fire and hit the deck, catching sight of another figure lying stiffly on the bed across the room.

Einstein reeled as if hit, then fired again. This time Novello was nailed. Pain like fire erupted in his left arm just below the shoulder. It was an effort just to breathe, let alone move. His ears were ringing, and he felt like a huge weight had been dropped upon him. He struggled not to pass out.

Just as he thought he was losing it, he was jarred fully conscious by the sound of a slamming door. Apparently Einstein had fled.

Novello marshaled his resources to attempt standing up. His arm erupted in another fiery burst of pain. He was seeing spots and feeling woozy. Apparently standing was out of the question. He crawled over to the bed and pulled himself up.

"Chris!" he croaked at the bound figure on the bed. "I'll get you loose."

The youth's eyes were wide and frightened above a cloth gag. Novello knelt beside him and fished in his right pocket, coming out with a pocketknife. It cost him another searing bout of pain before he managed to switch to a one-handed attack on the cord binding the bellcap's wrists.

"Push against me!" Novello commanded.

He realized that he was now sitting in a pool of blood that must have been his own. Beads of sweat were popping out on his clammy forehead, and the woozy feeling was becoming overpowering. He concentrated intently on sawing through the remaining fibers, made easier now by the man's resistance against the knife.

At last, the cord snapped apart, and his wrists were free.

"Go!" Novello whispered weakly. "Get help."

He was vaguely aware that Chris had left the bed. Somehow nothing mattered so much as being able to shut his eyes and lay down his head, even if it was in his own blood.

★ ★ ★

Brussels

Peter finished his blueberry cheesecake. It had been a great dinner. Moira claimed it was entirely home-cooked, including the candied yams. He believed it. And it had been good just to see Rick and Moira again and their two red-haired tykes, Jeremiah and Samuel.

Auburn-haired Moira was still beautiful, and the years apparently had softened the sharp edge of her tongue. Christianity probably had something to do with it too. Moira had undergone a foxhole conversion years ago, about the time that she and Rick were reconciling, eventually to remarry.

Carlotta gravitated to Moira as to an older sister. They began clearing the table together, deep in conversation about art and academics, while Rick steered Peter and Amos toward the den. Peter had been telling them about his debacle at the Executive Office Building. He had blown the entire morning waiting in vain for an audience with a Eurocrat who had been either fired or transferred to some other part of the Euro Union. It was impossible to get a straight story.

"And nobody would tell you what all the boxes and crates were for?" asked Stillman as they settled into easy chairs before the stone fireplace with mugs of coffee.

"Nope. It looked like the circus pulling up stakes for the next town."

Stillman smiled knowingly. "Then you haven't heard. Surprisingly few people have. The EU administrative offices are being moved from Brussels. I don't know why it's so hush-hush."

Sloat looked startled. "To where?"

"Rome."

"But why?" Peter asked.

Stillman shrugged. "Nobody will say. The administration is downplaying the whole thing, insisting the Parliament is staying here. But if the major ministries are moving to Rome, can Parliament be far behind?"

Peter didn't quite know what to make of all that. "Maybe my man at headquarters wasn't so much cashiered as just unwilling to move to Italy."

"Not unheard of for a management wanting to clean house," said Stillman. "You can't fire everybody, but sometimes you can make a lot of them want to quit."

"Well—" Peter looked at Sloat "—unless you have another rabbit in that hat, we might as well go back to Rome ourselves."

Sloat had the look of a magician temporarily between stovepipes.

"Now wait a minute," said Stillman. "There's more than one way to skin a . . . uh . . . rabbit. Did you forget about our friend Sir James Crisp?"

Peter blinked. "Yes, in fact I had."

Sloat looked from face to face.

"Member of the European Parliament," Peter said. "A Christian and a special friend of the Rhema Institute."

"Now even he is unlikely to get you in to see the chancellor, especially on short notice," Stillman went on. "But we'll ring Sir James up first thing in the morning anyway and see just who we might be able to plug you in with."

"Great."

"Meanwhile, why don't you update me on your investigations? You said something, for example, about a second clue."

Sloat fished out a folded paper from the breast pocket of his sport coat—it was the verse about Woden's hanging on the tree, wounded with the spear—and handed it to Stillman.

Rick scanned the sheet through his half glasses while Peter began recounting his recent visit with Rabbi Omar and Cardinal Ponzi.

Moira and Carlotta joined the men in the den with their own steaming mugs. They listened quietly to the account of the strange meeting at the temple headquarters of the New Order of Rome. Moira grimaced at the mention of the woman named Estelle Morgenthau who might be Elizabeth Morningstar. She had her own unpleasant associations with this woman.

Moira took the clue-paper from Rick and examined it while Peter continued.

"Amos has heard all of this," he said, "except for two details I left out."

Sloat raised his eyebrows. "And what might those be?"

"Two names. One was from Rabbi Omar—*Qabala*. And the other was from Cardinal Ponzi—*Gungnir*. I forgot to mention them before, Amos. They didn't mean anything to me. Are they important?"

Sloat frowned thoughtfully. "Could be. Gungnir was the name of Woden's spear. Qabala is a longer story."

"What is it?"

Sloat studied the inner depths of his coffee mug. "Ancient Jewish mysticism," he said at last, looking up. "Arcane symbols and esoteric readings of Scripture based on occult numerology. Invoking elemental spirits—not unlike ritual magic. A continuum of ten stages between the profane and the sacred. Chesed—mercy or love—is one of those stages, the fourth highest."

Peter recognized the name. "Like Rabbi Omar's Temple Beth Chesed?"

"Sure—House of Loving-kindness. But it also has other esoteric meanings."

Carlotta spoke up. "That's the fourth highest. What's the highest?"

"*Kether*. It means 'crown' or 'pure consciousness.'"

"As in 'Crown and Spear'?" she asked.

Sloat smiled ironically. "Before you jump to conclusions, remember 'crown' is a typical symbol for any head of a hierarchy."

"It just reminds me of something that's puzzled me," she said. She rummaged in her purse until she came up with a note card.

"This was stuck in Wendy Carlisle's *Holy Scriptures* from psalm sixty, verse seven: 'Ephraim also is the helmet of My head; Judah is My scepter.'"

Peter anticipated her. "So the helmet—or crown—is like the Kether. And the two together—the helmet and the scepter— are like the Crown and Spear."

"Yes," she said enthusiastically. "And that raises more questions. What's the biblical significance of this Ephraim and Judah reference? And—"

"And," said Peter, "why would Wendy Carlisle, a Scotland Yard detective on this case, be so interested in this verse as to write it down on a file card?"

For the first time, Moira joined in the conversation. "I can't help you with this Carlisle woman, but I think I can shed some light on the verse."

Stillman smiled. "Our ancient language expert and cultural anthropologist here has become something of a Bible student in recent years."

"Just shows there's hope for anybody," said Moira. "Put simply, Ephraim and Judah here mean the whole of Israel. The helmet and scepter, of course, are symbols of divine authority. And we also have the tribe here from which would come the Messiah to rule the nations with an iron scepter."

"Christians," Sloat said, shaking his head. "Wait till I tell you what the Qabala calls the whole system of ten stages."

"What?" asked Peter.

"The Tree of Life. And I suppose you're going to say that's from the Garden of Eden."

"Now you're cooking," said Moira.

"I am?"

Moira smiled. "Think *Yggdrasil.*"

Sloat looked startled, then nodded and fell into thoughtful silence.

"Think what?" Peter asked.

"Yggdrasil," Sloat repeated. "The World Ash Tree. The Tree of the World. We've hopscotched back to the Norse tradition now. It's the mythical tree that binds together heaven, earth, and hell."

Moira spoke in a hushed tone. "But isn't that the tree in your clue? The one from which wounded Woden hung in search of enlightenment? And that's your *Gungnir*—Woden's magic spear hewn from the magic tree."

"Wait a minute," said Sloat. "That's confusing two entirely different systems—ancient Jewish mysticism and Gentile paganism."

Suddenly Peter felt as if some of the pieces were starting to fit. "Yes! And maybe that's exactly the point. We might call it confusion, but to people like Rabbi Omar and the New Order of Rome, it's . . . it's . . ."

"Syncretism," said Moira affirmatively. "The belief that all religions can be reduced to a common denominator. The belief that Jesus was really a Hindu or Buddhist at heart. Or in this case, Woden is a Christ-figure, pierced and hanged on a tree. It makes perfect sense. As much as any of these things do."

"So," said Sloat, "if you're right, what do these Woden clues mean? Or are they really clues at all?"

Moira parried with another question. "Do you know what Woden represents?"

"Self-enlightenment," Sloat ventured. "Humans sacrificed to Woden were hanged and stabbed and strung up on a tree or gallows and then wounded with a spear. By doing the same thing to himself, Woden obtained some form of magical knowledge."

She agreed. "But I think you need to ask more specifically what kind of magic was revealed to Woden as a result of his tree-hanging. Rick, can you run more of the text for us?"

She gave Stillman the reference, and he instructed the computer to display the additional verses of "Havamal 139" from the Edda. In another moment, Cybersynchronic ALEX was audibly reciting the additional verses simultaneously as they appeared on the den wallscreen.

> "None gave me bread,
> None gave me drink.
> Down to the deepest depths I peered
> Until I spied the runes.
> With a roaring cry I seized them up,
> Then dizzy and fainting, I fell.
>
> "Then I began to thrive,
> Then my wisdom grew as
> I prospered and was fruitful.
> One word led to another,
> One word led me to many words,
> And one deed gained me many deeds."

"Runes?" Sloat ventured.

"That's my guess," Moira agreed. "You could try pursuing all of the interpretations of the verses, but I think they'd just be a lot of rabbit trails. I think the correct answer is the obvious one."

"What are runes?" Carlotta asked.

"Weren't runes the script of the Vikings?" Amos suggested.

Moira nodded. "And of Old Norse people in general. Runes had a dual purpose—ordinary writing and magic. On one hand, they're found in inscriptions, used just like letters of the alphabet. On the other hand, each character is invested with special meaning and is used for divination."

Peter was struggling. "But how does that relate to whatever clues our thieves are trying to communicate?"

Moira shrugged. "I don't know—unless they're planning to communicate in runes."

"Let me take a stab at that." Stillman paced the floor with his hands in his pockets. "It seems to me that these people are saying two important things. First, they're establishing their pedigree—'We're neo-pagans of such-and-such a persuasion.' Second, this statement here may not be so much a clue itself as a prelude."

"A prelude to what?" Sloat sounded unconvinced.

"Let me make an analogy. When two computers interface, they don't exchange data until they first do something called 'handshaking.' They establish a common format for data exchange before anything is ever transmitted. In this case, the message may be that the operative language is runes."

Moira looked bemused. "Isn't that what I just said?"

"So," said Peter, "we should be looking for runes? What do you think, Amos?"

Sloat was silent for a long moment, then sighed. "It's a little nutty, but I don't hear anybody coming up with any better ideas. I'm certainly open to suggestions."

Peter reluctantly had to agree, although the idea seemed a bit anticlimactic. "Where do we look for runes? And what do we do if we find them? Anybody here speak rune?"

"Not to worry," said Moira in a motherly tone. "I can give you some material to get you started. But if you do find something, you can always give us a call."

Stillman nodded at the screen. "That's right. There's nobody better at translating and deciphering than good ol' ALEX."

"However," Sloat said pointedly, "until we find a treasure map or something written in runes, we're stuck with good ol' shoe-leather police methods—pound the pavement and question everybody who knows anything."

Peter arched his back and stretched. "I just hope Sir James can open some doors for us."

"No question, Peter," said Stillman. "Sir James very much wants you to succeed."

At that point, someone mentioned Brussels again, and Peter voiced his regrets about not seeing the city. Moira rolled her eyes as Rick began promoting his homemade Brussels videos. In fact, he suggested, it would be just the thing if they would view them right then.

"You asked for it," Moira whispered to Peter as the lights dimmed.

22

Brussels

The autocab processor beeped assent to Peter's instructions and rolled off into the programmed flow of downtown Brussels's computer-assisted traffic patterns. Along the way, centuries-old markets, monuments, and storefronts vied with gleaming sky-scrapers and squatter, squarer structures such as the Hotel Water-loo, where he was staying.

Once again he regretted that he did not have time to explore more of this diverse and historic city. Carlotta was doing just that this morning, starting with the Musée Royale d'Art Ancien across town. She had been enthusiastic about the old masters Breughel and Rubens and Van Dyck, and now was her chance to witness these masterpieces for herself.

Peter had started his morning at the Rhema Institute, where Rick Stillman got Sir James Crisp on the telly right away. Sir James promised to make doors open for them—if not in the chancellor's office, then with Neumann's aide-de-camp, Population and Health Minister Jean Pierre Bardo.

The dignified MP impressed Peter as a man who played a close game with trump cards in reserve, a sly calculator of odds. With his shock of unruly white hair, twinkling eyes, and courtly manners, his aristocratic breeding too was understated. Peter had taken an instant liking to the man and told him he hoped they would meet again. With a sad smile, Sir James wished Peter Godspeed, told him to watch himself, and warned him not to trust the word of anyone over at the EOB, especially Neumann or Bardo.

Before Peter realized this wasn't just another traffic stop, he was there. The autocab beeped softly until he inserted his telecredit card in the rear port in payment. Then the curbside door swung obligingly open.

The Executive Office Building was another utilitarian glass-and-steel tower. Inside, a human beehive greeted him in the cavernous lobby. Peter threaded his way to the front desk and presented himself in the name of Sir James Crisp. Two armed United Nations officers in light blue uniforms escorted him to a security room down a short hallway. There one man relieved him of his portable to make sure it was not some lethal device in disguise. Two other middle-aged civil servants examined his ID card on a desktop terminal and performed face and voice scans to ensure that Peter was who he said he was.

He had time to recall a history-book picture of the terrorist bombing in New York City at the turn of the century. That had devastated the UN building and put an end to the institution as an international diplomatic community. Henceforth it had been relegated to a de facto multinational military police force for keeping larger states from bullying smaller ones and for performing routine diplomatic escort and courier functions among the European, American, and Asian blocs.

Soon a civilian security officer was escorting him to a high-velocity people-mover that expedited him to the other end of the building. Just as quickly, he was scaling the heights of the office tower in a priority elevator that made no stops on the lower floors. No one else was on the lift with them but a dead-faced functionary in a short-sleeved white shirt with a sidearm riding on his belt. When Peter's stomach returned to earth, the elevator light had stopped on floor thirty-two.

With an incomprehensible murmur and a vague gesture, the laconic guard indicated a passage to the right. Peter made strides for the heavy security door at the end. He recognized a standard visual ID port by the voice-lock. The guard spoke a few words, then turned to Peter.

"State name, please."

"Peter McBride."

In half a heartbeat, the door chunked open, and he found himself in a maze of modular offices separated by portable green dividers. Beyond was another great door, this one glass-paneled, where the real power types probably resided. Peter was escorted past the milling swarm of office workers, through the grand glass-paneled doors, and into a high-ceilinged, tastefully furnished antechamber, where a stunning English-speaking young woman came around an immaculate desk to attend to his beverage needs. Hardly had the woman gone, than she returned with a plastic smile and a delicately enameled demitasse full of thick, dark espresso.

Bardo—what did he know about the man? Not much beyond the fact that he was a crony of Neumann's and he ran Population and Health with an iron fist. But that might be noteworthy, since even now Neal was investigating the use of behavior modification tactics by government—especially Population and Health officials.

The only image, however, that Peter could conjure up of the man Bardo was something from the news, a vague impression of wavy hair and glasses.

Soon something beeped on the secretary's desk console, and she was summoning him down a hallway to another security door. The woman murmured again in French to a mike port, and the oak-veneer door swung open. It appeared to be one of those doors with metal plates inside and bullet-proof glass in the center panel.

A man with graying, wavy hair and steely eyeglasses like a precision instrument rose from behind a large and tidy glass-topped desk. Here, clearly, was a man at the top of his organizational pyramid. And he wasn't smiling.

Bardo extended his hand however. "Are you the young man who is trying to get himself killed playing Sherlock Holmes all over Europe?"

His grip was cold and firm. The accent was more British than French—maybe an Oxford influence. The tone was acid.

He was clearly an intimidator who wasted no time sizing up an opponent. Peter felt it was crucial not to yield ground at the outset. "Are you the old fellow who's been losing genome files all over Europe?"

The color drained from Bardo's face. "Sit down." He gestured curtly to the supplicant's chair opposite his desk.

As Peter did so, he watched Bardo with clenched jaw stiffly do the same.

"So. Did you come here just to insult me? And what do you know about genomes?"

"I came neither to insult you nor to discuss genomes," Peter began. "But since you mention it, I do happen to have a question on the subject."

Bardo stared back in stony silence.

Peter took that as a signal to proceed. "Do you have any idea why my genome should travel across the Atlantic to end up in Paris in the hands of a woman who was apparently murdered for some stolen items in her possession?"

Bardo considered the question for a moment. "The Hofburg articles? That is your mission, is it not?"

Peter nodded. "That's correct."

"Do not flatter yourself. Foreigners, especially Americans, have been of interest in some quarters. Do not ask me to account for crazy people who are looking to anoint the next caesar. Why are you bothering me with this?"

"That's funny—for a couple of reasons."

"Oh? Share the humor with me."

"For one thing, some people think Chancellor Neumann is a leading contender for that anointing. And some people think Population and Health is planning to give him the social controls he needs to accomplish that."

Bardo gave a dismissive wave. "Some people simply do not know what they are talking about. What else?"

"Gwydian Brandt. You may not have to account for crazy people, but what about employees? Are you going to deny that she worked for your organization?"

"I can assure you that any intrigue involving *Doktor* Brandt had nothing to do with her employment in Population and Health. But you must appreciate that it would not be appropriate for me to discuss ministry business with you. Will there be anything else?"

Peter felt his time slipping away. "What do you know about the Crown and Spear?"

Bardo's eyes grew evasive, then intense. "I do not know where they are. But I do know where they belong."

"Where is that?"

"Not in the Hofburg, for certain. They belong with those who can ensure their security and keep them out of the hands of fanatics and crazies."

"Like maybe with yourself—or Chancellor Neumann?"

Bardo showed his teeth in an unpleasant grin. "If they were here, we would not have junior gumshoes such as yourself traipsing about the world on sophomoric adventures to recover them. What is the Hofburg paying you for your services?"

"Enough. And it's not up for bid. If we find the *Reichskleinodien,* we intend to return them to their rightful owner. I would prefer to do that with your cooperation."

"I see. What do you think of your prospects of success?"

Peter answered without hesitation. "If the regalia can be found, we will find them eventually."

"Do you have any leads—I mean real, promising avenues to pursue?"

"Certainly," said Peter warily.

Bardo put his fingertips together as if he were an oracle about to prophesy. "How much do you think these articles—this Crown and Spear—are worth?"

Peter shrugged. "I don't have any idea."

Bardo looked incredulous. "What? Is that not the very first thing any novice investigator would establish? And you do not have any idea?"

Peter refused to let himself get defensive. "You mean officially? Officially, a footnote in the international registry cites an estimate of twelve million dollars. They're insured for ten. But as you surely must know, that's all nonsense. These items are priceless and irreplaceable."

Bardo fell silent, his eyes downcast somewhere into the maze of his fingers. Then he rose from his chair and wandered across the room, hands clasped behind his back. Finally he turned and fixed Peter with a penetrating gaze. "You are a very lucky young man, Mr. McBride."

"Why is that, Dr. Bardo?"

"Why? Because you are about to become a multimillionaire. That is why."

Peter shook his head to get the marbles back into proper alignment. "Repeat, please?"

For the first time, Bardo's face showed a smile that looked halfway genuine.

"I will explain. We assist you in your investigation, give you everything you need—security backup and so forth. You find the Crown and Spear. You bring them to us—"

"Wait a minute," Peter interrupted. "You forget my own liability. We already have an agreement with the Hofburg—"

"A detail." Bardo gave another dismissive wave. "Perhaps we take care of that legislatively. Anyway, we obtain legal title by paying the twelve million dollars—ten million to the insurance company, which reimburses the Hofburg for its loss, and two million to you for your efforts."

"Besides being unethical, sir," Peter said slowly, "that smells of trouble—claims, counterclaims, lawsuits for years."

Bardo was behind his desk now, easing himself back onto his throne.

"Do you not listen? I just said we have Parliament at our disposal. What more could you ask for?"

"You and I both know there are no sure things where politics is involved. I don't believe for a minute that even you and Chancellor Neumann can control Parliament. And this assistance you speak of. Interpol and Scotland Yard have been on this case from the beginning. If they're so good, why haven't they already recovered the goods?"

"The same question could be asked of you."

"McBride and McBride is a two-man operation. We don't have hundreds of agents in the field and a vast intelligence-gathering network. Why don't you just get your own system to work for you, if it's that simple?"

Bardo looked faintly amused. "All right. Perhaps it is not that simple. But you impugn the integrity of some good people. It has come to my attention, for example, that two Scotland Yard officers—" he picked up one of the few papers on his desk and scanned it "—Witherspoon and Carlisle, have just apprehended a material witness by the name of Giselle DuChesne. I understand this could represent a major break in the case."

That certainly made things interesting. Maybe that had something to do with Bardo's zeal—fear that the case might be solved before he could get his nose properly stuck into it.

"If you really believed that, you wouldn't be trying to get me—"

"Wait." Bardo held up a hand. "I can see that you have little faith in the system. There is another way."

"And that is . . ."

Bardo had a sly look. "We do it all, as they say, under the table. We do not acknowledge that the articles have been recovered. In fact, we might create the impression that they have been destroyed or otherwise lost forever. We leave the Hofburg and the insurer to their own devices. You bring the regalia here, and we pay you a larger sum—say, *four* million dollars."

Peter stood up. "Thank you for your time, Dr. Bardo. I'm sorry that we can't—"

"Wait!" Bardo barked, then forced another smile. "We are not done—yet. If you have no appreciation of money, perhaps there is one other thing that might induce you to see reason."

Peter had an uneasy feeling. "And what is that?"

Bardo's sly look was replaced by something less definable but certainly more sinister. He clasped his hands together and affected a look of concern.

"I understand that you have, shall we say, a little complication with my counterparts in the USP in obtaining a procreation permit."

The uneasy feeling was now assuming real form. "How would you know that?"

"No matter. Let us just say that this complication need not be permanent. I think we might be able to . . . work something out."

For an instant Peter felt himself drawn to the idea as to a life rope in the rolling sea. But before it could get a firm hold on him, he tromped on it. Hard.

"Thank you, but no thanks. We are dealing with this little complication, as you say, in our own way. Your help is neither wanted nor needed."

Something flashed in Bardo's eyes. "We shall see about that, Mr. McBride. We shall see."

As Peter turned to go, Bardo stood. He was definitely not smiling.

"Georgette," he called to the desk communicator. "Will you show Mr. McBride the way out."

★ ★ ★

Columbus

Neal McBride was becoming unhappier by the hour, more frustrated by the minute. The more he looked at this European business, the less he liked it.

First, he had expected to be able to complete his investigation of the Hofburg employees back in the USP, using the notes from interviews already conducted plus a few long-distance phone calls. But the facts of the case only became more confused rather than less, especially in regard to Giselle DuChesne.

Supposedly the woman was the number-one suspect because she had walked off the job without notice. And yet, following up a tip from an employee-friend had led McBride to the fact that Uppsala University had awarded this woman a fellowship for ancient

Norse studies, which he was able to confirm with a couple of simple phone calls.

Things weren't adding up. It almost had the smell of a frame job.

Then there was the matter of Estelle Morgenthau. He had shown the computer-enhanced version of Peter's video to several people who had known Elizabeth Morningstar—including his own wife and Vince Salerno, a former deputy sheriff and retired security systems consultant. With no prompting, every person instantly identified the woman as Morningstar. That in itself was enough for McBride.

However, when he contacted old friends in the state Attorney General's Organized Crime Division, he was told that Morningstar's file had been lost. And so was any hope of producing a mug shot for comparative analysis. One staffer thought the file had been sent to the feds. An audit trail suggested it had gone to Population and Health.

And finally, he was getting the royal runaround from Population and Health over procreation permits for Peter and the others. He'd originally believed that the government was beginning to respond in good faith in hopes of averting a multimillion-dollar lawsuit, which he would not hesitate to unleash. But then came the unreturned phone calls, the passed bucks, the non-answers, the inaction. Clearly something had changed. McBride had to admit this looked like nothing more than a stall.

"Dyana!" he called to his desk console.

"Yes, sir?"

"Get me Radman Gerrick, please." He made a conscious effort not to bark. But he might be inclined to growl a little.

In less than a minute, an edgy-looking Gerrick appeared on the office wallscreen. McBride did not view that as an encouraging sign.

"Hi, Neal," the man said a little too casually. "How you doing?"

"Mostly cloudy," said McBride. "Buried in a big snow job."

"Oh? Well, what can I do for you?"

"That fire you promised to light under Population and Health."

"Yeah?"

"It's giving me frostbite."

Gerrick furrowed his brow a little too deliberately. "What's that supposed to mean?"

"Let's not play games. You know very well what I'm talking about. The procreation permits. Due process. The Fourth Amendment. My clients' civil rights and all that good stuff."

"Now, Neal. You're going to have be patient a little—"

"I don't have to do anything but look out for the interests of those who have turned to me in their hour of need."

"But—"

"No buts about it, Rad. I want you to listen to me now, and I don't want anymore buts. Do you understand?"

Gerrick looked as if it was going down hard, but he swallowed it. "Go ahead."

McBride held up a substantial, fourteen-inch-long document fastened at the upper lefthand corner with a thick staple. "You see this, Rad?"

"Yes . . . "

"My clock says it's approximately two fifteen P.M. You have twenty-four hours. If I haven't seen some results—tangible movement—by two fifteen P.M. tomorrow, this baby's going to get a date stamp in the clerk's office. You follow me?"

Gerrick rolled his eyes and bobbed his head faintly. "I hope you know what you're doing."

"You let me worry about that. Remember, Rad—"

"I know—twenty-four hours."

Gerrick's sour face lost no time dissolving from the wallscreen.

McBride's eyes stayed on the screen while his mind weighed the odds and options. He felt a little better getting that off his chest, but that was about all. He had little doubt that he'd be forced to follow through on his threat. His suspicious mind also was wondering wildly about possible connections to such craziness as the New Order of Rome and Elizabeth Morningstar and Peter's run-in with the European Population and Health czar.

He was also moving relentlessly to the conclusion that his

days back in the USP were coming to an end. This European remote-control stuff was for the birds.

He needed to be there.

* * *

Rome

Amos Sloat paid the autocab and hustled into the dismal gray lobby of a residential high-rise on the city's north side. He was required to identify himself to the security panel in the elevator before it would take him to the twelfth floor, where the Novellos resided.

Sloat was more anxious than he cared to admit over Tony. When he had started getting the telephone runaround in Brussels, he decided to leave immediately. Something was definitely wrong, and there was only one real option. Back to Rome.

After identifying himself once again outside the door of apartment 1220, Sloat was subjected to a sniff test by a mammoth black Rottweiler before gaining final admittance.

"Get back, Piccolo," commanded a familiar voice.

The beast stood down, its tongue hanging lopsided from its mouth in a lazy grin.

Tony Novello, left arm in a sling, held open the door to reveal a front room dominated by a recliner surrounded by empty bottles of mineral water, coffee cups, saucers, and paperback novels with covers picturing mean hombres, ol' paints, and blazing six-shooters. Tell-tale signs of convalescence for a man who was not used to vegetating.

Novello grinned sheepishly and clasped Sloat's hand with his own good one.

"*Amico,*" he said fondly. "Please sit."

Sloat gestured toward the sling. "Hangnail?"

Novello chuckled. "Fractured humerus—from a dead-eye physicist."

"What?"

Before Novello could answer, his wife—Gina—returned with a coffeepot and some bread sticks.

Amos finally remembered to sit.

When their refreshments had been disbursed, Novello began to recount his hazardous encounter with the Einstein character. It had happened so fast, he said, there wasn't that much to tell.

Sloat had mixed reactions. He was grateful not to have tangled with this blackguard but was sorry his old friend had had to suffer in his stead. Still, he also suspected, because of the ransacking, that the intruder had been less interested in the room's occupants than in its contents.

"So" —Sloat clutched his coffee cup tightly— "any clue to Einstein's identity?"

Novello shrugged. "Maybe another of DiFalcone's punks."

Sloat shook his head. "I don't think so."

"What makes you say that?"

"Just a feeling. DiFalcone was trying to grab Carlotta. It sounds like this fellow was trying to grab the goods—goods that DiFalcone knows we don't have."

"Yet."

"Yet. Was there any physical evidence?"

"No shell casings. He used a gasser. Really only one thing to speak of."

Sloat felt there had to be a clincher. He just couldn't feature Novello clueless.

With his good hand, Novello fingered a remote control for his wallscreen. In another moment they were viewing a dark-complexioned man in a Texas Rangers ballcap delivering a flower box to a young woman at the front desk of the Fiorello.

"That's from one of our security cameras," he explained. "Cerelia followed instructions perfectly. She notified me and had him placed under surveillance as soon as these flowers arrived for Ms. Waldo."

The video resumed with the man, hatless this time and wearing a different-colored jacket, strolling across the hotel lobby. As the man selected a tourist brochure from a rack, the picture tightened about his face for its clearest image.

"Freeze!" called Novello. "Look familiar at all?"

Sloat stared at the frozen image in disbelief. "Yussef Halima!"

"Who?"

Sloat explained how Yussef Halima had killed Gwydian Brandt for the Hofburg articles and then had been killed in turn by the Felici brothers.

"So if this happened only three days ago," he concluded, "it can't be Yussef Halima."

"Unless he has a twin."

"May I have a copy of this? I have friends who could check it out."

"Certainly, my friend."

Sloat drained more of his coffee while Novello downloaded the video for him. "What about the police?"

He stood up, and Novello handed him the microdisk and several five-by-seven hard copies. "The *carabinieri* took a token statement from the bellcap while I was in the hospital. To no effect. I would have tried to bring the Questore in on it if it wasn't already too late."

Sloat wanted to be going, but something began gnawing at him at the mention of Interpol's Italian National Central Bureau. "What do you mean?"

Novello held his thumb and forefinger a centimeter apart. "One tiny lead. A friend in the *carabinieri* tells me they could have pursued one suspect who matched this man's description. The clincher for me was that this fellow had a shot-up arm too. But they failed to do anything, and now he's gone."

"Gone where?"

"Out of the country. Flew to Stockholm."

"Stockholm!" repeated Sloat incredulously as the gnawing bit down hard. He began moving toward the door.

"What's wrong, Amos?"

"Maybe nothing. Maybe everything. In which case, we'd better pray it's not too late."

"Pray?" Novello escorted him slowly to the door. "Have you been hanging around those Christians too long?"

Sloat knew his friend was teasing, but he was also aware that his own moorings might be subtly but perceptibly shifting.

23

Stockholm

The sky was filthy with birds.

Hundreds of gulls wheeled overhead, shrilling, flapping, dropping into the brackish bay where the waters of Lake Malaren spilled into the Baltic Sea. The inlet roiled and glittered with teeming schools of small, silvery feed fish, hundreds of thousands of them, enticing the squawking seabirds.

"Bonapartes," said Carlotta, nodding toward the quay on their right.

Peter gave her an incredulous look. "Who?"

"Our feathered friends out there—Bonaparte gulls."

"Oh. For a second there, I thought I was flunking European history again."

Carlotta chuckled. "No, just ornithology."

Peter snapped his fingers in mock disappointment. "Are you sure they're not Habsburg gulls?"

Her hand found his as they resumed their slow powerblading along the strand south of the train station to the crossing to *Helgeands Holmen*—Holy Ghost Island. They could have taken public transit, but this was much more romantic. And it wasn't even a fine day. The sky was overcast and kept threatening rain, rendering everything in shades of gray like a dingy bedsheet.

But it was their first experience in Stockholm, and Peter intended to savor it.

"So what do you know about orthi . . . uh . . . bird-watching?"

"Ornithology. For a while when I was a student, I painted nothing but birds—ducks, geese, owls, swallows, chickadees, finches, yellow-bellied lawyers, you name it. It was all a part of the discipline of realism. And studying in Cleveland meant becoming familiar with gulls—Bonapartes, ring-billed, herring, glaucous, and black-backed."

"You can really tell them apart?"

She nodded. "Sure. It's easy, once you know what to look for."

"I'm impressed. I think."

Now they were approaching the Drottninggatan bridge that would take him across to the island. Already Peter thought he could make out the dark stone structure of the Riksdagshuset—the Parliament building—in the distance. Nearby, he had been told, could be found the offices of Interpol-Sweden.

"This is where I get off," said Carlotta lightly, slowing her powerblades and dropping back.

Peter did a one-eighty and stopped before he got too far away.

"Remember," she called. "meet me at eleven thirty in Kungsträdgarden in front of the Sverigehuset."

"That's easy for you to say," he said and blew her a kiss. "Just be careful."

★ ★ ★

The sign above the door on the second floor of the federal Rikspolistyrelsen told Peter he had found the right place. *"Interpol Sektionen."*

Carlotta had reluctantly agreed to hit the museums while he did business. This time there had been genuine disappointment in her face, but he couldn't bring himself to treat her like a full partner in crime fighting. His solo excursions had become wearisome, but it seemed less than professional to take a girlfriend into the ring with him.

This at least should be a lot tamer than his incursions into the enemy camp. Considering Carlotta's newfound fascination with firearms, maybe she was actually developing an interest in this business. That would take some getting used to.

Now the bulldog-faced police secretary was returning with his ID.

"Sgt. Arvidsson will see you," she said in passable English, handing back the card. "Second door on the left."

Within that door Peter found a four-man modular office with blue dividers and the obligatory blown-up wall maps with colored push pins.

"Mr. McBride?" said a chunky man in a navy blue uniform, glasses, and blondish hair that probably contained more gray than appeared at first glance.

He had the wholesome eyes and features of a simple and honest man with no surplus of cleverness or guile.

"Yes, sir," said Peter, extending his hand. "Peter McBride of McBride and McBride, Investigations."

"Sgt. Bertil Arvidsson." The man gestured vaguely toward the chair by his desk. "How may I help you?"

"I'd like to ask about Giselle DuChesne," said Peter, taking his seat. "Austrian woman, wanted for questioning in connection with the disappearance of certain valuables from the Hofburg in Vienna."

The man looked a bit uncertain. "You're the private agent for the institution?"

Peter nodded.

Arvidsson relaxed. "*Doktor* DuChesne, she is. Interesting woman. Curiously overqualified for her position. An expert, I believe, in Norse antiquities, Viking artifacts, and so forth."

Peter had an intuition attack. "Runes?"

"Yes," Arvidsson agreed. "Esoteric things just like that, you know. But if you want to know whether she stole the Hofburg valuables, two Scotland Yard art theft experts have already cleared her."

Peter was incredulous. "Cleared her?"

"Yes. I am sorry you have traveled so far for nothing."

"Maybe not for nothing if I can question her."

Arvidsson's expression changed to wry amusement. "Then you had better pack your bags once again."

Peter had a sinking feeling. "Why?"

"She has been released, of course."

"When?"

"Just last evening, when they finished questioning her."

"Which officers? Witherspoon and Carlisle?"

Arvidsson looked as though he might be tiring of the interrogation. "The same."

"And where did Ms. DuChesne go?"

Arvidsson began to balk. "Why don't you just talk to the officers themselves?"

Peter didn't want to reveal suspicions about another Interpol agent. "I don't know that I could reach them. They may have followed DuChesne to see what she would do—wherever she went."

"I doubt that. But—very well—she said she was going to Cøpenhagen to do some more research. Look, this woman appeared to have nothing to hide. She was even traveling under her own name. As far as Interpol is concerned, there may be reason to fear for her safety. She could be an important witness later. Now will that be all?"

"Has there been a specific threat to her safety?"

Arvidsson stood up abruptly. "Nothing that I may discuss with you."

Peter figured he could extract one last favor in exchange for getting out of Arvidsson's hair. "Could you just confirm that she actually went to Cøpenhagen?"

Arvidsson looked as though he were about to unload, then changed his mind. "One minute, please."

The big man moved around to the other side of the cubicle and spoke to someone in Swedish. A woman's voice could be heard making a phone call. Not much more than a minute later, he returned.

"Giselle DuChesne has been confirmed on a Maglev bullet this morning from Stockholm to Cøpenhagen. Now good day to you, sir."

Peter resisted an impulse to salute.

* * *

Cøpenhagen

Peter stared hard at Carlotta in profile and for once did not get caught up in the sight of her hair, lips, eyes, and other usual distractions.

"So are you going to tell me now?" he said, trying to contain his impatience.

It would be a long bullet ride from Stockholm to Malmö and then through the undersea Öresund tunnel to Cøpenhagen. He intended to spend as little of it as possible dying of curiosity about her activities. It was almost as if she enjoyed his bewilderment.

Peter had had to wait an extra hour at the Swedish tourist center, killing time until Carlotta got there. He had accused her of taking a long detour in the huge department store across the street. She had emphatically denied that, insisting that she had confined her expedition to a couple of the museums on Skeppsholmen.

"Uppsala," Carlotta said softly after glancing about the small compartment.

"Uppsala?" said Peter, baffled. "You went to Uppsala?"

That couldn't be right. Uppsala had to be twenty or thirty miles from Stockholm.

"No, no," Carlotta remonstrated. "Our friend *Doktor* Giselle. Stockholm was just a staging area for her apparently. It looks as though she spent most of her time in Uppsala—several weeks' worth of time."

"How do you know?"

"Lower your voice. I was able to log onto the Euronet at the Modern Museum. You can find out a lot about academicians by doing audit trails of their computer activity."

Peter was impressed. "How do *you* know about that kind of thing?"

Carlotta looked conspiratorial. "Research systems are designed to be auditable, especially for instructors. I've done it sometimes with my art students—to assess the originality of their papers. If someone cares to do an audit trail on me, for example, he'd discover that I've just done a pretty thorough research audit on *Doktor* Giselle."

"So how do you know she wasn't accessing this stuff from Stockholm—or even Rome?"

"Some of her requests were for hard copies—books and such —on interlibrary loan to Uppsala."

Peter's admiration was growing. "What kind of information?"

"Sixth-century pagan practices in Scandinavia. She was particularly interested in Old Uppsala, where there's a sacred grove where animal and human sacrifices were hung from a legendary mighty oak."

"Hmm. Shades of Woden and Yggdrasil."

"Perhaps. When paganism was overthrown by Christianity, they built a church on the site of Sweden's last heathen temple. Shades of Chartres Cathedral? A church is still there today, and I wouldn't be surprised if *Doktor* Giselle spent some of her time there."

"But what do you suppose *Doktor* Giselle was doing there?"

Carlotta shrugged. "Whatever scholars do. Not necessarily anything to do with the Hofburg items."

"Except for the fact that she appears to have been involved in the original heist."

"We don't know that for certain, do we? Did you assume that because you were told she had taken it on the lam? If that's true, then how come she was traveling under her own name?"

Peter didn't like the direction this was taking. "I don't know, but it certainly doesn't reflect well on Interpol's ability to pursue suspects."

"Or maybe something worse. You already know that Scotland Yard is compromised by the likes of Wendy Carlisle. And—"

"Yeah, and I also know that Interpol answers to Bardo and Neumann, who would love to get their hands on the Crown and Spear. Just as much as DiFalcone or Ponzi or the Imam of Babylon, for that matter."

"And what's that tell you?"

"That maybe it's just you and me, kid—and Amos Sloat."

"How do you suppose Amos is doing?"

Peter winked rakishly. "Couldn't be doing as well as us."

* * *

Stockholm

"Cøpenhagen!" said Sloat in surprise and frustration.

"Yes, sir," Bertil Arvidsson said wearily, as if he had been through it all before. "Cøpenhagen. That's all I can tell you."

Sloat picked himself up hurriedly, then stopped. "Thank you, Sergeant. I would like to beg your indulgence for just one more favor."

Arvidsson looked up with a jaundiced eye. "Let me guess. You want me to confirm that Mr. McBride actually went to Cøpenhagen."

"No, no. I have no doubt of that. But he and his fiancée may be in mortal danger from a suspect who shot a man in Rome. This man may be here in Stockholm now, or he may be on his way to Cøpenhagen. I would like you to notify the proper authorities, including your Danish counterparts. The man is armed and highly dangerous."

Arvidsson looked unconvinced. "In that case, why have the Rome authorities not already notified us?"

Sloat shrugged. "Who knows? You know the Italians."

"What is the suspect's name?"

"I don't know that either."

Arvidsson glared. "Physical description? We have to have something."

"Of course." Sloat reached into his inner jacket pocket and extracted one of the hard copies of Tony Novello's Halima-looking man. "Here."

Mollified by the photo, Arvidsson asked several more questions, scribbled some notes for a brief report, and even proffered grudging thanks for the information.

Sloat left the *Rikspolistyrelsen* in high gear, muttering as he went. "Cøpenhagen!"

At least he had reasonable hopes that Peter and Carlotta were still alive. He hustled to the corner and scanned the intersection to get his bearings. He would have to grab an autocab to the train station and catch a Maglev bullet to Malmö and Cøpenhagen. He briefly considered gambling on a flight out of Arlanda Airport, then discarded the idea. If he got lucky—or providential, as Peter would put it—he could make up some lost time. But if he wasn't, if the flight was filled, he could actually lose time. And that was not a chance that he was prepared to take.

Sloat saw that it had rained recently—not for long but heavily enough to leave a sheen on the pavement and some occasional standing water. Just then an autocab already occupied whooshed by. Its right rear wheel bumped down into a puddle-filled pothole, and instantly he was drenched. The cold water was like a taunt, rubbing his nose in the foolishness of not carrying an umbrella or wearing a slicker on such a mercurial spring day.

Several insolent, icy drops rolled down his face and dripped off the end of his nose.

"Cøpenhagen!" he cried, turning the heads of several pedestrians.

Overhead the Bonaparte gulls continued circling in their floppy trajectories. To Sloat's current frame of mind, they suggested marine buzzards.

He was in no better frame of mind when he arrived at the Central Station on Vasagatan to find he had just missed the mid-afternoon Maglev to Malmö. Now he would have to kill another two hours before the next bullet. He couldn't help ruing his decision not to gamble on a flight from Arlanda.

With no particular destination in mind, Amos walked out into the gray light of afternoon and let his feet find their own way. Was it too superstitious to think there could be a larger reason, a greater good, behind these snafus and snarls? He wondered. It wasn't like him to think this way. That sounded like one of Peter McBride's notions. Maybe he had been hanging around these Christians too long.

Not far from Central Station his feet led him past a sidewalk vendor, a short Greek-looking man presiding over a wheeled dispensary of enticing-smelling steaming meats. Sloat's stomach stood at attention. His hands took over where his tongue failed, making the international signals for "Give me that fat-laden Swedish equivalent of Italian sausage on a soggy bun slimed with gooey onions" and forking over cash in payment.

One step away from the vendor and two bites into the low-rent succulence, his eyes flitted across the face of the next customer and then on down the street where his feet would take him next. It was another long moment before his brain processed the image and responded with a double-take. Memories of Texas Rangers baseball caps and shootings in Paris and Rome bobbed to the surface.

Sloat spun on his heel and tried to spot the man who had somehow reminded him of Yussef Halima. He was, of course, gone. When the beetle-browed vendor finally understood what

Sloat was trying to ask in monosyllabic English, he had nothing to offer but a shrug and a vague gesture down the street.

Looking at the milling pedestrians, Sloat realized he might as well try to pick out one particular gull from the seashore. It would be equally impossible.

Maybe he was stressed and imagining things. Probably his mind was playing tricks on him with wishful thinking, dressing itself up as a perfect stranger who looked vaguely Arab to fit his preconceived image. Still, this kind of thing wasn't at all like him.

Sloat pressed on down the avenue with his cooling, half-eaten pastry, hating himself for loving junk food, and wondering what else he was going to do for the remainder of these two hours.

At the next corner, a curly-haired young man with a rabbinic demeanor and a well-trimmed beard was handing out small pieces of literature. His T-shirt said something in Hebrew about Y'shua.

"*Shalom!*" said the young man to Sloat as he handed him a leaflet. "Y'shua loves you."

"Aren't you a little confused?" Sloat asked. "Y'shua means Jesus, and he's for Gentiles."

The young man smiled warmly. "I used to believe that too—until I got to know Him."

Sloat was not going to let that pass. "I got news for you, pal. Jesus is dead."

Now the young man's eyes were twinkling. "So how come nobody could ever produce the body?"

Sloat shrugged. "His disciples stole it. I don't know."

The young man had stopped passing out leaflets and was now sticking them back into a sack.

"Do you have time for a cup of coffee?" he asked.

"Sure," said Sloat, hardly believing he had said that. "I've got time for coffee, tea, milk, a six-pack—you name it."

* * *

Almost two hours and a pot of coffee later, Sloat was back at Central Station, waiting to get his ticket punched. His head was still spinning from his tangle with Benny, the "messianic Jew" who seemed to have an answer for everything. Amos had misinterpreted Benny's soft-spoken approach. Behind the easygoing humor was a black-belt evangelist who knew all the moves.

Yet it hadn't been just finesse. Sloat had found himself nearly defenseless when it came to the man's messianic proofs about Jesus Christ. And he had been practically speechless when it came to the evidence of the resurrection. The way Benny explained it, it took more faith to believe that the resurrection had been a hoax than that Jesus actually had risen from the dead.

Still, Sloat needed time. He needed to think about this more. Maybe he was just having a bad day, and tomorrow he would think of all the counterarguments he had forgotten today.

He also had been preoccupied by another question—just how to connect with Peter and Carlotta. Cøpenhagen was a big place.

So Sloat, his thoughts chasing each other around heaven and Europe, was caught especially offguard when a similar coincidence happened a second time that day.

As the train doors slid open, the flat, synthetic computer/dispatcher voice was telling Maglev passengers to step lively and to move to the rear, when something clattered to the platform in front of him. It appeared to be an electronic device, smaller than a personal portable, and he feared that it would be crushed underfoot.

Reflexively he bent down and scooped up the instrument before it could be trampled in the crush. This was odd. In his hand it reminded him of the personal homing devices used by a number of intelligence services including his own. When he stood back up, he found himself looking into a pair of brown eyes in an olive-skinned face that froze him in his tracks. *Halima!*

The man was holding out his hand. Sloat felt momentarily paralyzed, as if he had seen a ghost. Recovering quickly, he handed over the gadget to this man who presented himself as its owner. The Arab snatched it up quickly, spun on his heel, and boarded the train. Not a word of thanks. Not even an acknowledging nod.

Sloat scrambled aboard, trying to stay in sight of him, but in the milling crowd that was impossible. At first he could tell where the man was headed by the space that cleared around him as he elbowed his way through the rear coach. But then the aisle narrowed to single file between the rows of seats, and Sloat lost sight of him.

He would just have to assume that this character would stay on the train. He also had to assume that the Arab did not know know who he was. But if this was the man who had shot Tony Novello, he certainly had some idea of who Peter and Carlotta were. In that case, maybe he also knew about their Israeli friend. It was a chance he would have to take.

For this, he realized, was how he would find Peter and Carlotta. This Halima look-alike might lead him there.

Lord willing, as Peter would say.

* * *

Cøpenhagen

"Cøpenhagen!" Sloat muttered as he debarked from the Maglev in the Danish twilight.

He loitered at the top of the passenger ramp, casually scanning faces. And then he spotted his quarry exiting from the third coach ahead and making tracks for the busy *stræde*.

Would the man head first for a hotel or immediately for his victims? Would Sloat be able to keep up and make successful pursuit in an unfamiliar city? He knew all too well that success—not to mention the safety of his friends—depended on it.

He descended the ramp leisurely, maintaining a safe distance from his prey. At the bottom his man headed away from the corner toward the middle of the block and a stand of several white-and-green autocabs. Sloat took off like a shot, elbowing his way through human obstacles, ignoring the glares.

Out of breath, he yanked open the door to the next autocab in line and threw himself into the backseat as the lead car pulled away.

"F—follow that c—cab!" Sloat gasped.

Nothing. He could see the other vehicle shrinking in the distance.

"Follow that cab!" Sloat shouted again, then frantically searched his memory for some of the little native tongue he knew. *"Lige ud!"*

He hoped he'd directed the cab-brain onward—straight ahead. But for all the response, he might have just asked for his restaurant check. Maybe it didn't recognize either his English or his Danish. More likely it was only programmed to proceed toward a destination, a geographical locale such as Christiansborg Palace.

Either way, Sloat was stalled, and his man was now a dwindling speck in the distance. He got out of the cab and contemplated his ill fortune. He was never devoid of resources, if he could just keep his head. Even now a plan was taking shape.

If "Halima" were stalking someone with his homing scanner, two could play the game. All he had to do was find an electronics store, purchase a police scanner and a few extra parts, pull the circuit board, plug in the components, make a few adjustments, and he should be able to scan the same frequencies his foe must be using. He had absolute confidence in his ability to distinguish a homing code pulse.

The problem was time. This was going to cost him a good hour or two, and he was afraid that might be too long. It wouldn't be the first time he had failed on a mission, but it would be the first one he cared about this much.

24

Cøpenhagen

Night had settled in to stay. Large stone and brick edifices slid by, looking gaunt and forbidding in their floodlit majesty. In the distance appeared the shimmering black surface of some body of water, which Peter identified from his guidebook as the Frederiksholms Kanal. In that case, the museum wouldn't be much farther.

Carlotta had insisted that the National Museum, with its extensive collection of rune stones, Viking artifacts, and inscriptions to the god Odin, was the logical place to look for Giselle DuChesne, even at this late hour. The research annex, she said, was open after business hours for scholarly purposes.

"There it is," she announced in a whisper that still startled in the strange, quiet dark.

Peter followed the line of sight from Carlotta's index finger against the car window to the approaching institutional-looking structure and noticed what had caught her attention. Lights were visible through several large ground-floor windows in a wing on the far side of the darkened building. That should be the annex.

"Pull around back," he instructed.

The autocab bumped gently into the narrow drive and coasted to a stop in the spacious rear lot. Peter couldn't shake a peculiar, disquieting sense of vulnerability. He stole a glance at Carlotta, who gave no sign of nerves.

"Why don't you wait here while I check it out?" he suggested casually, reaching for the door handle.

"And let you hog all the credit? Not a chance."

Before he could reply, she was out her side.

Peter decided he'd feel better having her where he could keep an eye on her. But then, what was he worried about? Really?

Carlotta's hand found his in the dark. Her fingers were cold.

Up ahead were the large double glass doors of the flood-lit entrance, bearing a lengthy inscription in Danish.

"Even if this place isn't open," Peter said reassuringly, "there's bound to be some staff present—a security guard, at least."

He pulled on the handle and found that the place was indeed open. They entered a small lobby that was much too dark. Even after he had stood still for a half minute, his eyes did not adjust. The only light came from around the corner and down the hall. This was not the most encouraging sign.

"Hold on." He moved toward a logical place for light switches. "Oops."

His foot had made contact with something like a bunched-up rug. He made a course correction and finally fingered the light switches. A burst of light stabbed his eyes.

"Oh, Peter!"

Then he saw what Carlotta had seen. The bunched-up rug was actually an older man in a gray-and-black uniform, lying on his back in a quantity of blood, his eyes fixed lifelessly on the ceiling. A pistol drooped from his right hand. There was an angry-looking hole in his throat.

"So much for the security guard," said Peter softly, pulling out his own gun.

Red streaks on the wall told the story of the man's last moments of life. He had probably meant to pull the fire alarm, which was a few meters farther down the hall. But under the circumstances, it was understandable that he would grope for the wrong switches.

Peter stole a glance at Carlotta, who was staring at the man with an ashen look on her face.

"You OK?"

She nodded numbly without moving her eyes. He was suddenly glad she wasn't out in the cab by herself. Together they stood a much better chance in case of trouble.

"Come on," he said with a movement of his head. "Whoever did this is probably long gone. Let's see if there's anybody else here—like Doctor DuChesne."

He spoke with greater confidence than he actually felt. That blood looked fresh, too fresh. But he wasn't about to tell Carlotta that.

She moved very close to him and stayed there as they turned the corner and crept down the hall toward the lighted area. Their footsteps echoed ominously in the flat silence, broadcasting their presence.

The lighted area turned out to be the main attraction. It was a huge, two-story, glass-walled chamber filled with conference-size tables, computer terminals, and rows and stacks of books and microdisks.

At the far end of the largest table, surrounded by several disorderly piles of books, papers, and notepads, sat a lone figure, as if lost in thought. As they approached, it took on the appearance of a woman.

Peter strongly suspected her lassitude involved something more serious than a mere daydream or runic meditation. And then he saw.

Even slumped in her chair, she was obviously a tall, big-boned woman, but nonetheless lean. She wore a long, heavy Scandinavian folk-type dress and a black head covering gathered behind her right ear with a brass ring and black braid hanging below. Tufts of very blonde hair peeked out from under it. Very blue eyes stared up from deep sockets above high cheekbones at a forty-five-degree angle. Very white, very straight teeth showed through her death smile.

Two large-caliber holes perforated her chest, one precisely over the heart. Peter wondered what the original color of her tunic had been.

Her arms dangled over either side of the hard-back chair, as if her assailant might have propped her there after a somewhat messier disposition. And it was obviously so recent that whoever had done this might still be in the vicinity.

Peter picked up a book from the table in front of her, ignoring his screaming nerves. The hair on the back of his neck was standing up. This had the terrible feel of a setup—an ambush waiting to happen. He could hear Carlotta's breathing, fast and shallow beside him, then a footstep in the doorway behind.

And then things went mad.

Peter's ears rang as the computer terminal by his right elbow exploded in a shower of plastic and metal and glass. Several shards bounced harmlessly off his arm.

He whirled to glimpse a shadowy figure wearing a baseball cap and pointing a gun toward his chest.

"*Halima!*" shouted a voice from down the hall.

The man whirled about and fired at the voice, and Peter quickly gathered his wits.

"Hit the deck!" he yelled at Carlotta, firing his own pistol at their assailant.

He missed. A huge glass panel by the door ruptured into myriad fragments as the man down the hall returned fire.

"Carlotta!" Peter yelled again.

Instead of ducking, she was thrusting both arms forward and sighting down them to her hands, clasped around her own pistol.

There was a crack, and their assailant spun around to face Carlotta. That was a mistake. There was another crack, and the man lurched forward a half step with a look of surprise. But when he tried to reposition his pistol on Carlotta, there came a third crack. Carlotta did not miss.

The man spun again, this time into the doorway, where he caromed off and then fell flat on his stomach onto the floor.

Carlotta stood with arms frozen like a petrified triangle, still training her gun on the spot where their assailant no longer stood.

Peter's ears reverberated from the lingering echoes of shouts and gunshots and bursting glass.

"Carlotta. You can put the gun down now."

As if she had heard a posthypnotic command, Carlotta's arms went limp, and the gun dropped to her side. Her eyes fastened upon the dead man and stayed there, as if in disbelief.

Another figure appeared in the doorway. "Well, well, boys and girls."

"Amos!" said Peter.

Sloat was mopping his brow with a handkerchief. "Excellent shooting, Carlotta. You saved both our lives. Too bad we couldn't have saved that one." He gestured to the woman at the table.

Peter moved to Carlotta's side and put his arm around her waist. "Sweetheart?" he said softly. "You OK?"

Carlotta's eyes never left the floor.

He tried again. "What's wrong, love?"

"I want to go home," she said in a pathetic, tremulous voice. She was crying quietly.

Sloat suggested that Peter and Carlotta sit down and relax and take some deep breaths while he made a couple of phone calls. Peter assumed one of those would be to the local police.

Carlotta dissolved slowly into a chair at the other end of the big table, as far from the dead woman as possible.

Sloat found a phone on the other side of the large chamber, not quite out of earshot.

"Carlotta?" Peter said again, gently.

This time she looked up and managed a weak smile. "I'll be OK. It's just not very often that I . . . kill somebody."

Peter glanced for the first time at the book in his hand—*Voyage au Centre de la Terre,* by Jules Verne. He couldn't remember how it got there. He set it down and scanned the other materials on the table.

By the illustrations, he judged these to be an assortment of documents regarding ancient myths and legends of gods and heroes and the underworld, plus pages and pages of weird symbols. One looked like the lightning bolts adopted by the Nazi SS. Another resembled the broken, inverted peace-sign cross turned right-side up. Some seemed variants of Roman letters, others like nothing he had ever seen.

There was little doubt that they had found *Doktor* Giselle DuChesne. And Peter had a good hunch about the symbols.

"Runes?" he asked Carlotta, holding up one of the pages.

She glanced at it and nodded.

Sloat was making a second phone call, this time speaking in the language Peter had learned to recognize as Hebrew.

"Can you read it?" Peter asked.

She closed her eyes and shook her head slowly.

"No. The only thing I know about runes is from a graphics perspective. Do you notice anything unusual about the character formation?"

Frowning, Peter studied the symbols intently. "Just that there are lots of vertical and diagonal lines, but no horizontal strokes."

"Very good."

"Why is that?"

"Runes were usually carved in wood, and horizontal strokes tend to disappear in the grain."

Uneasy silence fell again in the chamber, punctuated only by Sloat's one-sided phone conversation, apparently winding down.

"Thanks," said Peter as the Israeli joined them. "That could have been one of us down there." He nodded at the gunman on the floor.

Sloat only grunted and stooped by the body to check through the man's pockets.

"But how did you find us?" Peter persisted. "And just what do you think you're doing? There are laws about disturbing a crime scene, you know."

Sloat grasped the apparent object of his search and held it up for closer inspection. It appeared to be some kind of pendant with a broken cord.

"Here." He handed it to Peter. "Hold this a minute."

Peter held the cord and examined the gently swinging object. It was semicircular and made of some flat, highly polished, dark mineral substance, like an igneous formation. On its surface were obscure engraved characters that resembled the symbols on DuChesne's work papers.

ᚷᚨᛞᛊᛏᛟ

"This is how I found it." Sloat took a small electronic device from a pocket and aimed it at the pendant.

An obnoxious squeal began pulsing rapidly. When it approached the pain threshold, Sloat turned off the gadget and asked Peter for the amulet. The silence was delicious.

Sloat produced a jeweler's eyepiece and a miniature tool like a cross between tweezers and pliers. In another moment he had extracted a tiny object from the stone and held it up triumphantly. The obnoxious electronic device obliged with a squealing encore.

"You look in here," he said, pointing to a lighted display in a small viewport, "and it actually gives you rough coordinates in increasing resolution closer to the source."

"So," said Carlotta, "you tracked this thug with a homing device."

Sloat shook his head, and Peter immediately saw what must have occurred.

"Not quite," he guessed, holding up the knotted cord. "If you check our lady victim's neck, I suspect you'll find a telltale abrasion precisely where this cord was forcibly removed."

Carlotta grimaced.

Feigning clinical detachment, Peter went over and gingerly pulled the woman's collar back slightly. "Yep. Left side of the neck has a nasty welt like a pencil line. Our friend here apparently grabbed the stone and pulled from the right side, snapping the cord on the left. Just like an ordinary smash-and-grab artist."

He mimed the action the way he pictured it while Carlotta looked on, wide-eyed. "I imagine she was already dead when he grabbed it."

Sloat nodded. "Not bad. We'll make something of you yet."

He then returned to the man's body and removed another object from a jacket pocket. This was an electronic device similar to his own, only smaller and more professional looking. But its signal was just as unpleasant.

"You're right, Peter," Amos said. "Halima and I were both tracking the amulet worn by this lady victim—who I presume will turn out to be Giselle DuChesne."

"Halima," said Peter, incredulous. "That's what you yelled to distract him. But that's impossible. Halima's dead."

"You're thinking of *Yussef* Halima," said Sloat. "I found a hotel receipt in his wallet. This is *Kabir* Halima. Kabir Ali Halima, to be precise."

"A twin brother?"

Sloat smiled faintly. "Something like that. Some days ago I transmitted this fellow's picture to my friends and asked them to run a check on the Halima clan. I just now got their reply."

He paused.

Peter understood these "friends" to be the customary euphemism for Shin Beth. "And . . ." he prompted.

"Clones."

The word fell like a pebble into a devilishly deep well.

"Clones," Peter repeated, trying the concept on for size.

It didn't fit well. He'd heard of genetically cloned humans—identical twins, triplets, quadruplets—but these were fiercely suppressed by Population and Health ministries around the world.

"Isn't that against international law?"

Sloat nodded. "Supposedly. It's sort of like gun control—when clones are illegal, only criminals will have clones. In this case, terrorist organizations that spawn them for use as trained killers."

"But if Yussef and Kabir Halima are clones," Carlotta interjected worriedly, "then there could be more of them."

Sloat nodded again. "I'm afraid so. My friends believe there's at least one more. Maybe two."

"But what's their game?" she asked. "What are they after? And why are they killing people?"

Peter frowned. "The Crown and Spear?"

Amos held up a hand. "But what does this amulet have to do with the Crown and Spear, and why did Halima have to kill her for it?"

"You're asking me?" said Peter. "Maybe he got up on the wrong side of the bed. Maybe she wouldn't give it to him. Maybe *Doktor* Giselle knew too much—was too much competition. But I have no idea what this amulet means. What's carved on it?"

Carlotta scrutinized the characters. "Runes, of course. Where's that Roman-character conversion table I saw? I might be able to get a transliteration at least."

Another question occurred to Peter. "It could be this is some major clue toward the whereabouts of the regalia—maybe even something DuChesne found during her researching in Sweden. But how did it acquire a homing device?"

"That," said Sloat, "is something we may never know."

"Hmm, yeah." Peter glanced at the two bodies.

Carlotta appeared to have found what she needed. "Six characters," she said slowly, referring to a chart. "G-A-D-S-N-O. Gadsno."

"'Gadsno'?" Peter echoed. "What's that supposed to mean? Somebody's name? A location?"

Carlotta shrugged. "I told you I don't read this stuff. But you should be able to get Rick and Moira to crack it for you."

Amos asked for the amulet and then pocketed it.

"What are you doing?" demanded Peter.

Sloat implanted the homing device into the fiber of the necklace cord and took it across the room toward Halima's body.

"The police will be here any minute," he said, returning the cord to Halima's pocket. "They may need the homing device to close the case on this stalker with the scanner. But *we* need the amulet. Did you notice anything remarkable about its design?"

"Just that one edge is irregular," said Peter, "as if it was broken in half from a larger whole—as its semicircular shape suggests. Its curved edges, in fact, are quite smooth."

Sloat smiled. "Good. What does that suggest to you?"

"That there's another piece somewhere, maybe with the rest of some message—a clue perhaps to the location of the regalia."

"Where would you look for this other piece?"

Peter sighed. "Maybe DuChesne's research notes will suggest the answer. Maybe Halima was after those too. Maybe he thought he had to kill her to keep her from solving the mystery."

"There may be another reason," Sloat said quietly.

"What?"

"Baiting the trap."

"Oh." At once Peter realized what Sloat had to mean. "So he could ambush *us?*"

Sloat nodded. "He was already on your trail. Let me tell you about Tony Novello."

By the time Sloat had finished recounting the shooting incident in Carlotta's room at the Fiorello, Peter saw that she was crying again. "What's wrong, Carlotta?"

"I'm sorry," she sputtered.

"For what?"

She shook her head. "I should have listened when you tried to talk me out of following you around, playing tough girl, cops and robbers. But I wouldn't, and DiFalcone's man ended up getting killed. And now—now this!"

"Wait a minute," Peter objected. "That's different. Lorenzo Lonardo may have been after you, but I don't think your presence made any difference for Kabir Halima. Although if it hadn't been for you, it might have been Amos or me lying there on the floor."

Somehow that didn't seem to help. Carlotta began weeping again.

"*I* killed him. And it's not at all like shooting paper men on the firing range. Not at all."

The sound of footsteps and voices in the hall interrupted them. Reflexively, Peter's hand went to the butt of his pistol, but he checked himself as four figures came into view, including two uniformed policemen. With them were a man in plainclothes with a satchel and a young, frightened-looking woman.

The woman put her hand to her mouth and hung back while the three men came on in, each pausing momentarily to peer at the profile of the dead gunman. The plainclothesman opened his large black bag and began removing instruments. This had to be the medical examiner.

The elder of the policemen, a husky fellow with graying hair and a ruddy complexion, who identified himself as Sgt. Andersen, addressed them in adroit English. "First, let us have some names and identification from all three of you, please. You too, young lady."

This last he said to the woman with the hand to her mouth. Peter judged her to be about twenty-four and altogether unremarkable with light brown hair and average height. More remarkable were her darting blue eyes, which made her look as if she wanted to jump out of her skin.

The younger officer began recording the questioning, asking for spellings of each name.

When it was her turn, the young woman identified herself as Disa Sjölvaag, a graduate student in medieval Scandinavian history from Oslo who was studying at the University of Cøpenhagen and doing research at the museum.

Sergeant Andersen quickly explained that Ms. Sjölvaag, like Sloat, had called to report the crime, claiming to have been in the museum research center at the time of the shooting.

"Is this the man," he asked her, pointing to Halima, whom you saw do the shooting?"

She looked over at the figure on the floor, where the medical examiner was going through some personal effects. "I—I don't know," she said tremulously. "I can't really see his face."

"Well, go look," boomed the officer impatiently.

Disa Sjölvaag jumped, suggesting that the policeman's bark had been well advised. Otherwise she probably would have been disinclined to bring her face two feet from the dead man's and look into his vacant eyes.

"Yes," she said miserably when she stood up.

"Tell me about it."

There wasn't much to tell. Man appears out of nowhere,

fires a gun. Woman dies. Man rips something off woman's neck and puts it in his pocket. Man flees into the night.

"And where were you when this happened?"

"Over there." She pointed to the far glass wall by the phone. "I had gone to the restroom and was returning when it happened. I stood without moving until he was gone, and I was able to see it all through the glass."

"And then what did you do?"

"I used that phone over there" —she nodded toward the telephone Sloat had used— "and I called the police. Then I ran outside and hid behind some bushes until I saw your cruiser."

"Did you know this woman?"

"No."

"Speak to her?"

"A little."

"About what?"

"I told her what I was doing, but she did not reciprocate. She seemed a little . . . strange. I finally asked her what she was researching, and she just laughed off my question."

"How do you mean?"

"She just said she was going to hell. That is why I say she was strange."

"Did you ask her what she meant?"

"No. I decided I did not really want to know."

"Thank you, Ms. Sjölvaag. That will be—"

"Excuse me," Sloat interjected. "I would like to ask a question."

The officer looked surprised but offered no objection.

"Do you have any idea what 'Gadsno' means?"

"What?" asked the woman blankly.

Sloat spelled it for her.

She shook her head. It was obvious that they had exhausted her usefulness and that she wanted to get back to her own quiet life, where people didn't laugh about going to hell and madmen didn't shoot them in the chest for no apparent reason.

"Please have a seat while we finish up here," Andersen said, "and we will escort you home if you like."

By now the medical examiner, who had already performed a preliminary inspection of Halima's wounds, was preparing to do the same with Giselle DuChesne.

"I believe you will find," said Sloat, "that the ballistics will confirm Ms. Sjölvaag's account—and ours."

"Which is . . ." prompted Andersen.

"Which is that the security guard and Giselle DuChesne were killed with Kabir Halima's gun and Halima was killed with Carlotta Waldo's—in self-defense."

"Perhaps," Andersen said dubiously, shifting his gaze to Carlotta. "Since, as you say, it was Ms. Waldo's gun, I will ask you, Ms. Waldo, to give a full account of how you happened to be here and to kill Mr. Halima, as you say, in self-defense."

Carlotta looked like a deer caught in the glare of car headlights, but only for a moment. She quickly collected herself and began telling the story of their hunt for Giselle DuChesne and the hunch that had brought them to the National Museum and ultimately to this bloody outcome.

Peter was impressed with the clarity of her story and her economy of detail. He was even more relieved to hear her give her account without once mentioning the Crown and Spear or the weirdly engraved amulet. The way she told it, it seemed eminently sufficient just to say that they were looking to recover some stolen objects on behalf of another Euro museum before another thief—namely Halima—beat them to it.

Andersen nodded thoughtfully at the end. And then he asked a question that got Peter sweating once more. "What is the significance of this 'Gadsno' that Mr. Sloat asked about?"

Peter glared at Amos, since he was the one who had brought it up.

"Well—" Sloat sounded reluctant "—I guess we might as well level with you."

Peter winced as Amos explained that they had no idea what it meant but they had what might be a clue to the missing articles from the Hofburg in Vienna. He held his breath as Sloat briefly described, almost conspiratorially, the high-stakes game involved and even the gnat's-whisker homing device.

When he was done, Peter realized that Sloat—the old fox—had done it all without once mentioning the amulet. "Gadsno" got quickly lost in the other intrigue.

Andersen's expression indicated that he was suitably impressed.

"Well, Mr. Sloat, if there is anything the Cøpenhagen police can do to assist you, please do not hesitate to let us know."

"Oh, yes," Sloat said as if he had forgotten something, "it *would* be most helpful if we could have a full copy of *Doktor* DuChesne's personal notes here plus a list of museum references she was consulting. If that's not too much trouble, of course."

Andersen's eyes looked momentarily uncertain. "Did you hear that, Sven?" he said to the younger officer. "Can you manage that?"

"Oh, yes," said Sven. "Certainly by tomorrow mid-morning, anyway."

Amos smiled delightedly. "We could probably have somebody in Interpol send you the proper warrants, if that would help."

Andersen waved dismissively. "I am sure that will not be necessary. Just tell me where you would like these papers sent. Where are you staying?"

"Uh . . . Peter?" Sloat's smile faded. "Where are we staying?"

Peter wished he had been asked a question he could answer. "We're not yet, Amos. We've been kind of living out of pocket these last couple of days."

Andersen smiled. "Well, then, would you like me to recommend a place or two? In fact, we might as well just take you there after we run Ms. Sjölvaag to her place. Would that be acceptable?"

Peter looked at Carlotta, who looked at Sloat. Smiles broke out three times.

"Cøpenhagen!" Sloat declared, this time with satisfaction.

25

Cøpenhagen

ᚷᚨᛞᛊᚾᛟ

From their hotel, through the twenty-first-century miracle of macrocommunications, Peter hoped to get both Moira and Rick Stillman and the mystery symbols on the same split screen. Carlotta and Sloat waited with him.

Rick was at work, and Moira was at home, but they made themselves instantly available. Peter knew there were few things these two thinkers would rather be doing, anyway, than attempting to solve a good puzzle.

"'Gadsno'?" Rick squinted in puzzlement, then brightened. "Sure. You never heard of Flip Gadsno? Played third base for the Phillies. Or was it right field for the White Sox? I forget."

"You're such a card, Rick," said Peter. "Excuse me for not laughing, but it's kind of hard with the bodies piling up."

"OK, let me take a hard copy of this rune-a-ma-callit of yours and have ALEX chew it over."

Moira took this opportunity to interject, "Did this unfortunate woman have any famous last words? Isn't that the way it happens in the movies? The famous last words that prove to be the key to solving the mystery."

"Well," Peter said, "she did say something odd to the last person who talked to her."

"How odd?"

"Supposedly she talked about going to hell. And who knows what she meant by that."

Moira said, "You know what this reminds me of? Something out of Jules Verne."

"Jules Verne."

"Yes. Did you ever read *Journey to the Centre of the Earth?*"

A funny feeling was sneaking up on Peter. "Not exactly."

"Peter?"

"Well, I don't read French, but I think that's the book I was holding in my hand last night."

"So?"

"So it was among *Doktor* Giselle's research papers and notes and so forth."

"That *is* odd."

Peter agreed. "So what's the connection with Jules Verne?"

"In *Journey to the Centre of the Earth,* Professor Von Hardwigg discovers an ancient document that tells how to reach the underworld, once his young nephew stumbles onto the key to translating the weird inscription. The nephew figures out that the message was written backward in Latin but—here's the interesting part—in runic script."

The sneaky feeling caught up with Peter and struck him temporarily speechless. There were too many coincidences here.

Now Rick returned with a cryptic look on his face, Carlotta's paper in his hand, and a twinkle in his eye.

"Backward is relative," he said. "Do you read Hebrew, Amos?"

Sloat nodded. "And if I read it left to right, *that* would be backward."

Peter's mind was racing. "Are you trying to suggest—"

"I'm suggesting," said Rick, "that with runes it's AC/DC. Sometimes it reads left to right, sometimes right to left. Your magic word probably isn't 'Gadsno' but 'Onsdag.'"

Peter's imagination began conjuring ideas of magic cities and lost civilizations. "What's it mean?"

"Wednesday."

Peter felt as though a big bubble had burst. "Come on. You're pulling my leg."

"'Onsdag' is the word for Wednesday in virtually all the Scandinavian languages."

"So what's that supposed to imply?"

"Sorry, pal. That's your department. I just do the high-tech stuff."

"But—*Wednesday?* That's like finding the buried treasure map and it turns out to be a grocery list—a quart of milk, a loaf of bread, and a dozen eggs."

Moira interrupted again. "Not quite. Literally, Onsdag is short for 'Odin's Day.'"

"So what's the significance of a date that occurs fifty-two times a year? How does that help us?"

Moira wore a triumphant look. "I think that's the key. I don't think this is the Woden's Day that occurs once a week. I think you're probably looking for the one that occurs once a year."

"There's an annual Woden's Day?"

She nodded. "It's one of the old pagan festival days. Woden's Day each year is the Ides of May—May fifteenth. Hold on a second."

She disappeared momentarily, then reappeared with a dark green book and flipped through a blur of pages until she found what she wanted. Then her eyebrows went up.

"That's interesting. Woden's Day this year happens to actually fall on a Wednesday. That only happens every few years, which makes it doubly significant."

"So what's the significance of May fifteenth?" Amos asked. "What do you expect to happen then?"

Moira gave him an ironic look. "Like Rick says, that's not my department, pal. I just do the esoteric stuff."

"My suggestion," Rick said, "is that you take this one step at a time. One clue may lead to another."

"OK," said Sloat. "But Moira, do you have any suggestions about this talk about going to hell?"

Moira frowned. "Nothing substantive, but I keep thinking about Iceland. And maybe I've got Jules Verne on the brain."

"Why Iceland?" Peter asked incredulously.

"Have you ever been there?"

"No," he admitted.

"Then you might be surprised to know that down through history many people have associated Iceland with hell."

"That would indeed surprise me. Why?"

Moira answered with another question. "Pop quiz time. Why is the abode of the damned called 'hell'?"

"I do know that. In honor of its queen, the goddess Hella. Greco-Romans go to hades. Norsemen and other western Europeans go to hell."

"Very good. Now, you may be interested to know that there's a city called Hella in Iceland. It's not far from Mount Hekla—which happens to be a terrifying volcano that convinced people in the Middle Ages that Iceland was the very gate of hell. They didn't understand volcanism. Today Iceland is still a land of hot springs and geysers and occasional volcanic activity."

"Guess I missed that somehow."

"In fact, the Swedes used to have an expletive when somebody made them really angry—'Dra åt Häcklefjäll!'"

"What's that mean?"

"Go to Hekla."

Peter pursed his lips. "I see. So Giselle DuChesne may have been fixing to go to Iceland. And if we want to find the other half of this rune stone message, that's where we may have to go too, right?"

"Perhaps," said Moira. "I do know that Iceland was the last place where runes were still used in writing—as late as the seventeenth century."

Sloat frowned. "Iceland's a big place. Where would we begin?"

Moira shrugged. "Again, sounds like your department—especially if you're into mountaineering."

Peter hoped she was just kidding. Then he noticed a red light winking on the communicator panel, indicating a message at the front desk.

"Could be our package from Sgt. Andersen," Amos said.

"We're supposed to be getting photocopies of Giselle DuChesne's work papers, courtesy of the local constabulary," Peter explained. "We're hoping they'll shed a little more light on the subject."

Rick smiled. "Well, then. Happy hunting. Please call again when you need straightening out."

"'Bye," said Peter.

"Gud blessi thig. 'God bless you' in Icelandic," Moira said, as their images began to fade.

An electric silence descended on the room as the wallscreen went blank, leaving Peter and Carlotta and Amos to pursue the invisible rabbit trails of their own speculations.

"May fifteen," Sloat said solemnly at last. "The first substantive clue."

"Yeah," said Peter. "but what's that tell us? Is something supposed to happen on that day?"

Sloat rubbed his chin thoughtfully. "It's hard to think like our Hofburg thieves, especially when we have no idea who they are. All we know is they're playing a strange game with deliberate clues. I can only assume that if we can get both a time and a place, we may find the Crown and Spear. It's almost as if they *want* us to find them."

"May fifteenth is a couple of weeks away. Does that mean we're on hold until then?"

Sloat shook his head. "That may seem like a lot of time, but it won't be unless we start getting a lot more breakthroughs. I'm just afraid that if we overshoot May fifteenth, we may not get another chance."

"You've already put in a lot of time on this. How patient is your organization?"

"You mean are they going to reel me in?" Sloat smiled wryly and then shook his head. "My people very badly want this world-ruler business shut down. And now with the discovery of the Halima clones, there's even more interest. I'm good for another hundred thousand miles. If I fail in this assignment . . . " He let his voice trail off, then just shrugged as if he didn't want to contemplate the consequences.

Peter turned to Carlotta, who had been silent the whole time. She wore an odd expression, looking almost as if she had been crying or were about to do so. He put a hand gently on her shoulder. "What's the matter, love?" he said, looking her intently in the eye.

She looked at him a long moment as if unable to speak and then blurted, "Frankly, I wish none of us had ever heard of the Crown and Spear."

"It's been stressful," Peter agreed, "especially for you. But I think we're on the verge of our big breakthrough."

She shook her head sadly. "I know you've got to see it through. But I'm finally going to heed your original advice and go home. I just—I just don't like . . . bloodshed."

The last word tumbled out like a rotten apple at the bottom of a barrel. He was not surprised. Carlotta had been acting subdued, if not depressed, since the shooting the night before.

Still, he was torn. It was true that he originally had entreated her to go home before things turned ugly. But now that they had been through some of the ugliness together, he must have changed his mind without realizing it. There had been a progression on his part from mere resignation to her right to make her own decisions, to a genuine respect for her analytical abilities and her sheer bravado—both with and without a firearm.

He knew he should approach this with sensitivity. "Back to Cleveland?"

She nodded.

"Carlotta, if I ever thought you were a burden here with us, I certainly don't think so now. If you really want to leave, that's one thing. But I don't want you leaving under the impression that I don't want you here. Are you sure you want to do this?"

Carlotta nodded again, and Peter noted the deadened look in her eyes. He turned to Sloat. "Is it on to Iceland, Amos?"

Sloat nodded faintly without expression. "What else?"

Peter sat down beside Carlotta and took her hand. "Then will you go to Iceland with us? It's on the way, you know."

She shook her head firmly. "That may be, but it'll be tougher getting a timely flight out of Reykjavík. I can be out of Cøpenhagen in no time. Besides, you may be willing to go to Hekla and back on this assignment, but count me out."

Peter appreciated her attempt to make light. He knew she did it to ease his concerns about her state of mind. A huge, longing ache welled up from the pit of his stomach and lodged somewhere in the back of his throat. He longed to hold her, protect her, love her. Was his heart growing fonder already just by a contemplated absence?

All he knew was that he didn't want to let her go—and that, for her own good, was exactly what he had to do.

* * *

It was dinnertime when Peter and Carlotta returned to the hotel from an afternoon of exploring Cøpenhagen, sightseeing, holding hands, tossing coins in fountains, making wishes, and generally trying to pretend that nothing had changed.

They had even returned to the National Museum, this time as tourists instead of sleuths. Peter was particularly enthralled by the Viking artifacts, including reconstructed longboats, armor, and weaponry. It seemed incredible that these ancient Norsemen actually had plied the high seas in such relatively small craft, reputedly as far as "Vinland"—America—centuries before Columbus.

For a time, it even worked. He, and seemingly Carlotta, all but forgot that they were on the eve of their not-so-sweet sorrow of parting once more. But by the time they were making their return, the temporary amnesia had lifted, and the heaviness of reality began settling back in.

Peter tried to laugh it off with a few teasing remarks, but his heart wasn't in it, and his humor fell flat. He could only hope that their mood would improve over dinner.

But at the hotel Sloat was not in a dining mood. He curtly suggested that if they had to eat, they ought to have room service bring it in. There was work to be done.

"Uh-oh," said Peter, removing his jacket. "Amos is in one of those moods."

Then he noticed that Sloat apparently had spread out all of Giselle DuChesne's work papers on the desk as if he had been going through them. Maybe he had discovered something.

Carlotta occupied herself with the room service menu, contemplating what might be worth eating.

"Have you unraveled all of the mysteries of *Doktor* Giselle?" asked Peter.

Sloat blinked and scanned the papers spread before him as if seeing them for the first time. "Oh. This," he said dimissively. "I can't make any sense of this. As far as I can tell, it's mostly historical and scholarly stuff—and in languages that I can't read. My suggestion is that you upload it all to Rick and Moira and see what they can make of it."

"Well, then, what *is* eating you?" Peter grinned. "Guess you can tell I've got food on my mind."

"Well, you'd better get the Hofburg case on your mind, because I think it's starting to get more complicated."

"How?"

Sloat got up from the desk and began to pace slowly. He stopped by the window, appearing to find something engrossing down below on the *stræde*.

But in a moment he spoke again. "Doesn't it seem odd to you that our kindly *Hilfsgeistlicher, Herr* Werner Liebenfels, would point the finger of accusation at Giselle DuChesne and that *Doktor* Giselle would then be found traveling under her own name—hardly acting like a fugitive from justice? And then it turns out that she was actually on some research sabbatical in connection with a university program?"

"The thought had occurred to me. But go on."

"I have, by the way, taken the liberty of calling your father with this information. He says he's coming back to Europe in a few days, and he's agreed to see if he can document Giselle DuChesne's leave of absence and thereby prove *Herr* Liebenfels to be a liar."

"But why would Liebenfels hire McBride and McBride to solve this crime if he was part of it himself?" Peter objected.

Sloat's eyes twinkled. "Don't flatter yourself. Who said he hired somebody he thought would actually solve the case?"

Peter was speechless. The remark bothered him a bit more than he cared to admit.

"But you're getting ahead of me," Amos said. "I took the opportunity to do a little research of my own this afternoon—some historical, genealogical things. You mentioned the swastika in Rabbi Omar's temple, and that's been preying on my mind. I decided to revisit some sources through the old information superhighway."

He paused dramatically and cleared his throat before plunging into his story.

"Once upon a time, nearly two hundred years ago, there was a journalist in Vienna by the name of von List who renounced Christianity and became a worshiper of Wotan."

"Wotan—like Woden?"

"Exactly. He founded an occult order dedicated to the old German warrior paganism. He gathered some followers, revived the old pagan salutation *Heil,* and created a banner employing the swastika, based on the Nordic hammer of Thor."

"OK," Peter interrupted, "but what's that got to do with the Hofburg case?"

"A lot. Just listen. Von List was a big influence on another fellow who later was a big influence on Adolf Hitler. He was a defrocked monk by the name of Lanz. This man too became a neo-pagan and promoted a philosophy of Aryan racial purity. He also founded a society that dabbled in the occult. Lanz also adopted the swastika as *his* symbol."

Peter's head was beginning to swim. "OK, Amos. So Hitler derived his Nazism from some mystical racism. But—"

"Listen. Here it is. In 1900, Lanz changed his name and birthdate, reputedly to confuse astrologers. He invented a phony lineage and began calling himself Baron Lanz von Liebenfels. Young Adolf Hitler was a known acquaintance of his."

Peter was stunned. "Liebenfels?"

"The same."

"You said you did genealogical research. Is our *Herr* Liebenfels a descendant?"

"It appears so. Again, Neal will attempt to confirm the connection with some personal inquiry."

Now Peter got up and began pacing. This was a disturbing development in several respects.

"It's almost too neat," he said at last. "Even if *Herr* Liebenfels is a descendant of this kooky baron, what does that prove? Isn't that guilt by association?"

"When you put that all together with the other aspects of this case—Giselle DuChesne and so forth—my gut tells me this is more than coincidence."

Peter stared at him for a long moment. "Yeah, Amos. Mine too."

There was a knock at the door, and Carlotta jumped up to answer it. Peter had long forgotten that she had ordered food. He wondered what it would be. Then his stomach answered that it didn't matter.

26

Cøpenhagen

Ordinarily Carlotta would have been upset to be awakened by an insistently bleating phone in the middle of the night. But it so happened that when the call came, she was suffering a pulse-pounding nightmare involving guns, bullets, and blood. At first it was only paper men coming out of the shadows for her to blow away one after the other. And then they started shooting back. It was no longer paper that she was blowing away, but flesh and blood.

Under the circumstances it was a relief to snap awake in her darkened hotel room and reach out for the reassuringly tangible substance of the phone.

"Hello?" she said breathlessly as if she had been running instead of sleeping.

The voice was female, faintly British-inflected, and oddly familiar. "Is this Ms. Carlotta Waldo?"

"Yes."

"I apologize for waking you. This is Scandia Airlines."

"Uh . . . what time is it?"

"It's three fifteen A.M., Ms. Waldo. I'm calling because we have had a cancellation on our earliest London–New York flight, and you have the first standby option for it."

Carlotta tried hurriedly to collect her thoughts. "Well, I . . . uh . . ."

She was packed; that wouldn't be a problem. The problem was Peter. She might not be able to tell him good-bye. Then she realized that wouldn't necessarily be all bad.

The woman continued, "We're sorry for the short notice, but it could be a while before there's another opportunity."

"No, that's fine. What time is this flight?"

"That would be Flight One-Oh-Nine at five ten A.M."

"Oh!" said Carlotta, realizing that the logistics would be daunting. "That's less than two hours. I don't even know that I could get to the airport in time. I know it's some distance."

"That may not be such a problem. There's an airport shuttle that leaves just down the block from your hotel on the hour. We could arrange for it to pick you up out front if you wish."

"That would be four o'clock?"

"Correct."

Carlotta felt the silent pressure for her to come to a decision. It was unlikely that this woman wanted to waste much more time on this phone call, especially if it might not pan out. In her half-asleep, thick-headed way, the only thing that made sense was to go for it.

"OK," said Carlotta. "I'll be out front at four."

"Good," said the woman, sounding pleased. "It'll be a dark green passenger van."

* * *

Actually, forty-five minutes was more than enough time. All she needed was a quick shower, a cup of coffee, and a piece of hotel stationery to write Peter a note. Convinced it was best to skirt the maudlin good-byes, Carlotta padded down the hall to Peter's room and slid the note under his door.

Five minutes later she was out front with her two bags. It was still dark, and the rest of the city seemed to be asleep. The only exceptions were the distant sounds of motor vehicles and the occasional lighted window of another early bird.

In another minute, one of those vehicular noises drew closer and louder. A dark van became visible behind a pair of headlights. It was only when the vehicle stopped at the curb under a streetlight that Carlotta could tell that it was any shade of green. The side door popped open invitingly.

Carlotta glanced at her watch before climbing inside. Right on time.

"Good morning, Ms. Waldo," said a vaguely familiar female voice.

As the door chunked shut behind her, Carlotta slid across the first bench seat, aware of another woman in the seat behind. The woman who had greeted Carlotta gunned the engine and began navigating the streets of Cøpenhagen, presumably in search of a freeway.

"Have some orange juice," said the woman behind Carlotta, passing forward a disposable container.

It sounded appealing, and Carlotta pulled the tab and took a sip. She made a face. It had a strange medicinal taste. She could see the driver's eyes watching her in the rearview mirror.

"Drink it," said the woman behind her.

Carlotta couldn't believe her ears. "I beg your pardon?"

"I said drink the orange juice."

"What *is* this?" said Carlotta, outraged.

The driver laughed. "It's not Scandia Airlines—that's for sure."

"Hold still," said the woman behind her.

"What?" Carlotta half turned to see what she was doing. Her breath caught as she found herself staring into the business end of a pistol. The woman reached over the seat and began patting Carlotta down. Her eyes lit up when she felt the bulge of her shoulder holster and the butt end of her gun.

"I thought so," said the woman. "Don't make a move, sister."

With the deftness of a pickpocket, the woman relieved Carlotta of her pistol.

"What's going on here?" said Carlotta, fighting back tears in her tiredness.

"Be quiet and drink the juice," said the driver.

Carlotta suddenly placed the driver's voice. It was the woman who had called, claiming to be from Scandia Airlines.

"Drink," said the woman behind her.

Maybe it was the gun barrel that snuggled up to the back of Carlotta's head that convinced her of the woman's seriousness. She drank.

"Where are you taking me?" she asked, suppressing a shudder at the noxious taste.

The driver laughed. "How about let's go to the cathedral and do a few laps around the triforium?"

Carlotta felt as though she were beginning to lose it. The remark made no sense. And yet she had the strange feeling that maybe it did, if only she could make an elusive connection. There was a distant buzzing in her ears, and her head was beginning to swim. The orange juice.

"Odd that you don't remember me, Carlotta," the driver said, half turning toward her. "After all we've been through together."

Carlotta had never realized how comfortable the bench seat of a van could be. She felt like melting into the fabric of the upholstery. Maybe if she just closed her eyes . . .

For an instant a passing streetlight illuminated the driver's profile like a lazy strobe. And then Carlotta finally realized who this woman was.

Wendy Carlisle. How nice.

* * *

Peter awoke reasonably early at a few minutes past six. He decided to get up even though his alarm wouldn't go off for another twenty-five minutes. This way he could take his time in the bathroom before Sloat even awoke.

He finished showering and had started to shave when Amos rapped on the bathroom door.

"I think you'd better come out here," he called.

"What's up?" Peter emerged wrapped in a towel.

Sloat nodded at the wallscreen. There looking back at them was the urbane visage of Sir James Crisp. A wry smile tugged at the corners of the white-haired gentleman's mouth upon Peter's appearance.

"My apologies," said Sir James in his polished tones. "Considering the earliness of the hour, you needn't have dressed for the occasion."

Peter retreated a half dozen steps to the bathroom, took his robe off the back of the door, and quickly shrugged into it.

"Excuse me," he said, returning. "I just never know when to expect these calls from MPs. How may we be of assistance, Sir James?"

Sir James' expression was opaque. "I would be most appreciative if you could bring me up to date on your progress toward recovering the *Reichskleinodien*. There have been some . . . developments . . . that may militate in favor of an accelerated timetable."

That sounded ominous. But Peter knew better than to question anything—yet.

"I am happy to report," he began, "that we have had somewhat of a breakthrough. There's been another clue and the promise of more. Unfortunately it was not without some bloodshed—"

"Yes, yes," the older man said somewhat impatiently. "That business at the National Museum. These things happen. I know all about that."

"You do?"

Sir James looked surprised that Peter would doubt it. "Of course. It was I who made certain that Sgt. Andersen's people got those papers to you. I don't want to know details. I just want to know if you hold out favorable prospects for success, how soon, and whether you require any additional assistance that I may be able to lend."

Peter was taken aback. It was certainly encouraging to have friends in high places. "Yes, Sir James, we have a good deal of confidence that success will be ours. As for timing, all I can say is that we may have only a two-week window to wrap this up. After that, I don't know."

Sir James nodded meditatively. His silence suggested that wasn't a totally unreasonable time frame.

"Sir James," said Peter, "can you tell us anything about these urgent developments you mentioned?"

The older man rolled his eyes tiredly. "Everything is coming apart at the seams. Interpol is compromised. Scotland Yard is corrupted. One of its key agents has gone south. There's almost no telling friend from foe anymore. Those are just the things you won't hear in the news."

"Where we're going," said Sloat, "we might not hear a lot of news."

"There's more?" asked Peter.

"Much," said Sir James. "I'm afraid some of this can only lead to armed conflict. Neumann and DiFalcone, don't you know? Have you heard of this P3 business?"

"Just rumors."

"Well, Neumann and Bardo are making moves, mostly against DiFalcone, and accelerating their population control measures—behavior modification, public health decrees, procreation permits. Both sides are taking hits.

"Intelligence indicates that if things escalate, we could see dock strikes, public-employee job actions, financial terrorism with electronic megafund transfers and counterfeit currencies, and so forth. That's on DiFalcone's side.

"Meanwhile the chancellor is threatening to round up all DiFalcone operatives, seal borders, suspend civil rights, and go to a genetic identification marking system for everybody."

"I'm glad all we have to worry about is finding a crown and a spear," Amos said.

"You had *better* find them—and fast!" Sir James's eyes flashed.

"Uh . . . what's the connection?" asked Peter.

"Why, the Crown and Spear are the big destabilizer. It's like the old nuclear arms race. Each side is worried that the other is going to get them. And if one of them actually does acquire the regalia, I hate to contemplate the monster that would create. These characters think it gives them title deed to the planet. And I haven't even mentioned the spiritual pretenders to the throne."

"The Imam of Babylon, Cardinal Ponzi and the New Order of Rome—" Peter said.

"And don't forget Father Zell."

"Who's he?"

Sir James looked mildly surprised. "Adrian Zell. You haven't heard of him? You ought to check him out. He was a bishop and Emmanuel Ponzi's former number two man in the original break with Rome. That only lasted a year or two until Ponzi and Zell themselves had a falling out over the usual sort of things."

"What sort of things?"

"Doctrine, power, who gets to use the private jet on weekends. Ponzi was into superecumenism, but Zell renounced Christianity entirely in favor of a brand of ancient paganism or some such rot. Nobody seems to know quite what became of Father Zell."

Peter shot a wondering glance at the Israeli, who wore his usual poker face. But he would have been willing to bet that Sloat was thinking what Peter was—how much this smacked of *Herr* Liebenfels all over again. Peter decided to take a small risk with this member of Parliament whom he had come to thoroughly trust. "We'll start a check on Zell at the earliest opportunity," he said. "But getting back to your earlier offer of assistance—"

"Yes, Mr. McBride. I am at your disposal."

"The greatest threat to the mission at this point is internal. I haven't even told the other half of McBride and McBride this yet, but we now have some information that may tend to incriminate our own employer on this case."

Sir James's eyebrows arched. "Are you concerned about your financial remuneration then?"

Peter shook his head. "It's not so much that. The insurer is our real paymaster. But what if *Herr* Liebenfels terminates our employment? Our next adventure involves a recovery expedition in Iceland, which will incur some considerable expense. Attempting it out of pocket could be a problem."

"Hmm. I understand. Well. Two things. One, under no circumstances should you let *Herr* Liebenfels know that you suspect him in any way. Two, if you are flying into Reykjavík, look up an Einar Njálsson at the Geophysical Institute. Use my name. He's a mountain guide and outfitter. My credit is good with him, if need be. Einar's worth using either way. He may be a little on the superstitious side, but he's also a geologist, which could come in handy."

Peter asked Sir James to spell the name while he wrote it down on a note card.

"Thank you, sir," he said when he was finished. "We'll look him up."

"When are you leaving?"

Sloat answered, "Very soon. We're assured seats on one of two flights this evening."

"And what about the young lady? Carlotta, I believe."

"She won't be going with us," said Peter. "She's going back to the USP as soon as she can get a flight today or tomorrow."

Peter noticed Amos giving him an odd look.

"Very well, gentlemen," said Sir James. "That is all. Go with God."

With that, his image evaporated like a genie reassuming the incorporeal.

Sloat still wore the odd look. He held a folded paper in his hand.

"What's that you have there, Amos?"

Wordlessly, Sloat handed the note to him. Peter unfolded it.

> Dear Peter,
>
> I'm sorry I didn't get to say good-bye, but I got a very early standby call from the airline. By the time you read this, I'll probably be a thousand miles away. It's probably better this way. If we had time to do this properly, I'm sure we'd only cry, and I'm tired of crying. Be very careful. If you get yourself killed, I'll never forgive you. Come home soon. *Gud blessi thig.*
>
> Your Carlotta

The rest of the room seemed to dissolve away. Peter was standing on a beach with his bare feet in the wet sand, the wind in his hair, the sun on his back, and her hand in his. It was one of those timeless moments that haunt lovers with what may never be recaptured. Within that moment he could almost smell the mingled Riviera fragrances of mimosa and sidewalk cafes and salt sea and hear the lisping waves again like the flood of memories sometimes unleashed by an old tune.

And then it was gone, as completely as a disconnecting image on the wallscreen. The ache was back, sharper this time. If he could have just seen her one last time, embraced her, made sure she knew how he felt—made sure he knew how she felt. But would he have been able to let her go? And then he realized that maybe Carlotta was right. Maybe it was better this way.

He told Amos about her departure.

"You OK?" asked Sloat, looking both concerned and awkward.

"Sure," said Peter. "What'd you think? I'd jump off a bridge?"

"No, but—"

"As much as I'll miss Carlotta, I still think she's better off going back home. Especially since that nasty scene at the National Museum."

Sloat looked skeptical. "*She* might be better off, but what about you?"

"I'm OK," Peter insisted with an assurance he knew was exaggerated.

While they packed and paced and periodically called the airport, Peter took the opportunity to ask Sloat a question that was on his mind and close to his heart.

"Amos, were you ever in love?"

Sloat ceased making checkmarks on a list of paraphernalia he had been assembling and got a distant look in his eyes. "Oh, yes," he said slowly, "a long time ago. Her name was Sarah."

Just as slowly, he dug out his wallet and fished inside. Then he handed Peter a yellowed newspaper clipping, folded in quarters.

It was a few paragraphs about a terrorist attack a dozen years ago in a crowded Tel Aviv market that left two maimed and one dead. The fatality was a Sarah Kleinman, twenty-four, a social worker.

"We were engaged," he said with a coolness in his voice that came from somewhere deep inside.

Suddenly Peter was awash in multiple emotions—vicarious grief for Amos beside his own blues. At least Carlotta was alive and well. He also felt as if he had just been given a window into his companion's soul.

"I'm very sorry, Amos. I didn't know, of course."

Sloat shrugged as if it were no matter.

Peter decided to press a bit further. "So is this revenge?"

"This what?" He looked puzzled.

"Your career of pursuing terrorists and other enemies of Israel. Is it for Sarah, Yaakov?"

"So," said Sloat with an ironic expression, "you know my real name. And you also know my heart, you think. But no, it's not for Sarah. It's for myself as I'm forced to live out this meaningless existence without her."

"Have you . . . ever considered forgiving her murderers?"

Sloat's eyes sparked. But when he spoke, it was in a low, carefully controlled voice. "No. And you'd better hope I don't—for the success of this mission."

"You mean if you ever gave up the hate, you might lose your motivation?"

"Something like that."

"Then why don't you do it for the love of your country, rather than for hatred of her enemies?"

"That's just not real. No man can forgive or love like that."

"Not the natural man."

"Oh, boy," said Sloat ruefully. "I walked right into that one."

Peter smiled. "How shall I exploit the opportunity? Let's try this one: There once was a man from Galilee. He stretched out His arms on a cross—" Peter demonstrated "—and loved this much."

"Yes," said Sloat with an edge of bitterness, "crucified by Jews."

"The Romans crucified Him," Peter corrected. "But He rose again. He's alive."

"Yeah, that's what Benny said."

"Who?"

The phone rang. Sloat grabbed it and said only a few words before hanging up.

"OK, boys and girls. Saddle up. We're flying to Iceland in two hours."

27

Rome

Carlotta awakened once briefly, wondering why Scandia Airlines flew such small planes. It appeared to be no more than a six-seater. But before she could process the information, somebody was sticking something in her arm. It stung.

A glimpse of the face reminded her of the woman who had sat behind her in the van. And then she was out again.

Now she found herself awaking, lying on her back in a darkened room, with flickering vision. Carlotta realized she was in a bed. She moved her arms and found they were under a sheet and spread. In one motion she threw the covers back and rolled out.

The moment her feet hit the floor, however, she realized that was a mistake. Her legs were insubstantial, and her knees would not support the rest of her. Feeling foolish, she prevented herself from hitting the floor only by grabbing the bed on the way down. There she clung for a moment while she caught her breath.

She felt headachy. There was a metallic taste in her mouth, and her pulse was racing as if something involving her adrenal glands had been set biochemically out of kilter.

Slowly, when the racing moderated, Carlotta worked herself back onto her feet and sat weakly on the edge of the bed. Her eyes seemed to have adjusted in the half-light. She now realized that the flickering was not her own vision but came from the light of a candle on a mantel on the opposite wall. Above it was a large crucifix bearing a battered Christ, sagging in death's embrace, His head hanging down in abject defeat.

Carlotta found herself unable to look away, yet repulsed at the same time. This was not for her the symbol of victory over sin and death that she associated with the cross. This was something dark and malevolent, almost diabolical.

She knew she was not where she was supposed to be, but maddeningly she could not recall where that was. Something had been done to her mind, and in her ignorance it was frighteningly difficult to know what might be real and what might not. For even now the image of the Lamented One was changing before her very eyes, that grimly marred visage swelling as if viewed through a zoom lens.

And then the eyes were open—and upon her.

"My daughter," said the Lamented One in a sepulchral voice of infinite sadness, "do you love me?"

"Y-yes," said Carlotta, the word nearly sticking in her throat.

How could this be?

"Then you must obey Father," replied the Christ.

"'Father'?" she repeated uncertainly. "Who do you mean?"

"Father Zell," was the solemn reply. "Obey him, my daughter."

It was too much to absorb. Carlotta felt like a punch-drunk fighter in the latter rounds of a title bout.

"All right," she murmured as she fell back onto the bed and found the pillow with her head. "Whatever you say."

She let herself go, turning her face partly into the pillow and inwardly collapsing without bothering to pull up the covers. And then she was gone, back into the soft womb of sleep.

★ ★ ★

Reykjavík

Peter looked out his hotel room window and thought that this was going to take some getting used to. It was after ten in the evening, and it was almost like high noon outside. Like Alaska at this time of year, Iceland was a land of the midnight sun.

It seemed he ought to be washing up for dinner about now, although he and Sloat had already eaten on the plane from Cøpenhagen, and he was not hungry. Having unpacked and arranged his clothes and toiletries to his liking, he resisted the impulse to turn on the TV and decided to go check on Sloat. He punched his room number on the phone and asked if he could come over.

"It's about time," Sloat said.

Peter noticed immediately upon entering Sloat's room that a text with foreign characters was displayed on the wallscreen, and they were not runes. Peter recognized it as Hebrew, but its meaning was closed to him. He decided to hold his tongue and see if Sloat offered any explanation.

"Is mountain climbing in your repertoire, Amos—if we have to do any?"

"I've done a little here and there," said Sloat. "How about you?"

"About the same—enough to wonder if we shouldn't be starting a training program."

Sloat shook his head. "We don't really know that what we're looking for is going to be found on Mount Hekla—or on any other mountain for that matter. We don't know where Giselle DuChesne found the first object, although it probably wasn't on a mountain."

"We have a pretty good idea it was at a site at Uppsala."

Sloat idly picked up his homemade scanner from the coffee table and switched it on. Instead of the familiar piercing homing signal, the device emitted only a low, flat hum. Obviously they were nowhere in range of their rune stone—assuming it was even here and had a homing device.

"If it's any help," Peter added, "I've done a fair amount of rappelling. But that's descending—and a far cry from ice climbing."

"You probably have all the skills you'll need. I understand that Iceland's reputation for ice is somewhat overrated. And Mount Hekla is not exactly the Matterhorn. It's only about five thousand feet."

Peter was surprised to hear that. "Less than a mile?"

"I just read some tourist information. Its fearsome reputation owes itself entirely to volcanism. And it's dormant now, I presume."

Peter gestured to the wallscreen. "What's that, Amos?"

"Oh, that," Sloat said almost evasively. "You don't recognize that?"

"Uh . . . no. As far as I know, it could be a refrigerator warranty."

Sloat called out to the wallscreen, "English program!"

Peter recognized the words instantly—"My God, my God, why hast Thou forsaken me? Far from my deliverance are the words of my groaning."

"Psalm twenty-two."

Sloat nodded.

When it became apparent that he wasn't about to volunteer further information, Peter prodded him. "What's the deal here, Amos? Why are you all of a sudden reading the Bible?"

Sloat wasn't budging. "It's a good book. Why not?"

"Does this have something to do with that 'Benny' you mentioned?"

"You might say," he conceded. "Benny was a so-called messianic Jew who accosted me on the street and tried to get me to accept Y'shua, as he likes to say, as Messiah."

"And did you?"

Sloat shook his head. "He showed me a number of quite persuasive things, but it was all too pat. I thought I needed to test the things he said to see if I was missing something."

"So what about Psalm twenty-two?"

"The guy sort of tricked me. I thought he was having me read something from the New Testament about the crucifixion—the mocking, the victim's bones out of joint, thirsting, His hands and feet pierced . . . I knew enough about Christianity to identify that as Christ. Then he showed me it was Psalm twenty-two and that David wrote it a thousand years before Y'shua. Talk about feeling a little stupid."

"So what was your conclusion?"

Sloat shrugged in bewilderment. "He was right, of course. I referenced some Jewish histories and confirmed the time frame. I agree it's striking—too striking, probably, for a coincidence. But there's something else that bothers me."

"What's that?"

"Why the mystery about Messiah's identity? If all the other aspects of His birth, death, and resurrection were prophesied in detail, why the conspicuous absence of His name?"

Peter shook his head. "No mystery. It's there. All through the Old Testament."

"Oh yeah? Like where?"

"Lots of places. Isaiah's a good place. Can you get your database to display chapter twelve? And, I think, sixty-two?"

Sloat so instructed the computer, including parallel columns in English and Hebrew.

Peter read Isaiah 12:2. "Behold, God is my salvation, I will trust, and not be afraid; for the Lord God is my strength and song, and He has become my salvation."

"OK, Amos," he said. "Check me out. I can't read Hebrew, but I submit to you that the righthand column literally says, 'God is my Y'shua,' and, 'He has become my salvation.' Am I right?"

Sloat stood there for a half-dozen heartbeats, his brow furrowed and his eyes focused on the wallscreen like laser beams.

"Yes," he said with some reticence. "I will concede that 'Y'shua' means 'salvation.' But it's a bit of a stretch to turn that into a person, don't you think?"

"OK, then, try the next one."

Peter directed him to cue up Isaiah 62:11: "Behold, the Lord hath proclaimed unto the end of the world, Say ye unto the daughter of Zion, Behold, thy salvation cometh; behold, his reward is with him, and his work before him."

"Literally," said Peter, "that reads, 'Behold, your Y'shua comes.' Right? And would you agree that this is a *person* whose reward and work are with him?"

"Oh," Sloat said deflatedly, "you're as bad as Benny."

"In fact, in the last book of the Bible, Revelation 22, those are among Christ's final words to His followers when He promises to return: 'My reward is with me.' So we know beyond doubt *who* this person is. Both testaments tell us."

Sloat fell silent for a long moment.

Peter finally suggested, "I think I know what's holding you back."

"Oh, you do? What?"

"Your will. Part of you—your mind and your emotions—were responding to what the man said. Yet you still feel you need to reason it out some more. I don't think you need more information, Amos. You need an act of the will—to make a commitment—to act on what you already know."

"But how do you believe when you're not sure?"

"In a sense, the willingness to trust comes first and then faith. Would you like to pray?"

Sloat's eyes grew wide, and his voice climbed the scale. "Pray? I'm definitely not ready to pray."

"OK. Are you afraid you'll stop being a Jew?"

Sloat shook his head. "No, it's not that. Benny was pretty convincing that he's just as Jewish as I am, except that he believes his Messiah has come. I'm just not quite ready for that."

"Well, then," asked Peter gently, "could we just ask God to confirm somehow if that's what you should do?"

Sloat looked for a moment as though he were going to resist, then finally nodded. "I guess I can handle that."

★ ★ ★

The next morning brought them to Reykjavík's Geophysical Institute, where they had left a phone message for Einar Njálsson that was careful to mention Sir James Crisp.

Njálsson met Peter and Amos in a sunny lobby with floor-to-ceiling windows and indicated they should follow him through a door and down a long corridor to an attached building. He was a big, strapping, saturnine man with unruly shocks of strawlike hair and a burly, flaxen beard. He looked as if he should have a big blue ox for a pet. Peter guessed Njálsson was pushing seven feet tall.

In his red-and-black plaid flannel workshirt, jeans, and hiking boots, he looked out of place in his office among other workers —scientists mostly—in shirts and ties or expensive-looking handmade wool sweaters and dress pants.

He noticed something else too. Nearly everybody he had encountered since yesterday—at the hotel, on the street, and now at the Institute—made him feel like a pygmy. At just over six feet, Peter was used to looking his peers straight in the eye. Most of these men, however, had eye-level clavicles. Only the women seemed the right height for good eye contact.

The attached building was a large two-story, barnlike utility area with unfinished walls and scores of racks and shelves for equipment storage. There were picks and shovels in more sizes and shapes that Peter had imagined possible, backpacks and other canvas and nylon items hanging from hooks, and dozens of other implements he could not easily identify. Farther down the concourse a lone figure was negotiating a large wooden crate into place atop several others with a forklift.

Njálsson escorted them to a battered desk covered with hand tools and odds and ends of hardware. Peter and Amos seated themselves in folding chairs facing the desk where the big Icelander sat down and gazed impassively at them with cool blue eyes beneath a craggy brow.

"And so," he began in a rumbling voice and a lilting Scandinavian accent, "why did Sir James think I could be of help to you? Are you planning an adventure of some kind?"

His inflection on "adventure" suggested to Peter that he might be taking some secret amusement at their expense. Then again, it might be his imagination. Peter glanced at Sloat, who was watching Njálsson with narrowed eyes and a stony expression.

"We've had enough adventure," Peter began. "We're looking for a particular . . . stone."

"Ah!" said Njálsson. "You have come to the right place. Stones we have plenty of. One is all you want?"

Peter found himself beginning to redden. He was about to ask the man if he knew of any outfitter/guides with all their marbles when the forklift squeaked to a halt beside them and its driver stepped off.

"Godan dag," said a smiling young woman with a turned-around baseball cap, who towered over them.

Peter and Sloat hopped to their feet, and Peter noticed that the woman still dwarfed them by half a head. She wore immaculate gray overalls and a blue workshirt, and her blonde hair hung halfway down her back in a ponytail.

"'Tag," said Peter, realizing too late that she wasn't really speaking German.

"Vígdis Njálsdóttir," she said, extending her hand first to Peter, then to Amos. It was soft but had a surprisingly powerful grip.

"Beg your pardon," said Peter. "Sorry, I don't speak Icelandic."

The woman let slip a giggle. "That happens to be my name."

Peter felt himself redden the rest of the way. He apologized and introduced himself and Sloat.

"Welcome," said the woman. "I am the one you spoke to on the phone—Einar's public relations protection. I try to undo the trouble that Einar causes with his insolent tongue."

"I hadn't noticed," said Peter.

"She is my sister," said Njálsson. "My older sister. Much older."

"Don't listen to him," said the woman with a weary smile. "He is six years older."

Peter was puzzled. "What did you say your last name was?"

"Njálsdóttir. Oh, you may not know, but yes, it is the same as my brother's. We do not have the same system of surnames that you have. It is a little like 'Nielson,' except that Einar is Neil's son, and I am Neil's daughter."

"Does the name carry down through the generations?" asked Peter.

The woman shook her head. "*Nei.* I keep my name after marriage, but my son, Olaf, is Olaf Thorvaldsson, after my husband, Thorvald. And my daughter, Gudrid, is Gudrid Thorvaldsdóttir."

Peter nodded. "I see. Then I must be your honorary American cousin."

"Oh?" said the woman with polite surprise. "How is that?"

"As an Icelander I could be Peter Njálsson. My father—my adoptive father—is Neal McBride, which would make me 'Neal's son,' right?"

"I think you have it," Vígdis said, giggling again. "Except you would have to start growing again to pass as an Icelander, let alone a Njálsson."

Peter chuckled, warming to this woman. "I'm afraid it's too late for that. What is the . . . uh . . . story behind the stilt-legs around here? Something in the water?"

She shrugged. "It is a fact. Why, I do not know. But Icelanders are the world's largest people. Men average just over six feet tall and women just under six feet. Some say it's environmental —fish oil in the diet. Others—"

"Giants—Vikings and Valkyries," Njálsson rumbled, startling Peter.

"I beg your pardon?"

"It is hereditary," said Njálsson. "It is said we are descendants of Vikings and the Valkyries."

"The daughters of Odin," said Sloat, speaking up for the first time. "Maidens who rode on horseback through the sky in armor, conducting warriors killed in battle to Valhalla, the hall of the slain, to feast and fight forevermore."

Njálsson's stony face looked almost impressed. "Well spoken, for an outlander. But enough of this. What is your destination? Surely you do not wish to be conducted to Valhalla. That is for dead men."

Sloat fished inside his own flannel shirt and pulled out the rune stone on its tether. "We're looking for the other part of this."

Njálsson's eyes fastened upon the dark stone, and his hand reached out for it. For a long moment his fingers felt it, rubbed it, turned it over and around, while his icy blue eyes roamed the surface.

"Apalhraun," he murmured under his breath, then looked up. "Volcanic rock. What does this runic inscription mean?"

"Wednesday," said Sloat.

Njálsson looked as if Sloat had just tried to sell him Greenland.

"And where do you propose looking for the other half?" he demanded. "All of Iceland is volcanic."

Peter spoke up. "We have reason to believe that it could be in the vicinity of Mount Hekla."

"Vicinity?" said Njálsson incredulously. "The vicinity of a mountain can take in a rather large area."

"If we knew exactly where to go, we wouldn't be here," Peter said with an edge.

Njálsson's eyes narrowed into an expression that Peter did not know how to read.

"What is so important about a piece of rock?" the man asked in a voice that gave more of a clue. It sounded like suspicion.

"All I can tell you," Peter said carefully, "is that we are trying to solve a crime and recover some stolen items. I'm afraid I can say no more—especially if you aren't able to help us."

Peter flipped open his wallet to his professional ID.

The Icelander gave it a glance but was not visibly moved. "I am sorry," he said with a condescending smile. "There are two problems, both of them insurmountable. First, this is like looking for a—what's the American expression?"

"Needle in a haystack."

"Yes—"

"That's where we hope you're wrong," said Sloat. "We have reason to believe that our object may have a homing device attached to it. In fact, that's how I found the first piece."

Njálsson shut his mouth while he thought about that.

"What's the other insurmountable problem?" Peter asked.

"Eldfell!" declared the Icelander, thumping his fist on the desk for emphasis. Several metal bushings lying upon it did a little dance.

"Fire mountain," Vígdis translated. "This may not be a good time to talk to Einar about volcanoes."

Njálsson looked positively emotive. "Only fools, Americans, and the *afturganga* are unafraid of the *eldfell!*"

"Who are the *afturganga?*" Peter asked.

Vígdis rolled her eyes. "In English you would call it a zombie. In this case, it is a dead man who has the power to take a person to hell, just as the Valkyries took the warriors to Valhalla."

"We heard about the old superstition that Hekla is the gate of hell," said Peter. "You don't really believe that, do you?"

Njálsson opened his mouth to say something, but Peter noticed Vígdis flashing him some cryptic gesture, and he held his tongue.

"Of course not," she said. "But this is a bad period of seismic activity in the region."

"Just how soon do you intend to go stomping around Hekla?" demanded Njálsson. "Can you come back in about six months?"

Peter was just as adamant. "Out of the question, I'm afraid. We have only days to accomplish this—not weeks and certainly not months."

"Then I am truly sorry," said the giant Icelander, rising to his feet. "But it is impossible. We are overdue for the earthquake of the century. When that happens, I do not want to be anywhere near Hekla—and neither do you."

Peter glanced at Vígdis, who looked vexed. Somehow he did not believe the pique was directed at himself or Sloat. It had more the feel of longstanding sibling conflict. He and Amos stood and prepared to take their awkward leave.

"Come on, Peter," Sloat said. "I think we can do better on our own."

"Yeah," he said. "But Sir James is not going to like this."

Vígdis followed them to the door. When they shook hands in farewell, she surprised him with a conspiratorial wink. Now that would give him something to think about.

28

Rome

When she next awoke, Carlotta was ravenous. She was also a bit more clear-headed. She glanced at the mantel. The candles still burned below and to either side of the crucifix, where the dead Christ still hung in defeat.

She rolled out of bed, and this time her legs supported her weight. She crept toward the mantel and then received a start. Upon closer inspection, the cruciform image in the flickering light appeared to lose its three-dimensionality. It was as if she had hallucinated an object from the canvas of a painting.

But—her mind must be playing tricks on her—hadn't it spoken to her? In fact, she seemed to recall something about a Father Zell and her need to obey him.

Carlotta surveyed the room and then sought out the curtained wall. She found the traverse cord and gave it a pull. There was no give. She inspected the intersection of the two large brown drapes and saw why. Someone had sewn the two halves together.

She swept back the fabric and stuck her head around the drapery. A large double window gave a view of a brick wall a dozen feet away. Unfortunately even this modest view was obscured by steel mesh.

Without quite realizing it, Carlotta was entering stage one in her grief over her loss of freedom—rage. She flipped the curtain down and stomped across the room to the door, grabbed the knob, twisted. As expected, it too was inviolably secured. She turned and pulled and pounded anyway.

At last she gave up and began pacing in silent fury. Why was she here? Who had done this to her? What was this place? How long would they leave her here? Would they allow her to starve? How many days or weeks might that take?

Half-baked plans began racing through her mind. She tried to remember some of those incredible stories she had read as a girl about escape artists who blasted their way out of jail cells with compounds made from the color dyes in an ordinary deck of playing cards and other bizarre scenarios. Was there any way to remove that mesh from the window that its creators may have overlooked?

She checked again, but it looked sufficiently well designed to repel a charging rhino. Yet it only intensified her belief that there must be a way out of this chamber, if only she could figure it out.

And so Carlotta was prevented from realizing that she had entered the grief stage by virtue now of entering upon stage two—denial.

She realized there was at least one thing she could do. She grasped the curtain by its bottom seam and began rolling it up like a bedroll. On the second try, she managed to toss the fabric the last foot and a half and made it stay over the traverse rod. Now, at least, the room was flooded with light.

She took serious inventory. There was a single bed, a straight-back chair, a barred window, a locked door, a tiny half bath, and the weird mantel. She did a double take. There were no longer any candles. There was no crucifix. In their place was a boxy wall-screen, possibly a rear-projection hologram imagizer. So she might have been drugged but not crazy when she had thought the Christ image was speaking to her.

But had the image been washed out by the sunlight or simply turned off? Carlotta looked more closely. An image was there, that of a face, arguably female.

"Close the curtain," came a familiar female voice from the screen.

Without questioning the command, Carlotta pulled on the traverse cord a couple of times, causing the curtain to topple back into place, darkening the room once more.

The face on the wallscreen grew more distinct by the moment.

"Open the bottom panel of the door."

"What?" said Carlotta, confused.

"Open the bottom panel of the door."

She moved to the door and stooped to inspect. It was hard to see in the half light, but her fingers found a knob and pulled. Flush against the outside of the door was a tray, visible in the brighter light outside. Food smells filtered into the room. She reached out and slid the tray toward her.

"It's so dark in here," Carlotta said half to herself as she stood up with the tray.

"Is this better?" asked the voice.

A recessed light in the ceiling came on.

Carlotta set the tray on the bed and found a covered bowl of chicken noodle soup and some kind of brown-bread sandwich. Instantly she began attacking the soup with a plastic spoon and tearing off bites of sandwich. It was half gone before the flavor registered—tuna salad.

When she next looked up, Carlotta saw that the wallscreen image had come into sharp focus. The face was vaguely familiar in that maddening way that verges on recognition. Carlotta's feeding frenzy slowed as her hunger began to be sated. Sensations of new strength and vitality were radiating out from the depths that she had been filling.

And then she remembered Wendy Carlisle. She knew she had not dreamed it. Wendy Carlisle was the one who had kidnaped her, the one who was responsible for her being in this place. Then who was this woman on the wallscreen, and why did she associate her with Wendy Carlisle?

Carlotta took the last spoonful of soup and thought about that, watching the image on the screen out of the corner of her eye. And then it came to her. The orange-juice woman. The one sitting behind her in the van. The voice echoed in her memory, matching this one now speaking.

Then came the awful thought, the suspicion about what she may have just done to herself again by ingesting this food. That would explain the lingering telltale metallic aftertaste.

"Who are you?" Carlotta demanded as she pushed the bowl away. "And what do you want with me?"

The woman on the screen smiled in a professional way. "I am Estelle Morgenthau. I am your keeper for a while."

Carlotta's mind raced. She recalled what Peter had said about Emmanuel Ponzi and the New Order of Rome. And yes, this woman did bear a resemblance to Elizabeth Morningstar. She could see that with a little creative visual editing. It was not a face she would easily forget even after ten years of aging and possible cosmetic surgery.

"However," the woman continued, "it is not for me to say what is to be done with you. That is up to Zell. He will decide."

"Who is Zell?" Carlotta queried. "What does *he* want with me?"

"That is for him to say, in time. Perhaps tomorrow. For now, you should rest."

"Rest?" Carlotta asked, as if presented with an alien concept.

Yes, she did know what that meant. It just took a moment to compute. Numbly, she recognized that fading sensation that she associated with the drugging. And the ringing in her ears. Next time, she resolved, she would refuse the food. She would be strong.

Now she just wanted this woman, this Estelle/Elizabeth, to know that she would not go down without a fight. A symbol of defiance—that's what she needed before she was chemically overcome. But already her associative abilities were slipping away and soon would be gone entirely.

"Why don't you stretch out and rest?" the woman suggested.

Even as she realized that the psychotropic drug was magnifying her suggestibility, Carlotta found the urge to recline on the bed irresistible. Yet there was still an ounce of resistance left.

"Estelle?" she managed to say as her head sank into the pillow.

"Yes?"

"Give this Zell a message for me, please."

"A message?"

"Yes," said Carlotta, struggling to put it together. "Tell Mr. Zell to go jump in a kite."

There. Now she could rest a minute. Or two.

* * *

Reykjavík

"What is that?" asked Sloat.

They powerbladed to a stop where the street terminated at a harbor crowded with fishing boats of all sizes and descriptions.

He was pointing across the water to a shimmering vision of snow-capped triple peaks on the horizon. It was one of those frequent clear days in this pollution-free capital, and visibility was distinct as far as the eye could see.

"Let's see," said Peter, extracting a tourist's guide from an inner pocket and thumbing around until he found the right place. "Here it is. Faxaflói Bay. And sixty miles away on the other side, if you can believe it, is a glacier called Snæffellsjökull on the Snæfellsnes Peninsula. It says the ice cap covers an extinct volcano—the one that Jules Verne's heroes descended to reach the netherworld."

"Like with demons and the *afturganga?*"

"I don't think Verne's Professor Von Hardwigg actually reached hell."

"Speaking of which," said Sloat, looking at his watch, "it's about time to get back to the hotel for our appointment."

Einar Njálsson had called and asked to meet them at the Hotel Leif Eiríksson. There could be little mystery as to the reason.

As predicted, Sir James had not been pleased to learn of Einar's intransigence. He must have called the big Icelander to tell him so.

Sloat had wanted to have nothing further to do with this Njálsson character, but Sir James insisted that they at least get outfitted by him, whether he accompanied them on the trek or not. Any other way would be exorbitantly expensive and possibly inadequate.

With a last glance across the bay at the majestic snow-capped peaks, Peter and Amos began powerblading back down the black-topped pedestrian path to the main street, which would take them back to the hotel.

"Metropolis" may have been stretching a point in the case of Reykjavík. Even an hour's powerblading covered a surprising amount of territory in this city of the "smoky bay," so-called because of the prevalence of steamy geothermal springs.

Peter was mildly surprised and even a little charmed to find this to be a capital city with few skyscrapers, no major traffic jams, and no discernible urban blight. It reminded him of an overgrown Scandinavian fishing village. Yet half the people of Iceland lived here.

By the time they found their way back to the hotel, it was a few minutes to the other side of the hour and a half that Njálsson had given them to expect him. Out front and just down the block were parked two rugged-looking Swedish four-wheel-drive Udas. Peter had little trouble imagining where those had come from.

He and Sloat removed their blades and climbed the steps to the hotel entrance. Inside, the brother and sister Icelanders rose from the seats where they had been waiting.

"It is about time," said Njálsson, conspicuously checking his watch.

Vígdis, on the other hand, gave them a warm smile that half engulfed her eyes.

"Sorry," said Peter. "We were just taking in the beauty of your charming city."

Njálsson seemed unmoved. "Where are your rooms?"

"Two-eighteen and two-twenty . . ."

"We will help you bring your things down, of course," said the big Icelander. "You are ready to leave, are you not?"

"Leave?" said Sloat incredulously.

"Do you not want to go to Hekla?"

"Yes," said Peter, "but right now? This minute?"

Njálsson frowned darkly. "Our mutual friend, Sir James, is already displeased with me. Do you want to share that displeasure?"

"But the seismic activity and—" Peter sputtered.

The Icelander nodded his head vigorously. "That is exactly why we must waste no time. If we are to do this, we must be quick about it."

⋆ ⋆ ⋆

Hella

It didn't take long for civilization to recede like vapor from a thermal pool. Peter found the hydrogen-powered Uda easy enough to handle, but Njálsson was cutting him no slack. Peter wasn't sure if he should be worrying about highway patrolmen. He wasn't even sure about the speed limit, but whatever it was, Njálsson had to be breaking it.

The Icelander obviously had traveled this highway enough times to know just how fast he could take its curves and bends. More than once, Peter, not so advantaged, fell behind on such stretches and had to make up time on the straightaway. But he learned quickly to pay particular attention to those places where Njálsson slowed. There was always a compelling reason, generally an unrepaired, axle-busting section of pavement that threatened to shake the teeth out of their heads even at Njálsson's slower pace.

Sloat looked bored. He sat staring out the passenger window at the passing scenery or lack thereof.

It was a rolling, windswept, rugged terrain with many giant rock formations and few trees. There were occasional farms with tidy barns, herds of sheep, and picturesque A-frame sodhouses, which appeared to be an organic part of the landscape. They passed several quiet hamlets where there was little sign of commerce other than an occasional hardware store, post office, or grocery. The only signs of life were a few older folk on horseback and some youths playing soccer. The country was surprisingly green.

Peter and Amos's Uda had a public band radio, but conversation with the other vehicle had lapsed since the start of the trek. Peter stifled impulses to ask Njálsson questions such as how he knew Sir James or exactly where they were going. None of those things would be fit for public consumption over the airwaves. There would be time enough when they got to their destination.

They had been on the road not quite two hours when Peter began seeing signs for Hella. If possible, the landscape was becoming even more rugged and forbidding. He wondered if it was his imagination.

"Warning," said Sloat, reading an imaginary sign. "Troll Crossing."

"Don't joke about that in front of Einar," said Peter. "I think he believes in that stuff."

"Probably. I wonder how two such different people ended up being brother and sister."

Sloat's statement, spoken wistfully, was just enough out of character to make Peter wonder. "What do you mean?"

"Oh, nothing. Just that Einar is so cold and morose. And Vígdis is so—"

"Warm and wonderful?" Peter supplied.

He sensed Amos stiffen and realized that he may have unartfully touched a nerve. He figured the only way out of it now was to proceed in the same lighthearted vein.

"She's too tall for you, Amos. I can't picture you with a woman you have to look up to." Then an idea struck him. "Amos, how tall was Sarah?"

"She played college basketball," said Sloat in a tone that did not invite further discussion.

"But at least Sarah didn't have a couple of kids," Peter continued. "We're probably talking married woman here, Amos."

Sloat shook his head. "Widow."

Peter was awestruck. "How'd you know that?"

"I'm in the information business, remember?"

They were traversing a particularly green and grassy area, punctuated by expanses of the peculiar black sand and gravel Peter was learning to associate with the creek beds in this region. Off to the north, the horizon had taken on a dark, hump-backed appearance that he realized must be a mountain of some significance. Was this his first glimpse of the notorious Hekla?

Before he could pursue the question, Peter saw the Icelanders' Uda up ahead was slowing, although it didn't look like a problem with the roadway. In fact, some buildings and traffic signals indicated they were about to enter Hella.

"We are going to take a back road here on the left," came Njálsson's voice over the car speaker. "The road conditions will not be quite so excellent. So pay careful attention and keep up your speed so we do not get separated. Use that pedal on the right."

"Smart guy," Peter muttered.

Njálsson's left turn signal came on, and Peter followed him onto a road that was narrower but not perceptibly different in quality. So much for Hella. Maybe he could plead for some sightseeing on the return trip. On the other hand, by then they might have some more urgent priorities than sightseeing.

Within minutes the houses and farms grew farther apart, and the terrain became more stark and forbidding. He could tell they were on a gradual uphill grade. Soon the pavement became black gravel, and eventually the gravel yielded to sand and dirt.

"How far are we going?" Peter radioed. He was beginning to wonder if Njálsson was planning to drive to the top of the mountain yet tonight.

"Not much farther. We will stop for the night at the outpost and go up the mountain early in the morning."

Peter thought about that. He knew the Icelander's concern was not for daylight. It was still as bright out as a summer evening in Columbus, although the dashboard clock said it was after 10:00 P.M. But Njálsson would be concerned that they be rested and sharp when they began challenging this mountain.

After roller-coastering in and out of a series of bends and curves, hills and dips, they suddenly came out onto a broad plain that appeared to be the last flat stretch before a chain of foothills building up toward the black mass in the distance. Peter could see they were approaching what might have been a small farm. It didn't take much imagination to picture this area as once a pastureland for sheep and dairy cattle.

Now they turned right and headed up a bumpy dirt lane toward a cluster of buildings that gradually grew before his eyes—weather-worn, sunbleached structures that could be arguably identified as farmhouse, barn, and various out-buildings having white sides turned to gray and red roofs turned to dull orange.

Posts near the dilapidated frame house stood as possible vestiges of a fence. The lane passed between two of them, overarched by a signboard inscribed in large letters with the name *Sæmundurholt* and a few other Icelandic words in smaller letters peppered with diacritical marks. Peter guessed that being a signmaker in Iceland was more challenging than in some other places.

He followed Njálsson's vehicle behind the house toward the barn, where, at an invisible command, the large peeled-paint door began clocking aside on an electric track. They parked their Udas in adjoining pens that could have been horse stalls at one time.

Peter and Sloat got out and stretched. Vígdis and Njálsson did likewise before starting to pull bags and bedrolls out of their Uda.

The next thing Peter knew, his feet were straight out before him and his head was swimming from a shock wave telegraphed up his vertebrae from his seat, which had just suffered a major collision with Mother Earth. In the moment before he started breathing again, he heard a familiar giggle and looked up to see Vígdis putting her hand over her mouth and turning away quickly.

"What was that?" He felt ridiculous.

"Oh," said Njálsson, "about a three-point-five."

Vígdis circled back and, extending one long, slender arm, pulled Peter to his feet by his hand. She grinned mischievously. "Three-point-five on the Richter scale."

"It was a temblor," said Sloat. "You had your mouth open, yawning, and you were leaning backward, off balance, with your hands over your head when the earth came up and hit you."

Peter was incredulous.

Njálsson gave a solemn nod. "Welcome to quake country. Loki struggles in his chains."

Peter glanced around, reluctant to utter dumbfounded questions.

Once again, Vígdis came to his rescue. "Loki—the god of mischief, the father of lies. For having caused the death of Odin's beloved son, Baldur, Loki is shackled in the underworld and tortured by dripping venom from a poison serpent. When it hits his face, he writhes in agony. Those convulsions are said to be the earthquakes we experience here in Midgard."

They moved with their bundles toward the rear of the old house, where Njálsson unlocked the back door.

Sloat asked Vígdis, "Is that what *you* believe?"

She giggled again. "Mercy, no. But while he is sure to deny it, I know that Einar more than half believes these things. He is the heathen one; I, the Christian."

Peter thought Sloat almost stumbled.

"Christian?" said Sloat.

"Yes," she said pleasantly. "Sir James introduced my father to Christ, and my father led me. Pray for Einar."

Peter saw consternation in Sloat's eyes. As Vígdis disappeared ahead of them into the house, Peter clapped him sympathetically on the shoulder.

"Well, look at it this way," Peter said softly. "You wouldn't prefer a pagan like Einar, would you?"

29

Hella

With his shoes off and his chair leaned back, Njálsson had shed his guarded look. Peter and Amos were staking out their own cots in the otherwise bare front room with its ancient, peeling wallpaper, and commenting on the anomaly of going to sleep with the sun still out. From the heavy-duty shades on the front and side windows, Peter guessed he wasn't the first person to have this consideration.

He felt like taking the opportunity to ask the Icelander a few questions.

Vígdis came in from what passed for a kitchen and proffered four steaming mugs of tea on a battered plastic tray.

"Hot water too?" asked Peter, accepting his mug gingerly.

"Of course," said Vígdis. "Around here we do not even have to heat it. That is the way it comes out of the ground. Tonight you can even take a shower before bed."

"Yes," said Njálsson. "In the morning we will not want to take time for such things."

Sloat looked around the room. "So this is what you call the outpost. Does it belong to the Geophysical Institute?"

Njálsson shook his shaggy head. "The government owns the land. The Institute leases the buildings. Several of the out-buildings house seismic station equipment."

"What is the meaning of the name on the sign in front?" Peter asked.

"Sæmundurholt? Ah, that is a story."

"I am not sure you want to encourage him," said Vígdis.

Sloat gestured magnanimously. "That's all right. We'd like to hear it."

"Well," began Njálsson, "it is one of the abandoned farms in this area that endured one too many volcanic shellings from Hekla. The name comes from Sæmundur, the man with no shadow. Sæmundur the Learned was a wizard who studied at the school of black arts in Paris."

"But why," asked Peter, "did he have no shadow?"

Njálsson did not smile, but his eyes held a kind of twinkle. "It is said that the devil stole it. The devil almost appropriated his soul as well in exchange for ferrying Sæmundur back across the ocean to Iceland without getting him wet. Sæmundur outwitted him by swimming the last short distance to shore, thereby getting wet but preserving his soul."

Vígdis set down her tea mug firmly. "I will take my shower

first, if you gentlemen will excuse me. I have heard these fairy tales before."

Peter couldn't help noticing that Sloat's eyes followed the tall, young woman's every move about the room. He also observed that she was, in fact, a lovely person in several respects, and Sloat certainly could do a lot worse. Unlike Amos, however, this did not distract Peter from the questions on his mind.

"Einar," he said, "does the sun ever go down this time of year?"

"A little. But he is down after you are asleep and back up before you rise. And if you wonder about seeing the aurora borealis, the answer is to come back in the fall or winter. It has something to do with the charged particles of the atmosphere interacting with the earth's magnetic field in relation to the sun. That would be the scientist's explanation."

"There's another explanation?" asked Sloat.

"Two, actually. One, this is the Valkyries' shields flashing on their way to Valhalla. Two, this is the time of year that Thor lights his campfire."

An easy silence visited briefly while the three men mulled those two opposite poles of ancient myth and modern science—Thor and meteorology, Woden and seismographs.

"So," said Peter finally, "was that quake that knocked me down something we should be concerned about?"

Njálsson's face held the slightest hint of amusement. "Do you mean do I expect something catastrophic to happen, like the mountain falling on us?"

"Well—"

"Listen, if it were not for Sir James, I would not be anywhere near this place. The seismic forces are in a bad cycle right now. Who knows? In the right place, a three-point-five like we just experienced could pop Hekla's cork. And it is possible that we could have a stronger shock at any time. It would be most unfortunate if that happened while you were up there."

"Uh . . . Einar," said Peter warily, "where are you going to be?"

"Vígdis and I will be right beside you—to a point."

"What point is that?"

Njálsson's eyes grew distant. "We will not go inside."

Peter was baffled. "Inside? Inside Hekla?"

"The great fissure. In 2024 there was a series of quakes and a minor eruption that opened up a substantial new crater. It has been dormant ever since, and crazy people from the continent like to come here and rappel down inside. Some day one of them is going to get launched into orbit—after being deep-fried. I hope it is not you."

Peter and Sloat exchanged searching looks.

"It makes sense," said Sloat. "If I were hiding a rune stone, this sounds like the place I'd put it."

Peter nodded gravely. "Why don't you try your scanner now?"

Sloat reached under his cot, dragged out his duffel bag, and rooted around until he came up with the homing device. He flicked it on and studied its readout while a subdued, low-frequency warble indicated it was picking up some weak signal. After a moment, Sloat looked up. He hooked an inquisitive finger toward the right front corner of the room.

"The source is that-a-way, forty-some kilometers. What do we have there?"

"You tell me," said Njálsson, getting to his feet and crossing the room. The Icelander pulled the shade up to reveal the familiar dark, hump-backed, foggy-topped piece of horizon Peter had seen on the road to Sæmundurholt.

"Hekla," he declared.

Peter was troubled by a thought. "If farmland this far away was ruined by Hekla's eruptions—tell me, Einar, how great are the chances of something happening while we're here?"

The big Icelander shrugged. "Who can say? The Institute is concerned about the frequency of the temblors. They have issued a Level-Two alert, which means no activity has been detected within the volcanic system, but conditions are ripe. Something is likely to happen sooner or later. At this point, we would expect at least twenty-four hours' warning after reaching a Level One, but there is no guarantee."

"That's not very reassuring," said Peter.

Njálsson's eyes flashed. "I am sure you know I would be delighted to terminate this foolishness right now. So do not expect reassurance from me. If you want my opinion, we are overdue for the eruption of the century. Guess when the last major lava-spewing event was."

Peter shook his head.

"Nineteen forty-seven—exactly a century ago. Eruptive forces the equivalent of ten thousand hydrogen bombs. And there were worse eruptions in the Middle Ages, some lasting a year, two years, ones that covered half the country in ash and caused terrible famine and disease."

"I think I see how it got its reputation as the gate of hell," said Peter.

Njálsson laughed aloud. "I will ask Thor to grant us a quick getaway. Who knows? Perhaps your object will even be found outside the gate."

At that moment, Vígdis returned, attired in fire-engine-red sweats and green thongs.

"Next," she announced, vigorously toweling her hair. "And, Einar, please keep your heathen superstitions to yourself, if you do not mind."

Njálsson gave her a slightly contemptuous look. "As opposed to Christian superstitions?"

"Don't look at me," said Sloat. "I'm not a Christian."

Vígdis's towel missed two beats. "Oh? Maybe we could talk about that. Would you like to go for a stroll?"

Sloat looked like a man who had just won the lottery but didn't want to let on.

"Sure," he said too casually.

"Uh," said Peter quickly, "I think I'll get my shower now, if you'll excuse me. Early to bed, early to rise, you know."

* * *

Peter actually was the last to rise. From the sounds and smells, he guessed that Vígdis was preparing some food in the crude kitchen and Sloat finally was getting his shower. Njálsson had just raised the shades in the front room, and it was as if the sun had never made it below the horizon. There it was again, somewhere behind the clouds, the only difference being the direction of the shadows.

Peter noticed that the others had rebagged their belongings, and he proceeded to do the same, encouraged by the wafting aromas of breakfast.

Sloat came in with unruly, wet hair and carrying two plastic plates of food. He was followed moments later by Njálsson and Vígdis with their own plates. Sloat handed one to Peter. It was toast and fried ham slices and a small cluster of red grapes.

Somehow that was especially satisfying.

Vígdis disappeared for a moment and returned with last night's mugs, this time filled with black coffee. While they chewed and sipped, sitting silently on their cots, Peter noticed that Sloat seemed particularly subdued, almost glum.

He waited until they were back in the Uda and heading once again toward Hekla before inquiring.

"Why the long face, Amos?"

"Huh?" said Sloat as if rousing from a slumber.

"I know you don't have a dog to get run over. So did Vígdis snub you?"

"Oh, no. We get along fine, in fact. It's just—"

"She tried to proselytize you?"

"She's as bad as you are. When I told her I'd already heard all that stuff from you, she got a little rough on me. Said I didn't need more information—I needed *transformation*."

Peter smiled. "Good for her. She's right, you know."

Sloat fell silent.

"So," said Peter, "has that got you bummed out?"

"Not exactly. I'm just thinking."

* * *

Less than an hour later, they were there. In that time Hekla had grown from a molehill on the horizon to a towering, mottled mass of blackened basalt and patchy snow and ice.

"Listen to this," said Sloat, turning up the volume on his scanner.

The difference was dramatic. Now the pulsation was strong and rapid.

"Sounds like we're almost on top of it," Peter agreed. "Or rather, it's almost on top of us."

For the last few minutes they had been traveling in Hekla's ample shadow, and now Njálsson parked his Uda at the crest of one of the last foothills that leveled out onto a small plateau, which looked almost like a man-made parking lot.

"What's this?" Peter asked.

The Icelander appeared intent on getting gear unloaded. *"Thyrla,"* he said tersely.

"What's that?"

"Whirlybird," said Vígdis, coming to Peter's assistance. "Chopper. They are still used for rescues. This is a landing area. Let us pray that there be no need of it."

"Yes," Peter agreed. "Amen."

Njálsson quickly parceled out a variety of implements at their feet, most of which Peter recognized. There were well-worn backpacks, military rations, first-aid kits, protective rock helmets, bunches of carabiners for their line, spiky pitons to anchor the carabiners, special gloves and boots, four serrated tomahawklike ice axes, and eight toothy contraptions resembling small animal traps.

"Crampons," said Njálsson. "We'll carry them on our packs until we need them for crossing ice and snow."

Peter had seen such exotic footgear before but had never worn it. He had never climbed an ice face. He was, however, familiar with the use of carabiners and line in rappelling.

"Going up the mountain may be strenuous," Njálsson said, "but if you do it right, it is the less hazardous part. Hardly anyone has been known to fall *up* a mountain. Coming back down can be a different story, through overconfidence or inattention. So please pay close attention as I demonstrate a few techniques."

In the space of a few short minutes, the big Icelander showed them how to attach the crampons, how to tie several types of knots including the bowline and sheepshank, a few ways to gain purchase with the *piolet* ice ax, and a variety of belaying techniques with the bucklelike carabiners and line to ensure that anyone getting in trouble could be pulled back by the other three. Peter's head was swimming.

"Not to worry," Njálsson asserted. "These things will only be required a few times as we go. We shall review the techniques and try them out on an easy snowfield not too far up. Very soon you will get the hang of it."

"For all its destructiveness," said Vígdis with an encouraging smile, "Hekla is not big, as mountains go. We shall be having lunch at the top before you know it."

Once their packs and gear were secured, the climb got under way. Njálsson led them up a winding trail in zigzag fashion to minimize the steepness of the ascent. Vígdis brought up the rear, with Sloat next and Peter right behind Njálsson.

"Switch on your helmet radio," he told Peter after they had been on the march for a few minutes. "Pass it on."

Peter did so and told Sloat to do likewise. When Vígdis completed the chain, Njálsson offered some explanation.

"You need to become accustomed to communicating this way. After we cross the big stream up ahead, we will come to our first ice field. There I will review the belaying technique. After attaching our carabiners to the line, we will need to spread out. If there is any hidden crevasse, it is better that only one of us slip into it than all four—and then even that one may be saved."

"Not that there is much chance of that," Vígdis quickly amended. "We are dealing with no glaciers. But we also want no surprises."

Before they rounded a high, angular rock wall, Peter could hear the roaring of fast water somewhere beyond. When they had come to the other side and in sight of the stream, he was surprised by the size of it. Green water churned and twisted like an Olympic slalom toward the plain below, in places rushing in angry patches of whitewater.

"That is the downside of these natural footpaths," explained Njálsson. "They also serve as natural funnels for falling ice and rock and as channels for ice and snowmelt runoff. As we approach the bank of this stream, I would like you two gentlemen to select a crossing point for us."

Nowhere did the stream narrow to a span that could be vaulted. It was time to get wet.

"How about there?" said Peter, pointing to a place upstream that looked as though it could be crossed in a half dozen well-chosen strides, depending on its depth.

Sloat looked where Peter indicated and nodded.

Njálsson began leading them toward it. As they approached, it looked even more promising, the waters apparently slower and calmer.

"It was a trick question," Vígdis warned before her brother spoke again.

"I have plumbed this point myself," said the Icelander. "If you were to step off here, you would most likely drown. Its depth is about twenty meters. The channel's narrowest parts are usually also the deepest. We will have much better success upstream at a shallower but broader point before all of the feeders have joined."

Peter and Sloat exchanged ironic glances. This fellow might not be Mr. Congeniality, but he certainly knew what he was doing.

"Why don't we just stay on this side?" asked Peter.

"That is not an option. This side becomes a steep rock face farther upstream. It would take you many more hours of very difficult and dangerous climbing. And then you would probably have to camp overnight."

"No, thanks," said Peter, and they trudged on upstream.

This section was a longer hike than Peter had expected, although that impression might have been influenced by its greater difficulty. For now they were climbing at an increasingly steeper angle. More than once, Peter found himself scrambling to maintain forward motion as the rocky ground crumbled under his feet.

"Right around these streams are some of the few places you will find sedimentary rock," said Njálsson.

"The entire land mass is volcanic, isn't it?" Peter asked. "At least, that's what I believe I read."

"That is correct," the Icelander agreed. "There are two main types of volcanic formations—subduction and rift—both related to continental drift. Subduction is where two continental plates are in collision, and one slides under the other. Rift is where they are pulling apart, and magma from the molten interior rises to the surface. Both produce volcanoes and earthquakes."

"We are the rift type in Iceland," added Vígdis. "This island is basically one big ooze right over the middle of the Mid-Atlantic Ridge. We will continue to experience volcanism as long as Europe and North America continue to pull apart, which should be indefinitely."

"OK," said Peter, "but what does that have to do with Loki, writhing in his chains?"

"Troublemaker," Vígdis muttered.

Njálsson ignored the remark.

Now they were at the point that the Icelander had chosen for their crossing. Indeed the water seemed less massive and turbulent. It was also broader.

Without a moment's hesitation, Njálsson stepped into the current and began sloshing across, reaching knee depth. Peter followed and found himself immediately forced into a kind of quick shuffle. The longer the interval between steps, the greater the sense that he was about to lose balance and lift off the bottom on one foot. He compensated by shortening his steps and maintaining a strong forward motion.

It was probably less than thirty feet to the other side, and all four were across in as many seconds. Peter was impressed with the boots and how they kept his feet perfectly dry, but his calves between boot and knee felt painfully cold after the numbness wore off.

Soon even the roar of the river was lost behind them.

"All right," Njálsson announced when they had gone a few minutes farther. "Crampon time."

Peter knew what that meant. They were approaching their first ice field.

Njálsson reviewed the belaying technique, involving the careful placement of pitons and ice screws and carabiners as they traversed the face, roped together through their own carabiners. Then he reviewed the use of the ice ax for step cutting, plus the techniques of *piolet ancre* and *piolet ramasse* for actually pulling oneself up the face a chop at a time.

Finally they tied up their individual harnesses about their midsections, attaching the carabiners at belt level. Crampons in hand, they scrambled up a steep table of bare basalt.

At the top Njálsson pointed ahead, then sat down to put on his crampons, and Peter saw their first ice face. What had looked like one tiny patch of snow from the bottom of the mountain now looked like a vast sheet of white, treacherous and cold.

"Not to worry about wasting pitons," said Njálsson when they were up and moving again. "We will use the same anchors on the way back down."

Once on the ice, Peter was glad the big Icelander was the lead man. He appreciated Njálsson's slow pace. It allowed Peter and Sloat the opportunity to get the feel of the ice and the crampons without the pressure to advance quickly.

Progress was tricky until he stopped moving his feet parallel to the surface and learned to approach the face on the perpendicular, where the teeth found their best bite.

"You are doing fine, Peter," said Vígdis when he got the hang of it. "You too, Amos."

By the time they were halfway across, Peter ventured to look down. It wasn't quite as bad as he'd expected. He could even imagine surviving a fall from this point.

"So what's so tough about this, Einar?"

"I am glad you are so confident," said Njálsson. "We have several more of these, each one a little more dangerous than the last. But I am sure you will do OK."

He was right. By the time they could begin to make out the summit, they had an ice field to cross that was so vertical they had to proceed at a crawl, clinging to the face with each step, grabbing for handholds, and learning to increase their purchase with well-chosen chops of their *piolets*.

When Peter looked down this time, he felt as if the bottom had fallen out of his stomach. For a moment, he closed his eyes and just clung to the ice face until the vertigo passed.

They were in clouds now, which seemed odd at this relatively low altitude. The wind had become a factor too. Peter squinted in the patchy sunlight that alternated between cloud shadow and snow glare, never giving his eyes a chance to adjust properly. Several times he thought he spied large, dark, soaring birds at a distance.

"Einar," he said as they were exiting the ice field, "we're not about to get some bad weather, are we?"

"The weather is good. If you mean the clouds, they are here most of the time. Hekla means 'hooded,' because of the clouds around it. It is a little thick here now, but it should change. You can remove your crampons now."

Then he pointed up another rise, this one gentler than most of the others.

"That is our destination—the beginning of Crater Row, where older eruptions have occurred. We shall stop there for lunch, and you can see the little drop we have to make to get to your big fissure. If that is where you think you need to go."

"Amos?" said Peter.

Sloat extracted the scanner from his pack and turned it on. The signal was reassuringly shrill and insistent. When he turned it obliquely to the far side of Crater Row, the tone flattened into its familiar bull's-eye drone.

"What's over there about eight or nine hundred meters?"

"That would be the fissure."

"Bingo," said Sloat.

"Let's eat," said Peter.

Rome

When next she awoke, Carlotta realized groggily that she had company. Two short, dark young women told her in clipped Italian that they would help her prepare for her shower.

She complied willingly, as if she had always had personal attendants. It did not occur to her to question their instructions.

She even drank the strange-tasting tea they offered without questioning. It was uniquely satisfying. The more she drank, the better it tasted and the better she felt. She didn't quite understand what these things were all about anymore, but somehow that no longer concerned her.

The important thing was that these two women who could have been sisters held the key to her door. What was more, they were prepared to use it. As soon as Carlotta had shed her stale, slept-in clothes with some genuine pleasure and donned a plain, white robe, they escorted her into a darkened corridor.

While her eyes were still adjusting, she caught sight of an imposing figure just outside her door. It was that of a hulk of a man, arms crossed upon his chest, dressed in monklike garb, who had to be a security guard. The "sisters" nodded at him as they passed, but he remained as impassive as granite.

Carlotta next found herself in a bathroom with a tiled floor and a sunken tub. In less than a minute in the warm, swirling waters she felt the stress dissolving away. She felt light and warm and peaceful and a thousand miles from worldly care.

She swished her toes lazily and watched the galaxies of bubbles and foam pursue each other. To her artist's eye, this was golden imagery—the world in a grain of sand and heaven in a wild flower.

If she could paint this in full-motion video, there would be no lack of metaphors, starting with the physical universe itself. As the waters rise, the teeming constellations on the surface represent the expanding universe, island civilizations on the stretching fabric of the space-time continuum. And then there would be the human mind with its myriad neurons and synapses. Perhaps even her own mind, disjointed and . . .

They were beckoning to her now and holding up towels. One of the women said something in Italian about Zell. She thought she remembered him. He was perhaps the reason she was even here. Would she see him now?

There was more tea, warm and sweet and deeply satisfying. There were fresh new clothes for her to wear, including a casual, oyster-white dress that fit her like tailored fabric, and special golden slippers that seemed made for walking on moonbeams. And there were her attendants to brush her hair and murmur encouraging nonsense with meaningless smiles.

It was easy to think of herself as some kind of princess, maybe under the sway of a magical spell in an enchanted castle. The only thing missing was a prince to break the spell and set her free. The very thought was vaguely unsettling, as if there was something she should remember.

She was to follow these attendants now, according to the older one, and see *him*. That would be Zell, Carlotta knew without knowing how.

And then there was another walk farther down the same murky corridor and down a flight of stairs. The older sister guided her elbow as they entered a murkier basement and spoke some encouraging words. It was timely encouragement. Otherwise Carlotta would have been tempted to balk at this unlighted path, these indistinguishable objects, these worrisome shadows.

Before anything like that could happen, the younger sister switched on a flashlight. It gave just enough illumination to make out the goal before them, apparently an open door at the end of a very long passage.

At the end, Carlotta realized that the little room she was entering was actually an elevator. There was an ominously hollow crashing as its doors collided, closing off the basement from her. The floor pressed strongly against her feet as this well pulled its bucket to the top. Then the doors rumbled open and disgorged its three passengers into a high-ceilinged chamber with dark wood paneling and large wrought-iron sconces. Substantial candles cast flickering shadows. The entire effect was medieval.

The older sister grasped a large brass doorknob on a section of paneling and pulled. The partition opened onto a half-lit, cavernous chamber that appeared to be a kind of sanctuary. The woman motioned for Carlotta to follow. The younger sister brought up the rear and closed the door heavily behind them.

In the eerie overhead illumination of backlit stained-glass, Carlotta was gazing up rows of pews toward a dusky chancel. She believed she could make out another one of those dead-Christ effigies behind the altar. At first she thought she and the sisters were alone in the auditorium until they moved closer and she noticed a lone figure in a hooded cloak standing by the altar.

When they reached the front pew, the sisters stood aside. Carlotta paused uncertainly until the figure by the altar beckoned for her to mount the three steps. It appeared she was being invited to witness something. Atop the carpeted platform, she sensed that it was something on the waist-high altar, though it was lost in shadow.

The hooded figure—a woman, she saw—applied a small flame to a long-handled implement and handed it to Carlotta. It took her a moment to recognize it as an acolyte's candlelighter. In the glow of the sputtering wick, she could see that two candles awaited her. She applied the flame, and a larger light grew to effulgence all about them. She returned the acolyte's instrument to the hooded stranger and looked back to the altar.

Now she could make out the objects upon it—the business end of a spear, ancient and gnarled, and a jewel-encrusted crown that seemed overdone and gaudy until an intuitive flash informed her that this might be a genuine article. She was momentarily on the verge of an insight, maybe a remembrance, and then it was gone, leaving nothing but that unsettling sense of déjà vu like that disquieting thought of the long-awaited prince.

Carlotta had no idea how long she stood there, enraptured by these mesmerizing objects, as if sustained meditation would reveal their secrets. Time was forgotten until an odd sound returned her to self-consciousness. After a moment, she realized it was coming from the hooded figure. The sound had the simultaneous qualities of a chant and a lament, a kind of ancient dirge in a lost tongue.

And then it ceased. Peripherally Carlotta was aware of the sisters stepping up behind her as if to resume their escort. The hooded woman walked to the end of the platform by a door and turned.

"Come," she said simply in English.

Carlotta shuffled forward a few steps, then stopped at the foot of the slain Christ and looked up. Something was wrong here. Even in reduced scale and dim light, this tragic figure in enameled ceramic was clearly different. Carlotta could see that this Lamented One was neither dead nor crucified. The wounded form was bound with fetters to a tree rather than to a cross. His gaze seemed to bore through her with one good eye. The other appeared missing. It was highly disconcerting.

"Come," the woman called again from the doorway, more insistently.

Carlotta tore herself away from the strange sight and obeyed. The woman opened yet another door, and they entered a smaller chamber that could have been a pastoral study. Inside were book-lined shelves, an antique mahogany desk, and two figures conversing by a spartan-looking couch. One was seated, the other standing.

Upon Carlotta's entry, the two men broke off their conversation. The larger man, a beetle-browed young fellow in a khaki jumpsuit, stepped aside to reveal an ascetic-looking, white-haired gentleman in a vestment like a priest's but for its olive-green hue.

His eyes found Carlotta's like a compass needle and held tight. She saw his face break into a radiant smile as if he had uncovered buried treasure, and her heart rate inexplicably quickened.

The sisters nudged her forward.

"Welcome, daughter," the man said, half rising, half bowing.

He took his seat again and addressed the sisters in Italian. "Bring us tea, please."

The two women exited the study with a dispatch that suggested unswerving devotion to unquestioned authority.

The hooded figure removed her head covering, and Carlotta saw that it was that strange woman Estelle Morgenthau, wearing a strangely satisfied expression.

"Come here, daughter," said the man. His robust, commanding voice belied the advanced age that his white hair suggested.

"Who—who are you?" asked Carlotta.

"I am Father Zell," he said, patting the couch beside him. "Come, sit and tell me about yourself, daughter. It appears that you were born for a high purpose. We shall have tea, and you will tell me the things of your heart."

Carlotta found her feet willing to obey and her heart ready to believe. Born for a high purpose? If Father Zell said it, it must be so.

* * *

Hekla

Peter was reassured to learn that he was not taking leave of his senses. Those birdlike things he thought he had been seeing were, in fact, big black ravens. An impressive number they were, flapping, gliding, soaring about Hekla's summit and their make-shift picnic spot.

The flock apparently failed to have the same salutary effect on Njálsson, who watched their growing numbers and closer proximity with a jaundiced eye, a set jaw, and occasional mutterings.

"This is not good," he declared from time to time, shaking his large head as he looked up at the sky.

"What's the big deal?" Sloat finally asked as they were taking their last bites of a wholesome, nutritious, and less-than-flavorful dessert bar. "What's wrong with the birds?"

Vígdis rolled her eyes. "Omens, you know. Gloom and doom. You ask me, I think these feathered friends just sense the possibility of a free lunch."

"They can have it," said Sloat, regarding the half-eaten bar in his hand with a jaundiced eye of his own.

When they were all on their feet, the big Icelander gave a nod of his head and a wave of his hand like a cowboy at roundup. "Let us go."

The next thing Peter knew, he was down again with the wind knocked out of him. Like yesterday's spill in the driveway at Sæmundurholt, he noted as the mountaintop spun about him. Except if the last one was a three-point-five, this one felt more like a four-point-five. He hated to think what the next one could be like.

He wobbled to his feet and immediately realized that the temblor was not over. The ground under his feet continued to quake gently but quite perceptibly.

"Careful," Njálsson warned. "There could be aftershocks."

Peter turned and saw that the Icelander was bleeding from the mouth and nose. He apparently had hit the deck face first. Sloat was stumbling about, shaking his head as if to clear it.

"Everyone reattach to the line!" Njálsson called out.

"Vígdis!" cried Sloat.

The tall blonde woman was nowhere to be seen.

"Vígdis!" Sloat bellowed, whirling about frantically.

A weak cry could be heard in response. It sounded afar off, but Peter realized it wouldn't have to be far to be faint if it were from down the mountain.

Sloat seemed to find what he was looking for over a drop not far from the spot where Vígdis had been standing. Instantly he was lashing a line around a small but solid-looking rock formation, hooking it to his carabiner, and going over the side.

"Wait!" cried Njálsson, tossing him another line. "We don't want to lose both of you down there."

Peter looked over the edge and almost wished he hadn't. It was a sheer drop. He could see Vígdis now, clinging desperately to the rock face. She seemed to be engaged in a slow-motion slide into oblivion. Sometimes she appeared to find a purchase, but it never lasted more than a moment before she slipped another foot away.

Sloat's catlike agility and the speed of his descent surprised him. This was obviously not Amos's first time rappelling. He let the line run out at a breakneck pace as he backpedaled down the face in a reverse hopping sprint faster than Peter thought possible —or safe.

Suddenly the payout stopped, and the two figures visually merged.

"Got her!" Sloat yelled over the helmet radio.

Peter realized he'd been clenching his fists and holding his breath. He consciously relaxed.

"Snap her online!" Njálsson shouted.

"I'm way ahead of you," Sloat retorted. "She's as secure as a kangaroo pup."

"Is she hurt?" Peter asked. "Get her to turn her helmet on."

The next voice was that of Vígdis, sounding a little shaky but otherwise intact. "I'm all right except for a couple of scraped knuckles and a bruised knee. I am not so sure about Amos."

"Amos," called Peter, "are you OK?"

Vígdis answered. "If I did not squeeze the life out of him when he got to me."

Njálsson interrupted the chatter. "Listen, both of you. Plant your feet, and we will start bringing your line up."

"No, thanks, Einar," said Sloat. "I think we're going to head for the crater from here."

"Now, just a minute—"

Sloat cut him off. "We're closer than you are. You have to go all the way over and down again. We only have to come up a few feet, and then we're at a section that looks like a straight lateral move with decent footing."

The big Icelander switched off his radio and commenced stomping about, muttering things in his native tongue that were probably better left untranslated. Peter noticed that his face had reddened again.

"We're just about up to the lateral," Sloat reported. "Go ahead and pull up the second line. When I've got our first anchor, I'll ask you to untie the first line and let it drop."

"OK." Peter began pulling up the second line. By the time he had finished, Sloat already was asking him to untie the first.

From this point, Amos and Vígdis were on their own. Peter said a silent prayer for them.

As they made their own way down the longer, more gradual descent toward the big fissure, Peter held his tongue. But when he believed Njálsson had had sufficient time to cool off, he sought to satisfy his curiosity.

"Einar, are you afraid what they're doing is too dangerous?"

There was another Icelandic epithet before he responded in English. "No. My concern is the fissure. It is too dangerous now to go inside."

"Since the last tremor?"

Njálsson stopped in his tracks. "You think it is over? Think again. Feel the earth. Loki still writhes."

He was right. Standing still, Peter could feel a faint trembling up his legs as if his knees were weak from fright. There was also that telltale quiver in the pit of his stomach and his inner ear. No, it wasn't over yet.

But he did not want any misunderstanding. "I'm sorry, Einar. I guess that's a chance we're going to have to take."

The Icelander resumed his silence. They were approaching the fissure, and they had to shinny down several hundred feet of treacherous mountainside to reach the plain.

Njálsson went first, deliberately breaking off the rock pieces that could prove disastrous if used as handholds or footholds and tossing them to one side.

Peter was careful to observe the places Njálsson availed himself of and did likewise. Occasionally, a hand or foot slipped, but he was always sufficiently anchored on his remaining points to recover with nothing worse than a racing pulse.

At the bottom, he could hear Sloat and Vígdis before he could see them. Sloat had turned on the scanner, which was emitting a double-time signal that meant they were getting warmer.

Then as they rounded a bend, Peter saw them. He also saw the fissure, a long, ugly scar where the mountain had pulled itself nearly in twain.

Sloat was holding the scanner in front of him like a divining rod. He followed the signal another hundred feet, where he stopped and pointed down. It was the widest part of the fissure, which made sense. Any good descent route most likely would have to start wide at the top.

It was not exactly a joyous reunion when brother and sister found each other once again. Vígdis and Einar commenced an animated dialogue in their native tongue that was clearly about something more heartfelt than the weather. After a minute, Njálsson broke off, looking disgusted and red-faced again. He walked away, muttering more Norse expletives, and sat down off to the side.

Large, black ravens wheeled about them, expressing their own opinions in shrill inflections. Unexpectedly the sky had become crowded with large, sullen clouds that enveloped them in a gathering shroud of gloom.

"This is not good," Njálsson muttered again, shaking his head.

While Vígdis rummaged in her pack, Peter sidled up to Amos. "You have any idea what that was all about?"

Sloat grimaced. "A fair idea. She told me she's going inside with us. I imagine what you saw was her breaking the news to Einar. I think he's about ready to sell her to the lowest bidder."

Peter chuckled. "Now's your chance."

Sloat cracked a tiny smile and walked away—toward Vígdis.

Peter followed at a respectful distance and quickly became aware of two things. The first was that they were standing on dangerous ground near the dark, gaping mouth of the fissure. One more quake like the last one, and they could lose members of their party all over again. The second thing was an elusive, acrid aroma the closer he got to the chasm.

Sloat wrinkled his nose. "Fire and brimstone. Maybe this *is* the gate of hell."

Vígdis attached a small black device to one of their lines and tossed it into the abyss. When the entire three hundred feet had paid out without hitting bottom, she began hauling it back in. Then she unhooked the little black box, pushed a couple of buttons, and consulted a readout.

Her lips moved, but her words were drowned in an explosive crack of thunder and a blinding shimmer of lightning, followed by eerily silent darkness. And then it happened again. *Zot! Boom!*

This time Peter felt a tingle from his toes to the fillings in his teeth. It felt as if the megatons of basalt under his feet were reverberating with the echo. Or was that more of Loki's writhings?

Now the sky was black with roiling thunderheads, and a cold wind began to press in upon them.

"By Thor!" cried Njálsson. "This is madness!"

"Sulfur dioxide," said Vígdis calmly, putting away her instrument.

"What?" said Sloat behind her.

"Sulfur dioxide is what we are smelling from the fissure," she explained. "It would probably be best if we got this over quickly."

Njálsson said something in angry Icelandic to his sister. She replied calmly in the same tongue, and Peter thought it sounded like a command. Reluctantly her brother handed her another small hand-held device.

She aimed it at the chasm and appeared to take some kind of reading.

"About two hundred and fifty meters to the bottom." Then she added, "Ultrasound to time the ultrahigh frequency echoes and a magnetic anomaly detector to give additional dimensions."

Next she produced three filter masks from her pack and distributed two of them to Peter and Sloat. With the third she demonstrated their proper use and watched as the two men tried it for themselves.

Peter looked at the troubled sky and then at the huge rocky cleft before them. The moment was upon them. All three exchanged knowing glances.

"Let's go for it," he said.

Peter insisted on going first. "Amos," he said, "you'll have to carry the third line down. When you're on the second line, I'll let you know when to drop the rope to me. OK?"

Amos nodded.

"In that case," Vígdis said, handing him several long, red tubes, "set off a couple of these once you get a good start. Do you remember how to do it?"

Peter mimed striking the end of a flare against the rock and tossing it over his shoulder behind him.

She nodded approvingly. Then she reached up, switched on his helmet light and radio, and secured his filter mask with its hook-and-loop closure.

"Cheerio," said Peter in a muffled voice, backing up to the brink.

Sloat shined his flashlight into the abyss. "You're cleared for take-off, flyboy."

With a silent prayer, Peter hopped out backward into the void, letting his line pay out slowly. If there were any obstructions, he preferred a slow-motion collision. This was the worst part, before his eyes adjusted and the first flare was lit.

After he got out of direct line of sight of the fissure mouth, Peter tightened up on the carabiner to halt his descent and planted his feet against the face. Then he reached into his backpack, grabbed a flare, struck it against the rock, and tossed it over his back as it sputtered into incandescence. Looking over his shoulder, he watched the flare fall—and kept on falling.

"Holy Roman Empire!" Peter heard himself exclaim.

"What is it?" Sloat's concerned voice sounded in his ear.

Peter had almost forgotten about their helmet radio. "In addition to my European history, remind me to bone up on my metric system. Two hundred and fifty meters is a long way down."

At least it looked like a relatively clean descent with no dangerous outcroppings to work around. Now he let the line pay out full speed, like a spider's dragline. After the first hundred feet or so, he put on the brakes long enough to toss another flare and then looked for the bottom. He saw the two flares illuminating a broad, rocky floor and guessed it was another five or six hundred feet down. It was going to be a long, hard climb back up.

Peter resumed his descent, more slowly this time. When he got to within twenty feet of the end of his line, he found a good spot and stopped. There was a nice horizontal crevice about the width of a pencil. He inserted a screw anchor and began torquing it down with a small wrench. It was an excellent fit. He was so pleased with the results, he began setting a second one about six inches away to distribute the weight on the line.

"OK, Amos," he radioed. "I'm setting the anchors into the face now, right below a small outcrop. I'll set a flare on it to mark the spot for you."

"Got you."

Peter next attached his line to the anchors, let it drop, hooked it to his carabiner, and unhooked the first line.

"OK," he called. "I'm off the line."

He was in business again, dropping rapidly down the face. When his second line ran out, he set two more anchors and a flare and called to Amos to drop the third line. He could see the bottom more clearly now. This time when he dropped the rope, nearly half of it piled in a heap on the rock floor.

Peter gave it the gas. Just before hitting bottom, he heard a crackling about his head that he thought was radio interference. After his feet touched down, he realized it was something more serious. The floor was rumbling and pulsating beneath him in the now familiar throes of another tremor.

He wiped off a layer of grit from his hands and face and realized the crackling must have been a bombardment of tiny pebbles shaken loose by the temblor.

"Is everything all right up there, Einar?" Peter radioed.

"No!" cried the Icelander. "If the earth does not kill us, the sky will!"

"What are you talking about?"

"Quakes! Hailstorms! I have tied myself to a rock so I do not blow away. Thor's mercy!"

"Hang in there, Einar. We'll be back up there before you know it. It may be safer in here."

Sloat, who didn't have to spend time setting anchors, was now finishing his descent. Looking up, Peter could see Vígdis not far behind.

In the metallic glare of the flares, Peter squinted down both directions of the subterranean canyon, but it was not about to reveal its secrets so easily.

Sloat whipped out the scanner, muted the audio, and checked the display coordinates.

"This way," he said, pointing left up the north passage. "It's not much farther now."

From this point, Amos assumed the lead. Now they got out of range of the flares, and the rock walls appeared to press in around them, threatening them with blackness.

Around a gentle curve, the darkness took on a shifting, almost shimmering characteristic. Peter stopped, thinking he was imagining things when the phenomenon grew into an orangish glow. It reminded him of flickering firelight seen at a distance.

"Do you see that?" he began, but nobody was in a talking mood.

Sloat plunged forward, and Vígdis quickened her pace to keep up. Peter hung back, sensing something amiss.

"What's that?" he said, hearing some low-frequency rumble at the edge of hearing.

But then he was tossed like a piece of straw, and his own lights went out.

31

Hekla

When he came to, Peter's head was swimming. His helmet light had been extinguished, and he was lying in total darkness on a pallet of rock with his head up against the cliff face. His mouth was full of grit. He tried to spit out the worst of it.

When at last he stood up tentatively, his head began to throb with an intensity that almost dropped him to his knees. He strained his eyes for any available light, no matter how feeble. That only further convinced him of the totality of the darkness that now held him.

This was not the darkness of a moonless, starless night with cloud shadows floating on the ground. It was not the darkness of a child's hiding place with a pencil line of light at the bottom of the closet door. It was not even the darkness of eyes pressed tightly shut, face down in a pillow, where the corneal pressure produced its own miniature auroras.

This was the darkness of oblivion, blackness itself, the place of abandonment. Peter tried to shake off rising panic, but it degenerated into a craven shiver. He wanted to scream.

He suppressed the urge to bolt and run, knowing he'd only get himself further lost and probably hurt. Maybe he was already hurt. There were apparently no broken bones, but his mind seemed confused. He could have sustained a mild concussion. As he forced his dulled brain to approach the problem logically, he remembered the radio.

"Amos! Vígdis!"

He repeated the cry twice more before conceding that either the radio was dead or they were. Maybe he was the dead one. Peter stopped himself before it really did turn to screams. If he were dead, this most certainly was not heaven.

"Einar!" he cried again. "Einar, can you hear me? Answer me, please!"

Surely it was only his radio that was dead. His difficulty thinking a straight thought and the silent radio must be from the same thing—head trauma. He wiggled out of the helmet and craned his head about for any sound he might pick up in the darkness.

He stood for a long moment, straining his ears to the maximum. Even now he could almost believe he was hearing a distant cry, a hideous sobbing and moaning. But he knew that had to be some inner projection, the influence of suggestion, like hearing the ocean inside a seashell.

Where was everybody? And where was he?

He wanted out of there, and he wanted out now. His panic seemed almost to threaten sanity itself. Was this what the "outer darkness" meant—the very hellishness of hell? Crashing about terrified in darkness, blind and insane, cursing God?

Peter said a prayer to restore a measure of calm and began to move slowly along the rock wall, extending his arms to guard against knocking himself out again. He knew there was no such protection from ground-level hazards that might trip him up.

He progressed for several minutes more before deciding to stop and reconnoiter. Had it been minutes or hours since the last quake? Where were Amos and Vígdis? Were they even still alive?

Again he removed his helmet and listened. This time he was convinced it was not his imagination. Without straining his ears he heard it—a bone-chilling sound of weeping and wailing.

He shuddered. The noise was remote but unmistakable. It was the chorus of the lost, the shriek of desolation, the anguish of the damned. It was unnerving in the extreme. Everything within him shrank from it. In fact, there was only one thing worse—going back.

He had to go on, and so he did.

* * *

After what could have been several minutes or several hours, Peter began to wonder if he were losing his grip. The black void ahead now seemed to shimmer with a vague orange aura. Was he hallucinating? He had heard of sensory deprivation experiments in which the mind began to generate its own stimuli after an extended period of time.

Then he remembered. That aura was the last thing he had seen before that quake rocked them. He also dimly recalled an interlude of semiconsciousness in which he had stumbled around in the dark, half-delirious, until finally passing out. Only now was it coming back to him.

It was a little scary to think that his own mind was playing tricks on him. If he were suffering temporary amnesia, what else might he be forgetting?

But it made sense. During that semiconscious interlude, he must have wandered in the opposite direction, and now he was back approximately where he had started, where that strange orange light had played off the rock wall.

Peter blinked and stopped. The orange glow was gone. He tore off the helmet and listened for the eerie weeping and wailing. Gone too. It was maddening. As crazy as these phenomena truly were, they were preferable to the black hole of the void.

"Amos!" he shouted in frustration. "Vígdis! Somebody answer me!"

"*Peter!*" It was a woman's cry, distant, echoic.

Peter's heart leaped. Vígdis was still alive. All he had to do was find her.

"Stay there!" he cried. "I'm coming!"

After another several minutes of tediously picking his way through the rock-strewn cavern, he could make out a small beam of light playing on the cave wall. It was white this time, not orange. Vígdis apparently was shining a lantern or flashlight in his direction as a beacon.

The closer he got, the easier it was. The spare illumination was enough to give him some bearing. He could just make out the rocky obstacles he needed to skirt or climb over. Soon he was running.

He came out into a broader expanse that ended abruptly before what appeared to be another major drop.

Vígdis was standing there, waving her flashlight in his direction. She motioned him on.

Sloat was there too. Peter could see him in the light of a small lantern on the cavern floor that threw lurid shadows on the rock walls and ceiling. Amos was at the edge of the precipice, kneeling. Maybe he was hurt.

"Hi," Peter said to Vígdis as he closed the remaining distance. "You OK?"

She nodded. "You?"

He shook his head. "I may be a little punch drunk, but I'm still in the ring. Is Amos hurt?"

Vígdis gave him a small, cryptic smile. "Why don't you ask him yourself?"

He walked slowly toward the precipice. "Amos?"

Sloat looked up with a distracted expression. "Hello, Peter," he said softly.

"Are you all right?"

Sloat appeared almost startled by the question. "Peter, I finally understand," he half whispered.

Peter's throbbing head tried to process what was happening. "Amos, are you trying to tell me—"

"Peter," said Vígdis, "Amos prayed to receive Christ."

Peter stood stunned.

Sloat climbed slowly to his feet, holding something on a tether from his right hand.

Peter knew his brain wasn't firing on all cylinders. "And what's that?" he asked, pointing to Sloat's hand in the shadows.

Sloat held it up, and Vígdis shined her light on it. The object was some kind of pendant on a leather thong. At the end was a semicircle of dark volcanic material, etched with strange symbols.

Peter stepped closer until he could make out each character:

ᛃᛃᚱᚢᚲᚱᛖᛞ ᛞᚢᛚ ᛈᛞᛖᛏ

"Does this look familiar to you, Peter?" asked Vígdis.

"The rune stone! Where did—"

Sloat's eyes twinkled in the lantern light. "Watch."

He moved gingerly to the edge of the abyss and knelt again.

Peter squinted to make out what his friend was doing. It appeared that he was slowly letting down the rune stone into some receptacle just over the edge with needle-threading care.

All at once, Peter didn't have to squint anymore. The cavern erupted in a riot of shimmering orange light. It danced and played as if coming from a thousand fires. And the cries returned—the same weeping and wailing—only far louder this time. All seemed to emanate from somewhere in the abyss. Individual voices now were distinguishable, as if in the grip of some afflictor.

They were no longer at the outskirts of hell. They were at Hades Ground Zero. Or, at least, someone had created a clever illusion to make them think they were.

"Step back, Peter." Vígdis tugged at his elbow.

Just as he was about to ask why, an apparition materialized on the verge of the precipice, not far from where he had been standing. It was hideous to behold—a sexless, gray-skinned, dough-faced, amorphous human remnant, consisting primarily of head and torso with limbs nonapparent.

"Help me! Help me!" the loathsome creature cried. "Save me from the worm that does not die and the fire that is not quenched!"

And then it was gone.

Peter knew better than to credit reality to this apparition, but in his current state it only added to his disorientation.

Now he found himself caught in the gaze of a pair of malignant eyes that hung in the void, disembodied, appearing out of nowhere. There was something about this that bothered him far more than the apparition.

Peter turned to Amos. "What *is* this?"

The presence in the void answered first. "You tell *me*."

A body materialized about those baleful orbs. It was a giant in the mail-clad garb of an ancient weapons forger. "Vulcan, god of fire and sword."

Just as quickly, the figure transmuted into a deformed ogre. "Hephaestus, lord of volcano and fire, hurled to earth by Zeus himself."

And then it became a devious-looking miscreant, writhing in chains and uttering murderous expletives. "Loki, the trickster, shackled in the bowels of the earth."

Peter wanted the display to be over, but it continued still, this time in the form of a goat-faced satyr with cloven hoofs, horns, and tail.

"Beelzebub, the lord of flies and king of hell."

"End program!" Peter shouted.

But the metamorphic face had one more word to utter. "Come!"

Peter took several steps back as Sloat reached down again into the chasm.

Amos's hand brought up the rune stone again, and the demonic picture show died.

"Yikes!" said Peter. "Who would want to obey that character?"

"Apparently somebody did," said Sloat. He motioned with his flashlight for Peter to join him at the brink. Then he shined the light down into the inky depths.

Peter, peering over the edge, could barely make out another floor several hundred feet below them. And then his eyes focused on the object of Sloat's flash beam. Even at this distance there was no doubt that he was looking at the crumpled body of someone who had, in fact, gone over this very edge.

He stood up and retreated a step. "Holograms, of course."

Sloat nodded and pointed his flashlight at a shiny metal plate where the rune stone had reposed, acting as an on-off switch. "Interactive holograms, in fact. You could probably have all kinds of interesting discussions."

"No, thanks—"

And then he was suddenly pitched forward toward the void. Another quake!

He and Amos scrambled away from the brink, and Peter found himself looking at a step up to get back to where Vígdis stood. And then, with a jolt, he was looking at two steps up. Their small ledge was breaking off into the chasm.

"Jump!" Peter cried.

He reached the solid floor just as the ledge dropped yet again. And then it was gone.

"*Amos!*" Peter screamed.

He was answered only by an enormous smashing of rocky tonnage into stones and pebbles on the lower floor that made his footing reverberate with the deadly rumble. Peter's heart sank as if it were part of the defunct ledge.

"Peter! Back here," said a familiar voice.

He turned and saw the man he'd just written off as gone.

"Amos!"

Sloat clapped him affectionately on the shoulder. "You're slow, pal. I'd already jumped to safety before you yelled."

Peter was about to explain about the state of his head when the ground began to shake much harder.

"Let's get out of here," Sloat said. "This whole area could collapse next."

* * *

With decent light, they were able to make swift progress. But Peter was beginning to feel as if they were inside some cavernous womb in the throes of labor. And now the contractions were coming with accelerating frequency. He knew what that had to mean. They probably didn't have much time left before a cataclysmic grand finale.

Without a light of his own, he was forced to stick close to Sloat and Vígdis, who were wasting no time retracing their route. It was probably just as well, since without a helmet radio he had to stay close just to talk.

"Amos," he said as they neared their original point of descent, "you still haven't explained one thing."

"Only one?"

"Well, maybe two—your decision to trust Christ and what that hologram had to do with it."

Sloat managed a chuckle. "Actually, that little freak show had almost nothing to do with it—although I have to admit it was pretty intimidating to run into that in the dark."

They were in sight now of the wider canyon wall where they had made their descent. When Vígdis shined her light up the slope, Peter could even see the tiny fluorescent lines of their climbing ropes. The sight was curiously reassuring.

He noticed that Sloat's hand reached out in the shadows and found hers. He also noticed that Vígdis left her hand there in Sloat's as they walked along.

"About your trusting Christ—" Peter tried again.

But their stony womb was convulsing yet again.

"Watch out!" Vígdis yelled, whipsawing Sloat's arm to one side.

A boulder crashed out of nowhere and smashed into the canyon wall on the other side.

The three broke into a sprint for the exit. Peter knew the hard part was yet to come—pulling themselves straight up nearly eight hundred feet.

When they reached the bottom of the first rope, Sloat said, "Peter, I suggest you let me take the lead this time. I'll hammer in the new anchors. By the time I get halfway up the second rope, Vígdis can start. And then you can bring up the rear."

Peter silently agreed that under the circumstances Sloat probably could get them out of here more quickly than he could.

"Amos," said Vígdis, "should we not wait and try to time it so we're climbing in between tremors? We don't want to get knocked off almost at the top."

"That's a chance we're going to have to take," Sloat said as he attached the first line to his carabiner harness. "There's not enough time between quakes. They're coming too close together now."

"All right. But Einar says to hurry up. Something is going to blow soon."

It was a long, tedious climb. Several times Peter had to stop and clutch his anchors and pray while the rock face shook and rattled, threatening to toss him off into the void. Each time he felt a heavy adrenaline rush. He waited until his heartbeat slowed before resuming his climb.

And then it happened. Vígdis was just clearing the top, and Peter was halfway up the last line, when there came an ominous roar and rumble. Half a moment later came the accompanying shake, rattle, and roll.

Peter just prayed that somehow he would be able to hold on and ride this one out. He was thrown about so violently that his hands were torn from the wall anchors. He could do nothing but swing freely until it was over.

Now he was pelted and pounded by a small avalanche of loose rock from the top. A rock struck him in the face, and he tasted something salty. Another struck the back of his head, making him grateful once again for the helmet. And now he was taking a charge in the midsection that sent him spinning in gut-wrenching circles.

And then his head struck the cliff face a resounding blow. Stunned, Peter began to free-fall down the line. He felt as if he was going to be sick.

"*Peter!*"

Amos's distant, panicky cry from somewhere above snapped him back to reality. He jerked up on the line, braking its play through the carabiner. His free fall stopped with a nasty jerk that left him dangling and twisting over the abyss.

He looked down at the line and felt sick all over again. Only about six inches of rope were left in the carabiner. In less than a second, he would have been launched out into the abyss, plunging to meet Vulcan, Hephaestus, Loki, and Beelzebub in their counterfeit hell.

Fortunately the worst of the tremor seemed to be over. The quaking had died to a trembling. But Peter was beginning to wonder if he had enough strength left to make the climb. He felt dizzy, sick, faint, and failing. Maybe he'd better go for it while it was still possible.

He got his feet back on the rock face and hauled himself hand over hand up the line until he was back in the groove with the anchors as footholds and was climbing steadily again.

But this time it went much more slowly, and the higher he got, the slower it went. And then finally, he had to stop. He was out of gas. Maybe if he rested a minute.

He looked up. He could see the crest and someone's head bending over the edge.

"Just hold tight, Peter!" Sloat yelled. "We'll haul you the rest of the way up."

Wearily Peter planted his feet on the pitons and grabbed the line with the full strength of his grip as it began to pull him up.

Now he was walking up the rock face on the anchors almost effortlessly. But the dizziness was getting the best of him. He felt cold, clammy, and woozy.

The next thing he knew he was over the top with assorted hands grabbing for him. He fell to his knees in a near faint.

"Let him down," Sloat said.

And then he was resting blessedly face down on the ground. Now he could pass out or get sick or even die if he had to. He was vaguely aware that it was raining. The rest was just too confused to try to figure out.

* * *

Some time later Peter realized that he must have been dazed or dozing, but even so he had been walking steadily downhill with some assistance. One arm was up over Amos's shoulders and the other over Einar's.

Amos was trying to ask him something.

"Do you think you can make it just a little farther?"

Peter licked his dry, caked lips and croaked, "Sure, Amos. Race you."

He looked up and was dully surprised to see a big green machine with a lazily cranking rotor perched at the top. "Who called the cab?" he asked.

"Guess he's feeling a little better, Einar," said Sloat.

They were almost there. Peter felt rubber-legged and was glad for the support. Now that he was wide awake, he was even more grateful that it appeared they were not going to have to spend another half day climbing back down the mountain. He would never make it. And he suspected that time was probably too short, anyway, before something bad happened.

But he still couldn't make the picture fit. "Whose chopper?"

"The Institute's," said Njálsson. "Remember, I said they had one for emergencies? They say Hekla is about to blow. And I believe them."

They were there now. The big Icelander said something to the pilot and got in beside him while the other three climbed in the back. Vígdis strapped Peter in just as the rotor-thumping accelerated in pitch and the floor began to reverberate underneath them.

A moment later they were airborne and putting the mountain behind them. Peter tried to get a look at it, but they were at the wrong angle.

"Uh-oh," Sloat said, looking out the window on the other side. "Look at that."

Peter thought he was hearing more thunder. And then his stomach fluttered as the helicopter lost altitude, then recovered, while shaking and shuddering as if it had been broadsided by some kind of shock wave. Despite the excitement, he was feeling overwhelmingly drowsy. It was probably his head again. He noted that he ought to get somebody to look at it when they got back to wherever they were going.

He looked out the window again. Now he was at the proper angle to see what had impressed Sloat, but for a moment he didn't quite realize what he was seeing.

It was Hekla in full eruption, blowing its stack to high heaven.

In the front, Einar was shaking his head and muttering. "This is not good."

32

Rome

Father Zell smiled benevolently and poured Carlotta a cup of tea, the beverage that had become so dear to her. It was good of him to see her again, and she told him so.

"Nonsense, daughter," he murmured. "It is my pleasure. What is on your mind today? What can I tell you?"

Carlotta wrinkled up her nose, stared at the ceiling, and thought hard. There was something, if only she could think of it.

"Perhaps," Zell suggested after a moment, "you would like to know what this place is and why you are here."

Yes. She nodded brightly. That was exactly it. How remarkable that he seemed able to anticipate her very thoughts before she could think them.

"Yes, daughter. There are some things you must know. The time is short, and in just a few days we are expecting the prince who is to come."

Carlotta felt an odd sense of expectancy. "The prince?"

"Yes. He is the one who is qualified to wear the Crown and wield the Scepter—after he endures yet one more trial."

Something tugged at the corners of her memory. "Crown and Spear."

Zell nodded with his eyes closed. "Have you seen them in the sanctuary?"

"Yes. Yes, I did. What do they mean?"

"Ah!" Zell's eyes widened with fervor. "He who wears the Crown and wields the Scepter rules the world. The Crown is the ancient diadem of the emperor of Europe, the political ruler. And the Scepter is *Gungnir,* the symbol of military sovereignty and Woden, the warrior god."

Some of Zell's words rang bells. "Woden?"

"Yes, daughter. You saw his likeness in the sanctuary over the regalia."

"The man on the cross?

Zell smiled patiently. "A common confusion. That is a tree, not a cross. To obtain enlightenment and secret wisdom for himself, he sacrificed one eye and was pierced with the spear and hung on the tree. That is the other coincidence. Some Christians believe this spear to be the lance that pierced the side of Christ."

"It isn't?"

Zell shrugged. "Who is to say? Some even believe it to be the ancient rod of Hermes with life-giving powers. What is for certain is that it is a most remarkable ancient instrument. And to those who have understanding, it is all one and the same—Hermes, Mercury, Woden . . ."

A brief silence elapsed while Zell let her dwell on those things.

"We shall begin your formal instruction very soon in these things—tonight, perhaps," he continued. "But daughter, what questions do you have now?"

Carlotta tried to sort through the dull confusion in her mind. "What sort of instruction?"

"A very good question, daughter. Little do you realize it yet, but you may play a quite significant role with the prince who is to come."

"What kind of role?"

Zell was silent for a moment, seeming to choose his words carefully. "This young man is a true champion of royal lineage, but he has not attained enlightenment. In fact, he apparently has been influenced by some kind of fundamentalist Christian cult. Your role will be to help open this young man's eyes."

"Who is this prince?"

Zell got up and moved slowly about the booklined study, hands clasped behind his back, his head bowed thoughtfully. Then he stopped and looked searchingly at Carlotta.

"His name is Peter Carpenter McBride."

"Oh," said Carlotta, puzzled. If the other things rang a bell, this set off a fire alarm.

Zell was smiling beatifically. "What is it, my daughter?"

"I believe I know a Peter McBride."

"Indeed. That is why your assistance may be so invaluable."

"But what can I do?"

"You can help him overcome this Christian fanaticism and liberate his mind to receive the truth."

"How can I do that?"

Zell smiled mildly. "Love, child. Does he not love you?"

Carlotta found her memories as elusive as eels. "I—I don't know."

"I assure you that he does. And you love him, do you not?"

Maddeningly, she could not even conjure up an image of Peter McBride's face. But something inside her was answering the question powerfully in the affirmative.

"Yes! Yes, I'm certain that I do."

"Yes." Zell was nodding. "And so, if you are the prince's betrothed, what does that make you?"

"A princess?"

Zell put his hands together. "Think of it. The mate of the ruler who is to come—a position of very great consequence. And so I must have an equal concern for your spiritual well-being as well."

Carlotta could only blink in uncomprehension. She was coming in touch with her own dysfunction, a vague kind of impairment that would not reveal itself.

"But I too am a Christian," she blurted.

"Yes, I know," Zell said condescendingly. "And I do not condemn you for it. There is some truth in Christianity, as far as it goes. It will be my responsibility to move you beyond the elemental into deeper spiritual truth."

"But . . ." she faltered. "But what if I don't . . .want to?"

Zell's smile faded, like the sun passing behind a storm cloud. "Have some more tea, my daughter. Drink deeply."

⋆ ⋆ ⋆

Reykjavík

Something kept nagging at the edges of Peter's tortured mind and fevered brain. It had to do with automobiles and helicopters, although much was jumbled. By turns he was reliving the climb out of the volcano and fantasizing nightmare images that would have frightened an opium eater.

He dodged lightning bolts on the mountaintop. He climbed hand over hand with arms that had no more strength up a rope that had no end. He slid down and down, faster and faster toward the abyss, unable to find the brake handle before he ran out of line. He tried to run through black molasses, dreading confrontation with the Prince of Darkness and a legion of demons around the next corner.

There was an utter blackness that sucked at his eyes and ears and threatened to plunge him into terror and madness. There were ants and snakes and lizards and ravens and bats and centipedes. There were booming thunderclaps and whirling chopper blades and abandoned cars on a burning mountain. And why wouldn't somebody do something?

"Peter!" someone was saying. "It is all right, Peter!"

Peter clutched a soft hand and pressed it to his cheek. "Carlotta," he murmured.

"No, Peter," said the woman, cupping his hand with both of hers. "You can open your eyes now."

He did so and realized his mistake. This was Vígdis. What was she doing here? And there was Amos by her side.

Then it came back to him. His head. He reached up and touched his head. It was oddly numb. Then he remembered the medicine. The memories were coming in reverse order until he put his mind to it.

They had brought him to this hospital, where a red-bearded doctor with an unpronounceable Icelandic name had informed him that he had a concussion. But not to worry; with modern medication and a decent night's sleep, he would be nearly good as new again.

The doctor had spoken of intercranial pressures and contusions and some other terms Peter did not recognize. There was a good deal of wheeling about on a gurney, first to a diagnostic holographic imager in a darkened, antiseptic room, then to this room, which appeared to be his own for now. And there were five injections—two in the neck with a local anesthetic, followed by two more with some miracle biotech pharmaceutical to counteract intercranial pressure, and finally a sedative to induce sleep.

It had done a pretty good job—until now.

"Was I . . . " he faltered.

"Were you what?" Vígdis prompted.

"Was I . . . raving?"

Amos stepped in closer with a mischievous grin. "You kept calling a woman's name. Wait till I tell Carlotta."

"Oh, Amos!" Vígdis remonstrated.

Peter didn't get the joke. "What woman?"

Amos chuckled. "Uda."

Vígdis giggled. "That is not funny, Amos."

"Then why are you laughing?" he rejoined.

Peter's alarm resumed. "The Udas! Did—"

He half sat up, but he was met with Vígdis's fingertips against his chest.

"Take it easy," she insisted. "None of that yet."

"Don't worry about the Udas," said Amos. "A couple guys from the Institute drove them away, just ahead of the eruption."

"Oh," said Peter, relieved. But then he developed a sudden new concern. "Einar! Where is he? Is he all right?"

"Relax, Peter, please," Vígdis said pleadingly. "He is no worse off than you—or not much, anyway."

"He got himself snakebitten, Peter," Amos interjected. "He thought it was just a little thing, but by the time we'd evacuated, his leg had swollen to the point that his pantleg had to be cut off. They're detoxifying him now. He's expected to be OK. Like you, he'll probably just spend the night."

"Snakes?" said Peter. "I don't remember any snakes."

Vígdis smiled and squeezed his hand.

Peter had forgotten she was holding it. He felt a twinge of affection and hoped once again that Amos might give his heart to this very good woman.

"That is how Einar knew to radio for help," she said. "When the vermin start to flee, you know things are all over."

"Like rats," said Sloat, "deserting the sinking ship."

She nodded. "They seem to know."

With a shudder Peter found himself back on Mount Hekla in his mind's eye. "Snakes, plural? What kind?"

Vígdis shrugged. "Some kind of viper. Nasty reptiles. All over the place. Did you ever hear of the eruption of Mount Pelée in 1902?"

"No."

"On the island of Martinique. About thirty thousand people died. But before the eruption, the town of St. Pierre was inundated with swarms of ants, foot-long centipedes, and poisonous snakes from the mountain. But that is not even the most remarkable thing."

"What was that?" asked Sloat.

"Martinique had been a haven for the libertines of Europe. By 1902 it had become hostile to the gospel and to the missionaries. On Good Friday someone sacrificed a pig on the altar of the cathedral in St. Pierre. Then they sent the missionaries packing. But as they left, Mount Pelée erupted—killing all but two people in St. Pierre."

"Reminds me of the judgments of Revelation," Peter said. "Amos—did you really have a conversion experience inside Hekla, or did I just dream that?"

"No dream," Sloat said soberly. "If you recall, I was starting to tell you it had nothing to do with our hologram from hell when we were interrupted by the quake. It was bad enough facing those images to get the amulet. But my real jolt came when we got separated right after that first big quake. Somehow my helmet light went out, and I was left stumbling around in the total dark. That was far more terrifying."

"I know what you mean."

"I've always been pretty much the fearless type, which is one reason I'm in this line of work, I guess. But that total darkness really got to me. For a minute I thought I was going to lose it. I couldn't shake the idea that this must be something like hell, and I didn't want any part of it. But then I realized that might be exactly what awaited me some day. And then something kind of strange happened."

Peter was hanging on every word. "What was that?"

"I fiddled with the helmet light and found out it wasn't broken—it had just gotten turned off. And then it came to me that that was like my spiritual condition. I was stumbling in the dark when the light was within my grasp. I just needed to avail myself of it. It was as if Someone was suggesting this to my mind, if you know what I mean."

"Yes, Amos. I know exactly what you mean."

"So as soon as we got the hologram shut off, I told Vígdis about this experience, and she offered to pray with me."

"How do you feel about your decision?"

Sloat gazed out into space. "Cleansed, set free—and a little frustrated. I don't know the Bible. I want to ask questions. I want to know what I need to do with this new faith."

Peter smiled. "That's natural. I'm sure there are places in Reykjavík where you can buy an English Bible. Vígdis and I would be delighted to take a stab at your questions."

Peter thought it would be interesting to see how Amos handled his bitterness. He suspected Vígdis could be a bigger help in that area than he could.

She cleared her throat and touched Sloat's arm. "We probably ought to let him get some rest."

"Oh, nonsense," said Peter. "I feel OK. You don't listen to doctors, do you? What do they know?"

"Well, if you want to get better and be discharged in the morning," she chided, "you will have to follow medical advice and rest. Get a good night's sleep and take your medicine. Listen to those doctors."

Peter grinned. "Yes, Mom. Oh, but wait! The amulet. Where is it?"

Sloat reached inside his shirt and extracted the carved stone on its thong around his neck. He pulled it off and offered it to Peter.

"No," Peter demurred. "I trust you."

Sloat shrugged and hung it back around his neck. "No reason not to. But it's not my job to return the regalia to the Hofburg—that's yours. Mine is just to get it out of enemy hands—which we have done."

"That's OK," Peter insisted. "I only wanted to make sure it was secure."

"It's secure." He patted the small bulge in the breast of his jacket. "A Smith and Wesson manual security system. Very effective."

"You know what to do with it next?"

Sloat's straight face was betrayed by twinkling eyes. "Have it bronzed and hang it in the den?"

"I'll bet you don't have a den."

"I don't even have a house. Never in one town long enough."

"Listen. Just call Rick and Moira in Brussels and—"

"And get them to translate the runes for us," Sloat finished for him.

"Check. And then when I wake up in the morning, presumably I'll know whether to pack my bag for Rotterdam or Kiev or Istanbul."

Sloat shrugged. "I hope it's that easy."

Vígdis cleared her throat again, and Sloat glanced across the room at the clock.

"One more thing," Peter said, "what's happening with Hekla? How major was the eruption?"

Vígdis looked grim. "It is still in progress, Peter. This is more than just a colorful tourist eruption. There is no end in sight."

He gulped. "Thank God we got away when we did. How bad is it?"

"As Einar would say, not good. In prior centuries, Hekla has blighted the landscape for miles, darkened the sun, and destroyed crops and livestock, which led to widespread famine and disease. Thousands died in conditions like nuclear winter. Whether that happens again is anybody's guess. The only thing we can say for certain is that there will be more spectacular sunsets for a while."

"Oh. Tell me, does the Geophysical Institute track earthquakes and volcanic activity around the world as well as in Iceland?"

Vígdis nodded. "Correct. And yes, earthquake activity has been accelerating for some time, as you might suspect. The scientists get nervous trying to explain why—except the Christian scientists, of course."

"Excuse me," Sloat interrupted. "What do you mean by that?"

"Sorry, Amos," she said. "Famines, plagues, earthquakes in many places—signs Jesus gave for His coming and the end of the age."

Sloat looked skeptical. "The famous second coming? You're not suggesting it's imminent, are you?"

"Actually," said Peter, "the coming of the Antichrist is more imminent, because it sets the stage. That's why we're so antsy about this Crown and Spear business."

A nurse entered the room looking as if she had serious business on her mind. She was not quite as big as Einar, but she looked about as powerful.

"Vígdis," said Peter, "maybe you can bring Amos up to speed on end-times things."

She smiled. "I shall be glad to try."

"Get rested up, Peter," said Amos as they headed for the door.

"Gud blessi thig," said Vígdis.

"Say, 'Ah,'" said the nurse.

* * *

Rome

Olivia, the older, darker, and more solicitous of the two sisters, watched uneasily as Carlotta reached once again for her teacup and, also once again, found it empty. She was doing that frequently.

"Why not leave the tea alone for now?" said the woman. "Too much is not good for you. I am afraid it will addle your brain."

Mirabella, the younger, quieter sister, traded a dark glance with Olivia. Her face wore a disapproving expression.

Carlotta was feeling vaguely anxious. "What—what do you mean?"

"You know," Mirabella interjected quickly. "Too much theobromine in tea. Like caffeine, it can make you hyper."

Carlotta nodded, but she wasn't really buying it. Her brain might be addled, but it was not from overstimulation. She wasn't hyper. If anything, her nervous system was depressed. Carlotta, for once, thought to say a silent prayer. What was Olivia really trying to warn her about, and why was Mirabella trying to quiet her?

Then, as if in answer to her prayer, came a moment of crystal clarity. It was like a lifting of the fog of confusion, and in that instant Carlotta thought she saw the menace confronting her. It came in the form of a flashback.

"Have some orange juice," said a vaguely familiar female voice.

And then she actually recalled the name *Estelle Morgenthau.* That was how she had been ensnared in the first place—by drugging. Just beneath the surface, darker, dimmer memories stirred of a woman named Elizabeth Morningstar in a castle basement. Just as quickly another scene was coming to her. In her mind's eye she pictured the triforium of a Gothic cathedral in which a demon named Belen was assailing her in the guise of a woman named Wendy Carlisle.

"Something wrong?" said Olivia, wearing another worried expression.

Carlotta wondered what her own face had revealed. She glanced at her hand and saw that it was shaking. She quickly stuck it into her pocket and manufactured a cavernous yawn.

"Excuse me," she said. "I must rest before I see Father Zell."

The two sisters nodded approvingly and began clearing out of her room. Actually Carlotta intended to do more praying than resting. She needed a plan for getting her head clear.

33

Rome

Have some tea, daughter." Zell smiled like a doting uncle as he set the cup and saucer on the coffee table before the couch.

"Thank you." Carlotta pretended to take a sip.

It was maddening. She actually wanted the tea—really wanted it. She said another silent prayer and commanded her trembling hand to be still. Surely this had something to do with chemical addiction. She was determined to get free.

"Daughter—"

A knock sounded at the door, and someone entered.

Carlotta tried not to start at the sight of Estelle Morgenthau. She concentrated on remaining expressionless no matter what she saw or heard or felt.

Morgenthau looked as though she wanted to speak privately until Zell motioned her to join them.

"You have a status report?" he asked, and she nodded. "Please join us. I think Ms. Waldo would profit from hearing about it. Have some tea?"

Morgenthau's sour look did not escape Carlotta's attention. The older woman seated herself on a chair opposite the couch and got right to the point.

"Our sources report that Peter McBride and his Zionist sidekick have secured the rune stone in Iceland."

Zell clasped his hands in delight. "Excellent! Right on time. Does he know its meaning? Is he on his way to Rome?"

Morgenthau shrugged. "I have no doubt he's figuring it out. He did before. But he's being treated in a Reykjavík hospital for some kind of injury, apparently minor."

Carlotta almost jumped. Peter—her beloved—hurt? Her heart hammered at the news. Then it started coming back to her—the rune stone, the shootout in the museum, their betrothal. Clearly the sedation, some kind of designer drug, was dissipating in her system.

Zell's smile faded. "Is this injury a problem?"

"I don't think so," said Morgenthau. "Wendy Carlisle says he's scheduled for discharge in the morning."

"All right. What about Khalid?"

"Wendy says Sgt. Witherspoon has seen to it that Halima has the same information that Peter McBride and the Zionist have."

"Very good. Thank you, Ms. Morgenthau. Is there anything else? How is Ponzi? Has he figured out we are right here in Rome?"

She shook her head. "No, I've made sure of that. But our other friends are acting up."

Zell frowned.

"Neumann and DiFalcone. It's in the news today. Turn on your wallscreen."

With a few commands Zell called up a report recorded earlier from One World News showing scenes of labor strife and police arrests juxtaposed with government buildings and financial institutions.

A woman's voice-over began to explain. "Tensions between crime lord Salvatore DiFalcone and the regime of EU Chancellor Waldemar Neumann escalated today with reports of a massive influx of counterfeit currencies in Italy, France, and Germany.

"Financial markets tumbled to their lowest point in three years as confusion prompted many investors to shift their assets into commodities and precious metals and other presumably safe havens, triggering a large sell-off of stocks.

"At a meeting of World Trade Organization ministers and economists in Brussels, Neumann blamed DiFalcone for what he called financial terrorism and threatened to initiate a currency recall throughout the entire EU."

The scene changed to a packed meeting room, where the smartly attired, balding, and steely-eyed chancellor gestured with an admonishing finger from the podium.

"If need be," he said, "I have a solution for financial terrorism, for mass counterfeiting, and for the hoarding of billions in ill-gotten gains from criminal enterprises. At a future date, we eliminate all further use of paper currency and coin in favor of exclusive reliance upon the smartcard/electronic telecredit system already in use throughout the European Union. Those who can legitimately account for their accumulations of capital may convert those into electronic European Currency Units.

"This will effectively flush the system of billions in illegitimate ECUs, which are, in fact, claims against the government. This also would serve to strengthen the EU fiscally while breaking the back of the professional criminal element."

There was building applause, cut short by the return of the woman reporter.

"Chancellor Neumann," she said, "did not say if or when he planned to implement this bold initiative, which presumably would require parliamentary approval. Some government sources indicated this might be a bluff, but at least one—MP Sir James Crisp—suggested something more sinister might be afoot."

The reporter's face was replaced by that of a genteel, white-haired man speaking calmly despite the grim subject.

"I have been warning for some time," he said evenly, "of covert government plans to convert to a totally cashless structure based on a government credit system. If that were to occur, the ability to buy and sell would become totally government controlled, depending upon one's good standing with the authorities. And then Population and Health will have its strongest device yet for total population control. I have no doubt whatever that a crisis such as this present one could be employed as an excuse to implement such a system."

Sir James's face was replaced with the earlier scenes of labor strife and police arrests.

"The conflict worsened yesterday," noted the reporter, "when Italian police began rounding up key members of DiFalcone's organization in Rome, Milan, Venice, Naples, Genoa, Bologna, and several other locations. This was in apparent response to crippling dock strikes that have been occurring throughout Italy. Nobody knows what started the conflict, although various sources have suggested a major power struggle is in process. Nor does anyone know quite where this frighteningly escalating conflict will finally end. For One World News, this is Crystal McKenzie reporting."

As the sound and picture faded, Carlotta became aware that Zell was laughing. To her ears, the laughter sounded a bit manic. And then it ceased abruptly.

"What a simpleton!" he exclaimed. "'Nobody knows what started the conflict.' And she was the very one who broke the story about the Crown and Spear! Ms. Morgenthau, I want you to contact this Crystal McKenzie and clue her in. No—even better, have Sgt. Carlisle brief her."

Morgenthau looked troubled. "Uh . . . are you sure you want to do that?"

Zell smashed his fist into the palm of his other hand. His face was livid. "Yes!" he thundered. "Not only that, but I want Sgt. Carlisle to see to it that Crystal McKenzie is here to witness the main event on Wednesday for the waiting world. And for your information, I'll do the thinking around here, Ms. Morgenthau. I suggest for your own sake that you not forget that."

At that, Morgenthau reddened and rose to her feet. "Yes, sir."

"Please keep us informed of these developments. You may go."

The woman shot Carlotta a cryptic, frigid glance and spun on her heel.

Zell followed her to the door.

Carlotta took this opportunity to empty her cup into the philodendron on an end table by the couch.

Upon his return, Zell's dangerous dark side was gone without a trace, replaced once again by a sunny expression that may have been intended to reassure. But the swiftness of his mood changes and the explosiveness of his wrath were frightening.

"Well, daughter," he said with a kindly smile, "the prince approaches. Everything is falling into place at the proper time. You can see the whole world awaits its deliverance from chaos and confusion by the one who grasps the Scepter. Do you understand any of this?"

Carlotta shook her head. "No. I await the deliverer from Zion, the one with nail prints in His hands."

She wanted to say that anyone else would be a counterfeit. She wanted to insist that Peter McBride could not be the prince who was to come. But realizing the grave danger, she held her tongue.

Zell looked mildly surprised, then made a dismissive gesture. "For that, I would suggest you not hold your breath. What if I told you that Jesus did not die on Calvary but lived on, even to have descendants? No, we do not have to wait for—as they say—pie in the sky. We have the opportunity to grasp history now and make things happen. Apparently there are things about Mr. McBride that you do not know."

He gave her a penetrating and unsettling look.

Carlotta, trying to stay in character, continued to hold her tongue.

He assumed the smug expression of someone who holds trump cards. "Do you know Peter McBride's real name?"

"That is his real name."

Zell's eyebrows rose slightly. "Not 'Carpenter'?"

"Well, yes, that was his name when he was very young, before his mother remarried and Neal McBride became his adoptive father."

"Do you know anything about the biological father?"

Carlotta shrugged. "No, other than that he was killed in the Second Korean War when Peter was very small. He doesn't remember him."

Zell smiled slyly. "Captain Louis Carpenter was descended from an old French family—Charpentier, actually. That's where it becomes interesting. Have some more tea, daughter."

He poured her another cup and then got up to pace the room, seeming to be gathering his thoughts.

Carlotta surreptitiously watered the philodendron again.

"Royal blood flows in his veins," Zell said carefully. "Possibly of the highest order. We believe we have traced the genealogy to the fourteenth century and the Charpentier and Plantard royal families of Merovingian descent. It was a most exciting find, especially since he was also engaged in a quest for the Crown and Scepter. All of the signs are right."

He paused and scrutinized Carlotta's face.

She was having trouble taking any of this seriously. "What does 'Merovingian' mean?"

Zell's eyes brightened. "This is the heart of your history lesson, daughter, so you can help Peter McBride realize his destiny. 'Merovingian' refers to the dynasty of Merovee, fifth-century king of the Franks, who drove the Romans and Huns out of France. Through the centuries most of the ruling families of Europe have come from the royal Merovingian line. Charlemagne, who founded the Holy Roman Empire, married into this line to establish his own dynasty. During the Crusades, the first king of Jerusalem from the Knights Templar was a Merovingian. In the modern era the Habsburgs were of this bloodline."

"The Habsburgs?" Carlotta blurted, reminded of Peter's perplexities.

Zell appeared not to hear her. "The Knights Templar supposedly established an international banking system that financed entire kingdoms. Kings and popes conspired to exterminate them, but they were never totally successful. In fact, to this day a remnant is alive and well as a very secret society."

Carlotta's thoughts raced. There were many questions she wanted to ask, but she couldn't appear too eager.

"How do you know this, sir? Are they involved with the Crown and Spear?"

Zell's expression turned stony. "Let's say we are in contact. Their single desire is to see the establishment of a one-world government with a bona fide Merovingian sitting on the throne. And to think that it may be within our grasp even now!"

"How do you—they—plan to get people like Neumann and DiFalcone and Ponzi to move over and make room for this upstart?"

Zell smiled. "It is simple. Money. Our friends exert considerable control over international commerce and banking—behind the scenes. If that little man Wally Neumann is threatening a mass currency recall, it's because someone told him to do so."

Zell stopped pacing and sat down. When he spoke again, it was in a hushed tone. "History records that Merovee himself claimed descent from Woden."

"Woden the god?"

Zell looked mildly amused. "Why not? Many of the famous Greek and Roman heroes were half-god, half-human."

Carlotta nodded, vaguely remembering the stories.

"Legend has it," Zell continued, "that Thor, the slayer of giants and dragons, was a Trojan, and one of his descendants was a wise-man–magician named Odin."

"Like Woden?"

Zell nodded. "Odin led his people north into Germany, France, and Scandinavia. Scholars say the mythology of these men of the north—the Norsemen—was a corruption of the Greek myths. In place of Hermes—Mercury—they substituted Odin. For Ulysses, archenemy of Troy, they substituted Loki, the blackguard who is destined to bring about the downfall of the gods at the battle of Ragnarök."

"Is that the Norse Armageddon?"

"Yes, daughter—Götterdämmerung. I want you to learn about these last things. If Peter Carpenter McBride is not successful in his quest, it could be the beginning of the end."

Carlotta was genuinely puzzled. "The beginning of the end of what?"

Zell frowned. "You saw the news report. If you don't think this is serious business, just wait. You will change your mind."

"But why is Peter supposed to come here? And how am I supposed to help him? And for that matter, who is this Khalid?"

Zell shook his head. "It is all part of Peter McBride's quest and trial, which he must satisfy to prove his worthiness. For now, I want you to learn the ways that Peter must learn so that he can hear it from someone he loves and trusts. As a young priest, it took me years to realize the underlying unity of all faiths. For you, we do not have that kind of time."

He took down two books from a shelf above his desk in the corner and handed them to her. "I think you will find many of your answers in these. In fact, I want you to spend the next twenty-four hours gleaning as much as you can, and we shall talk further. For now, what else can I tell you?"

Carlotta had no hesitation. "The Spear. What is its significance?"

Zell appeared to be appraising her through half-closed eyes. Carlotta began to feel uncomfortable under the prolonged scrutiny, but when he finally spoke, it was in calm and measured tones.

"That is a great mystery, daughter. One story says Joseph of Arimathea took it to Europe, possibly France. In the Middle Ages it disappeared entirely. Such a spear was presented to Pope Innocent VIII in the fifteenth century. Whether all of these are the same spear, or if it's the same instrument in our chancel, are good questions."

"Your personal feeling?"

"Perhaps it is none of those. Perhaps it is Woden's own spear. What we do know is that it has a mysterious and powerful effect on people. We also know that if Jesus did not really die on the cross, then this, of course, could not have been the instrument that proved His death."

Carlotta could not resist expressing her own opinion. "I have very little faith in holy relics. But I have the utmost faith in the fact of Christ's death on the cross."

The piercing expression returned to Zell's darkened face. "Peter Charpentier," he muttered, almost too low for Carlotta to hear.

"I beg your pardon?"

"Jesus and Mary Magdalene may have fled to France. Do you think it a coincidence that one line of nobility would bear a name so reminiscent of the Carpenter of Galilee?"

Carlotta was dumbfounded by the sacrilege.

"You asked me a minute ago how you could help Peter."

When Zell let that hang, Carlotta said, "Yes?"

"The best thing you can do to help him, daughter, is simple —renounce this childish Christian faith and open your spiritual eyes to a deeper reality."

Carlotta felt the shakes returning. How she needed a cup of tea.

34

Rome

Peter was never so glad to see a hotel as he was to see the familiar Fiorello with its vigilant pines and leaded glass and rose marble and gleaming brass, not to mention its quaint and colorful house detective, Tony Novello.

Novello appeared his old, garrulous self, cracking jokes and capering about as if he had never intercepted flying lead.

Novello and Sloat slapped each other playfully and traded good-natured insults before the detective turned his scrutiny upon Peter.

"How is that head, Peter?" he asked as they shook hands vigorously. "You look like you could use a little chianti to put some color back in those cheeks."

Peter chuckled. "I had a good deal of color a couple of hours ago—green."

"Green?"

"Airsickness. I've never been sick on a plane before. Must have something to do with the concussion or the medication. And when I walk, it feels like I'm moving around on a trampoline. Other than that, I'm OK—as long as I take my headache medicine and cross my fingers and hold my mouth just right."

"Ah!" said the detective with a dismissive wave. "We shall have you feeling like a new man before you know it."

Novello escorted them upstairs to their rooms. Peter was pleasantly surprised to discover that they were old, familiar 314 and 316. The detective said the rooms had been reserved just for them ever since they left.

"The Fiorello is not exactly hopping with business right now," he explained.

The moment Peter laid his eyes on the bed, it was all over. "Uh . . . fellows, I think I need to recharge my batteries for a while."

"Beg your pardon?" said Novello.

"He needs some shut-eye," said Sloat.

Novello smiled and nodded. "By all means. And when you awake, Peter, someone else may be here who would like to see you."

Peter wanted to ask who that was. Surely Carlotta wouldn't be back in Europe. Maybe Neal. But he was already on his back on the bed, his respiration slowing. It would have been too much effort to interrupt Amos and Tony on their way out the door.

"So what's new with you, Amos, you old scoundrel?" Tony was saying.

Their voices faded as the door opened onto the hall.

"As a matter of fact," Amos was saying, "there is something very new with me. Let me tell you about it."

And then the door closed onto blessed quiet.

* * *

They strolled a moonlit beach on the Côte d'Azur, hand in hand, the chill waves lapping at their bare feet. The still-warm air from the defunct day carried the nip of salt sea. Carlotta's fingers wove themselves among his, a nonverbal expression of an intimate bond.

Yet there was a tension in the calm. For reasons that make sense only in dreams, Peter was convinced that they needed to quicken their pace, to distance themselves from something unspeakable.

Their feet were jogging through the loose sand when there came a terrifying sound like distant thunder.

"Quick!" Peter cried. "The mountain—it's about to explode!"

Without questioning how he knew, he pulled Carlotta by the hand, but their efforts seemed to spend themselves in the crumbling sand. And now the harder they struggled, the faster the beach seemed to erode beneath their feet.

Suddenly Peter realized their progress had been entirely erased and they were actually losing ground, as if they were on a treadmill gone out of control and threatening to carry them out to sea. Or it was as if the sea was devouring them progressively from heel to ankle, calf to knee. And the deeper they slid back into the ocean, the less traction their feet could find in the disintegrating sand.

And then Peter felt Carlotta's grip fail, her fingers slip hopelessly through his. Something was rumbling and rupturing massively in the distance.

"*Carlotta!*"

His cry seemed to break the spell. The quaking beach was gone, and his tormented mind was set free from its hall of horrors as a man called his name.

Someone had taken his hand and grasped it with reassuring flesh and blood. Peter opened his eyes to see who.

"Dad!" he cried.

"Take it easy, Pete," Neal McBride said. "You'd better stop eating Italian cuisine before taking a nap. It'll give you lunatic nightmares every time."

The familiar crow's feet crinkled at the corners of McBride's smiling eyes as he helped Peter off the bed and onto his feet for a warm bearhug. In the embrace, Peter caught the fleeting aroma of home. It was an enormous encouragement to have Neal here now.

With the two of them together, no challenge seemed beyond possibility.

"They didn't tell me you were here," Peter complained and then peered into the next room. "And for your information, I've had nothing to eat."

He could see Sloat and Novello in animated discussion, Tony waving his hands in the air and Amos nodding.

"I just got here," said McBride, moving toward the other room. "Are you hungry?"

Peter's stomach whispered the answer. "Yeah, come to think of it. I guess I am."

"Good. *Signore* Novello has arranged for some food in the conference room."

Peter was playing catch-up. "We have a conference room?"

"That's right," said McBride. "There are four of us, and we have a lot to discuss."

Sloat and Novello gave Peter a wave and a nod and headed out the door, talking all the way. Peter felt sufficiently revived after his nap to suppose that, with some food in his stomach, he might make it. But first, a dull throb in his head reminded him to take some medicine.

Their conference room was on the fourth floor. There the men found cold cuts already laid out on the table, and they began building themselves some serious sandwiches.

Peter pointed Neal to the head of the table.

McBride shook his head.

"This is your baby, Peter. You run it."

A little reluctantly, Peter sat down and looked around at the munching faces. A large screen dominated the opposite wall.

"Then let's see if we can get Rick and Moira on the line while we finish our sandwiches," he said.

Novello spoke up. "Give me the numbers, Peter, and I'll set it up."

While Novello did so, Peter recounted to his father their perilous descent into Mount Hekla for the rune stone. McBride's eyes lit up when he heard of Amos's conversion experience in the pit.

"Congratulations," said McBride. "But that must have been a pretty traumatic experience."

Sloat stopped chewing and took a swallow. "You might say it was like finding heaven in the midst of hell."

McBride nodded. "In a way, that's how it is for many of us."

Now the images of Rick and Moira Stillman took their places on the split screen, Rick from the Institute and Moira from home in Brussels.

"So are you ready to tell us why you had us traipsing back to Rome?" Peter said after the pleasantries had been exchanged.

"Sure," said Rick, "Not only that, but I think we can give you a pretty good idea where in Rome to look."

Peter held up a hand. "For the benefit of Tony and Neal, please start at the beginning with the rune stone."

"Fine," said Rick. "Are you satisfied with the security of this conversation?"

Peter nodded. "If you're referring to the signal, we've got it scrambled."

"And if you're referring to *Signore* Novello," said Sloat a little stiffly, "he's the only one of our group who has been shot for the cause. There is no security concern here."

"OK, Amos," said Rick with a conciliatory tone. "My apologies. Now, let me display the inscription as it actually appears on the rune stone."

Rick pressed some keys off camera, and the familiar characters appeared across the bottom of their wallscreen:

ᛊᛊᚱᚢᚲᚱᛖᛞ ᛞᚢᛚ ᛈᛞᛖᛏ

Below that appeared another, more legible, inscription:

Templum Mercurii

"That's the literal Latin translation," said Rick. "Temple of Mercury."

Peter was getting that eerie feeling again about lost civilizations and magical mysteries. "And that supposedly is where we'll find the *Reichskleinodien?*"

"That," said Rick, "is anybody's guess. My mission is simply to help you find the place."

"And it's somewhere here in Rome?"

Rick hesitated. "It wouldn't *have* to be in Rome, but the name pretty much narrows it to a handful of places in the general vicinity of Rome and Ostia."

"But why the Temple of Mercury?" Peter asked. "Because of the parallel with Woden?"

"I'm sure that's part of it. But who knows what else these people may have in mind?"

"So don't keep us in suspense. Where do you think this Temple of Mercury is?"

Rick rustled some papers offscreen. *"Mons Aventinus."*

A large graphic inset appeared on the wallscreen, eclipsing the lower portion of Rick's image. It was a map, apparently of the Eternal City. But it took Peter a moment to realize that the feature names were in Latin rather than Italian. This was ancient Rome.

"The Aventine Hill," said Rick. "I'll let Moira explain her theory to you. I happen to agree with it, and I think you will too."

"It's not too difficult," she said. "There are three possible sites, and this place on the Aventine Hill is the only one with a building upon it."

"Why does it have to have a building on it?" Peter objected.

"It doesn't *have* to, but unless you think your thieves are just playing games with buried treasure—"

McBride interjected, "We can eliminate those two possibilities in short order with a metal detector. Just give us the directions."

Novello spoke up. "I'll have it done first thing."

"OK," said Rick, and two locations outside the city lit up on the electronic map with some precise coordinates displayed underneath.

Novello carefully jotted down the vital information. "I think I know exactly where these are."

"Tell us about the third location," said Peter. "The one with the building."

"OK," said Moira. "The historical record is incomplete, but here is what we've been able to piece together. Most standard references give verifiable locations for the other ancient temples—Jupiter, Apollo, Venus, and so on. You can go visit them today. Several references also mention a Temple of Mercury on the Aventine Hill but don't give a precise location. I defy you to find that one today."

"But," said Peter, "I take it you overcame that little problem."

Moira rolled her eyes. "You owe me one, Peter. Let's say it was a bit more than a little problem. It took hours of research, but I finally eliminated every site in the vicinity of the Aventine Hill but one. The problem was that there was almost nothing recorded about it. So I decided to start calling some other scholars. That's when it got really confused—everyone gave me a different story."

"So what made you decide this particular place was the site of the Temple of Mercury?"

Moira shook her head. "I didn't. Believe me, Peter, these scholars don't go out on limbs without facts. I think they were all correct. I think this particular site was probably many things at various points in time. Give us the coordinates, Rick."

A tiny red dot appeared in the middle of the *Mons Aventinus*. After a moment, that image was replaced with a modern map that took a jump in magnification, showing the entire grid of cross streets in the immediate neighborhood.

Peter could not make out any printing. "That's a church?"

Moira nodded. "Yes—San Giacomo—although not an active one today. According to another colleague, it was a small Marianist church until the twelfth century. And maybe a thousand years earlier it had been alternately a temple for the worship of Cybele, Mithras, even Mercury, all the way back to before Christ. If I were going to set up some New Age cult or something like Woden worship, I'd probably go to a place just like this."

Peter had hoped Moira's analysis would be a little more conclusive. He was going to have to trust her judgment. Why did these things always boil down to an issue of faith?

"OK," he said slowly. "Tell me about San Giacomo."

"I don't believe it's had a service for more than forty years. It was bombed around the turn of the century. That's when priests who denounced the Mafia were getting blown to bits by car bombs and drive-by shootings."

Peter was thinking hard. "But who owns this property today?"

Moira shook her head. "I don't know. Not my department."

"Well," said Peter slowly, glancing at Neal, "that'll be our first assignment this afternoon. Woden's Day is only thirty-six hours away."

Neal nodded and smiled faintly. In the old days, it would have been McBride dispatching the troops to courthouses and clerks' offices for incriminating public records.

"Godspeed, Peter," said Rick. "By the way, where's Carlotta?"

Peter smiled. "Oh, she went back to the USP several days ago, before we left Copenhagen for Iceland. I think she had her fill of playing cops and robbers for a while."

Rick nodded, but Peter couldn't help noticing that Neal had reacted with *that look*—something that only a wife or a son would catch—a stiffening, a narrowing of the eyes, a troubled set of the mouth.

Rick was speaking again. "We'll leave you with some thoughts from the greatest authoritative reference in the world, the Bible. For some divine perspective on the Crown and the Spear, check out Genesis forty-nine, verse ten, and Ezekiel twenty-one, verses twenty-six and seven."

Peter asked him to repeat the references, and he wrote them down.

"There's one more," Rick said. "Isaiah forty-six. God speaks of the idols of Bel and Nebo, that must be carried about by beasts and have no power to rescue anyone. And then, in contrast, listen to this great promise: 'You who have been borne by Me from birth, and have been carried from the womb; even to your old age, I shall be the same, and even to your graying years I shall bear you! . . . I shall bear you, and I shall deliver you.'"

"Thanks, Rick. That *is* a great promise."

"We'll be claiming that promise for you while you enter the lion's den and engage the enemy, Peter. Just remember, underneath are the everlasting arms."

"I'll remember. 'Bye, Rick, Moira."

Peter had intended to ask his father about Carlotta as soon as the screen image faded.

McBride beat him to it. "Say, Peter. Did you and Carlotta have a fight or something?"

"Uh . . . no. Why?"

"Well, if she returned to the USP, she didn't bother to tell us. I would think she would have touched base with us through Dyana, at least."

Peter had that airsick feeling again, but without the airplane. Something had to be very wrong here. He stuffed down his rising panic and determined not to let himself get too carried away.

"I'll call Dyana. Maybe she just forgot."

McBride said nothing.

Peter was sure he wasn't buying it. Neither was he.

"OK," Peter said, scanning the faces of the other three men. "Let's talk assignments. Division of labor. Tony, you're going to check out those two alternative locations with a metal detector?"

Novello shook his head. "No need. I can have it done by a couple of maintenance people who know how to keep their mouths shut. Why waste our time where we don't really expect to find anything?"

"You're right." Peter changed his mind. "We're going to need you more on the Aventine Hill job. But by the same token, we can't have anybody outside the inner circle scrabbling over these other sites. What if they actually find something? We must always assume that we could be wrong."

He was answered by silence. No one was willing to challenge that irresistible reasoning.

"That's why," he continued, "I'm going to ask you, Amos, to take over that job. You seem fated to pursue hidden objects with scanners and metal detectors. Sorry, pal."

Amos shrugged. "No problem. It's got to be done, and the sooner started, the sooner finished."

"OK," said Peter. "Then, Neal, I'd like you and Tony to find out everything you can about this Aventine Hill location. You know—current ownership, occupants, if any—"

"Floor plans," interjected McBride. "Color schemes, wiring diagrams, birthmarks, dental records. The usual stuff."

"You got it."

McBride smiled. "OK, chief. We'll report back at the end of the day."

"Uh . . . Peter," said Sloat. "What will *you* be doing?"

Peter got a faraway look. "Taking a long walk, exercising this battered body." And getting alone with God.

* * *

Actually he changed his mind and rented a bike and headed out to the Aventine Hill for a firsthand look. The trek would be challenging, but he needed to shake this malaise with a jump start. Then he would spend some time praying.

At first, Peter wondered if he had erred. Even in the lowest gear and the fastest crank speed, several of the hills nearly beat him. He stopped once after cresting a knoll to let his heart rate ease. But after a while, he felt some strength returning to heart and legs and lungs. From that point, he began challenging the hills and beating them. Even the dull background headache from the residual effects of the concussion seemed to abate.

Peter found that running and cycling were often conducive to reflection and problem solving. This time, he really had something to think about—the whereabouts of Carlotta.

Before renting the bike he had placed a couple of phone calls, one to Dyana and the other to Carlotta's housemate, a woman named Vida. Both women had been in bed still, owing to the time differential. Neither had seen Carlotta or even knew of her plans to return to the USP. Peter played down his fears and suggested that it could be some kind of misunderstanding. Maybe.

All the way up the *Mons Aventinus,* he brooded about what kind of trouble Carlotta could be in. He prayed as he pedaled and tried to resist a feeling of despair.

At long last Peter realized he was approaching the street of San Giacomo. A few more blocks, and there it was. He slowed and looked up and down the strada of little mom-and-pop *bottega* and low-rise *appartamenti*. A few pedestrians were trafficking the shops and apartments, but nothing to cause concern. He felt relatively inconspicuous dismounting and walking his bike to the next corner, where the apparent object of his search stood in dark relief against a backdrop of scudding clouds.

Dominating the entire short block were two dark and battered buildings encircled by chain-link fence crowned with three strands of barbed wire. The foremost structure had no visible name. It was obviously a church, though every piece of glass had been punched out and replaced with crudely cut lumber. The building to the rear was cut from the same architectural cloth, an archaic style in dark stone, perhaps something Gothic. He guessed it must have served at some time as a friary. It was too large for a parsonage and had more the feel of a dormitory about it.

There was no sign to identify this place, and the conclusion that any observer was compelled to adopt was desertion and abandonment. And yet. . . .

Peter leaned his bike against a utility pole and clutched some of the galvanized links, peering through into the churchyard. Something didn't fit.

Then he spotted it. The window boards were freshly cut and still the raw yellow of pine that has not been long exposed to the elements. Along the edges he could see little splinters from the saw cuts, exactly the kind of thing that does not stand up to long exposure. And obliquely along some of the boards at random angles could be seen the stenciled name of the lumberyard—Bellini. This too should have been bleached out and washed away seasons ago.

Something very recent—and very anonymous—was going on here.

Suddenly two brown-and-black snarling dervishes out of nowhere hurled themselves at the fence. Peter yanked his fingers away from the snapping while they were still attached to his hands and backed away, his heart in his throat.

It was curious how little reassurance was provided by cyclone fence restraining a pair of foaming Dobermans. Obviously somebody still owned and cared about this property to protect it in this old-fashioned but deadly effective manner.

Peter retreated toward his bike as the dogs continued to bark and bay, lifting their snouts to the sky. He became aware that those sounds had been joined by a higher-pitched yipping that grew louder.

He turned and saw an old man being led by a dwarfish mutt that had to be at least part dachshund. In any case, it was one of those dogs with an outsized sense of itself.

Its master was an overdressed fellow with black-rimmed glasses, a beaky nose, salt-and-pepper mustache, threadbare trench-coat, snap-brim hat, and a fuming Meerschaum pipe. At this moment he was jerking on the leash and reviling the dog in a torrent of Italian. But as he drew nigh, Peter could see he was also eying Peter with some apparent interest through the thick lenses.

"Good afternoon," Peter said.

"Eh?" The old man cupped an ear with his free hand and jerked the dog with the other.

"I say, '*Good afternoon!*'" Peter repeated over the dog din.

"Yes," said the man. "But the church, she is not for sale."

"I beg your pardon?"

"She has been vacant for years," continued the old man. "Everyone says it is haunted. Then two months ago, the sign comes down. People hear things in the middle of the night. Suddenly the windows are boarded up. It is not good, I say."

"Have people seen something? Who's in there now?"

The old man lifted his free hand above his shoulder, palm up, and waved it slowly, as much as to say, "I know nothing—and I want to keep it that way!"

Instead he said, "You know how people talk. Black masses and all kinds of things. All I can say to you, young man, is to stay as far away from this place as you can if you know what is good for you. Good afternoon."

And then the little mutt was towing him away once again down the street.

35

Rome

The return trip was mostly downhill. Peter found he had more than enough punch left to keep going past the Fiorello and on into the Villa Borghese. It was time to find a good spot under a quiet tree and begin lifting up the concerns of his heart.

Since it was afternoon siesta time in Rome, a few other people had similar ideas. But at last Peter found a place at the foot of an olive tree that he could call his own.

Leaning up against the trunk, he got out his portable and called up the electronic Bible with commentary. He prayed silently for discernment and then tapped out the command for Rick's verse, Genesis 49:10.

> "The scepter shall not depart from Judah, nor the ruler's staff from between his feet, until Shiloh comes, and to him shall be the obedience of the peoples."

Peter scanned the previous verses and identified the passage as the blessing of Jacob upon his twelve sons. What struck him, as Rick probably had intended, was the business about the scepter and ruler's staff.

He sensed that the only spear or scepter that really mattered in the eternal scheme of things was the one that Christ one day would wield over the nations. And that was a divine perspective that Peter needed.

He noticed that the commentary cross-referenced Ezekiel 21:26–27. He called that up next and read God's command to remove the crown of Judah "until He comes whose right it is; and I shall give it to Him."

Again this was the Messiah, who would not only wield the scepter but also wear the crown.

On impulse Peter turned to the end of 2 Kings and read how the Babylonians tore down Jerusalem's walls and burned the Temple. And so Zedekiah, the last king of Judah, was removed from the throne and fell into the hands of the conqueror.

He thought he saw what the passage was saying to him in his present circumstance. Though the nations be in an uproar with would-be kings vying for Earth's throne, it is the Lord who anoints kings and establishes kingdoms. No one assumes the crown without His consent.

So then, what about Carlotta? Where was she? Should he be here playing private eye when her life might be in danger? Could he trust God for her safekeeping?

Peter bowed his head and began laying it out before God. It was God who would have to bear them and deliver them, as Isaiah had said.

* * *

It had been a difficult night. Cold sweats and shakes had come upon her in the wee hours. Carlotta knew what she could do to end it—drink the tea. But that was the very thing she had forbidden herself to do.

Instead she used the time to pray. She prayed for herself and for Peter and especially that Peter would find this place and deliver her. But she had no Bible, so she ended up despite herself delving into the two books that Zell had given her. She wondered how he would respond to her ultimate refusal to bend to his warped world view.

From Zell's texts she began to understand the man's burning pursuit of a deliverer. In his own belief system he was on the losing team, and it was imperative that the ultimate conflict be postponed as long as possible. To that end, a champion, a pretender, might appear to be the best guarantee.

Carlotta concentrated her reading on *Ragnarök*, marveling at how it paralleled the Christian version of the last battle of the ages—except in reverse. In the Norse version, Loki, "the father of lies," would break free from his underworld confinement to launch the final battle of the gods and giants. It was the evil giants who were fated to win.

She was astounded by the *Muspilli*, a ninth-century prophetic poem that attempted to combine both pagan and Christian perspectives. Here Satan and the Antichrist were allied with the giant werewolf of paganism, Fennis, in a climactic battle against the forces of good. The good guys were defeated in the end.

Yet she knew from Scripture that in the end it was Christ who would defeat every foe, including the last enemy, death.

In numerous places were handwritten notes that were mostly unintelligible to her. At several points they might have made some sense if she had known what their author meant by the term "guardian."

Finally, at dawn, she found herself dozing with her face on her hands over the open pages. She was awakened by a woman's voice calling her name. It was Olivia with a tray of tea and biscuits.

"When you have breakfasted and bathed, Father Zell will receive you," she said softly. "But please, not too much tea."

Feeling thick-headed and irritable, Carlotta devoured the biscuits and poured the tea down the sink. But an idea was forming in her mind, a plan for dealing with Zell.

⋆ ⋆ ⋆

The man received her once again in his study.

"Well, daughter, do you know what day this is?"

"Yes," she said dutifully, recalling her instruction. "*Lunedi*—Monday. Day of the moon and enchantment. Tomorrow is *Martedi*—Tuesday. Day of Mars, god of war, and *Tiwes,* the sky god."

Zell nodded approvingly. "Very good. And the day after tomorrow?"

"*Mercoledi*—Wednesday. Day of Mercury and Woden, wisdom and magic."

"And most important," said Zell, eyes twinkling, "the day the world may have a new prince. Have you decided upon your role in this?"

"Yes, Father Zell," she said demurely.

"And what is that?"

"Whatever the prince requires."

Zell fell silent for a long moment, his eyes boring holes into her head. And then he spoke in a softer voice that Carlotta thought actually sounded more menacing.

"The prince may not yet know what is needful. You, who hold the key to his heart, may have to persuade his mind."

"Yes, Father."

"We have already discussed this," he said with a slight edge. "Are you ready to give me your response to the teachings I had asked you to study?"

"Yes, Father," she said, hoping her performance would be convincing. "I have been reading those books you gave me."

"Very good, daughter. And . . ?"

"And now I think I understand what you mean by the fundamental unity of the faiths."

Zell again nodded his approval.

"And," Carlotta ventured, "the last days—Armageddon, *Ragnarök,* the Twilight of the Gods? You believe that time approaches?"

"Yes, daughter. The end of all things is finally at hand. Winter gets longer each year."

Carlotta was baffled.

Zell smiled patiently. "Signs of the end—greed, strife, lawlessness, and three years of winter. We see all the signs now, especially with Mount Hekla."

"Hekla?"

"A major eruption began several days ago, daughter. Last century they worried about global warming. Now we worry about global cooling with so much ash in the upper atmosphere from accelerated earthquakes and volcanic activity. If we were to have another Hekla . . ."

He let the thought hang in the air like a toxic cloud. Carlotta's thoughts turned to Peter and Iceland.

"Do you have further questions, daughter?" Zell persisted.

She wanted to ask about Peter's rune quest, but she suppressed the urge.

"Who are the 'guardians,' Father?" she managed to ask.

A pregnant silence ensued as Zell's eyes narrowed to slits. Carlotta had no idea whether Zell was buying her naive act. He got up and began pacing once again.

"I have already told you all you need to know about this," he said at last.

"Perhaps I have forgotten."

"I told you of the modern remnant—the financiers of the old world powers. Their identities may not be revealed."

Carlotta held her tongue and nodded. The scary thing was the likelihood that Zell might not be a lone crackpot.

"And now," he said, fixing her with his disturbing gaze, "what about Christ?"

Carlotta's palms were perspiring.

"What do you mean, Father?"

"You now claim you have received the truth. Are you ready to give up your childish Jesus-loves-me religion?"

"It's not a religion. It's a relationship with—"

She knew she had blundered. But then, what else could she do? She considered backtracking. Based on the literal question, which assumed a distorted version of her faith, she perhaps could have played along, renouncing a meaningless straw man. But she knew what he meant, regardless of how he had expressed it.

"Interesting," Zell said, low and mean. "Would you care to explain?"

Carlotta lowered her eyes. "I don't think so."

"That was not a request. I want to hear your position. Speak, please."

He now stood immediately in front of her, so that she had to look up at him. She could feel the adrenaline coursing, her heart hammering.

"I want my freedom," she said, quietly defiant.

Zell looked surprised. "You wish to leave, just as things are getting interesting?"

"What would happen if I tried?" Carlotta was envisioning guards and guns and dogs.

"Well," said Zell with phony-sounding innocence, "you would miss Mr. McBride's arrival here on Wednesday."

Carlotta's brow furrowed in uncertainty. "How do you know he'll be here?"

"He'll be here. He's already in Rome—and it is not for an audience with the pope."

"If you know where he is," she cried, "let me go to him!"

And then she realized the hopelessness of her situation. They had her. Her only hope was not in escape but in finessing her way through her situation. And now she had let herself get caught fatally out of character.

"Daughter," Zell said in his menacing tone, "you sound like you need some tea."

He poured a cup and set it before her.

"It is not a question of duress," he said with a sigh. "It is the fact that you need to be here. Willingly or not, you will provide the incentive for Peter McBride to realize his destiny. But I am afraid that you have condemned him to mortal combat to achieve it."

Carlotta was wondering what Zell meant by those ominous words when she looked up to see him glaring down at her. She was startled to see that despite his apparently calm words, his face was a stony mask of wrath.

"Drink the tea," he commanded, some of the anger cracking in his voice. "And this time, do not pour it into the flower pot."

* * *

Peter was stepping out of the shower when he heard the front door opening. Too late he realized that his sidearm was on the bed and out of reach.

But then a familiar voice called out, "Peter!"

"Yeah, Neal! Be out in a second."

As his heart rate returned to normal, Peter toweled himself off and wondered if he were going to have to start taking a gun into the shower. He figured he ought to feel safe in any hotel secured by the likes of Tony Novello, until he remembered that Tony had been shot in his own bailiwick.

Then he heard two voices and realized that Tony must be there too. Peter worked over his hair with a towel and then climbed into a pair of jeans and a T-shirt.

"Good! Good!" Novello effervesced when he saw Peter. "That's what we like to see—color in the cheeks."

"Yes," Peter agreed, "and no chianti. Just a bike trip up the Aventine Hill and back."

"Oh?" said McBride, eyebrows arching. "Sightseeing, were we? See any interesting sights?"

"As a matter of fact, I saw the most interesting old church. I'm no expert on these things, but I'd guess it was more like an abbey with maybe a whatchmacallit—friary?—to the rear. Did you fellows have any luck with the records?"

"You might say," said McBride. "It would appear that what you found was San Giacomo. Was it on a cul-de-sac off Via di San Anselmo?"

Peter nodded. "Exactly."

"Notice anything remarkable?"

"Well, yeah," Peter admitted. "It's not something you can walk right up to. It's got barbed-wire fencing and guard dogs. Somebody's put new wood in the windows not very long ago, and an old Mustache Pete said it's supposed to be haunted. Warned me to stay away or the bogeyman would get me. What did you find out?"

"I cannot vouch for pagan temples and all that," Novello said, "but it appears that Mrs. Stillman's other information was correct. Records show there have been several different structures on that site going back into the Middle Ages. Then there is a gap in the sixteenth century. Sometime in that period the Benedictines built a small monastery there, although apparently neither of the current structures."

McBride, wearing his reading glasses, looked up from his notes. "In the nineteenth century the Benedictines relocated. Then, sometime after the turn of the century, there's a transaction involving the local diocese that resulted in the establishment of the San Giacomo parish.

"And no, I don't know who Saint Giacomo was. What's important is what happened after that. In 2001 the church was still fighting the Mafia when San Giacomo's pastor was gunned down while celebrating Mass. The diocese brought in another priest, who was nearly killed a few months later when the church was bombed. The young man was so shaken, he fled the country and left the priesthood."

"So where was the bomb damage? I couldn't see any from the street."

"Ironically, confined entirely to a modern wing in the back. News accounts said everybody thought at first that the priest had been blown up with it, but then he was seen escaping from the friary—which is supposedly connected to the church by a tunnel.

"The next priest balked at the assignment, and they threw in the towel at that point. Now this is the interesting part: the building remained vacant for forty years until the title transferred three years ago to a certain party you would recognize."

Peter had a strong hunch. "The New Order of Rome?"

"Bingo, Sherlock. Anybody ever tell you that you ought to go into the private investigation business?"

"But Emmanuel Ponzi," Peter muttered. "That doesn't make a lot of sense. He doesn't have the Crown and Spear. I'd bet the farm on it."

"There's more," McBride said.

Just then there was a rap at the door between the two rooms, and Sloat appeared, nodding in mute salutation.

"Hey, Amos," said Peter. "Bring back any wild geese?"

Sloat shook his head and with a sigh settled himself into the lone empty chair. "No buried treasure, I'm afraid. I certainly hope you fellows had better . . . uh . . . providential circumstances than I did."

Peter and McBride smiled. Novello shook his head slowly in bewilderment.

"That's what we were just assessing, Amos," said McBride. "Our Temple of Mercury seems to be the defunct San Giacomo Church on the Aventine Hill, recently owned by the New Order of Rome until its title transferred one more time."

"Oh?" said Peter expectantly. "To whom?"

"Optima Securities."

"Optima Securities?" Peter frowned. "What's *that?*"

"It's a subsidiary of state-owned Telesis Industries—a capital improvements contractor for the EU and a major supplier of technological services to the Population and Health ministry."

"Wait a minute," said Peter. "Now we're talking Neumann and Bardo?"

McBride shook his head, and Novello spoke up. "Not quite. This may be a state-owned enterprise, but its people owe their allegiance to the Public Employees International Union."

"Salvatore DiFalcone," McBride said.

"Yikes!" Peter exclaimed. "How do we make any sense of all that? Ponzi, Neumann, Bardo, DiFalcone—and none of them has the Crown and Spear."

Sloat stood up. "Maybe that's not all the players. Let me show you something."

He withdrew into his own room for a moment, then returned holding a rolled-up document. He took it to the flat panel, fed it into the scanner, and waited for the display to appear on the wallscreen.

"I wasn't only chasing wild geese with metal detectors this afternoon," he explained. "I had asked home control some time ago to send me some visual IDs on key operatives in P3. I think you'll find this one interesting."

A grainy color image appeared on the screen, consisting of a dozen individuals seated around a conference table. It had the kind of low resolution resulting from major enlargement. After some manipulation with the enhancer, Sloat managed to rid the picture of most of its fuzziness.

"It's interesting that you mentioned Optima Securities." He directed a square halo to highlight the face of one of the figures at the table. "This picture happens to be the board of directors of Optima Securities about ten years ago. Half of these characters were reputed members of P3, including this one, Simon Morgenthau, a powerful investment banker from Zurich and chairman of the board of Optima Securities."

"Any relation to Estelle Morgenthau?" Peter asked.

"Ex-husband. His primary occupation is running a thing called Guardian Holding Company in Zurich. It owns a chain of banks, plus assorted credit life insurance and personal finance companies. And a major security system for commercial telecredit networks."

Peter digested the information slowly. "OK. Others?"

"These are zeros," said Sloat as he turned six of the figures into black silhouettes with the enhancer. "Plain vanilla business-persons, nonplayers, having nothing to do with P3 or anything else we're interested in. But look at the rest."

He began spotlighting each of the remaining five, one at a time, in the square halos.

Peter jumped at the sight of the first face and then began calling out names. "Waldemar Neumann. Jean Pierre Bardo. Salvatore DiFalcone. Emmanuel Ponzi. I don't recognize the last one. Who's he?"

"A fellow," said Sloat, "named Adrian Zell."

Peter blinked.

Now maybe we're getting somewhere.

36

Rome

McBride's puzzled eyes darted about over his half glasses. "Who's Adrian Zell?"

"Ponzi's former right-hand man," Peter said, "and probably the missing link in this weird chain. He was a bishop who left the church along with Ponzi to form the New Order of Rome. Then he left that to form his own breakaway sect that's apparently gone underground. As a matter of fact, Sir James said we should look into this guy. Looks like he may have been right."

McBride still looked uncertain. "Why would people like this be on the board of an investment company?"

"Ten years ago," said Sloat, "was before Ponzi and Zell were cardinal and bishop. Today they are no longer on this board, but those positions have gone to others just like them in P3."

"OK, Peter," said McBride, as if calling a bet, "what do you make of all this?"

Peter shook his head. "You think I'm stumped?"

McBride smiled faintly, holding his tongue.

Peter decided to raise the stakes. "I'll make you a deal. If you can explain the original heist, I'll tell you how it all adds up."

"Which means what?"

"You owe us an update on the Hofburg. Give us the low-down on Liebenfels, DuChesne, and Brandt, and I'll explain the rest. Deal?"

McBride was smiling broadly now. "Deal. Of course, this is going to require a drink. Hey, Tony, do you really have cream soda in this establishment?"

Almost before Peter knew what was happening, Tony was at Neal's side with a towel draped over his forearm and a bottle in his hand.

"A wise choice, *Signore*," said Novello, pouring the sparkling redpop into McBride's glass.

McBride took a sip, savored it, and swallowed thoughtfully.

"Well, as you know, Giselle DuChesne was a legitimate scholar. Little did she know that her leave of absence would put her in such jeopardy—or provide such an opportunity to create a convenient scapegoat."

"But," said Sloat, "do you believe Liebenfels passed the relics to Brandt?"

McBride nodded. "Especially after what you told me about his Nazi/occult roots. I checked him out. He is indeed a direct descendant of his infamous namesake."

"So," said Sloat, "what did you do with that information?"

"Well, I didn't confront him—not after you told me Sir James had advised against it. I went over his head. I consulted with an insurance executive at Griswold—the ones we're really working for. But it's your classic good-news/bad-news story. The good news is that they've become *our* insurance policy."

"How's that?" Peter asked.

"Turns out Liebenfels had been telling them we were muffing the case, and he was going to fire us. It was probably no coincidence that this was just when we had started making real progress. Griswold was already suspicious about Liebenfels in connection with an inside job, and I confirmed their suspicions. So if Liebenfels tries to fire us, he'll have a fight on his hands."

"So what's the bad news?"

"There's a company trying to buy Griswold."

"Uh-oh. Who?"

"Guess."

"Optima Securities?"

"Bingo."

That gave Peter pause. "After tomorrow night, it won't matter much what they do."

"How is that?" asked Novello.

"We should have the goods. The last thing they'd want to do is fire us then."

"Yes," agreed McBride, "but then we'd be working for the thieves themselves, wouldn't we?"

Peter nodded. "Maybe we just hold onto the Crown and Spear until we can return them to their rightful owner."

There was momentary silence while the men chewed over that one. Peter wondered if anyone else was pondering the same thing he was—how they could physically secure the Crown and Spear from all of these ruthless players.

Finally he said, "OK. What about Gwydian Brandt?"

McBride frowned. "Brandt was a government scientist for Population and Health. Ostensibly she was working for your friend Bardo. It's pretty interesting that the only two people who could incriminate Liebenfels—Brandt and DuChesne—are now both dead. I suspect that Brandt was shot because she double-crossed her boss in some fashion."

"Such as . . ?" Peter prompted.

McBride spread his hands. "Not delivering on the goods."

"How do you explain why she was analyzing my genome?"

McBride shook his head. "I can't. There's too much that still doesn't make sense about this whole affair. But I'll tell you one thing—my experience with the Population and Health people back home has got me thinking that they and Bardo are somehow in collaboration."

Peter got up from his seat. "Let's think about that a minute."

He began pacing slowly about the room, while ideas gnawed at the corners of his attention like rodents in the dark. He was standing by the window, his back to the other three men, looking out toward the Villa Borghese, when it seemed as if the dark were beginning to recede a few degrees.

McBride broke the silence. "Are you ready to tell us how this all adds up?"

Peter, still lost in thought, answered indirectly. "You may be right about Bardo influencing his colleagues in the USP. He practically threatened as much to my face when I met with him."

"But . . ." McBride apparently anticipated Peter's direction.

"But I think you're wrong about Brandt. Liebenfels may have been hoping to bilk the insurance company or play up to Bardo and Neumann, but it doesn't appear that the EU had a hand in Brandt's murder. The fact that she was shot by an operative of the Imam of Babylon and that Optima Securities is trying to acquire Griswold leads me to a different conclusion."

"Which is . . ."

"Think of Amos's picture—all the players sitting around the same table. Seems to me that's the only way to make sense of this thing. If there's a conspiracy, I think they're *all* part of it—Liebenfels, Neumann, Bardo, DiFalcone, Ponzi, and this mysterious Adrian Zell. The difference is that Zell seems to be the one holding the cards. And the Imam and I seem to be the outsiders."

"Uh-oh," said McBride. "He's free-braining now. Hold onto your hats."

Peter ignored him. "I think Zell has disqualified all the insiders in the power struggle. These clues we've been chasing seem designed to draw out a particular individual—and I'm beginning to believe I'm the one, though I'm not sure why. And I feel like these Halima characters have been my shadow all along. I wouldn't be surprised if there's one more Halima waiting for me at the OK Corral."

Novello, the devotee of Zane Grey and Louis Lamour, grinned. "You mean San Giacomo?"

Peter pointed a finger at Novello's nose. "Exactly. Two champions engaged in battle ordeal for the prize—as in the days of yore."

"But," interrupted Sloat, "how can you be sure of Zell? We know almost nothing about him. We don't even know if he's actually holed up in that old church."

Peter snapped his fingers and reached for his wallet. "Maybe we do." He pulled out a slip of paper. "Tony, can we have this number traced?"

Tony gave his no-big-deal shrug. "Sure. There is a *goomba* in the *carabinieri* who owes me one."

"What is that number, Peter?" said McBride.

"I'd almost forgotten about it." Peter handed the slip to Novello. "When Wendy Carlisle and I were going through Brandt's effects, we got some numbers off her computer—people who had been receiving transmissions from her. One of those parties was named Zell. I just considered it something to file away for later, since Zell hadn't been a player as far as we knew—until now."

"Too bad we couldn't just get a warrant for the *carabinieri* to kick the door in,"McBride said.

Novello threw up his hands. "Nah! With heavies like DiFalcone involved, the last place you want to go with information like this is the authorities, I am sorry to say. Perhaps things are not so bad in the USP . . ."

"Tony," said McBride. "I'm afraid our system is just as compromised. That's one big reason there's lively business for people like McBride and McBride."

"Come to think of it," Peter mused, "we ought to add Wendy Carlisle to our list of conspirators. I can see now how she was guiding me at the beginning to get me started on the right track."

"But *why*, Peter?" asked McBride. "Why you?"

"I told you I'm not sure why. Did I say I'd make it *all* add up? OK, so maybe I spoke a little hastily."

"What happened to never-say-die and free-braining?"

"Well . . ." Peter was somewhat reluctant to voice his thoughts. "Actually, I do have an idea, but it's a little bizarre even for me."

"Let's hear it. You know the rules."

Peter sighed. "All right. You asked for it. If Zell has the Crown and Spear—which everyone else is seeking—why hasn't he either quietly traded it for some weapons-grade plutonium or had himself crowned Imperial Majesty? Why is he advertising it with clues and all?

"Suppose Zell isn't a would-be king like the others, but a king-*maker*—like that twentieth-century fellow Rick told us about who tried to bring the next Buddha out of the closet. Suppose that after studying the genetic profiles and personal histories of various and sundry individuals he comes to the irrational conclusion that his candidate for prince of the realm is a shrewd and clever bachelor private eye from the USP who is hot on the trail with—well, I said it was bizarre."

Sloat shifted in his chair. "You said something earlier about a 'battle ordeal.' Why do you assume that whoever this prince candidate may be has to fight for the treasures?"

Peter shrugged. "Just a wild guess. Based on the fact that the serious contenders all along have basically been two—myself, perhaps, and another guy named Halima with interchangeable first names. Anyway, it doesn't seem as though this Zell just wants to hand the stuff over. He wants something—even if it's nothing more than some proof of worthiness."

"Well," said McBride uncertainly, "when you said you'd make it all add up, I guess you didn't claim it would necessarily be a rational number."

Peter nodded. "Zell may be counting on people's natural desire to make sense of things in order to draw us in."

"It does look," conceded Sloat, "as if the only way to find out is to jump in and play the game. So what's our game plan for the church? You mentioned tomorrow night. Are you thinking of staking out San Giacomo at midnight tomorrow?"

"Maybe," said Peter, glancing at his watch. "Let's talk about that. Tony, do you know a good restaurant with authentic cuisine and a place where we can talk?"

"Oh, yes," said Novello, licking his lips. "I know just the place. Why don't you fellows get ready while I make a couple of calls. I'll reserve a table for seven o'clock and get my *goomba* tracing that phone number."

"That'll work, Tony."

* * *

There was more in the air at Giuliani's than just garlic and oregano.

From the moment they walked in the door, Peter wondered what the excitement was about. At the bar in front, several old men were laughing uproariously and raising their glasses in an ecstatic toast while several younger men disputed some point in equally loud voices. Still others were gathered silently around a television at the end of the bar. Peter couldn't make out what it was all about over the racket from the jokers and debaters.

Tony indicated Peter and McBride and Sloat should wait by the cashier's counter while he attempted to catch the eye of a short, gray-haired man with thick glasses who was coming their way from across the room. As he approached, Peter recognized him as the grinning gentleman who appeared in a score of pictures on the wall with assorted VIPs who had dined at Giuliani's.

And then their eyes met. Tony waved. The older fellow smiled in recognition and returned the gesture, hurrying over.

"Good evening, Tony." He nodded cordially at the other three. "Follow me."

He led them at a good clip toward the far end of the long restaurant, past a dozen other dinners in various stages of consumption.

"What's going on, Vincenzo?" asked Novello. "Some news?"

"You might say so," *Signore* Giuliani replied, half-turning his head. "The Falcon is about to fly."

Peter watched Novello's face turn ashen.

"What was he talking about?" he asked when they were finally seated and Giuliani had withdrawn.

"Salvatore DiFalcone," Novello muttered. "I was afraid of this."

A matronly waitress appeared with a pencil behind her ear. They deferred to Novello, who ordered a tableful of food for them in Italian.

When she was gone, Sloat spoke up. "I think I heard something on the news earlier. Does this have anything to do with an uprising at Aldo Moro?"

"It does," said Novello. "The inmates have taken over—as if they didn't already have control. There's only one way this makes sense."

"What's that?" asked Sloat.

"A prisoner-hostage exchange. Right now, they are making all kinds of outrageous demands—resignations of government officials and so forth. Soon we shall see what they really want—commutations of sentence for the Falcon and his boys, better conditions for the rest of them. Clean needles, dirty movies, and so forth."

"They must be serious. I heard that Bardo already has fired the minister of corrections."

Novello nodded. "Yes, but that did not satisfy them. They are demanding the ouster of Bardo himself. I think their real goal is to stop Neumann's plan to recall all currency and go to a cashless system, because it would kill the underworld economy."

Peter frowned. "Then why wouldn't they go after the finance minister?"

Novello snorted. "No juice. Getting Bardo strikes directly at Neumann."

Just then there was a stir at the front of the restaurant and a sudden hush as two men in black uniforms entered.

"Nazi pigs!" snarled Sloat as the men came their way.

The two swaggering storm troopers pushed past Vincenzo Giuliani's fruitless attempt to corral them. The leader thrust the old man away with a hand to his chest. Peter watched to see what the proprietor would do, but it appeared Giuliani was afraid of these characters. He simply walked away, wagging his head.

The men commandeered a table nearby, and one whistled shrilly for a waitress. Peter believed he had seen flickering glances from the pair, as if they had deliberately chosen a table near his group.

Their own food was arriving now, and Peter stole sidelong glances at the neo-Nazis, who were having some animated discussion with a young, made-up waitress with big hair. The next moment she stomped off, red-faced, while the men roared with laughter. Peter guessed they hadn't been discussing the soup *du jour.*

The red-haired ruffian with a big mouth and jack-o-lantern teeth appeared to be the leader. His sidekick was darker, swarthier. He might have been native Italian.

Conversation lapsed as Peter and company dug into their food. He felt apprehensive about discussing the sensitive issues of Woden's Day with such an audience close by.

The big-haired waitress reappeared with a pitcher of beer in each fist and a scowl on her face. There were more snickers and suggestive remarks as she set down the pitchers and retreated.

Peter noticed that Sloat was bristling.

"Easy, Amos," Peter murmured. "This is an opportunity for you to practice your forbearance."

Sloat's scowl only deepened.

Novello set down his fork and frowned at his pasta. "Perhaps I should get Vincenzo to move us to a different table."

"No!" Sloat snapped. "Don't give those pigs the pleasure."

Peter's stomach knotted up. There was no way Sloat's words could have escaped the hearing of the men at the next table.

"Amos," he said warningly, tapping Sloat's foot under the table with his own. "Don't be a bad dog."

But it was too late. The swarthy roughneck was out of his chair and heading their way, an unlit cigarette dangling from the corner of his mouth. As he reached their table, the man stopped, touched a flame to the cigarette, and fired it up.

"You have a problem, Jew?"

Sloat stood up to look the man in the eye. "You must have mistaken me for someone else. I don't believe we've ever met."

The man laughed humorlessly and flung an insult.

Peter winced as the chances of salvaging this encounter headed irretrievably south.

Now the hooligan was blowing smoke in Sloat's face. Amos shoved the trooper away from him, and the man responded with a fist to the face that snapped Sloat's head back.

The men at both tables stayed in their seats, momentarily transfixed. Sloat rocked back to his toes and launched himself at his adversary, catching him with a blocked punch against a forearm, which was probably a feint, and then the real move—a nasty jab on the point of the jaw that sent the man reeling backward into the Nazis' table, noisily spilling one of the pitchers. The red-haired man rescued his own glass and grabbed the second pitcher before it spilled too.

Now the swarthy man was coming back with murder in his eye. Sloat ducked a roundhouse, but the left fist caught him squarely on the nose. A knife flashed in the other man's grasp, and Peter instantly had his gun out.

"That is enough!" a voice said.

It was Novello, on his feet with his gun in hand too.

"Vincenzo!" Novello bellowed in the tense silence. "Would you be so kind as to show these gentlemen the way out before I have to waste some perfectly good bullets on them. I will take care of their check."

Giuliani hurried forward as a dozen human statues thawed.

"I will take the knife too, my friend," Novello told the hoodlum, extending his hand.

The man smirked at Sloat, who was wiping a generous nosebleed from his upper lip with a napkin, and gave the knife a toss. Novello snatched it in mid-air while Peter kept his gun trained on the red-haired man, rising from his seat.

The two walked stiff-legged toward the front door.

Peter followed. He might have been holding a zucchini in his right hand, for all the attention he was paid by the other diners. There were plenty of mouths munching spaghetti, but most eyes were studiously averted.

At the door, *Signore* Jack-o-Lantern Teeth flashed Peter a gap-toothed grin.

"Get out!" Peter snapped, pushing the door open with his free hand and waving them on with his gun.

In another moment they were gone, and the tension evaporated like a soda bubble.

"Grazie!" Giuliani exclaimed, clapping Peter on the shoulder. "You are welcome here any time, *Signore* McBride. This dinner is on the house."

"Thanks," Peter murmured, wanting to get back to Sloat.

At their table, the three other men had resumed eating as if nothing had happened, although McBride wore a curious, wan smile.

"Guess you guys like pasta a lot," Peter muttered as he took his seat again. "If the place was on fire, would you ask for a doggie bag?"

Sloat looked up with an innocent expression.

"You act like nothing happened. *You* especially—how can you eat fettuccini with a busted nose?"

With a completely straight face, Sloat dipped a finger into the tomato sauce and smeared it across his upper lip. "You mean like this?"

Suddenly Peter suspected he had been had. "Was that whole fight staged?"

Sloat shrugged, wiping off his lip.

"That Nazi with the schnozz who clipped me," he explained in a voice barely above a whisper, "is actually an agent from my organization. He's a Russian Jew—Gregor. Show him the knife, Tony."

Peter took the proffered blade, a red switchblade affair with a black swastika on the handle, and turned it over in his hand. He pushed the button and watched the four-inch blade spring forth.

"Keep it," said Sloat. "Its blade is metal-detector neutral. It could come in handy."

"Nonmetallic? What's it made of?"

Sloat shrugged. "Some New Age hardened polymer silicate."

Peter looked more closely at the blade and wondered at a tiny marking at the base:

שב

"What's that?"

"My mother company," said Sloat. "Shin Beth."

"I see. But I still want to know why the phony fight?"

Sloat shrugged again. "Two reasons. It seemed that Gregor needed a little validation with the group he's infiltrating."

"By picking a fight with a Jew?"

Sloat nodded.

"What's the other reason?"

Sloat hesitated, apparently thinking. "He may be sending us a message."

"What kind of message?"

"I'm not sure. Maybe he's letting us know that the Fourth Reich is on our case. Anyway, I have a feeling this may not be the last we'll see of these characters."

Peter chewed thoughtfully. "So both of you were pulling your punches? It looked pretty convincing."

Sloat smiled and tossed his head to one side as if he had just taken a shot to the jaw. "Just like in the movies. It's part of our basic training. I'll show you sometime."

After a moment McBride spoke up. "I have a question for Tony."

"Yes, sir?" said the Roman detective.

"Was your *goomba* successful in tracing Peter's number from Gwydian Brandt's computer?"

"Ah, yes. You will be interested in this. According to my friend, the phone company records indicate it's an Optima Securities extension on the Aventine Hill, taken out by an E. Morgenthau."

"That's our place," said McBride.

37

Rome

The next morning Peter awoke entirely clear-headed for the first time in days. There were no fading bad-dream memories of exploding mountains or demons from the pit. He felt rested and ready to take on any number of Nazis with garlic breath and bad teeth.

He tested the floor with his feet and found the unsteady trampoline effect was all but gone. He was further heartened by the thought that tomorrow was Woden's Day and that the object of their search might be within their grasp as early as midnight tonight.

"Hey, Peter!" Sloat called through the door from the next room. "Look at this."

Peter entered Sloat's room to find him engrossed in a scene on the wallscreen.

Amos ordered the computer to replay, and a moment later the green mandala logo of One World News flashed on the screen. A middle-aged newsperson in unisex smock and haircut appeared briefly to begin a report on some upheaval in EU Chancellor Waldemar Neumann's government.

"It is not known today," said the commentator, apparently female, "whether the European Parliament will follow through on yesterday's threat to call a no-confidence vote for the government of Chancellor Waldemar Neumann. Speculation also has centered on what further steps Neumann might take after yesterday's cabinet shake-up."

The newscaster's face was replaced by that of a familiar character with wavy hair and glasses.

"Population and Health Minister Jean Pierre Bardo resigned last night amid charges of government incompetence and mismanagement in the wake of the uprising at Aldo Moro Penitentiary, where thirty-seven prison guards and other corrections personnel are still being held hostage. The ouster had been one of the demands of Mafia boss Salvatore DiFalcone. Neumann said he had not asked for Bardo's resignation and he accepted it with deep regret."

The image changed from Bardo to some B-reel of the Falcon whispering to his lawyer at his trial several years ago for the attempted assassination of Pope Gregory.

"The question now is whether Neumann will follow through on his threats of a currency recall if DiFalcone does not end the Aldo Moro uprising. Neumann and Bardo had been promoting the idea of a cashless system as a way of destroying the underground economy—and the alleged source of DiFalcone's power. But in light of the threatened no-confidence vote, it would appear that such a bold move might have to wait."

DiFalcone's image was now replaced with a split-screen display of two other individuals—Pope Gregory and Chancellor Neumann.

"How long is yet another question, as powerful forces have begun choosing sides. Pope Gregory appealed for law and order and an end to the prison uprising and political infighting, an appeal that appears to strengthen the hand of Chancellor Neumann. At the same time, however, Emmanuel Ponzi, pontiff of the powerful New Order of Rome, has condemned the Neumann government and, without endorsing DiFalcone's forces, called for their demands to be given serious consideration. But former Cardinal Ponzi had a more unusual demand."

Peter was not prepared for the image that took shape next—twin photos of the Crown and Spear.

"He demanded that Neumann's government explain why it has failed to recover the Crown of Charlemagne and Holy Lance that were stolen weeks ago from the Hofburg in Vienna. He predicted that strife and chaos would only intensify until they are recovered. The former cardinal did not explain, although rumors have persisted that the ancient regalia is being held somewhere in secret for a future world ruler."

Sloat halted the report, and Peter suppressed a shiver.

"Bardo," he marveled. "How the mighty have fallen."

Sloat appeared to be channel surfing. "I thought you'd find that interesting. Here's something else interesting on the local news. A messianic Jewish congregation in Trastevere is having some kind of rally today that's drawing protests."

Peter watched as the camera panned across a sea of faces, some ecstatic and exuberant, others angry and defiant. Over the heads of the happy was a huge, royal-blue banner exclaiming in gold letters, "The King Is Coming!" There was some pushing and shoving from the not-so-happy. Among both groups, mouths were working, but the audio was some inane commentary about block parties and street festivals.

Just then a knock came at Peter's door. Sloat switched channels to closed circuit, and Peter saw that it was the elder McBride and Tony Novello out in the hall, one room over. They also saw a cart of some sort.

Sloat stuck his head out the door and called the men in. With McBride and Novello came the pleasing aromas of breakfast, which explained the cart.

While they munched rolls and fruit and quaffed coffee and juice, Peter recounted the international news report about Neumann and Bardo.

McBride listened, nodding at appropriate points. When Peter was done, he said, "I have some news of my own."

"Uh-oh," said Peter apprehensively. "What is it?"

"Griswold. It's been sold."

Peter stopped chewing and forgot to swallow. This was not good.

"To Optima Securities?"

His father nodded.

"How do you know?"

"I had a message at the desk to call someone at Griswold I'd never heard of. Something told me not to return this call until I'd checked it out. I looked in the newspaper, and, sure enough, in the business section I found an item about Griswold's being sold to our Optima friends."

Peter whistled. "For how much?"

"Terms not disclosed. But you know it's big—very big."

Peter and Sloat exchanged troubled glances.

"What does that mean for us?" Peter asked after a moment.

McBride pursed his lips. "Well, I'm certainly not going to return that call and let them tell me to drop the case."

"But that doesn't mean we're not off the case," Peter pointed out. "And off the payroll—so far as they're concerned."

"Look," Sloat interjected, "that should be the last thing on your mind right now. If we recover the Crown and Spear, the objects themselves are worth millions."

"You're not suggesting," said Peter, "that we sell the regalia to the highest bidder?"

Sloat shook his head. "Not at all. But what happened to just doing the right thing? Who knows? Maybe McBride and McBride will score other international business as a result."

"Not to mention how the Lord may repay," McBride added.

"Well" —Peter was only partly mollified— "there's something else that bothers me. Who now is the rightful owner of the regalia?"

"Peter," Novello spoke up, "it will not help to borrow trouble. You need to take these things one at a time. First get the goods, then worry about where they go."

"There's something else that bothers me," McBride said. "How did this Griswold character know where to find us?"

"That's an unsettling thought," Peter agreed. "It certainly wasn't Directory Information."

"Look," Novello put in. "Rather then worry about how they did it, we need to formulate a response. I suggest we simply move you to another establishment for now. We can have you out and set up again before you know it. And, more important, before *they* know it. Agreed?"

Peter nodded, then looked at his father, who nodded too.

"OK," said Novello. "I'll have your things moved to the Hotel D'Amico right away. That's across town on Via Gioacchino Antonio Rossini."

Peter nodded again. "All right. Now, how about the authorities? Can we arrange any backup from the police?"

Novello shook his head firmly. "It is the same problem as before. Until a crime is committed—"

"No," Peter cut him off. "I know they're not going to investigate rumors and superstitions about missing relics. But I'd appreciate it if you would alert your highest-ranking trusted contact that San Giacomo may become the scene of a crime anytime after midnight tonight. Maybe they'll keep an eye out. It might save somebody's life."

Novello nodded solemnly. "That much I can do. No problem."

Peter turned to McBride. "What are your plans today, Neal?"

McBride blew air out slowly. "Oh, I'll probably be burning up the phone lines to the USP. I have a lot of business back home to check up on. Then I'll probably take in a museum or do some other sightseeing. I think we all ought to take the rest of the day off and relax—maybe even take a nap this afternoon, so we're fresh tonight if we're going to hit San Giacomo at midnight."

"Good idea. And what are you going to do, Amos?"

"Me? I need some exercise more than rest. I think I'm going

to rent a bike and pedal over to Trastevere. Then maybe come back and take a nap."

A blue banner with gold letters flashed in Peter's memory bank. "Maybe take a spin by a certain messianic Jewish establishment?"

Sloat nodded. "Something like that. Want to join me?"

Peter hesitated.

"Doesn't matter," Sloat declared. "I'm going—with or without you."

"All right," said Peter. "I'll go and make sure you don't get into trouble. We can't afford to lose you. You may have to teach us how to breach barbed wire and fight off Dobermans."

"Piece of cake," said Sloat with a straight face.

Novello's eyebrows began dancing like woolly-bear caterpillars in shock therapy. "OK, tough guy. Please tell us how you fight through barbed wire and attack dogs like a piece of cake."

Peter knew Sloat well enough by this time to tell that the expression on his face was too straight now.

"Sure," the Israeli said. "First, you get yourself a pair of bolt cutters—"

"Fine," Peter interjected in Sloat's pause. "That will take care of the dogs. But what do you do about the barbed wire?"

Novello chuckled.

"Easy," said Sloat. "Just smack it with a rolled-up newspaper."

The detective's laughter burst out like a thunderclap.

"See?" said McBride. "You don't have a thing to worry about. You guys blow this assignment, you can always start your own comedy team. You're a scream."

* * *

Mirabella, the younger, fairer, and colder of the sisters, handed Carlotta a towel as she emerged from the bath and told her to move a little faster. Zell awaited.

But, Carlotta wondered, *faster than what?* It was all relative, wasn't it? Maybe it wouldn't seem so arbitrary if her veins weren't so full of chemicals. She knew she was operating partly impaired. The difference was that this time she knew it, and she had specific memories of her lucid hours in this place to judge by, no matter how jumbled.

There was another difference too. They were taking no chances with orange juice and tea. They were shooting her up with the drug now. Sometimes Mirabella did it; sometimes Olivia, and then it didn't hurt so much.

Once she had wriggled her way into clean clothes, Olivia took over. The elder, friendlier sister escorted her down the elevator, through the basement passage, and into the sanctuary.

Carlotta was mildly surprised to see that Zell was not in his study. He was standing at the front of the altar, before the Crown and Spear, and beneath the one-eyed god of divination hanging from the tree.

"Come here, daughter," he called, beckoning. "There are some people I would like you to meet."

It was amazing that all she had to do was relax and her feet obeyed, carrying her up the center aisle to the front. Now she could see that others were sitting on either side in the front pew.

Zell himself was flanked by a couple of strapping thugs in khaki overalls, part of the shadowy security force that seemed to swarm in the recesses of this infernal place.

"Estelle," said Zell, "will you do the honors, please?"

Morgenthau rose from the right front, as Olivia handed Carlotta off to another khaki-covered guard, who directed her forward by a firm hand above her elbow.

A very pretty young woman with blue eyes and sandy hair rose to squeeze Carlotta's hand and proffer a vapid smile. Carlotta experienced a fleeting flashback of stained glass windows in a French cathedral and a demon's breathing in her ear.

"You remember our good friend Sgt. Wendy Carlisle from Scotland Yard," said Morgenthau unctuously. "She will be your . . . protector."

Carlotta nodded numbly as Carlisle took her place by her side. She understood the meaning to be closer to "captor" or "handler."

Then came a bedraggled, olive-skinned man with clothes hanging in tatters. It took Carlotta a moment to realize that the streaks on his torn shirt were blood and that his hands were behind his back because they were cuffed in restraints. Dully she wondered why this man also looked vaguely familiar.

"This," said Morgenthau, "is our newest guest—Mr. Khalid Halima. I'm sure Mr. Halima regrets his untidy appearance at the moment, but he had to climb a nasty fence and cut the throats of a couple of guard dogs to get here. And, believe me, Dobermans don't hold still for that."

Carlotta could see some unpleasant cuts on the man's arms and one on his neck. She also saw cold fury burning in his eyes.

"I believe you met Mr. Halima's brother in Copenhagen, daughter. Kabir was his name. Perhaps you recall that brother had the misfortune of being on the receiving end of a gun you were firing. He is now as dead as those two Dobermans. Do you remember that, my dear?"

Carlotta nodded woodenly. How could she forget? Through the haze, she realized that if this man's hands were not tethered, they might well be around her neck.

"Why—why is he here?" she managed to say.

Zell smiled condescendingly. "The Crown and Scepter, my dear. Perhaps he may be interested in you too—a little consolation prize for the loss of his brother. Winner take all, you know."

Carlotta's mouth worked, but her brain froze and nothing came out.

"But," Zell continued with a careless gesture, "perhaps Peter McBride will have something to say about all that. I certainly hope so. It would be so tiresome to see the Saracens back in the driver's seat after all these years. They're worse than fundamentalist Christians."

Sometimes Zell spoke as if he lived outside the historical confines of a normal lifespan.

Carlotta was getting the general drift that this was the mortal combat Zell had spoken of before. Was Peter expected to challenge this dog-butchering Arab for possession of the regalia? The thought that she herself might be part of the booty was exceptionally distressing.

"Ah, yes," a third figure was saying. "The old damsel-in-distress routine. How picturesque."

A diminutive man about forty with wavy, salt-and-pepper hair, a smoking jacket, a pencil-line mustache, and an ascot slithered toward Carlotta with the unabashed curiosity of a visitor to the primate cage.

"Hmm," he murmured, reaching up and fluffing out her hair. "Let's get her a trim and a set. And we need to talk about her wardrobe."

He took a step back and surveyed her figure from head to toe with a hand thoughtfully at his chin. "Yes, the body is OK. But can we get her into something a little more provocative? Something more foo-foo?"

Carlotta felt suddenly naked.

"Foo-foo?" repeated Zell, dumbfounded. The words sounded misplaced in his mouth.

"Yeah, baby," said the man tartly. "You know—low-cut, come-hither. Certainly not this . . . this dreadful nun's habit."

This must not have been in the script, for Zell was now sputtering.

"Who is this person? How did he get in here?"

Morgenthau stepped in. "This is Roldo Javier-Carstairs, Crystal McKenzie's producer for One World News. He is in charge of all the setup for tonight—lighting and so forth. McKenzie herself will come a bit later."

"*That,*" said Zell in amazement, "is the producer of One World News?"

"*A* producer," Morgenthau clarified.

Javier-Carstairs suddenly grabbed Carlotta firmly by the chin. "You'd be surprised how much show biz goes into the news. I'm going to make this damsel a star."

Either there was liquor on his breath, Carlotta noted, or somebody had just spilled some nasty solvent.

* * *

It was a long hike by bicycle across town and over the bridge to Trastevere, but it was worth the ride.

Peter and Amos stopped astride their ultralights at the corner, watching the action swarming about the former ghetto synagogue that had become home to a messianic Jewish congregation.

Bearded young men in jeans and T-shirts emblazoned "Y'shua" and young women with braids and sandals offered leaflets to each passerby. Most of their overtures were rejected, since by this time most passersby were carrying protest signs.

Peter tried to identify the different persuasions by their placarded messages. There were outraged Orthodox Jews, agitated anti-Semites, riled-up Roman Catholics, put-out Protestants, nettled neo-pagans, and more. What animal rights or pedophilia had to do with this scenario was beyond him. Not only were they all galled by the messianic Jews, but they appeared to have animosity left over for one another, judging by the raised voices and occasional pushing and shoving.

And high overhead, stretching between two utility poles and spanning the street, was the blue-and-gold banner he recognized from the video report— "The King Is Coming!"

Someone blew a shofar, and then began the slow, building strains of some bittersweet, folk-sounding melody, punctuated by the offbeat jangle of a tambourine. The bearded men and braided women lifted their voices in rhythmic jubilation, though the words —Hebrew?—were unrecognizable to Peter. There was excitement and expectancy—and danger—in the air.

"What are they singing?"

Amos craned his head a moment, then translated. "'The kings of the earth take their stand . . . the rulers take counsel together against the Lord and against His anointed. . . . But as for Me, I have installed My King upon Zion."

Peter nodded. "Psalm two. The Messiah."

The hypnotic beat increased in tempo until he wanted to link arms with the singers and dance.

It was then that he spied the Nazis.

There was a small battalion of them in their ersatz Fourth Reich uniforms, goose-stepping and swinging clubs as they advanced, cutting a swath through the crowd. Those who fell were trampled, a few beaten. Their quarry parted in confusion as panic began to incite a stampede in the opposite direction. The music faded into cacophany.

Considering their neo-Nazi encounter the night before, Peter was alarmed. "Are you sure we should be here?"

When Amos didn't answer, Peter turned to see the Israeli with hands in the air and a pistol inches from his belly in the hand of a jackbooted, leering Nazi.

And then Peter felt a hard jab in his back. He glanced over his shoulder to see his own version of Sloat's predicament staring back at him.

"Come with us, swine." The Nazi waved the pistol under Peter's nose and grinned.

Their captors indicated they should march toward a waiting car with its rear doors standing open.

As he turned to obey, Peter knew he had seen that face before. Not long ago. *Herr* Jack-o-Lantern Teeth.

38

Rome

The one with the bad teeth called himself Adolfo. Gregor, the double agent, was going by the name Heinrich.

Peter silently thanked God for Heinrich/Gregor. He had no idea how far Adolfo would go to even the score for their humiliation at Giuliani's. At least, with Sloat's Shin Beth friend here, there was a reasonable chance they would come out of this alive. The question was whether they would get out of it in time to keep their appointment with destiny at San Giacomo's.

The thought made him anxious. After these weeks of sweat and blood leading up to the big event, to have it fall apart now—Peter rejected this useless line of thought.

He was also minding his tongue. His jaw was still sore from

where Adolfo had backhanded him just for asking where they were going.

With their wrists cuffed behind them, the ride was increasingly uncomfortable. Peter's hands were falling asleep. And since Heinrich was driving and Adolfo sat between them in the backseat, it was impossible to change position enough to get relief.

Peter hoped Sloat knew where they were going, because he had long since lost his bearings. It seemed that they had been heading into the northern reaches of Rome for some time, but in the past few minutes their route had become so circuitous that he was quite disoriented. They had entered a seedy warehouse district with junk on the sidewalks, junkers on the streets, and junkies in the doorways.

It seemed an appropriate place for a Fourth Reich headquarters, but, if so, where were the blindfolds? Peter shivered involuntarily. Maybe it didn't matter. Maybe they weren't expected to walk away from this.

Then they were crunching and lurching along a narrow gravel alley to the rear of one of countless warehouses. Heinrich jerked the vehicle to a stop beside a loading dock, and Adolfo ordered them out.

"Up the ramp," he snarled, motioning with the pistol from his shoulder holster.

Peter and Sloat mounted the ramp into the afternoon shadows. At the top was a heavy-looking black door that chunked open upon their arrival. They were marched down a darkened corridor, through a dimly lit gymnasium with mats on the floor and weights on racks, and on into a long, narrow room. A scarred conference table was in the center, and a pair of red-and-black swastika banners hung on either side of a fly-specked window.

On the table were some tubular objects that reminded Peter disturbingly of saps or rubber hoses. It was all disquietingly reminiscent of an interrogation room.

Mentally he fled to the refuge of God's promises, especially the one that Rick Stillman had singled out for him. "I shall carry you, I shall bear you, and I shall deliver you." He was fervently claiming that promise when Sloat coughed, then quickly whispered, "Let me handle this."

Adolfo picked up one of the saps and slapped it enthusiastically into his left hand. "Sit down!"

"Where are your two friends?" Heinrich demanded.

"It doesn't matter," said Sloat. "I'm the one who showed you up yesterday. If you want a rematch, you're more than welcome."

Heinrich pulled himself up to his full height but ignored the challenge. "What were you doing at the Zionist rally?"

Sloat snorted. "Shows how much you know. Those were messianic Jews. The Zionists were among the protesters."

Heinrich stuck his chin out. "You talk pretty tough for the spot you are in. Who are you two, and where are you from?"

"I'm Peter McBride, and I'm a lawyer from the USP."

It was always much easier that way. Lawyers were expected not to talk about their clients or their business.

"And I'm Dennis Scovill. I'm an agent for P3, and our business is none of yours. You mess with us, and you're going to have a lot of explaining to do."

Adolfo put down the sap. He leaned against the door and rested his handgun against his chest. He gave a derisive snort.

Heinrich frowned. "Why should we believe you?"

"We're on special business. You can ask your own field marshal."

"And I suppose you know his name," said Heinrich scornfully.

Sloat smiled. "Old Kuppermann? I know Manny better than you do, I'd guess. If we fail to show for a very important appointment at midnight, you'll get to know him a lot better. But probably not the way you'd like to."

Heinrich hesitated.

"Want his number?"

Amos gave it to him, and Heinrich wrote it down on a slip of paper with apparent reluctance. Then he shot Sloat and Peter a withering look. "If you are telling stories, you're going to be very sorry."

With that, Heinrich vacated the room, leaving Adolfo and his pistol.

"Strictly room-temperature IQ," Sloat said in a normal voice, nodding in Adolfo's direction.

Adolfo ignored them.

"Adolfo doesn't know it," Sloat continued, "but I think the two of us could take him, even with that gun."

"Silence!" the red-haired man snapped.

Considering that their hands were still cuffed behind their backs, Sloat's suggestion would be a good trick to pull off. Peter understood that the Israeli was playing mind games—at which Adolfo was clearly outclassed. Maybe Amos was right about the low wattage.

Silence hung as heavily as Adolfo's eyelids for the next few minutes until Heinrich returned.

"We've got to cut them loose, Adolfo."

"What!"

Nevertheless Adolfo reholstered his gun and pulled out a knife. It looked like the one in Peter's own pocket that had come from Heinrich/Gregor in the mock fight. The Nazi severed the plastic cuffs, and Peter and Amos commenced rubbing the pinch out of their wrists.

"Our apologies," said Heinrich, "but the filthy Zionists are everywhere. Where do you need to go for this appointment? Do you need food?"

Sloat smiled. "I take it the Field Marshal had a few choice words for you."

Heinrich did a decent job of looking uncomfortable. "He vouches for you."

Peter didn't know exactly what was going on, but he did know one thing—he wanted out of here.

"Can we just go back—" Peter began, then stopped when he saw Sloat shaking his head faintly. "We can't just—"

"Heinrich will leave a phone message at the hotel," Sloat said quietly.

"Our orders," said Heinrich, "are to take you to your engagement."

"Well," said Sloat, "our destination is a place on the Aventine Hill. Have you heard of San Giacomo's?"

Adolfo began snickering.

"What's with him?" demanded Sloat. "An orphanage burn down somewhere?"

"San Giacomo's has the reputation for being haunted," Heinrich explained. "Perhaps Adolfo never met a pair of ghosts before."

Peter thought the red-haired Nazi still looked as if he wanted to get in some batting practice with the saps, new attitudes notwithstanding.

"Actually," Sloat continued, "we have an appointment with a priest of Woden."

"'Woden'?" Heinrich repeated, sounding incredulous.

Peter wasn't certain what Sloat was up to, but it wouldn't be out of character even for Nazi retreads to know about Woden, since he was one of their traditional icons.

"That sounds like Zell," said Adolfo without leering. "Is that where he is casting his spells these days?"

Amos shrugged noncommittally. "Maybe."

Now Adolfo looked almost friendly. "Some of our people have worked for him. He is supposed to be more than a little crazy, but his people are friends of ours."

"But can you get us inside?" queried Sloat. "The place doesn't exactly roll out the red carpet."

"Certainly," said Adolfo. "If there is anybody home."

"Do you need anything else?" Heinrich wanted to know.

"Uh . . ." said Peter, "did you say something about food?"

Sloat shot him a quizzical look.

"Well," Peter said a little defensively, "it's still a long time till midnight."

* * *

The shadows were lengthening and the breeze cooling when their car pulled up at the gate to San Giacomo's.

Peter and Amos got slowly out of the back while Heinrich and Adolfo walked to the fence and surveyed the property. They eyed the barbed wire and stepped back when a couple of Dobermans began stalking toward the fence, barking their warning.

"What was the deal with Field Marshal Kuppermann?" Peter asked Sloat softly. "Surely you don't know that character."

"Of course not."

"So what was with that phone number?"

Sloat smiled. "Time and temperature."

Peter suppressed a laugh.

"Adolfo had no idea that Gregor was talking to a recording. Talk about fast ones—I don't think he could catch anyone pulling a slow one."

The Nazis walked back to the car.

"I think we are going to need that other number," said Adolfo.

"Sure thing," said Sloat, fishing in his wallet.

He read it off while Adolfo punched the numbers into the carphone. There was something familiar about the sequence.

"Hmph," said Adolfo after a moment, banging down the handset disgustedly. "A recording—some security firm."

"'Security,' as in private police?" said Heinrich. "Or 'securities,' as in investments?"

Adolfo shrugged. "There's a difference?"

Sloat rolled his eyes.

Peter realized why the number sounded familiar. Optima Securities.

But now around a corner came two armed guards in khaki overalls. One made the dogs sit at ease. The other did something that caused the gate to buzz and begin clanking open along its track.

"Thanks, Heinrich," Sloat said over his shoulder as he and Peter slipped through the widening aperture.

Peter waved at Adolfo through the chain links, and Sloat gave a silent "*Sieg, heil!*" salute.

"Don't worry," Heinrich/Gregor said in a low voice through the fence. "I'll leave word for your friends at the hotel."

Now the San Giacomo guards were marching them away from the boarded-up church and toward the ancient friary. Peter remembered that there should be a tunnel between the two structures and speculated that the friary might be the only access to the church. He supposed they would have figured that out eventually, assuming they had overcome the barbed wire and the dogs. But this was certainly less stressful.

Suddenly Peter saw Rick's verses in Isaiah 46 in a new light. There were obviously the strong, masculine aspects of God the Father in this promise of His protection. But when he thought about the actual words—God's "carrying," "bearing," and "delivering" His own—that was an entirely different picture. He saw himself now in the position of a beloved child, in the arms of a nurturing mother. It was a touching and humbling concept.

Once inside the dark, cavernous friary, two more khaki-attired guards escorted the Israeli to one room and Peter to another.

Peter realized there was probably good reason for his being shown to a furnished room. He and Sloat were something more than prisoners but something less than guests. On reflection, he suspected that the padded archway they had passed through in the foyer was a metal detector.

In Peter's room were a couch, a table, and a bed. On the table was a plate of cookies and milk.

"Until it is time," said one of the guards in clumsy English, "you will get some closed eyes."

The door shut behind him with a sound of finality. Peter tried it. No dice.

There was only one thing to do. So he did it.

The milk was tepid, but the cookies were good, some kind of pecan sandies. By the time he finished them, he realized there was one more thing to do—get some rest. He recalled Neal's suggestion that they take naps to be ready for a long night. Now the urge was becoming irresistible. He stood over the single bed on wobbly knees and reluctantly succumbed.

Dimly Peter wondered if there were something more potent in this bedtime snack than the sandman's kisses. By the time his head hit the pillow, he realized that the guard was right—he would get some closed eyes.

* * *

Hours later Peter seemed to be dreaming. In this confused semireality a man's black silhouette escorted him down a darkened corridor to a flight of stairs that led into a shadowy basement, then down another corridor of gloom that appeared to have no end.

The darkness faded slowly, and the passage terminated with an open door into a very small room, which was the sole source of the faint illumination. Inside, he could see that this was from nothing more than a green digital readout that said "1201" and several backlit buttons. The silhouette man pushed one of them, and there was an ominously hollow crashing as two doors collided shut a cubit away from the end of his nose.

Peter, his brain hazy and his thoughts leaden, was just dreaming that he should know the significance of "1201" when it changed to "1202." Somehow that seemed equally significant, if not slightly more so. And then the floor pressed strongly against his feet, reminding him of hospitals and office buildings.

The doors rumbled open, exposing an entirely different scene, though just as dark. He stepped out like a sleepwalker into a high-ceilinged chamber with dark wood paneling and large wrought-iron sconces holding substantial candles that cast flickering shadows. The silhouette man was gone, apparently swallowed up by the rumbling doors.

Peter was alone and without a plan. He stared at the dark woodwork for half a dozen heartbeats before spying a large brass doorknob.

The formidable door opened onto a half-lit, yawning chamber that appeared to be a kind of sanctuary. He gazed past rows of pews toward a dusky chancel where a lone figure in a hooded cloak stood by the altar.

Magnetically Peter gravitated to the front and paused until the figure beckoned for him to mount the three steps to the carpeted platform. He sensed he was being invited to witness something lost in shadow upon the waist-high altar.

The hooded figure applied a small flame to a long-handled implement and handed it to Peter. Its grasp was cold brass, like an acolyte's candlelighter. In the light of the sputtering wick, he could see two candles awaiting him. He applied the flame—and almost awoke.

Suddenly a larger light grew to effulgence around him. He returned the acolyte's instrument to the hooded stranger and looked back to the altar. The man was gone.

Now he could make out the objects upon the altar—the business end of a spear, ancient and gnarled, and a jewel-encrusted crown that seemed gaudy and overdone until intuition informed him that it might be the genuine article.

Usually, when he dreamed he thought he was awake. Now, if he thought he was dreaming, did that mean he was really awake?

Peter offered up a silent prayer for the clearing of his head. As if in answer, a picture-memory formed in his mind's eye. He was inside a mountain that was about to explode and trying to find his way out. What did this mean?

And then it came to him. He had had to compensate for something wrong with his head, a concussion that clouded his thinking. Was that his situation now too?

How long he had been standing mesmerized by this crown and spear, half-lit in the dancing shadows, Peter didn't know. But his reverie was broken by the growing awareness of a presence, like the echo of one's breathing and like a reflection in the mirror. Peter realized he was seeing the aqueous gleam of a pair of eyes opposite him across the altar.

He also realized that the auditorium was growing brighter, as if someone was raising the houselights. And then a woman's voice across the room spoke his name. But she was not addressing him. It was a kind of description or report. Maddeningly, again it seemed he should know this voice.

And then he heard something else he recognized—the name *Khalid Halima*—and memories started rushing back in a flood. "In the name of Allah, the one true God—praise be unto His name—" said the man opposite, now more clearly visible, "and Muhammad, His only prophet, I claim these articles for the Imam of Babylon—may he live forever."

Now Peter was fully awake. These were the long-sought Crown and Spear! He shook his head, as if to rid himself of any lingering chemical impairment. As quickly as the Arab's hand reached for the Crown and Spear, Peter slapped it away.

Halima locked eyes with Peter for a long, intense moment. There were no words for what passed between them. Peter's impression was a succession of nonverbal images—exploding cars, piled-up bodies, dead dogs, cut throats.

The rumination cost him. In a flash Halima snatched the Spear from its case and held it aloft like a royal scepter.

Two khaki-uniformed guards appeared to cart away the altar on its casters, like stagehands changing scenes.

"Too bad you are weaponless, Yankee pig!" said the Arab, though his voice offered anything but remorse. "This is a fight to the death."

"Too bad you are clueless," Peter retorted. "I have no intention of killing you—or of being killed."

He became peripherally aware of the presence of others in the auditorium now that the houselights were up, but he didn't dare take his eyes off this crazed Halima. He offered up another brief, silent prayer and then wondered momentarily about Sloat Like the cavalry, maybe he would bring last-minute reinforcements. But then, he realized, Sloat was more likely locked away in his own guest room, zonked on juiced-up milk and cookies.

Like a boxer in the ring, Halima warily stalked him. As if still in a dream, Peter thought he heard a familiar female voice call his name, but just as quickly Halima was speaking again.

"Then, coward, do you renounce all claim to the Crown and Spear?"

"No," Peter answered, "and if you take them, I will track you down and take them back."

Halima grinned humorlessly. "Either way, we fight to the death."

Just then the hooded figure stepped back into their theater. He pushed back the hood and showed himself to be a white-haired, priestly looking man.

"Just so you understand, Mr. McBride," said the man, "we will not surrender the Crown and Scepter to either of you without mortal combat. There will be no nonaggression pacts here." He stepped back into the shadows without further explanation.

Peter wondered briefly if this was the mysterious Zell. His mind was still stuck on the woman's cry that continued to nag at his recollection.

Halima maneuvered him to the edge of the stage, but Peter judged it better to defend himself on the platform than down below in closer quarters.

As Halima lunged forward, Peter dodged to his right. Halima went over the edge, landing on his feet. He leaped back onto the stage, demonstrating impressive leg strength. But just as quickly, Peter was there, planting a foot against the Arab's chest at the moment he had regained a perch.

Peter kicked, and the man went flying backward, taking an ignominious pratfall in front of the stage. The Spear, knocked free from his hand, rolled sideways about a meter.

Peter knew he should jump after Halima in this moment of opportunity and seize the Spear, but . . .

"*Peter!*"

He froze. It was that voice again.

He looked up and saw two figures on the balcony, both female, who took him back in time to the triforium of Chartres Cathedral. And this wasn't just a flashback. With mixed feelings of joy and horror, Peter realized that the two figures were Carlotta and Wendy Carlisle. But this time, they weren't struggling. In fact, Wendy was patting Carlotta's arm supportively, as one would a fragile child.

Peter's heart raced as the full force of his longing for Carlotta hit him. There was so much more at stake here than the Crown and Spear—starting with his own skin and extending through all his future hopes and dreams.

It was as if some cosmic croupier had raked all of his chips onto the table and wagered them all on one number.

39

Rome

Halima was back on the stage, Spear in hand. "You do not seem to understand. I will kill you, then take the Crown and Spear —*and* the woman!"

Suddenly Peter wanted to fight.

Just as quickly Halima lunged again, thrusting the Spear toward Peter's heart. His reaction was quick enough to avert a direct hit, but not to avoid contact. There was a tearing of shirt fabric and a jagged catch in his side.

It took a moment for Peter to register the searing pain and feel the matting of the shirt to his chest that meant blood. But he would never give Halima the satisfaction of knowing he'd been hurt—at least, not so long as he could stand.

Already the man was coming back for more. But his lunges were becoming predictable. This time Peter jumped to the left. In the moment of Halima's off-balance recovery, he rapped a fist off the Arab's chin. It was enough to knock him back a step but not to stop him. Halima swung the Spear like a broadsword and caught Peter against the side of the head.

And then he was back inside the exploding mountain, his head ringing from the impact of solid rock. He knew he had to get back up before Loki writhed in his chains again and Hekla blew its top. But he could not find his feet, and his head was spinning.

In this confused transport, there was One before him whose side had been pierced with a spear—it was more a knowledge than a vision. Then he seemed to see a kind of cross, black on red, growing larger, revolving. *There was death here!*

Peter rolled to one side just as the Spear bit into the carpet beside him. He was on his feet without quite knowing how. His head still spun, and he felt as if he were walking on a trampoline again.

He tried a feint. He stumbled and shook his head as if he couldn't see. He pretended not to notice Halima closing in from the side.

An instant before the thrust, Peter dropped the feint and seized the Spear with his left hand. With his right he delivered a bruising smash to Halima's face. The Arab fell back, but his grip on the Spear did not relax. Peter wondered if anything short of death would make that happen.

Halima started to fall, then caught himself, tripping Peter over his extended front leg. The Arab grabbed the Spear with both hands now, twisting until he broke Peter's grip.

They regrouped and stalked each other for the next engagement. Peter realized he was becoming winded despite the adrenaline. And the wound in his side was beginning to throb. The injury was obviously more than superficial. He wondered how long he could continue to hold his own without a weapon against this man who was clearly his equal in physical strength.

And then he was seeing again that black cross spinning on a field of red. This time the black figure appeared more clearly as a swastika and—*the knife!*

Gregor's Nazi switchblade with its metal-detector-neutral blade had been riding all the time in his pants pocket.

Halima thrust again and missed as Peter jumped out of the way.

He worked on another feint, pretending to be out of breath and slow of foot. He tried panting.

Sadistic glee burned in Halima's eyes. "You are finished, Yankee pig. I will think of you when I take your woman."

The threat cut far deeper than the Spear.

Halima lunged again but did not thrust with the weapon. This time the blow was a fist aimed at Peter's mouth.

Peter's reaction shifted it to his nose, and his head snapped back. His ears were ringing, and there was a salty taste in his mouth. But none of that seemed to matter now. He was in a kind of rage beyond reasoning. He was a rocket's red glare. He was a bomb bursting in air. It was kill or be killed.

With a cry from the depths of his angry being, Peter was on Halima, oblivious to the pain in his head and the searing in his side. He held onto the Spear with his left hand and grabbed for the Arab's throat, coming away instead with a rent piece of shirt.

Halima landed a blow to Peter's punctured side, filling him with blinding pain.

They were close to the rear wall now as Halima retreated. It was Peter's turn to lunge again, knocking the Spear aside and landing a blow in the middle of Halima's face. Blood now ran from the Arab's nose.

The man fell forward and pulled Peter down with him. They wrestled, smearing each other with sweat and blood. A knee in the stomach cost Halima his breath, and Peter had the Arab on his back. He sat on the man's chest, holding off the Spear with one hand and reaching into his pocket with the other.

Halima's eyes widened in terror when Peter hit the button and the blade sprang at his throat. Then he shut his eyes, his mouth working faintly in a silent incantation.

Peter put blade to throat—like a carving knife to a roast—and froze. This was not a roast. This was a man—a despicable specimen perhaps, but a man nonetheless.

Halima opened his eyes and frowned, his breathing labored both from exertion and from the weight upon his chest.

Peter was panting too, this time for real. Sensing that the beaten man had relaxed his grip, he wrenched the Spear from his grasp in one quick motion and held it aloft.

From somewhere down deep, Peter found his voice. It was ragged and harsh. "So much for invincibility! Your magic Spear seems to be a dud."

Hatred clouded Halima's face.

"I knew you were a coward, Yankee pig," he gasped with contempt. "But you must not deny me an honorable death."

It was Peter's turn to snarl. "I choose not to kill you. I give you back your life."

"Then let me up," Halima challenged, "and I will show you how a man fights. Your shoes will shine with your own blood."

"No!" cried a voice. "I declare the contest over. You are finished, Halima."

Over his shoulder Peter saw a figure emerge from the shadows. It was the strange old man he had thought to be Zell. By his side was one of the security men carrying a rope.

"You have won, Mr. McBride," the old man continued. "But what you offer the Arab is not yours to give."

As Peter numbly pondered the meaning of that, the security man knelt and secured Halima's wrists. He nudged Peter to get up, and Peter complied on legs suddenly grown weak and heavy without the adrenaline's raging.

"Throw him out," said Zell.

Several things happened too fast for Peter to track. Halima was thrust upon his feet and marched down the three steps from the platform. The beaten man needed some rough encouragement to keep walking toward an exit door. Heading toward them from another part of the auditorium were a man shouldering a TV camera, a diminutive fellow with a pencil-line mustache and wavy hair, and a blonde woman in a bright green dress who reminded Peter of Crystal McKenzie.

"Hurry," the greasy little man was saying as another security man opened the side door. He and the woman reporter apparently didn't want to miss a second of this.

And then Halima was being shoved unceremoniously out the door into what appeared to be a fenced-in parking lot bathed in the stark radiance of towering floodlights. It was past midnight, after all, Peter recalled.

Peter was not far behind the cameraman and the reporter, close enough to hear a startled cry come from Halima. And then he saw why. Two snarling Dobermans stalked the Arab on stiff legs, their hair spiked up on their necks and tails. Perhaps they were litter-mates of the ones Halima had dispatched.

Before the door swung shut, Peter saw something he would not forget for a long time. Halima tried vainly to fend off the dogs' assault with his tethered hands. He was dead in his tracks.

Peter noticed that the reporter's face looked as green as her dress. But one thing was even more striking—the floodlit sight of blood shining on the Arab's shoes.

* * *

Peter awoke to a rapping at his door—a door he didn't know he had. He stared at the ceiling, wondering what he was doing in a strange hotel. The last thing he wanted was to get up and answer the door. His head felt wretched. His body felt as if he had been run over by the Fourth Reich. Maybe whoever it was would just go away.

Unfortunately he had not counted on whoever it was having a key. It was Tony Novello with an older, balding gentleman who carried a large, black briefcase. Novello toted a small, black coffee pot on a tray with some cups.

"Good morning, Peter," he said with a smile. "This is Dr. Vito Angelotta. He wants to look you over. He is a sports medicine specialist—treats soccer players and boxers."

"Yes," said Angelotta, sitting on the edge of Peter's bed and opening the black bag. "And you certainly look as if you have gone a few rounds—black eye, swollen nose."

"You ought to see the other guy," Peter managed to croak.

"Let me see what else you have. Can you sit up?"

With some difficulty, Peter scooted up in the bed as Angelotta propped him up with two pillows and Novello poured him a cup of coffee. The doctor parted Peter's hair to look at the side of his head, palpated his neck, rotated his head, felt his nose, shined a light into his eyes, and told him to follow his moving finger with his eyes.

"Do you remember everything that happened last night?"

"Everything," said Peter, "until the point when the police arrived and Tony put me into his car. I don't recall coming here. Wait—where's Carlotta? And Neal? And Amos?"

"They are here, Peter," said Novello. "You will see them in a little while."

"OK," said Angelotta, turning off his light. "The right pupil is dilated fractionally larger than the left, which is consistent with the contusion. There appears to be little or no aphasia and only incidental amnesia connected to proximate events. That is a good sign. If there is a concussion, it is slight. I have some medicine."

Angelotta reached into his case and placed several small plastic bags on the nightstand. "I want you to put icepacks on that knot on your head and on your nose. The nose is not broken, but there is much swelling. Try to remember more from last night as you can."

Peter immediately remembered one thing. "I think they drugged me, Doc."

Angelotta reached back into his bag and placed a small computer on the nightstand. "I shall take a blood sample from you and do the same with Miss Waldo next door."

Next door! She was only a few meters away at this very moment?

Angelotta drew some blood from Peter's arm and inserted the syringe into a port on the little computer. While that percolated, he opened his shirt and looked at Peter's chest. He frowned.

"This will hurt a little," he said, shaking a squirt bottle, "but not as much as the old days when they closed such things with catgut and nylon."

Looking down, Peter saw an ugly-looking cut, about five inches long. Angelotta began cleansing it with antiseptic, which burned like fire for a few moments until the topical anesthetic took effect.

While the doctor prepared to apply the Epi-Bond wound-closer, Peter worked at recalling what else he could from the night before. Now he remembered waking in the night, confused, and being sick in the bathroom. He didn't remember getting back into bed.

Other pieces were coming back randomly. Zell and his henchmen disappearing into the night when the *carabinieri* arrived with their flashing lights. Sloat blinking in confusion after he was let out of his room to join them in the auditorium. Carlotta, looking dazed and numb, coming into his arms. Wendy Carlisle giving them an odd sneer before vanishing like a specter. Someone trying to put a crown on his head.

The least coherent recollection was of a strange conversation with Crystal McKenzie in her green dress and of lights and a camera and the quirky character named Roldo hovering in the background. He couldn't reconstruct any of the dialogue.

"Hmm," said Angelotta, having finished with the cut and now studying the blood results on the computer display. "Acedia—a potent designer drug that interferes with specific neurotransmitter sites, making the subject especially compliant and open to suggestion without major impairment of higher mental faculties. It is a favorite of cult groups that depend on unquestioned devotion to a strong leader—which is most of them. I will give you some medicine for the residual neurotoxicity."

Angelotta stuck a needle into his arm and delivered a dollop of something pink.

"Cordrazine," the doctor explained. "To stimulate your own metabolic detoxification."

Angelotta gave him instructions for the two kinds of pills he left on the nightstand, then repacked his bag and stood up.

"Be sure to get much rest—and congratulations."

Sloat and McBride were waiting outside. They came in, beaming and congratulating Peter, who was availing himself of the coffee and savoring the gratifyingly warm sensation it produced from the inside out.

"I don't get it. Why is everybody congratulating me?"

Sloat chuckled. "Through the miracle of modern telecommunications, half the world now knows that Peter Carpenter McBride has been crowned Grand Dragon of the Unholy Roman Empire."

"Terrific," Peter said glumly.

Sloat's smile faded. "Oh. We are not amused this morning. I guess you're pretty banged up."

"You were a big help last night, Amos."

"Sorry. I guess I forgot to set my alarm."

McBride sat down on the bed where Angelotta had been. "How *do* you feel? What did the doctor say?"

"I'll live. It seems I have the equivalent of a giant hangover and assorted bumps and bruises from a knock-down-drag-out bar fight. Nothing serious. I should avoid death matches for a while."

"That's a lot better shape than we thought you'd be in," McBride said. "From our vantage point outside the fence, Tony and I thought at first that was you feeding the dogs. That put a little damper on the evening for a while."

"I wonder if One World News will show that scene," said Novello.

Peter frowned. "Just what *did* I say to Crystal McKenzie on camera? Or do I really want to know?"

McBride beamed again. "You were pretty smooth. You declared that the power struggle was over and that you would have the Crown and Spear returned to their rightful owner. When McKenzie asked if you planned not to assert any royal authority, you said you would step aside as soon as the current dispute between Chancellor Neumann and Salvatore DiFalcone has been settled."

Peter was incredulous. "I said all that?"

"We can get it off a news channel if you want to see it. The initial reaction from both sides, according to One World News, was very positive this morning. Neumann and DiFalcone couldn't put the toothpaste back in the tube, but you can—in a way that will allow both of them to save face. They seem to place a lot of credence in this emperor business—or at least fear what it could do to their own authority."

Peter frowned in frustration. "But what should I tell them?"

McBride paused and looked off into space. "I don't know. Just getting things back to status quo would be something. I'd like to hear your own ideas."

Peter closed his eyes and said a silent prayer. His head was clearing and his mood beginning to lift. Maybe the coffee and Cordrazine were starting to have some effect.

"Where are the Crown and Spear?" he asked suddenly.

"Right here," Novello said. He fished a key out of his pocket and unlocked a utility closet beside the bathroom. "Here you are, Your Majesty," He brought the regalia to Peter's bedside.

Peter grasped the cold metal of the Spear and eyeballed the Crown of Charlemagne. The imperial authority they conveyed was staggering.

"Knowing DiFalcone," said Peter, "I don't believe he really expects to stay out of prison. He's already toppled Bardo. If Neumann agrees to cancel the cashless telecredit system and Bardo's population control measures, agrees to stand for a parliamentary confidence vote, I imagine DiFalcone will agree to fold his tent.

"I know he'll talk to me. Maybe he'll have some other issues like prison conditions, but I wouldn't expect anything very problematic. I mean, he already runs half of Europe from Aldo Moro anyway."

The other men were nodding thoughtfully.

"The only question," Peter continued, "is how to get hold of DiFalcone and then get Neumann to agree."

"No problem," said McBride. "I'm sure Crystal McKenzie knows how to reach DiFalcone, and we know how to reach Sir James, who can get to Neumann. Consider it as good as done, Your Majesty."

Peter ignored the gibe. "I have little doubt that Neumann will see the wisdom of this. In fact, I'd bet he'll jump at it. And while we're at it, there ought to be a little something in it for us too. Neal, do you think Neumann could help our cause in the USP?"

"No question," McBride said without hesitation. "My government sources back home say EU pressure was the only thing keeping them from settling out of court with us on the procreation permit litigation. And with Bardo gone, all it should take is a phone call to the right place to get the whammy off your case. I think with Neumann's cooperation Sir James ought to be able to work that out before day is done."

Peter's heart leaped as he thought of Carlotta sleeping next door and of all their hopes and dreams now almost within their grasp.

"Great," he said. "The only remaining question, then, is what to do with the Crown and Spear."

"Oh, is that all?" said McBride wearily. "Back to square one. We can't in good conscience hand them over to that crook Liebenfels, and we're going to go home penniless with Griswold out of the picture. I suppose you have another bright idea?"

"Maybe." Peter was enjoying himself now. "How about we find ourselves a smart lawyer and file claims against Liebenfels, Griswold, Optima Securities, and the government? We can make favorable treatment of those claims, our other condition to Neumann. In the scheme of things, I think that would be fairly easy for Sir James to pull off. Don't you?"

McBride agreed hesitantly. "I could imagine Sir James pulling that off with just the *threat* of legal action. That might, in fact, make us whole."

Peter looked at Sloat, who nodded agreement.

McBride, however, still wore a shadow of a frown. "There's . . . uh . . . still one thing I don't understand," the older man said when their eyes met.

"What's that?"

"Why you? Why did Zell fasten this prince identity on you?"

Peter shrugged. "Who knows? Maybe Carlotta will be able to shed some light on that. To us, this whole bizarre affair was just solving a mystery. To Zell, it seems to have been some kind of qualifying ritual."

"Sure," Sloat agreed. "In fact, it could have turned out much differently. I suspect that the 'prince' probably could have been just about anyone—even Halima."

There was silence in the room while that grim notion sank in. The consequences of the Crown and Spear's falling into the hands of the Imam of Babylon were almost unthinkable. Jihad. The "liberation" of Jerusalem. The "time of Jacob's trouble."

"All right," McBride said slowly. "But back to the original question—what *are* we going to do with the *Reichskleinodien?*"

This time something began to click. There might be one sure way to squelch this prince business and all of the neo-pagan hype and superstition.

"I propose," Peter said, deciding on a course, "that in our final interview with Crystal McKenzie we announce that we have decided to turn the Crown and Spear over to Israel for safekeeping until there has been a permanent and equitable resolution of this matter—or until the return of the King of Jerusalem to claim them Himself."

Three pairs of eyes widened, but no one objected. It was an idea that took a little getting used to. But there was something poetically just about it. The King of Jerusalem. King of kings. Lord of lords. Forever and ever. Hallelujah.

"Amos," Peter continued, "would you be willing to undertake the transfer of these articles to Jerusalem on behalf of your government?"

Suddenly Sloat began laughing. He didn't stop until he had wiped a tear from the corner of each eye.

"OK, funny guy," said Peter. "What's going through that brain of yours?"

"Oh," said Sloat, "I was just thinking how much I'd like to see the prime minister's face when he's told these items are being held for the Messiah—Y'shua."

That thought produced a few more smiles. But Peter was totally serious. He looked squarely at McBride. "Do you concur?"

His father nodded, still smiling. "Once again you come up with the angle nobody else would ever think of. But that's been your style throughout this oddball case. And I have to admit, your analysis has been completely on target."

It was Peter's turn to smile, knowing that was his adoptive father's supreme compliment. He threw the covers back and stretched, squeezing life into his legs.

"Amos," he said, "what are your plans? Do you get a vacation?"

Sloat assumed a cryptic expression. "Sure. Long stretches on. Long stretches off."

"I suppose you might do a little traveling?"

"I might."

Peter suppressed a chuckle. "Maybe around and about Europe? Say, Scandinavia?"

"Could be."

"Iceland?"

Sloat smiled and said nothing.

Peter tried standing. The trampoline effect was back. The worst part was a dull throbbing in his head. Under the circumstances, he wasn't going to complain.

"Just where do you think you're going?" said McBride, looking a bit concerned.

Peter fastened a couple of buttons on his shirt and smoothed down his hair in a mirror over the dresser.

"Well," he said, opening the hall door, "there's a beautiful young lady next door, and I have a proposal to discuss with her."

EPILOGUE

Brussels

The small brownstone church attended by Rick and Moira Stillman, not far from the public gardens and the Rhema Institute, was crowded with flowers and well-wishers.

They came from all over. Carlotta's sister, Dyana, and mother came from the USP with Peter's mother, Judith. Tony Novello and Gina came from Rome with Neal McBride. Vígdis Njálsdöttir and Einar Njálsson came from Reykjavík. Amos Sloat came from Jerusalem. The Reverend Darnell Jones came all the way from the Sudan, where he administered Scripture translation projects among some of the hundred or so major language groups along the Blue Nile. Even Vida Beasley, Carlotta's roommate, came from Cleveland.

It was a week since Peter had abdicated a throne that the world had tried to give him and, in a widely publicized and highly controversial appearance on One World News, had taken the Crown from his head and consecrated it to the Lamb of God and the Lion of Judah. DiFalcone had returned to Aldo Moro. Waldemar Neumann had gone into sudden retirement when it developed that he might not survive a confidence vote.

But to Peter McBride, nothing was as momentous as this occasion with the one he loved in the presence of friends and family and in the sight of God. It was the moment he had been awaiting for more than ten years.

The rich baritone of Darnell Jones rose majestically through the "dearly beloveds" and the other flowery preliminaries, and his aging brown face made crow's-feet as he took obvious pleasure in doing these honors.

Peter's heart hammered almost as hard as it had inside Mount Hekla and San Giacomo's as he watched the flicking of Carlotta's eyelashes under her veil.

"Do you, Carlotta Waldo," said Jones, "take this man, Peter McBride, to be your lawfully wedded husband, to have and to hold from this day forth, for richer or for poorer, in sickness and in health, to have and to hold, forsaking all others, so long as you both shall live, so help you God?"

Carlotta's voice was soft and tremulous but nonetheless emphatic. "I do."

Jones turned to Peter. "Do you, Peter McBride, take this woman, Carlotta Waldo, to be your lawfully wedded wife, to have and to hold from this day forth, for richer or for poorer, in sickness and in health, to have and to hold, forsaking all others, so long as you both shall live, so help you God?"

Peter found his voice oddly hoarse and tight. "I do."

"Then by the power vested in me through the ministry of the Word and the church of the Lord Jesus Christ, I now pronounce you man and wife."

As the old-fashioned electric organ struck up the powerful strains of the wedding recessional, Peter was almost overcome by a battery of emotions—love, joy, relief, amazement, and even momentary disbelief. After all this time, it was almost too good to be true. She was so beautiful—and he loved her so much—he feared for a moment that he was dreaming. But it was just a flicker of unreality from the electricity in the air and the floorboards vibrating from the music that reminded him of dreams and concussions and trampoline walking.

No, this was real.

Carlotta had swept away her veil and was making a face at him that didn't quite erase her radiant smile.

"Kiss me, you fool," she breathed.

He did, and in that long moment of embrace he was finally overcome, this time by the melting sensation of two becoming one.

"Come with me, Mrs. McBride," he said finally, leading her down the steps from the altar, hand in hand.

They threaded their way out the front door and down the steps to the reception room in the basement to await their guests.

"What is *that?*" asked Peter, pointing to a large, vaguely conical lump of white on a silver tray in the middle of the room.

Carlotta chuckled. "Our wedding cake."

"Then why," said Peter, "is it so . . . misshapen?"

"Don't you recognize it?" she said with contrived reproach in her voice. "It's not misshapen. It's supposed to be Mount Hekla."

"Oh, no." Peter groaned.

"It was Rick's idea. Moira tried to talk him out of it, but he insisted. Pretend to be surprised when he lights the interior and it erupts."

"Just like those volcanoes that kids take to the science fairs?"

Carlotta nodded.

Now the guests were streaming down the stairs behind them. Peter realized there were many more faces than he could recognize, probably friends of the Stillmans from the local congregation. Judith McBride and Lena Waldo wanted to hug their children and dampen their shoulders with mothers' tears. Even tough old Neal McBride looked a little damp-eyed as he hugged Peter and kissed Carlotta's cheek.

"Cut the cake, you two," Moira was saying.

"Not yet!" Rick cried. "Where are those matches?"

Peter turned his head, aware that Carlotta had left his side. "Where do you think you're going?" he called after her.

"There's one more very important thing to take care of," she said, heading back up the steps.

At the top, she turned and held up her bouquet. Every woman in the room seemed to know exactly what she was doing. It took Peter a little longer to figure it out—the flower toss.

And then the bouquet was sailing overhead in a gentle arc. Amid all the uplifted arms, one especially long and slender arm and hand reached out to intercept the flowers. When the little crowd cleared, Peter saw who it was.

Vígdis.

When he saw Vígdis raise the flowers in a victor's gesture and flash a homecoming queen smile, he chuckled. When he saw Amos Sloat off to the side with a dumbfounded expression, Peter laughed out loud. Slowly, Amos crossed the room to her side.

No doubt about it, they made a great-looking couple—Vígdis with her long, blonde hair, beaming expression, and pink cheeks, and Sloat with his penetrating brown eyes and a face that concealed many deep and dark secrets, now inducted into the greatest one of all, the mystery of godliness. Peter hoped that this was one flower toss that would prove truly prophetic.

Above the buzz and chatter, laughter and acclaim within the room, Vígdis could be heard proclaiming loudly and earnestly to one and all, *"Gud blessi thig! Gud blessi thig!"*

As if in concert, Rick's sugar-frosted wedding volcano across the room began spewing and sputtering like a sparkler and burping a tiny cloud of smoke.

Carlotta returned to Peter's side. As if seeing her for the first time, he took hold of both her shoulders and gazed deeply into her eyes. Then he took her into his arms and murmured into her ear.

"Yes, Mrs. McBride," he said. *"Gud blessi thig!* Forever and ever."

Moody Press, a ministry of the Moody Bible Institute,
is designed for education, evangelization, and edification.
If we may assist you in knowing more about Christ
and the Christian life, please write us without obligation:
Moody Press, c/o MLM, Chicago, Illinois 60610.